MULTIPLEX MAN

and

THE ONE PENNY ORANGE MYSTERY

For the collector!
Morris Ackerman

MORRIS ACKERMAN

This is a work of fiction. The events, characters and dialogue are from the author's imagination.

Copyright © 1995 by Morris Ackerman.
All rights reserved.

Library of Congress Card Catalog Number 97-91725

ISBN Number 0-9657743-0-9

Published by Chevy Chase Publishing Co.
Chevy Chase MD 20815

Printed by Signature Book Printing, Inc.
Gaithersburg, Maryland, USA

First printing: May 1997

10 9 8 7 6 5 4 3 2 1

Prologue

The subtropical island's typical dawn began faintly with the sounds of chirping birds and pulsating surf breaking on the shore. Vigorous trade winds rustled through the ten foot tall sugar canes. A kestrel's screech pierced the undertone as it overtook its prey. The scent of lightly salted air and fresh fish from the nearby ocean mingled with the tangy aroma of eggs and breadcakes frying in oil. Heavy mists in the eastern sky cast blue and gray streaks of light which slowly faded into the sun's yellow warmth. This was the prelude before the usual honking of auto and bicycle traffic became audible. Normally, as the morning outlived the dawn, the raucous rush-hour traffic would drown out the sweet, quiet sounds of nature and the day's work would begin.

But not on that day. The calmness gave way to the sound of shouting as thousands of clamoring people, not vehicles, clogged every downtown street, pushing and elbowing their way toward their destination, the Government House in Port Louis. The British flag, the symbol of colonial empire, flew there, soon to be replaced by the flag of independent Mauritius. The rumbling noise made by the crowd resembled the sound of an approaching train that drowned out all other sounds. As thousands of natives surrounded the Government House, their white shirts and jodhpurs like a billowing sheet splashed with brightly colored swatches provided by their turbans, fezes and straw hats.

From his office window, Major Edward Postmark, watched the large, noisy crowd approach his building as members of the staff left their typewriters, files and unfinished paperwork to gather in the Major's office. Perhaps they sensed that he, Major Postmark, the military attache for the British government on the island of Mauritius, would protect them. Edward tensed as he turned from the window and faced the dozen persons who now filled his office, nervously watching the windows and talking to one another to stay calm.

"They are carrying torches," said one of the men. We could get trapped in a burning building!"

"They are holding something else," said another. "Looks like grenades!"

To Edward the grenades looked more like fruit but the torches were growing in numbers and the smoke, at first seen only hovering above the crowd, now permeated through the building. Frowning, he turned and looked at his desk and files. *These documents date back to the rule of Queen Victoria and I know each faction would interpret the contents of the documents to suit their political aims. I had better take them with me.* He quickly stuffed them into a satchel. It crossed Edward's mind that his own future too was at stake. The British would leave Mauritius just as they had done after India's independence. It was time to move to a new post. Where would he go? He did not dwell on it. Instead, he took his pistol from his desk but did not expect to use it. He knew these people, many of whom had come here from India, where he had been posted for many years. He believed that beyond the clamoring of their protests they would not hurt anyone. Nevertheless, Major Postmark was keenly aware that a riotous crowd could lose control. He hoped his pistol might deter the crowd long enough for him to lead his small contingent out of the building.

"Can you see what's going on?" asked one person.

"Yes," another answered, "the crowd is heading this way, like a mob."

Some of the women even pressed against Edward, as if to get under his protective wing. One woman near the window cried.

"They are carrying knives; I'm afraid they will attack us." Hearing that, a woman beside Edward began weaving back and forth, holding her head and moaning.

"Penny," she sobbed. "Please stay with me. I know they will rape us. Why can't we leave?"

Penny took her hand to reassure her but the woman became more hysterical.

"Major Postmark will get us out," Penny said.

Edward pondered his situation. He had not seen crowds like this since he was on duty in India before she became independent of colonial rule. Now it was happening here in Mauritius. He noted it was the year 1968 and the British colony of Mauritius, an island six hundred miles east of southern Africa, surrounded by the Indian Ocean - a speck in this vast body of water - was about to become a Republic, free of British rule. Independence, he knew, would not come without a struggle.

Edward remembered the hard fought general election of last year that had been won by a coalition of Hindu and Muslim parties. Opposing them was a party consisting of French and Creole representatives who held control of the island's politics until the election. The French-Creole party viewed the new regime as oppressive, looking down on them because of race. Now, both factions marched to protest to the British government personnel.

Why the protests, he wondered? The British had already planned to leave. He saw placards under his office window which seemed to arrive just to answer his question. Some read:

"BRITISH GO HOME."

Others read, "BRITISH STAY."

Many signs said, "OPPRESSORS- GO BACK TO INDIA."

The majority party wanted the British out faster while the minority party complained of oppression by the new majority party.

Edward watched the police and British Army personnel move about in squads seeking strategic locations, but they were too few in number to keep the two factions separated. Edward turned to the group which grown and had now filled up his office.

"Just stick together and we will get out of here," he told them. "These people are not normally violent."

The door to his office suddenly flew open revealing a small group of protesters. Through the open door, the Major watched as other protesters ran through the halls apparently seeking the head man. Edward and some of the men attempted to clear the doorway, fearing that the marchers would try to cut off their escape route. The women, clearly disturbed by the escalating turn of events, candidly expressed their fear.

"They are going to get us. Help!"

"Stay close together," Edward shouted. "I will get us out of here!"

Shots could be heard inside the building and Edward moved quickly. As the staff pushed toward Edward, he positioned himself in front of his small flock to try to protect them. He then waved his pistol in the air to frighten the crowd which had grown in numbers. He knew he had to somehow maneuver his people through the crowd and downstairs to the basement which would allow them access to the rear door of the building.

Meanwhile, the crowd grew aggressive and began to push and shove, threatening to overwhelm his small group. The air suddenly smelled of rotten fruit as tomatoes and melons were hurled into the room. Major Postmark now held his satchel in front of his face as they slowly made their way to a door that led to the basement.

At that moment, somewhere behind the first crowd came the opposing sects and a battle ensued. Shots rang out. Edward brandished his pistol as he moved his small contingent closer to the stairway door.

Before Edward could make the next move, he was confronted by a fierce looking native. His beard curled up from his face like a snarling lip, his turban and beard were in Edward's face, his knife was pressed close to Edward's throat.

"Take us to your leader! Where is he?"

Edward pushed the knife away.

"If he is here, he is in his office upstairs."

The native pushed the shouting, jostling crowd toward the stairs. The torches carried by the mob inside the building had filled the halls and rooms, the dark, acrid smoke making it hard to see and breathe.

"Move downstairs to the baggage room!"

Edward's group stumbled ahead to the stairwell and down to the baggage room in the basement, all the while coughing and trying to spit out the acid taste of the torch smoke. Just as they got inside the baggage room, the Major shut the door before the clamoring crowd could get in. There was another door at the far end that could be used as an exit if the crowd was held in abeyance long enough for them to reach it.

The baggage room was used to house large containers belonging to the staff for shipping pets and belongings to their homelands. The smell of animal fur and food reminded Edward that some of these baskets and crates were occupied. He quickly moved a large basket toward the door where the screaming crowd gathered, trying to force open the door. Smoke now filled the room causing more coughing.

"Don't leave!" they chanted. "Take us to your leader!"

"Here," said Edward to the men. "Hold the door closed while I push this basket in front of the door."

"What's in it?"

"Don't open it, just hold the door!"

As soon the basket was at the door, Edward opened the door and removed the lid of the basket. Suddenly the largest king cobra he had ever seen began to emerge from the basket, hissing and weaving! The crowd suddenly came face to face with the awesome sight of the huge flat hooded head, its deadly fangs thrusting out of its gaping mouth. The king cobra's movement had a hypnotic, yet kaleidoscopic effect. Edward himself was even momentarily mesmerized while some of his party screamed at the sight.

"Watch the snake; it's coming out of the basket!"

The effect on the people was instantaneous. As the giant asp rose taller and more animated, its fangs jutting forward, the crowd drew back. One man from the crowd lunged forward to kill the serpent with his bolo knife but others, who did not wish the cobra harmed, restrained him.

As planned, this gave Edward and his contingent enough time to exit the rear door of the baggage room. They then followed him through several doors and out of the building. Another group of rioters was already there and began to hurl threats.

"We do not want the British to leave! We will not let you pull out!"

More police had arrived and were pushing the crowd away from the building. Edward and his group immediately dispersed and ran for their respective bicycles and cars. The crowd, intent on finding the British governor, did not pursue them.

Edward returned exhausted to his house on the outskirts of Port Louis, the capital of Mauritius, eyes burning and throat choked up from the smoke. He poured a double scotch and water and collapsed on the sofa. Even with the drink, he could still taste and smell the sour stench of the smoke.

Fate had determined that Edward would be responsible for the long-hidden documents from Queen Victoria's reign held in that satchel. Later, once calm, he would clean the splattered remains of rotten fruit and put the satchel containing the documents, unread, away in his attic.

He pondered the events of the day and the ferocity of the protestors; with independence coming there were already a number of dissidents. The caste system of the East would prevail.

It was a race riot.

Chapter 1

> *"Water, water, everywhere,*
> *And all the boards did shrink;*
> *Water, water, everywhere,*
> *Nor any drop to drink."*
>
> - *"The Rime of the Ancient Mariner"*
> by Samuel Taylor Coleridge

Major Edward Postmark was returning to Mauritius some twenty years after he had left. The tranquil, seemingly endless flight across the Indian Ocean was coming to an end as the pilot sought the entrance to the landing pattern at the airport. The crew listened intently to their radio signals and stared at their maps and instruments to ensure they were on course to that island, a mere pinpoint surrounded by thousands of square miles of glistening, empty sea. From the window next to his seat, Edward gazed at the purplish horizon, anxiously seeking a speck of land that he hoped would be Mauritius. The ocean was a virtual palette of color: white caps, aquamarine, emerald and velvet indigo. After watching the water for endless hours, he had yet to see a bit of land that would assure him the crew had located the island.

Edward spotted a tanker or cargo ship large enough to be seen at high altitude. How transportation has changed, he thought, since he had lived in this part of the world. The Indian Ocean was the scene of trade routes long before the early navigators reached the New World and the Pacific Ocean. Ships plied this ocean between the Middle East and the Far East as trade routes emerged between Arabia, India, China, Indonesia, Australia and Africa. European countries traded through the Mediterranean and Red Seas, then overland to this ocean. Picturesque dhows sailed from Zanzibar to trade their cloves and rice for sugarcane in Mauritius. The dhow, an Arabian boat with its tilted triangular sail, hardly looked as though it could make such a long journey - only the gentleness of the Indian Ocean made it possible. *I wonder if the navigators of long ago considered a route to the east to connect with Europe, the reverse of what Columbus and others had done in the fifteenth century?* Food from fish life was plentiful. Strange creatures - probably giant sea turtles and large poisonous snakes - were often reported by ships' crews. Aircraft transport now added to the traffic of commerce across this ocean.

When Edward had worked on Mauritius, he had paid little attention to the natural features of the island. He was not even aware that he resided on volcanic rock. He was too busy with work or partying with the English girls who also worked for the British government. Before leaving for this trip, he had purchased a travel book about Mauritius. He took it out of his pocket and read to pass the long hours of the flight. He learned that volcanoes on the sea bed had erupted long ago to create a number of small, isolated islands. In the tropic zones, coral atolls formed around islands such as the Maldives while coral reefs surrounded some of the less tropical islands. Edward did remember the coral reefs because he had gone to many beach parties. Edward did not remember Mauritius as a small island; there seemed to be plenty of space for everyone. The island's area, only about 700 square miles, held a population of well over one million.

Edward read further that the island was uninhabited when the Portuguese discovered it in the 16th century. After these early settlers arrived, new plant and animal life were introduced, resulting in the disappearance of much of the indigenous flora and fauna. Later, the Dutch arrived and tried to colonize it, naming the island after Prince Maurice of Nassau. The French took over in the early 18th century and established a sugar industry worked by slaves brought in from Africa. Eventually the sugarcane fields displaced much of the original rain forest. During the Napoleonic Wars, the island was used as a French naval and privateer base until 1810 when the British captured the island in a little-known naval skirmish. Slavery was abolished in 1833 and laborers from India began to replace the slaves. The book also mentioned dhow pirates docking on Mauritius to bury treasure. Edward remembered long-ago stories about treasure hunts, some of which were successful.

Edward put the book away, got up from his seat and headed aft to the lavatory. Towards the rear of the airplane he noticed a dark-haired woman staring at him. Her face was familiar. As he squeezed through the lavatory door, he thought: *Attractive lady and I know her from somewhere.* Heading back to his seat he saw her again but this time she was standing in the aisle. She smiled as she spoke.

"You must be Major Postmark."

"Why, yes. I am. And you are...?"

"You don't remember. I am Penelope Cancel. We worked together on Mauritius many years ago."

"Of course, you're Penny! You stayed here to work for the new government. Do you still live here?"

"Yes, I do, but I retired early from my position.

The aircraft was not full so they sat together and Edward ordered drinks while Penny fluffed her hair as she looked in her compact mirror.

"It has been a long time, Penny. You certainly look great."

"And so do you, Edward. I had no trouble recognizing you."

Edward was the quintessential retired British Officer, a product of bygone wars in the remotist part of the Empire. He was tall but no longer quite so lean with a posture still stiff as though at attention. The "stiff upper lip" was topped by a thin mustache against a ruddy complexion which was derived from his service in India. Spit and polish over-the-ankle boots complemented his tan suit which was adorned only with a subdued necktie. His British accent was still prominent, somewhat tempered by many years of influence by the French Creole and Sian languages.

"If I remember correctly, Penny, we used to go out together for a while."

"You did remember! I was not going to remind you."

Their drinks came and they reminisced.

"I shall never forget that day of the riots. Did you know, Edward, that you became a near legend to those of us who stayed on?"

He shifted in his seat and pulled the arm rest up.

"Oh, I am sure the legend grew in time like most legends do."

"Not this one. Remember, I was there!"

Penny excused herself and got up to visit the lavatory. Edward admired her figure as she swung into the aisle. After he sat back down, his mind, turned on by Penny's mention of the riots, reached into its memory and played it back. His mind connected the mention of the riots with the long-forgotten documents he had stored in the attic. Edward began to wonder if they contained anything important. If they did he would return them to the British government. Thoughts of the satchel full of papers conjured up an icy memory of the cobra he had placed in front of the crowd.

Penny was nudging him to let her into her seat, as Edward emerged abruptly from his reverie.

"I was thinking about the riots and similar outbreaks when I was posted in India."

He spoke reticently about his duty station in India but one could sense many adventures there. In the glory days of the British Empire, upon which the "sun never set," Edward had served as an officer in the army stationed in the southern part of

India. He was there in the days of Gandhi and predicted the end of Great Britain's hold on that country. His unit had stayed on until India's new government stabilized.

The aircraft was now losing altitude and Edward could see the small point of land from his window. There were ships below followed by great birds, the albatross and the frigate "man o'war" birds with their great wingspreads.

"Edward, are you returning to Mauritius or just visiting?"

"I am just visiting for perhaps a week. I have some business to take care of in connection with some property I own. You may remember the house, located on the outskirts of Port Louis. I liked living away from the British townhouses on the island but my stay at the house was brief. Soon after I bought the house, the island's struggle for independence began and I knew it was a matter of time before many of us would leave.

"While you are here, Edward," said Penny, the brightness of excitement showing in her eyes, "you must visit me. I may be moving back to England after all these years but I will tell you more about it later."

"Yes, I will come see you after I visit my house."

Edward glanced at Penny as she stared out the window. He thought she was even prettier than when they had dated. They had some fun times but she was quite a bit younger than he. Perhaps that was why he had not pursued a more serious relationship. Then again, he was never too serious about any of the women he dated. He noticed she was not wearing a wedding ring. She turned to Edward, her expression somewhat pensive.

"When I was single, I and the other girls spent our month's holiday in England, hoping we would meet a husband there. We bought new clothes in London, and tried new hair styles in anticipation of the revelry and romance to follow. Some were successful; most returned to Mauritius and began to plan for the next year."

"Were you successful?"

"Yes and no. I did marry, but not in London. I met someone here but it did not work out."

"Sorry to hear that. I never had that problem. All those years in India somehow precluded marriage."

Penny shifted uncomfortably in her seat and turned toward the window to hide her slight blush.

"I'm not surprised you didn't marry. You went out with so many girls but I don't recall your staying with one for very long -- including me," she added.

Edward turned toward Penny thinking that women from England had those clear complexions that seemed to go with the cool, dewy English weather. The climate in Mauritius was much different and although their skin remained clear, they gradually tanned. Edward had not recognized her because over twenty years ago, she was a mere slip of a girl, skinny and angular in build. Now, Edward could not help but notice her fuller, shapely figure. Of course, she was a woman now and Edward quickly appreciated her maturity.

"Do you still live in the compound?"

"Yes, I do," She said, handing him a card with her address and telephone number. "Call me as soon as you can."

The aircraft was descending. The island became larger as the aircraft was oriented into the landing pattern. Edward became inwardly more excited thinking about this trip. Penny again opened her compact and fluffed her hair.

"Edward, how did you come to Mauritius in the first place?"

Edward paused before answering. He also was thinking about the past.

"Following my assignment in India, I was invited by my former commanding officer there to consider an assignment in Mauritius. I accepted and was designated to the administration as a kind of military attache and aide-de-camp. Following departure of the British from Mauritius, I rather hoped for a position in British overseas government. However, the Empire's decline left little opportunity. So, I returned to England and was posted there until my retirement from the army."

Looking past her out the window, Edward commented on the sight of many acres of plantations. Looming on the horizon were mountains, jagged peaks of volcanic rock behind Port Louis.

* * *

After landing, Edward and Penny went through Customs and made their way outside to hail a taxi. Penny declined his offer for a ride but reminded him to visit her. As they parted, she gave Edward a warm embrace and kiss.

As soon as she had gone, someone called his name. It was Ashok Patel, his former colleague and tenant of his house. After the, he had leased the house to Ashok, who also worked for the administration. Ashok promised to act as caretaker in exchange for a very reasonable lease agreement. Edward had written advising Ashok of his intent to visit but had given no details.

Ashok grabbed Edward's hand and shook it hard.

"Welcome, welcome back!" he shouted, white teeth gleaming amid his trimmed black beard adorning his smooth, dark skin. Ashok had migrated from India to Mauritius just before the island became independent.

"Come, I have a car."

They pushed through the airport's people traffic, finally making it to Ashok's car, a Renault 4CV. Edward asked how Ashok was able to obtain the French model.

"Just after the British left, one of the staff sold it to me. I always wanted a 4CV. It is worth more today then what I paid for it but it needs work."

"Yes, I can hear the transmission," Edward replied, raising his voice over the metallic clamor.

As they drove, Ashok asked Edward about his itinerary.

"I plan to stay just one week," replied Edward. Distracted by the excitement of returning to the island and of meeting Penny again, he neglected to explain the purpose of his visit.

Ashok frowned but drove on without asking Edward again.

Edward mentioned the size of the crowd to Ashok.

"Yes, we wonder every day how the island can handle this growth."

"I see the airport is much larger and there are many new airline companies flying here."

"Yes, Mauritius is now a connecting link between Europe, Africa, India and Australia. Perhaps we will also have more tourists."

Edward grimaced as Ashok dodged a multitude of buses on the well-paved hilly roads. They soon arrived on the outskirts of the city. Looking down from the hills, the sea on the other side of the city was clearly visible. Along the road, many flowers displayed azure, aquamarine, reseda and emerald blossoms, spotted with scarlet, cerise and yellow petals. The fresh smell of the air, the cool breeze from the ocean and the faint fragrance of the colorful flowers flooded his senses. While Edward rambled on about the island sights, Ashok tensely gripped the steering wheel with both hands.

They arrived at Edward's house and Ashok's wife, Subhadra, and two small children came out to greet him. Edward would stay at his house with Ashok's family and they took him and his luggage to a room upstairs. He was invited to freshen up and join them for the evening meal.

As Edward unpacked, he could not help overhearing the conversation between Ashok and his wife. Subhadra looked askance at Ashok as though she could wait no longer to find out what Edward's intentions were.

"Maybe, Ashok, he is now here to evict us and live in the house?"

"Perhaps. Whatever he does I believe he will not put us at a disadvantage. I could be in error; it has been many years since he was here."

Then Edward realized he had not told them of his plan for the house. He would tell them as soon as the meal was completed.

"Ashok, what if he sells the house, where will we go?"

"I have thought about that and I have to assume that he will give us time to find another home. He was a decent man; he will do the proper thing. In any event, I shall ask him after our evening meal."

After cleaning off the dust of travel and washing up, Edward came down to the kitchen. Subhadra was impatiently stirring the food in the pots on the stove, splashing some out of the pot which sizzled noisily on the burner. The children helped set the table while she stirred the food again and again as if to hurry the cooking along.

Edward told Ashok he would like to look around outside while the meal was being prepared.

The house was built with a brick-like material from lava rock - a sturdy substance for a structure. The white paint which covered the bricks contrasted with the brilliant colors of the flowers surrounding the house. The roof was made from the same lava rock and shaped into gray slates. The first floor windows each had a window box overflowing with different varieties of hibiscus. A profusion of other flowers, with crimson, indigo and heliotrope hues, filled the flower beds along the perimeter of the house. Their fragrance softened the cool, early evening air.

Edward returned to the dining room where the evening meal was ready.

"Seeing the house," he said, "I feel as though I never left the island. It certainly brings back memories. The building appears to be well-kept which I do appreciate."

"I have tried, Major, to keep it from falling into disrepair."

"I noticed you have added to the landscaping. Very picturesque. I particularly like the flowering fruit trees in the backyard near the house. It looks like a small orchard. And the yard looks large enough to add two more houses. I did not remember the lot as being that big."

Ashok frowned at Edward but did not reply. Instead he stood and went into the kitchen.

The aroma of stewed chicken and vegetables drifted into thedining room. Curry and other spices sharpened the smell. Subhadra and the children appeared and began setting the food on the table, seemingly eager to get on with the meal.

Edward did most of the talking thoughout the meal, trying to reminisce over the days when he was stationed there and asking where mutual acquaintances were.

The meal was completed rather quickly and, while the children noisily cleaned the pots and dishes in the kitchen, Edward brought up the purpose of his trip.

"My reason for this trip is to sell the house."

Subhadra inhaled sharply; Ashok stiffened with his arms crossed in front of him.

"You will have first interest in buying the house if you so desire. I will establish a reasonable price and a loan for you with a local lawyer who can handle the deed."

Subhadra's face broke into a large smile and Ashok jumped up and grabbed Edward's hand.

"I am overwhelmed," said Ashok, shaking Edward's hand. "When I read your letter I thought you might want the house back so we talked about finding a new place to live. We are delighted with your offer!"

"I do not expect to return to Mauritius. I am settled in London and see no reason to keep the house. You have certainly taken good care of it for which I am grateful. Think of this as my way of repaying you for your efforts."

The family was excited about the offer and chatted with Edward into the evening. Finally Edward rose and took his leave.

"I am tired from the long flight," he said. "Tomorrow morning, Ashok, I shall begin looking through the attic. If there is anything worthwhile there then I shall ship it to London. By the way, I met a former colleague of ours, Penelope Cancel."

"Oh, yes, I remember her. Does she still live here?"

"Yes, in the old compound. I shall visit her before I leave the island."

"Do not forget, you must plan to take your meals with us."

* * *

Early the next morning he had breakfast with the family. After Ashok left for work, Edward climbed the dusty, creaking stairwell to the attic. Each step he took seemed to invoke some memory in his mind, like opening each chapter in an auto-biography. The door creaked as he opened it. He stood still and looked around; it was intensely quiet. For a moment, he thought it felt like looking at a mirror of his past. Although the floor beams were covered with plywood flooring, the garret had never been finished into a room. The rafters were exposed and, without insulation, a musty damp odor was noticeable.

At first, Edward did not pay attention to the sound which broke the silence. He stopped suddenly when he heard the scraping-like noise. He thought he had made the noise with his shoes. It stopped but as Edward exhaled the scraping began again and then became intermittent. Edward stood rigidly still and thought: *I am not alone; is someone here or is it an animal?* After a few minutes, he did not hear the sound and went over to examine his old belongings.

Edward methodically started with the trunks. The morning wore on as he plodded through each trunk, removing items he wished to keep and leaving the rest. There was little there to evoke much nostalgia for the past. He smiled as he picked up one old sweater which reminded him of a special outing with one of his girlfriends. He closed the trunk, pushed it aside and labelled it. He left the few objects that he wanted to keep on the floor for the time being. Behind the trunks was a satchel. His memory jolted back to the riots. There was the bag containing the files taken from the government building.

He decide to finish going through the trunks before tackling the papers in the satchel. He continued pulling the contents from each trunk. Soon he realized there was little to salvage. Edward listened once more for any noise, left the garret and went to his room to clean up for lunch.

After lunching with the family, he asked Ashok to take him to the car rental office at the airport so he could do some sightseeing. Ashok insisted that he use his car. If Edward would drop him at his office after lunch, he could use the car all afternoon and then pick him up. But Edward insisted on the rental.

Ashok drove off with Edward toward the airport.

"When I was in London planning this trip I worried that seeing the house and the island again would awaken a desire to return to Mauritius. In the attic today I was transported back many years to the Mauritius period of my life, but nothing there convinced me to leave London."

The noisy old 4CV arrived at the airport entrance.

"Don't get lost," yelled Ashok, above the noise of the aircraft. "The roads are good but there are not many of them, especially when you drive in the hills."

"I think I will recall some of the area when I get there, Ashok, but, to be sure, I will get a map with the car."

There was a long line at the car rental office. Edward watched the faces in the crowd; a truly international mix of people, sprawled throughout the terminal areas. Many were sitting or sleeping on their luggage. A brilliantly colored parrot suddenly hopped onto Edward's shoulder and then jumped onto a small child's hand. Animals in small travel cages were everywhere, their odor mingling with the oily smell from the vendor stalls selling versions of fast food, rice cakes with curried chicken. Coming from a crowd near the car rental was the sound of India, the reedy tones of an oboe-like instrument. Edward stared at the musician, half expecting to see a cobra weaving back and forth to the refrain.

Edward finally secured the car he wanted and drove from the airport to the hills behind Port Louis just to get the feel of the roads. It was not easy to get acclimated because of the heavy traffic. He stopped occasionally to familiarize himself with the map. Satisfied he knew where he was, he headed back to the house.

Subhadra met him at the door. Edward tried not to stare at her but she was a very attractive woman. He had to admit that Subhadra was quite striking when she looked at him with her wide, black eyes. The colorful, thin sari she wore did not hide her slim figure. Edward was very uncomfortable being alone with her in the house.

"Major Postmark, you had phone call from Ms. Cancel. She asked that you call her."

"Thank you, Subhadra. I will call her right away."

Subhadra smiled at Edward as though she were aware of hisdiscomfort. Penny answered after the first ring.

"Edward, I am rather anxious to talk to you. Can you come over tomorrow around tea time?"

"Yes, of course. I will be there before tea time."

Edward rang off and stared at the phone. He wondered what could be bothering Penny.

* * *

Edward went back up to the attic and continued looking through the trunks. He had accumulated some old silverware, lamps and several small paintings. As he pondered their destination, he heard that strange sound again, a sort of rustling, scraping movement. He looked around but did not see anything. The sound stopped, then started, and stopped again. He heard Ashok's noisy car drive up to the house so he decided to quit for the time being.

After supper, Edward told the family what he had found so far in the attic. He asked Ashok about the noise he had heard. Ashok was puzzled; he was not aware of any animals on the premises. If the sound continued, he would help Edward look for the source.

* * *

After breakfast the next morning, Edward returned to the attic and opened the rest of the trunks. He decided there was little in them of interest. He would leave them for Ashok to dispose of them as he saw fit.

He reported his progress at lunch with Ashok and his family, giving instructions to Ashok regarding disposition of the trunks. After lunch, Edward drove around the island seeking roads leading into the few remaining heavy forests. He did not remember so many farms; there were more woods and rain forests when he was last here. The extinct dodo bird had inhabited this part of the island.

After a while, he drove towards the ocean to see the coral reefs that still survived. He got out of the car and went down to sit near the water. The view and the invigorating scent of the sea wind brought back memories of the good times he had shared with the women in his life while on the island. They often came here to picnic and when the weather and ocean became too cool in the late afternoon, a fire was lit to keep warm. By nightfall, the couples would hug by the fire or sneak away from its light.

Leaving memories of his youth on the beach, he returned to his car and headed towards the city and the townhouses that at one time housed the British government personnel. These houses were attached to each other in the style of London's mews. He recognized the houses and stopped at the one with Penny's number. He rang the bell, soon answered by Penny.

"Hello, Penny. I found my way over here after all these years."

"Hello again, Edward. Do come in."

They sat and chatted in a lively fashion about the by-gone days when Edward lived on the island. Edward could tell that Penny was nervous from the way she frequently got up and paced.

"I wanted to see you Edward to let you know I have a relationship with someone in London. I admit I am a bit unsettled after meeting you again after so many years. You were one of my favorite companions."

Edward watched Penny as she paced. After she sat down again, Edward held her cold hand and restrained himself from embracing and kissing her.

"Who is he? Do I know him?"

"He is a friend of my former husband. I met him during one of our trips to London just before my husband and I broke up. I am going back to London to see him. I think he wants to get married but..."

"When will you be returning to London? I do want to see you there."

"I'm not sure but I will let you know before I leave the island."

To hide the flush of her cheeks, Penny pulled her hand away and stood.

"To tell the truth, we have been very chummy but he has not yet offered to marry me. But I think he will. I came back here to make arrangements to move permanently to London."

Penny walked over to the window, looking at the jagged peaks in the background.

"I shall see you in London but I wanted you to know that I may be committed."

Edward stared at her figure while he mulled over her situation.

Penny turned around, looked at Edward and smiled.

"It's time for tea; I shall bring in the service."

Edward stood up and looked around Penny's home which was furnished in a tropical motif, so different from an English home. It seemed her life intermingled the two cultures. Her home was warm and inviting with tan wicker furniture on bright Indian rugs designed with yellow, orange and green flowers. Light green sheer curtains draped the windows.

Edward stared out the window at the other houses and he could see the one he used to live in. He now thought it odd that he had never settled down with one of the many English women, including Penny. But, at the time, his heart belonged to all of them; he could not settle on one. He thought about Penny's status. His feelings for her were suddenly strong and yet how could he tell how she felt about him? He was not likely to become impetuous so he would see her in London and let events take their course.

Penny brought in the silver service tray along with crumpets and scones. She poured the tea a bit unsteadily, rattling the cups and saucers while Edward selected a scone. He took a small bite, savoring the creamy taste.

"One thing about Mauritius, Edward, the Indian tea is delicious."

"I dare say you are right. The brew has a decided aroma."

Time passed quickly and Edward said he had to leave. Penny invited him for dinner the next day and Edward readily agreed. Driving back to the house Edward thought how attractive she looked after all those years.

Edward was late getting back to the house for dinner. He was keyed-up and told the family he would have dinner with Ms. Cancel tomorrow. After dinner, Edward returned to his room still excited about his meeting with Penelope.

* * *

The next morning Edward continued his review of assorted boxes, the contents of which appeared to be worthless. Some of the boxes which contained old brochures. He labelled them to be destroyed. Near the boxes was the old satchel containing the files he had taken from his office so many years ago. He was about to pick it up when he heard the scraping, rustling sound again, only much louder. Suddenly there appeared before him a mask-like face! Edward was frozen in place! He found himself face-to-face with a king cobra, extended vertically almost full length, weaving and and hissing! Edward slowly backed away, scarcely breathing, mesmerized by the hooded serpent. He remembered the cobra in the basket during the riots. The snake slowly lowered its hooded head and curled around the satchel. Edward backed away, feeling his heart pounding and quickly disapppeared down the stairwell.

Shaken, he asked Subhadra for some scotch and water while he told her what happened. She immediately called Ashok at the office. Ashok soon arrived and heard Edward, now a bit calmer, repeat his story.

"I have never seen a snake in this house," said Ashok "Perhaps it climbed one of the fruit trees and got under the eaves. Come, we will capture it and I can sell it."

He found a sack, a box and then took an old broom.

"Here, Major, hold this broom handle."

He nailed a small piece of rope to the top end of the broom, then made a noose through another nail which allowed him to tighten it after he had the noose around the snake's head. They went into the attic and slowly approached the suitcase. The rustling noise began again and suddenly the dreaded hood appeared, at almost eye level to the men.

"You hold the broom and I will get the noose over the hood."

"I've got the snake, Ashok; hold its head."

With Edward's help Ashok placed the thrashing reptile into the bag. With the snake inside the bag, Ashok loosened the noose, removed the broom handle from the bag and tied up the bag. The bag seemed to move toward them, stirring up the dust until they grabbed it and placed it in the box. They carefully pulled the box down the attic stairs and Ashok placed the box outside.

They both sat down, brushed off the dust from the attic and contemplated the origin of the snake.

"Ashok, why was the snake positioned on that satchel?"

"Was there anything in the satchel connecting it to the cobra?"

"I do not know. Let's find out."

They climbed the stairs to the attic and listened for any noise to make sure there were no more snakes. Edward carefully opened the satchel, lifted its top gently with the broom handle and peered inside. All he saw were files; nothing moved and nothing unusual was there. He closed the top and they left the attic.

Still somewhat shaken, Edward joined the family for lunch and discussed the incident.

I cannot attribute anything significant or sinister to the snake," said Ashok. "There are those in India who would see the cobra as symbolic of something sinister and there are those who would see it as a positive sign."

"Well, having seen many cobras in India I did not see this one as mysterious. But I must say I was startled!"

Edward and Ashok had experienced enough excitement for one day and, after Ashok went back to the office, Edward drove out into the country. This time he drove toward the highest mountain, Piton de la Riviere-Noire, in the southwest part of the island. Bottle palms dotted the roadside until he started climbing up into the mountain as far as the roads would take him. Sugar cane fields had not yet taken over in this area and the flowers were prolific and pretty. He recognized the hibiscus plants which seemed to spread over the lower altitude terrain. As he left the hilly country, he was once again surrounded by sugarcane fields which grew near the road. The sugarcane grew well over ten-foot tall, dwarfing cars and people around them. The thick stalks were colorful, ranging from white and yellow to green and red. It was getting late so he drove back to the city to Penelope's house.

* * *

Edward looked forward to having dinner with Penny. He brought three different wines to make sure one of them would complement the entree. She made a traditional English roast beef dinner, served by candlelight which sparkled on the china and silver settings she had kept from her marriage. After Penny set the food on the table, she asked Edward to carve the beef. He professed a lack of experience and managed not to mangle the roast. The entree was delicious emitting a somewhat spicy aroma. Conversation was confortably interspersed with the clink of knives and forks against the plates and tinkling of glasses brought together to toast days gone by.

The wine flowed until well after dinner. Edward and Penny reminisced until they ran out of memories.

"It was a delightful evening, Penny, unfortunately, I will finish my business tomorrow and leave the next day."

"So soon?" she asked, trying to mask her disappointment.

"I would like to meet you in London. When are you returning?"

"I plan to go there shortly and I shall let you know my itinerary, although..."

Penny hesitated, then took his hand and continued.

"Edward, I told you that I may be seriously involved withsomeone there. However, if you like, I will still see you in London."

Her eyelids brimmed with tears, revealing her sadness at his leaving. Edward wondered if that was an invitation.

"Would it be awkward if I stayed the night?"

"It would be difficult; you have confused the situation! My plans in London appeared to be clear-cut until you showed up here. I am glad to see you but your timing was not good for me."

"Well, I had better go."

Penny walked with him to his car. The night was cool and clear but his head was not. Edward kissed her goodnight and yearned for more, but Penny returned to her house.

As he motored back to his house Edward wondered what to do about the emotions stirred up by his visit with Penny. *Although I always seem to have strong feelings for women but I could never seem to settle down. This time might be different. I will see Penny in London and see what develops.*

* * *

Despite the afterglow he felt from his dinner with Penny, Edward did not sleep well. The cobra haunted his dreams. He arose early and offered to help Subhadra prepare breakfast but she politely shooed him out of the kitchen. Ashok came down at his usual time and together they had breakfast.

After the meal, Ashok went off to work and Edward slowly ascended the attic stairs almost expecting to see his nemesis, the reptile, again. He approached the satchel with foreboding, fearing another snake would be inside. He opened the satchel with the broom handle and saw no snake. Instead, there were government documents concerning old diplomatic matters. Nothing seemed of particular interest except that the correspondence was historic, dating back to the mid-1800's. With the British government gone, the files had little significance to him so he decided to ship them along with his other objects. They might, he thought, be of interest to a university or museum. He would keep one file which contained personal letters, articles and some old envelopes given him by his predecessor. Some of the envelopes had postmark dates as early as 1850. One of them contained several unused stamps which showed a profile view of Queen Victoria's head. *In London, I shall ask a stamp dealer if they have any value to a collector.*

He walked slowly around the garret checking again the boxes marked for shipment to London. He had said goodbye to Penny, now he must say farewell to his house. At least he would see Penny in London. He closed the door, leaving the dusty attic behind.

After lunch, Edward and Ashok drove to the lawyer's office. On the way, Edward spoke again about the cobra. Was the snake protecting the suitcase? Was there something more to the snake's presence in the attic? Ashok could not explain it and did not appear to be superstitious about it. But Edward, stunned by the appearance of the cobra, could not shake an oppressive, ominous feeling.

"Major, did you discover anything unusual?"

"No, nothing of interest, only some old envelopes and stamps."

He showed him the letters and stamps he had found the night before. Ashok looked at them and commented that they were obviously very old after recognizing Queen Victoria's profile.

The business at the lawyer's office was concluded rapidly and Ashok had his house. Back at the house, Edward nursed a scotch while Ashok and Subhadra sipped nonalcoholic drinks to celebrate the occasion. Ashok's wife even hugged him and also repeated her thanks. They sat and spoke nostalgically about Edward's last night on Mauritius.

Subhadra normally stayed out of gentlemen's conversations but tonight was special. She smiled at Edward with her wide eyes as she spoke.

"You never married?" asked Subhadra.

"No, even though I had met many ladies when I worked here, including Ms. Cancel."

Subhadra could not resist a smile and then commented boldly.

"Would it not be an irony if you and Ms. Cancel reunited after all these years?"

Edward smiled but said nothing. He looked at his watch.

"Well, I had better finish packing for the long trip tomorrow," said Edward.

"Ashok, I am too excited to sleep," said Subhadra, putting away the glasses.

"I am also excited but I must work tomorrow after we see Edward off at the airport."

Edward went to his room as Ashok closed up the house, now Subhadra's and his house, and retired.

* * *

Early the next morning, Edward was up before the others and wandered around the outside of the house for the last time. Then he had breakfast with the family, packed the rental car and checking his luggage, Edward said good-bye at the departure gate. Ashok and Suhadra tearfully thanked him again for his kindness.

Soon Edward was airborne for the long flight that would include a number of stops before ending at London's Heathrow Airport. As the island faded from his view, so did the memories of the island. As the aircraft settled into its cruise altitude, the image of the cobra again loomed in his mind.

* * *

The boxes from Mauritus arrived a week after Edward returned to London. He removed the various objects and deftly placed them around the house. He came across the envelopes and stamps that he had brought back from his trip and wondered again if they were valuable. Not being a collector, he took the stamps and envelopes to a local stamp dealer.

"Good Morning, Sir" said the salesman behind the counter displaying a variety of colorful stamps. "May I help you?"

"Yes. I wonder if you might look at these items and tell me if they have value to a collector."

The salesman studied the stamps and envelopes. He referred to the envelopes as "covers." He looked up the stamps in the catalog on the counter, then picked up the phone and spoke to the owner of the store. His eyes were focused on one stamp in particular. The owner appeared within minutes and began to study the stamps with a magnifying glass. They conferred for a few minutes. With a pair of tongs the owner carefully selected an orange colored stamp and set it on the glass apart from the others. Edward was not prepared for the owner's next words.

"Sir," said the owner quietly, "if genuine, this stamp is worth over 700,000 pounds or over one million American dollars!"

Chapter 2

> *"The world is too much with us: late and soon,*
> *Getting and spending, we lay waste our powers;*
> *Little we see in Nature that is ours;*
> *We have given our hearts away, a sordid boon!"*
>
> *- A Sonnet by William Wordsworth*

Roger Essay's car was careening along the freeway through the light Sunday morning traffic heading for Chesapeake Bay. He had been awakened by his boss at 6 a.m.; there had been an explosion on the Project 006 power plant. Roger was an engineering manager at Power Engineering International in Washington, D.C. The plant being constructed along Chesapeake Bay was a fossil fuel power plant using coal instead of oil. He was responsible for the design of instrumentation, those dials and needles essential to the control of the plant.

He could not conceive what could have gone wrong and had been told only that the explosion occurred in his area of responsibility. His mind was now awake and in high gear. He thought about his job which kept him hopping nearly 80 hours a week at the office and at home, twice the so-called normal 40-hour week. But that was not enough; computer technology allowed him to do even more. What's the word? Ah, yes! multiplexing: doing two or more things at once. Now he could do 120 hours of work per week! Was he under some zodiac sign for speed? At the office he had many projects in work at the same time. More multiplexing: each project needed input everyday. He recalled a child's toy wherein six large ball bearings were randomly propelled by rotating cams to push six tin racehorses along their slots until one crossed the finish line. That was how his life seemed to be moving along.

He soliloquized half aloud as the car roared down the highway. *Is this my life? I need a change, an asynchronous diversion, to divert this dash to workaholism. I must spend more time with my hobby. I need a woman in my life.*

From his house in Maryland, the plant was normally two hours away. With the light traffic and driving at high speed he would make it in an hour and a half. He kept checking his speedometer He was now on the road to Annapolis, Maryland, the gateway to the Bay. After turning off to go south toward the plant, located just outside of Solomon's Island, he made a quick stop for coffee and a bagel and then resumed his pace. Seeing the Bay along the way, he should have enjoyed the scene of boats sailing through the morning mist, but his thoughts were preoccupied.

He arrived an hour later at the plant to find a fire engine and ambulance at the main building's entrance. He rushed inside and ran toward a crowd at the power plant's control console. "What happened?" Roger asked Bart, the foreman, a strapping, former football player who glared at Roger and leaned forward as if he were about to tackle him. He wore the usual baseball hat on top of his long locks of hair.

"That little lady engineer who works for you blew up a transformer."

"Is she hurt?"

"I think she's o.k., but she's still trapped inside. We had trouble shutting off the power; not everything is checked out yet."

Roger went inside the console, behind the instrument panels to console his engineer huddled against the steel structure while a fireman was cutting away burnt wires which blocked her path.

"Pamela, are you hurt?"

"A few small burns, Roger," she choked, "but mostly I'm upset at what I did. Just look at this mess. It made a hell of a noise but it looks worse than it is. I can work around it."

Roger stared at a small transformer which obviously had ruptured and was still spewing forth acrid smoke.

"What caused the explosion?"

As the fireman continued cutting the wires, Pamela explained that the meter for turbine ball bearing temperature appeared to be giving wrong readings at below 100% power output. At 100%, the reading was correct. She thought she had traced the trouble to a small instrument transformer but when she tried to test it, she inadvertently applied 220 volts and blew it up.

The fireman finished cutting the wires so Pamela could step away from the structure. Roger reviewed the test data with her. Meanwhile, the burly foreman returned and began yelling at both of them.

"You whizz-kids are putting me behind schedule. When will you fix this mess?"

Although he towered over her Pamela stood up to him. She was toe-to-toe with the furious foreman, undaunted by his size.

"Look, big bird, I'm working the problem instead of being out sailing my boat, so what are you complaining about?"

"Alright, little lady, I could be sailing too, but you're holding up the turbine system wiring changes."

"Go work around the problem like I'm doing! Move your ass now so I can get back to work!"

Roger and Pamela together did not equal the size of the hefty foreman but Roger quickly stepped in between them anyway. The foreman scowled and looked like he wanted to poke Pamela.

"Hold it!" Roger barked. "Let's break it up. I've got to get data for the staff meeting tomorrow!"

The foreman gave one last glowering look at Pamela and stomped off. Roger and Pamela went to the front of the console, sat down and went over a chronology of events which would help him at the staff meeting explain what had happened at the plant.

"Pamela, do you need some help?"

"No, Roger. The first shift engineer is here so I'll brief him and then leave. I'll come in early for my shift tonight after I calm down and get some rest."

Roger knew Pamela was a competent engineer. She had volunteered for the night shift to have more time during day light hours to sail. Roger knew he would be here all day. The multiplex man would be in full swing. It could have been worse. Roger collected his notes and went to the Test Manager's office and called his boss, the vice-president of engineering.

"Hello, Roger, are you still at the site?"

"Yes sir. One of my engineers was slightly hurt but she'll be o.k. We're fixing what happened last night but there is a problem that is unsolved."

Roger recited the details of the transformer fire and the continuing problem with the Turbine Temperature Indicator.

"Roger, you'd better stay there all week if necessary. The indicator problem will impact the delivery schedule if you don't fix it soon. Call me each day."

*　　*　　*

All week long the solution to the turbine temperature problem eluded Roger and his engineers. While Roger remained at the power plant site, he had three of his engineers at the Rosslyn office analyzing possible approaches which they passed on to Roger by phone calls and E-mail. The test team made the temporary changes both in hardware and software and then recorded the instrument readings.

Toward the end of the week, Roger sat in the test manager's office rubbing his eyes, tired from studying the computer printouts. Pamela walked in.

"Roger, we finished the last batch of code changes and we're still getting the same indications. Shouldn't we move on to other tests?"

Roger stared silently at Pamela, apparently unwilling to concede defeat.

"You're probably right, Pamela. I'm stymied, I admit. I plan to leave this afternoon. I need some time to decide where we go from here. I'll tell the Test Manager to move on to complete the other tests."

Pamela left and Roger located the test manager and recommended he continue with the test plan. Roger packed his belongings in one suitcase and the test data in another. He thought: *I can't believe this answer is so hard to find. I'll have to ask for help at the next staff meeting. Meanwhile, my plan to slow down and enjoy my hobby will have to wait.*

Roger picked up his two suitcases and left the building, walking with his shoulders hunched over like a tired travelling salesman.

*   *   *

At half past six Monday morning electrons began stirring all through Roger's house. In the room called the den, a computer screen lit up and presented a checklist of morning routine instructions. Suddenly, the kitchen was illuminated as the coffee pot on the counter made percolating noises. Computer monitors in the kitchen and bedroom were energized.

Soft music emanated from the bedroom and the aroma of coffee filled the house. Shortly thereafter the body in the bed began moving. A hand appeared from under the covers trying to shut off the music coming from a speaker on the table next to the bed. Controlled by the computer, the music would not cease so the hand retreated under the blanket. Five minutes of music

passed and then a tinny voice came through the speaker.
"Time to shine!"
Roger Essay bolted upright and then slowly slipped out of bed and headed for the bathroom. A sensor picked up his movement and spotted him there and shut off the wake-up music. *I wonder what day it is. Oh yes, it is Monday again, the day of the weekly staff meeting.* Now about half awake, he headed to the kitchen and poured a cup of hot coffee. He put on his sweat suit and went jogging. When he returned, he glared at the computer monitor screen in the kitchen and heard a raspy voice from a nearby speaker, 6:45 a.m. The monitor also reported the weather as fair and cool.

"Time for your shower, Roger," said the speaker, "Pick out a delicious breakfast and put it in the microwave oven."

Roger shuffled into the shower. By the time he finished he the computer energized the microwave oven, where the frozen meal would be heated and ready to eat by the time Roger returned to the kitchen table.

After his shower, Roger dressed and continued to think about work. A bad habit; and yet some of his best ideas occurred early in the day. The weekly staff meeting turned him off so his mind wandered from work to the recent breakup with his girlfriend. *Should I have been more serious? Was there a right time to get serious and get married? Was she the one? Where is "Ms. Right", or is it, when is "Ms. Right?"*

Women were always attracted to him. Although Roger had a tall, lean build, his pale, hollow cheeks under prominent cheekbones gave the impression he needed a solid, home-cooked meal. That was okay with Roger.

He was approaching what used to be considered "middle age" - the late thirties. His dark brown hair was slightly thinning but he did not wear it long as befitted someone from the sixties generation. Black, horn-rimmed eyeglasses contrasted with his light skin and made his face appear more gaunt yet more attractive. His somewhat thin lips made his nose look more prominent than it really was. Looking at the mirror he wondered if a mustache would help.

Roger's physique was standard as measured by suit sizes that were off the rack. He dressed well and despite his hectic schedule he avoided wearing tennis shoes and jeans to work.

He put on his dark blue silk suit, light blue shirt with an appropriately loud, multicolored tie. He enjoyed wearing his shiney loafers with the tassels. Most of his colleagues wore dull-colored shoes with a matte finish, and button-down, soft shirt collars. This was the uniform of this generation's managers and lawyers. Even the president of the company wore matte-finished shoes and a button-down collar shirt. *Not for me; I wear a straight collar and very shiny loafers.*

The multiplex man did not have time for relationships, much less marriage. He would miss the setup he had with his now ex-girlfriend. Other then bedtime meetings and occasional dining out, they hardly saw each other. And now she was gone.

A sensor in the kitchen sounded that the subject had arrived.

"Good Morning, Roger", said the speaker. "Your breakfast is ready in the microwave."

Roger removed his breakfast dish from the oven and began to eat as he perused his schedule for the day on the monitor. The staff meeting was still on at 9:00 a.m. If it finished before noon, he would go over to the London Gallery which was having a stamp auction sale this week, something he looked forward to.

His hearty breakfast of eggs and salami wasn't bad. He liked the breakfast meal and took his time. He read the paper and switched between the morning TV shows during commercials, hoping to catch something of interest. He always switched off the weathermen, most of whom were selling their personalities. It bothered Roger that the forecasts were so inaccurate. He remembered a small project in his eighth grade science class. The students collected the daily newspaper forecasts for a month and compared each one with the actual weather. The accuracy was a bit over 80% at a time when computers were not used. Now, despite billions of dollars worth of computers, the accuracy is not much better.

"Have a good day," intoned the computer. "See you tonight. The weather is a little cool so you might want your topcoat."

Meals were no problem for the multiplex man. They were cooked on Sunday and frozen, then alternated with commercial frozen dinners throughout the week. Sometimes he ate out for variety. He thought about taking more of an interest in cooking like so many of his male colleagues.

After brushing his teeth, Roger went back to the kitchen to clean up. Roger stared at the automation he had added to his home. It appealed to his sense of order. While he was not a hacker, he had extended the range of his computer to his house; scheduling of his time, preparation of food, security, and various sensors. When he had started his effort he expected it to help him accomplish more each day and it did. But now he worried that he may have overdone things.

Roger Essay headed off to work and a tough meeting. He knew last week's explosion would be the first order of business. He had a dozen engineers reporting to him yet he still seemed to be in meetings most of the day. The company had given him the responsibility to manage a group of very technical people but too little time to spend managing his team. Managing meant planning, organizing, leading and controlling. How could he accomplish all of this when he spent more than half of his day in meetings? *I wonder if I'll lose my technical skills because of my job; I know I'm losing my social skills.* Even with multiplexing his he found that he spent more time on work.

He picked up his brief case and laptop computer and looked around the first floor of his house before leaving. He liked his two-story, brick townhouse, what his parents used to call a row house. He had furnished it very simply in early American. He looked at the long sofas in front of the picture window and across from the fireplace. He had spent a lot of money for the oriental carpet which covered the shiny, waxed hardwood floors. Since four people could eat in the kitchen, he had converted his dining room into his computer office. A colorful oil painting hung on the wall near the window. Roger thought it a comfortable place to live.

He closed the front door and the house. Proximity sensors told the computer when he left the house. The computer then engaged the house alarm system. When Roger returned he had 20 seconds after he entered the house to key a code on his alarm control panel. The computer would turn off the alarm outside lights and set the timer for his dinner for the appropriate hour.

He got into his car in the driveway and drove less than ten minutes to the Metro train station where he parked and walked over to the tracks. Roger's townhouse was just outside of Washington, D.C., in Maryland near Rock Creek Park. The Metro subway, with one transfer, would take him right to the Twin Towers Center in Rosslyn, Virginia, where his company, Power Engineering International, occupies the 20th through the 25th floors. Every weekday he traversed three state lines - Maryland, District of Columbia and Virginia - to get to work.

The Company - Power Engineering International Inc. - was an old line organization that designed electric power plants for utility companies. Their plants utilized fossil fuels: coal, natural gas, oil or coal gas. With a very conservative management, they never built nuclear power plants although they did design systems that worked with the steam supply part of a nuclear plant.

PEI, Inc. was housed in one of the high-rise buildings in Rosslyn. "High-rise" in the Washington area meant twenty-some stories, not one hundred stories like in NYC. This small town, directly across the Potomac River from the Washington, DC, was composed mainly of tall office buildings and apartments. City planners, however, seemed to have forgotten how to handle pedestrians and parking. From the top of some of the buildings, the view of the nation's capital was spectacular; one could see all the way down the Mall, the Lincoln and Jefferson memorials, the Monument and the Capitol.

As the subway moved rapidly through the city, Roger thought about the company. PEI was successful; right from the start after World War II and had grown steadily. It was now the leading producer of fossil fuel power plants in the world. The Board of Directors and the top management remained steadfastly conservative through the years. They recognized the need to keep up with technological advancements such as the digital computer but they were reluctant to initiate sudden changes. Instead, they encouraged the younger engineers and managers to recommend state of the art improvements for new plants. In their instrumentation for example, they still preferred to use the old meter style instruments with large dials and needles instead of the newer digital type of readouts. When customers complained about this, the management was loath to redesign the control panel but would agree to put in a few digital products. Being a computer expert, Roger had converted over half the instrumentation to digital hardware and software.

The Metro train arrived at his transfer point. He boarded the line to Rosslyn, still musing about the company. Because the management was so proudly conservative, Roger was surprised when the vice-president of engineering announced a month ago that an outside company had been hired to do a BPR exercise. BPR - Business Process Reengineering - was the latest rage for big companies. Roger had read enough about it to know what BPR entailed but he never expected PEI, a very successful company, to engage in this latest corporate fad.

The Board of Directors had announced its decision publicly in an attempt to please the stockholders. Most of the stockholders, however, never even heard of BPR and they were already content with their consistent dividends. Roger knew the ultimate result would be a downsized corporation, whether the Board expected it or not.

The vice president of engineering did not expect much impact on his department but "be prepared," he had said, to work with the outside company to explain the current processes. Roger was not as optimistic as the vice president. The company had to come up with a substantial reduction in staff - flatten the organization as they called it - in order to justify the large contract the BPR company received.

The train roared to a stop in the station where Roger got off and made his way through the crowd into the express elevator that whooshed up to the 20th floor. It amazed him that he could not feel the acceleration needed to rise so high so fast. He strolled to his office through the bustle of a corporate workplace. His office was on an outside wall with a view of more buildings. The conference rooms and executive offices had the outstanding view of Washington.

After getting a cup of coffee from the pantry, he turned on his desktop computer, settled into his chair and began to prepare for the staff meeting. As a first-line supervisor of twelve engineers, he had to attend these meetings, held by his boss, Louis Watts, the vice president of engineering. He liked to hold these reviews on Mondays so that any bad news would not spoil his weekends and in Roger's line of work the news was seldom good. Designing prototypes posed many problems. On Fridays, Watts met with the Program Managers so that they could prepare for their monthly meeting with the senior vice president/general manager and his vice presidents. Accordingly, Roger hauled out his schedules and files for the seven projects running concurrently and began reading. The computer system at PEI was not yet advanced enough to put reports on E-mail so Roger had to read the paper reports. He reviewed the action items from the previous meeting and noted which ones were his. Following the last Monday meeting, he had reviewed his items with his staff to obtain answers to problems and determine actions to be taken. His list was still current since the last review.

Gathering up his papers, he headed for the conference room. Inside, he made a fresh cup of coffee and listened to the chatter of his colleagues. The main topics were sports and golf. While he loved baseball, he seldom played golf. The last time he played, he recalled, was as a substitute for someone in the company golf league. He remembered it well. In the middle of the course a heavy rain fell and he was soaked. He completed the remaining holes drenched to the skin and drove home with water squishing out of his shoes.

The vice president of engineering arrived and started the meeting. He always appeared to have just finished eighteen holes, panting a little as he spoke. And his complexion was ruddy as though he spent all weekend in the blazing sun. Well-built like an athlete, he was usually somewhat uptight at these meetings which probably added to his ruddy skin color. He started right in on the action items from the last meeting arranged by priority. This meant they were put in the order of importance as perceived by his boss, the general manager. The noise of the conference room subsided as soon as he began the meeting. Unfortunately, number one on the list was an item belonging to Roger and his group.

"Project 006," thundered Watts, "I see your section has shown no progress since the last program review and yet you continue to spend man-hours and dollars. Now, we have the explosion to deal with."

Roger's logical mind prompted him to explain in an orderly fashion, starting with the explosion and then explaining the 006 problem. Although he was answering the vp's question, he responded as though he was making a presentation. This took longer and made the vp impatient, but Roger knew he would cover all aspects, avoiding unnecessary questions.

"What led to the explosion was a problem we are still working on; that is, the Turbine Temperature Indicator reads correctly at 100% power but incorrectly at lower power levels. The engineer thought it might be the transformer in the circuit but, during testing, she put the wrong voltage on it and it blew. Luckily, she wasn't hurt and a replacement for the hardware is on the way. At this point we don't know whether the meter is a hardware or software problem."

He then proceeded to describe the solutions they had tried but did not work. Roger knew instinctively that this could not go on without outside help. He had learned the hard way that if you let your problems fester, someone else will solve them to your discredit. But if he exhausted his approaches and requested help, he would not lose his credibility.

"I've assigned three engineers but we haven't been able to solve this problem," said Roger. "I wish to request assistance from the technical director rather than wait another week."

"O.K.," said the vice president, "I'll request his assistance."

And so the meeting droned on as the vp went through his list. Roger daydreamed occasionally but he had to be careful because sometimes Watts would ask various members of his team for opinions. He expected you to "be here" and concentrate on the business at hand. But Roger wanted to get through the pile of paperwork he had brought to the meeting.

Roger began one of his more productive multiplex acts. As the meeting continued, he started reading his paperwork - proposals, memos from his staff, Program Managers' memos, expense reports, etc. - which had accumulated since Friday. The vice president continued discussing other projects and other problems, seemingly ignoring Roger's diversion. Roger knew the vp knew he was doing this and sometimes the vp deliberately interrupted him for an opinion. "Be here," Watts once admonished him. Roger knew he could get away with it as long as his section was doing its job. Roger felt it was warranted because the meetings often covered items that he was not involved in so he saved a lot of time by multiplexing; it permitted him to keep up with the paperwork without taking it home.

Roger used to take his work home every night and weekends. After supper, he would settle in with his attache case and spend two or more hours going through the papers. On weekends he used to do the same thing: spend hours reading and shuffling papers. When he had to prepare memos, he would type them at night and input them into the system the next day. This went on for nearly two years. The strange thing about it was that he never seemed to catch up; in fact the amount of paper he handled seemed to grow.

Then one weekend, he realized that he rather looked forward to it! He could not wait to get to a rendezvous with his attache case! His internal light bulb flashed and he suddenly realized that he was a workaholic, a common affliction in corporate America. That was the clue: when one would rather work on paperwork at home instead of relaxing or doing other things. If Roger had a date he felt disappointed; he would rather do his homework! And, in fact he had fewer and fewer dates. Paperwork was replacing love. His revelation saved him. From then on he would not bring work home and, except for a few emergencies, this worked well for him. And to his surprise, the paper load decreased.

Roger stirred out of his reverie and went to the coffee table. The coffee service was provided by a subcontractor and he had to admit it tasted good. Each day they featured a different blend; today it was amoretta.

He returned to his seat to finish his mail, then planned his next step to solve the problem on Project 006. He would meet with his three engineers after the staff meeting and lay out an approach and a work plan to solve the problem. He would use that a basis for his discussion with the technical director that afternoon. Most of his section's instruments were working well on the 006 prototype but this one instrument was giving peculiar readings. It measured the temperature of the generator bearings which made it a critical component. If the generator bearings failed, a serious loss of power and revenue would occur.

Suddenly Watts stood up, took off his glasses and paced in front of the table with a big smile on his face.

"You know, when there are days like this with all the complex problems I have, I wonder how it would feel to be the chief engineer at a factory that manufactures straight pins. I could spend all day deciding what the optimum radius under the pin head should be!"

Watts began to laugh at his own little joke. The staff held back at first and then joined in the laughter.

"That's my own little pipe dream," said Watts. "Let's move on to the next project."

The vice president continued through his list of problems for all programs. The engineering sections were organized so that each one contained specific skills needed to engineer prototypes. Roger's specialty was instrumentation of the vast fossil-fueled power plants produced by the company. His staff of engineers designed all of the instrumentation and controls needed for start-up and operation of the power plants.

Following a review of action items the vice president concluded with new business.

"We have a bid review coming up next week for a major proposal that you are all working on. I'll schedule a bid review this week. Please make sure your bid inputs have been sent to the proposal manager. And make sure you have identified all of your risk areas."

Roger checked his watch again. *I must get to the London Gallery today.*

The meeting finally ended and the managers stayed to discuss mutual problems. The vice president left the conference room and went over to the office of Dr. Arthur Newton, the technical director.

"Sit down, Louis; you look like you just finished another exciting staff meeting."

"Yes, Arthur, it was exciting alright. I have a problem for you. As soon as you can, talk to Roger Essay about the turbine temperature instrument on Project 006. He asked for your help."

"Okay, I'll call him this afternoon. Roger seems to know when to holler for help."

"Yes, he does," replied Watts, trying to relax after the tense meeting. "I have section managers on my staff who are very effective in the engineering disciplines that they supervise but cannot deal with their staff. They constantly have "people problems" which consume a lot of their time and mine. Conversely, I have some section managers who are just adequate technically and supervise their staffs very effectively. I need managers who are both technically competent and people-oriented. I find that Roger fits that category."

Roger lingered in the conference room, enjoying the panoramic view from the large window. Looking toward the Capitol from the conference room window, Roger always felt uplifted. The bright sun added a white glare to the already white gleaming structures while the multicolored trees framed the scene much like a picture. *I've got to visit some of these sights. All the years I had worked in the nation's capital, I still hadn't seen the Monument, the Capitol or the Art Galleries. I need to slow down. Perhaps I'll find a new girlfriend to share my interests.*

As Roger stared out the conference room window, he was thinking about his position as section manager. It took a lot of effort to become a manager. When he came to work as a young engineer right out of college, there was no formal training. His new boss hardly spoke to him; he had to seek help from his colleagues. Roger found out much later that his supervisor was afraid of new employees; it was not a personal thing. He had been directed by his boss to hire more engineers but he feared they knew more than he did. Subconsciously he thought that if he ignored them the new employees would quit or transfer.

Roger thought about the billions of dollars spent by industry and government to train better managers and the poor results to show for it. And how about the thousands of books on this subject - the "how to" books which assured the reader he/she would become better at getting along with their subordinates. After all that training and reading, supervisors still tended to dump on their staffs, the very people they needed to be successful. For the most part, a manager's performance is only as good as his staff's performance. As a manager, he was inherently responsible for delegating work because he could not do it all himself or he would not be a supervisor. Paradoxically, many managers put up with their people as a necessary evil.

Roger thought about a training session which was tailored to the level of the company's chief executive officer (CEO). The CEO invited his staff to attend. The upshot was the CEO never set one foot in the classroom! Roger recalled that course because of a simple acronym which defined what a manager did; PLOC, which stood for: planning, leading, organizing and controlling. A more correct order was "POLC" but "PLOC" was easier to remember. That was how the instructor defined the manager's job. The course was not bad but since the CEO did not attend, why should his staff take it seriously? The sessions were given at a resort so golf became the number one agenda item. All had a good time but the training was not taken seriously.

Of course, Roger was not naive. He knew that many people were promoted to managerial positions for reasons other than competence. This was why many who became managers could not supervise, so why train them? Their "champions" would not fire them no matter what. The "buddy system" was alive and well. Roger remembered seeing a calendar in an office in a vendor's plant he was visiting which read: "Good old American know-WHO." His boss, however, seemed to avoid the buddy system but he was stuck with some poor managers his predecessor had promoted.

Roger returned to his office and called in the three engineers working on Project 006 to bring them up to date. They were not thrilled with the idea of getting assistance from the technical director, but, as Roger quietly pointed out, they did not have a solution. Roger knew there would be hard feelings so he took the time to talk it out with them. He also knew they would all be better off with the problem solved, no matter who came up with the solution.

Lunchtime was nigh so Roger sent them back to their cubicles. Roger pushed himself to concentrate on Project 006 knowing he had to face a difficult meeting Dr. Newton. Roger knew he should work through lunch while he ate at his desk but he was determined to spend more time on his hobby.

Roger had collected stamps, on and off, since he was a teenager. After he did his homework, he would visit a local stamp store to seek missing issues. He tried to find at least one stamp per country in his beginner's album. It was a pleasant diversion for a kid. Now that he was older he needed the diversion more than ever and yet he was too busy to achieve it.

Roger had stopped collecting stamps when he went to college but renewed his interest in the bits of paper while travelling. Working for an international company, he visited many foreign lands. It was while he was on a trip to the Middle East, specifically Turkey, to troubleshoot a problem on one of their power plants that he re-awakened his interest in stamps. He had to stay over one weekend before he could get a flight out, even though he had finished his work, so he wandered some of the streets in Ankara. He stopped at a souvenir shop and the proprietor took him over to the stamp display where he showed him some old packets of stamps from Mesopotamia and Trieste. He bought some of them and later at the hotel looked them over with growing interest. He went back the next day to buy more packets of stamps from countries in that area.

When he had returned to the states and bought some albums for the stamps, he really enjoyed his new hobby, especially between relationships. He became more and more fascinated with the old issues. He bought a catalog to assess their values. Interestingly, most of them, even though they were nearly eighty years old, were not valuable. He soon learned that the age of a stamp did not necessarily make it valuable. In fact, as he became more knowledgeable of the hobby, he realized that the value of a stamp was very unpredictable. He once tried to create a math model wherein the projected value of a stamp was a function of age, quantity printed, quantity used for postage, popularity, uniqueness (like a printing error) and demand. Since he could not easily put numbers on some of these variables, he concluded that the value depended basically on supply and demand.

Most postage stamps are inexpensive but on occasion one of value could be discovered. Roger recollected one evening when he was studying his stamps and the catalog he came across an early issue from Mesopotamia which he learned was once a Province of Turkey which later became Iraq. During World War I the British issued occupation stamps in 1918. They had used Turkish stamps with an overprint reading, "IRAQ, BRITISH OCCUPATION" with the value of the postage. The packet he had purchased had several of these issues from the 1/2 anna value to the 8 anna value, all with the same overprint. But then he noticed that the 2 1/2 anna surcharge on a 1 piaster stamp was somehow different. He then observed the surcharge was inverted compared to the other stamps. The catalog listed its value as $3250! Later, he found out where to get the stamps checked for authenticity and sure enough the stamp was genuine. The thrill of the find encouraged him to look for old issues on most of his trips and slowly he built an impressive collection of stamps from Middle Eastern countries.

He left his office and headed for the London Gallery.

Chapter 3

*"Ah, but a man's reach should exceed his grasp,
Or what's a heaven for?"*

- *"Andrea del Sarto" by Robert Browning*

Informed that he possessed a rare postage stamp from Mauritius, Major Edward Postmark quickly placed the stamp in his bank's vault and pondered his next step. Once the shock of discovering such a valuable object had subsided, Edward decided to sell the stamp. He was not a collector and certainly had no objection to adding income to his pension. Knowing he would need advice, he called the dealer who had revealed the value of his treasure. The dealer said he would be pleased to make an offer once the stamp was authenticated as an original. The dealer mentioned the Philatelic Society of England, located conveniently in London, as a reliable source of experts. Edward decided to contact the Society immediately.

Without realizing it, his life was changing. Since retiring from his military duty, he had spent a considerable time with several archeology groups. On occasion, he was engaged by various companies who sought advice regarding localities in India where manufacturing might be practical. Once a week he met with old army acquaintances at a veteran's club overlooking Waterloo Bridge. These activities kept him very busy in a routine, comfortable way.

Now, suddenly, there was a shift in priorities. The stamp changed everything as he responded to countless telephone calls, resulting from the rumor mill, which had quickly reached the world-wide collecting community. In addition to calls from the press, collectors, and dealers, he had already heard from brokers and investors interested in handling money he had not yet acquired. He had received one call from a woman who wanted to spend an evening with him and to view the stamp.

Edward finally obtained an unlisted telephone number and installed an answering machine. Even so, he found that he was forced to spend more of his time on calls related to the stamp. He was more convinced than ever that he should sell it. Accordingly, he had made calls to the Philatelic Society of England and scheduled a meeting with a Dr. Seebeck, an expert on British stamps.

With so many people interested in his stamp, Edward knew he should be cautious. When the stamp was not in the bank vault, he decided he would hide it in his attache case that he would keep with him at all times. He created a niche behind the lining just large enough to hide the card holding the stamp. He then purchased ten sets of Mauritius stamps from a local dealer and put them in a packet along with an early issue that pictured Queen Victoria and was colored orange. This would provide a decoy to divert a thief. He put the packet on top of papers in the attache case.

It was a typical wet day for London and it started to rain again as he hailed a taxi to go to the bank. He would need the stamp for his meeting with Dr. Seebeck. When he left the bank, Edward did not notice the woman in a raincoat outside the bank door who spoke into her portable phone as soon as he got into the waiting cab.

At the Philatelic Society offices, Dr. Seebeck excitedly examined the one penny orange. Some of the Society's staff gathered noisily in the office for a once-in-a-lifetime view of the rare stamp. Edward fidgeted. *I am very nervous about this; I should have hired a security guard.*

The expert cleared the office and began his evaluation in his lab. Various chemicals emitted odors that worried Edward, hoping that Dr. Seebeck would not put the stamp in any of them. The buzzing crowd remained outside the door, waiting for the results as if it were an election night.

The stamp's paper was not watermarked as were later British issues so Dr. Seebeck could not easily establish its authenticity. Later British stamps had very distinctive and easily detected watermarks. He placed the stamp in a dry watermark detector to establish that there was no watermark, thus eliminating the possibility that someone had used very old, but watermarked stamp paper for a forgery.

He checked the paper quality by comparing it to other Mauritius stamps issued near that period. He had in his collection copies of the third and fourth Mauritius stamps which were printed on yellowish and bluish paper. His copies had poor impressions, typical of later issues.

"Edward, although the catalog does not describe the paper for the one penny orange, it appears to be of similar texture and tint but perhaps not quite as thick. I will have to depend on a microscopic comparison."

He sat at his desk, reviewed the catalog again and went to his microscope.

"I cannot come up with a direct way to check the paper, so I compared the paper of the three stamps under the microscope. I can only conclude the composition of the paper is similar.

There was no gum on the back of those stamps. Ultraviolet light was applied to check the paper condition and to look for possible repairs. He pointed out to Edward that the stamp had never been placed in a conventional album with a paper hinge which would have left a mark on the paper. The "never-hinged" condition of the stamp was added value and would command the highest price.

He then examined the stamp's engraving under a magnifier to verify that the engraver's initials, "J B," were on the bust of

Queen Victoria. The initials were where they belonged. Dr. Seebeck went to his files and pulled out a photograph of a one penny orange made by a collector who had had access to a used copy of that stamp. The picture had been enlarged to show details. Dr. Seebeck then took a camera and photographed Edward's copy. He developed the film there in the lab, dried it and produced a picture in color. Now, he was able to check the initials and the engraving. The two photographs matched perfectly. Because the stamp was cut square without perforations, he did not have to check the number of perforations per inch. The margins around the engraving were ample which further added to its potential value.

The color in the photographs appeared very close. In addition, Dr. Seebeck compared the stamp's color to specific color charts used for stamps.

"Well, Major Postmark," said Dr. Seebeck finally, "I am through with my tests."

"What is your conclusion? Is the stamp genuine?"

Someone from the impatient, noisy crowd rapped on the door. Dr. Seebeck opened it a crack and spoke to the group.

"Please do not interrupt. I shall let you know."

Dr. Seebeck shut the door and directed Edward from the lab and into his office.

"Yes, Major, I can certify that it is authentic. Let me shake your hand; it is a perfect specimen."

Edward looked at the stamp again and wondered how a postage stamp could be worth over seven hundred thousand pounds. For a small piece of paper? Dr. Seebeck prepared a certificate while expounding on the history of the stamp.

Mauritius, he said, was the first British colony to issue postage stamps well over 100 years ago in 1847. The engraver made a mistake in the first issue of two stamps, a one-penny orange colored stamp and a two-pence blue colored stamp, by engraving the words "POST OFFICE" instead of "POST PAID" on both plates. The error was short-lived; new stamps with the same design were issued with the correct words. Because of the error very few stamps were issued and thus not many were used for postage. The engraver put his initials on the bust; he would forever be credited with the error.

A side view of young Queen Victoria's head adorned the faces of the stamps, as was the case with most of the early British issues. Compared with the elaborate designs on modern day issues, the engraving was quite simple. A provenance of one of the same issue, which had appeared on the market, indicated it was discovered in 1869 and ended up in the collection of a Japanese philatelist. Another stamp known to be in the possession of the great collection of Th. Chapion was sold in nineteen sixty. The provenance for Edward's copy began with his discovery of it in his house.

Dr. Seebeck continued on.

"The earliest Mauritius stamps were considered the top collectibles of the stamp world. All of the famous collectors sought these issues. They would pay a fortune for the two first issues and any covers that carried them."

"I assumed," said Edward, "that all of the old stamps I had found were valuable."

"As the dealer showed you in the catalog," said Dr. Seebeck, "this was not necessarily true. Many stamps over a hundred years old were only worth a few pounds, yet there were stamps issued during your lifetime that were worth thousands of pounds. There appeared to be no clear-cut formula to determine what a stamp was worth. The stamp catalogs are the best guidelines but it is hard to predict which stamps would appreciate. Stamps, like any collectibles, are worth what someone is willing to pay for them."

Dr. Seebeck finished his discourse and handed Edward the stamp and its certificate.

"Major, you must be careful carrying this stamp around. Some collectors will go to extremes to acquire it."

"That has occurred to me. I intend to deposit the stamp directly into my safe deposit box at my bank."

"As word gets around, the threat will increase," Dr. Seebeck continued. "You must be very careful. There was a case in France many years ago where it was alleged that a chap named Leroux was killed by another collector who coveted a certain rare stamp in Leroux's possession. Leroux owned the famous two-cent Hawaiian Missionary stamp. That stamp, incidentally, was recently auctioned off for well over four hundred thousand pounds!"

Edward nodded solemnly and tucked the stamp away in the slot in the attache case.

"I would encourage you to sell the stamp through a large auction house," Dr. Seebeck said. "In particular, I would recommend calling Winston Watermark, an auctioneer who used to work at the most famous house here in this city. He now owns theLondon Gallery, in Washington, DC."

Edward agreed to talk to Watermark and placed a long distance call to him from Dr. Seebeck's office. Winston and Edward struck an instant rapport and reminisced about merry old England and their war service. Dr. Seebeck joined them on the call and confirmed his evaluation of the stamp. Edward agreed to produce the stamp one week before the day of the auction sale at the London Gallery in Washington, D.C.

Watermark would send Edward a contract to sign. Since he already had his quarterly auction set, Watermark would announce the addition of the one penny orange to the auction. Winston told Edward this would be the auction of the decade. Edward thanked Winston and hung up the phone.

"I do believe, Major, that you will find Mr. Watermark to be an honest merchant to deal with," Dr. Seebeck asserted. "While he worked in the local auction houses he had an unblemished record for fair dealing. I bought many British stamps from his auctions. He was meticulously accurate in describing a stamp's condition."

"That is good to hear," replied Edward, "since I am not knowledgeable of this hobby."

"Put yourself in his hands. He will teach you a lot in a short time. I understand that he designed a beautiful facility in Washington which has become a major attraction for philatelists. I am seriously considering attending the auction myself; it will be an international affair."

Edward took his leave from Dr. Seebeck. As a precaution, he looked around to make sure no one was following him. Because of the rainfall, he had to wait for a taxi. While waiting, he noticed a woman in a dark blue raincoat looking in his direction. As soon as Edward climbed into a taxi, she began speaking into her portable phone. Checking the lock on his attache case, he settled into his seat as he headed for the bank. When he arrived at the bank, a woman in a dark blue raincoat followed him into the entrance. He sensed a fleeting familiarity but proceeded quickly to the safe deposit office. Preoccupied, he did not observe the woman leave her raincoat on a chair nearby and follow him through the secured safe deposit entrance. Edward signed out his box as the woman surreptitiously picked up a file from a nearby desk.

The bank attendant took his key and removed his box from its slot. Edward went into a cubicle, closed the door and opened his attache case on the table. The cubicles were adjacent to the office where other bank personnel were working, thus, the woman who had followed Edward into the office was not conspicuous as she opened the door to Edward's cubicle and went in.

"What is it?" asked Edward, intuitively knowing exactly what she was after. The scent of her faint, gardenia-like perfume preceded her into the small room.

"Be still!" said the woman as she reached under her miniskirt and pulled out a small handgun.

"I want the orange stamp you are carrying."

Edward had not yet removed the one-penny orange from its secret pocket in the case. He reached for the attache case but the woman pulled it away from him.

"Stay put!" she said waving the gun which, Edward noticed, was quite small and yet had a silencer on its muzzle.

She took the packet of Mauritius stamps out of the open case and quickly looked at each set. Edward concentrated on the weapon.

"This must be it," she said, taking out the single orange colored stamp with the Queen on the face. "Don't move or make a noise!"

"Wait!" yelled Edward, but she was out the door and gone.

Edward sat down, mopped his face with his handkerchief and then got up quickly. *I must get out of here before she discovers she took the wrong stamp! I'm lucky she did not take the attache case.* He took the rare stamp out of its niche in the case and put it in the safe deposit box along with the certificate. Edward decided not to alert bank officials of the attempted robbery for fear he would be delayed by them and the police. He pushed out of the bank and hailed a taxi to get to his hotel. He arrived at his hotel and headed straight to the lounge for a scotch-on-the-rocks.

Sipping his drink and trying to calm himself, Edward thought through this predicament. *The would-be thief was not a collector or she would have known it was the wrong stamp. She must have been hired by someone. Interesting because I thought I saw the same woman outside the Philatelic Society's offices, but how could she get to the bank at the same time I did? I must call a security agency. I am going to need help to get to the U.S.*

* * *

In another part of London, a smartly dressed woman in a

dark blue raincoat entered an apartment.

"Do you have the stamp?" asked the woman seated on the sofa, sipping a dry martini.

"Yes, indeed! " she replied.

She took off her coat and changed into a dry pair of shoes. She went to a small bar in the dining area and poured from a beaker of martinis into a glass containing two olives.

She sat down in the living room, facing the other woman who looked exactly like her.

"Let's call the agency and report in."

Before going to the speaker phone, she poured a second drink, sipped it and puckered her lips at the dryness.

The apartment was beautifully furnished with contemporary blond furniture on a bright green wall-to-wall carpet. White couches surrounded the fireplace which was glowing with a low flame. Inexplicable but colorful abstract acrylic paintings adorned the walls cleverly intermingled with subdued pen and ink drawings. Except for the clinking sounds of martini glasses placed upon the table, the apartment was quiet, in contrast to the excitement felt by the two women.

She reached their supervisor on the speaker phone who put her on hold on to contact the client. While waiting confidently, she chewed one olive. In a few minutes he was back on the line.

"I have our client on a three-way conference call. He will listen but will not speak to you so as to remain anonymous. Procede to describe the stamp."

"The stamp," said the woman, "is colored orange and has a profile of Queen Victoria on the face. The lettering says 'Mauritius, Four Cents' and has the word 'Postage' on each side."

There was a prolonged silence on the other end, then, suddenly, the supervisor yelled.

"Dammit! You have the wrong bloody stamp! Stay put. I will call you back within the hour!"

The women were twin sisters - Diane and Violet - who had

established a well-noted reputation in the private detective comunity. They were highly skilled professionals who kept physically fit by taking martial arts. They had petite, well-proportioned figures and shapely in all aspects. Each had naturally blonde hair often covered with dark wigs for camouflage when on assignments. Strikingly attractive to look at, their prey usually thought them to be actresses or models, not private investigators. This worked to their advantage because they seldom aroused suspicion even as they closed in on their targets.

The agency they worked for handled in private investigations of almost any sort. If they specialized in any one area it was industrial counterespionage. This meant they sought out individuals who stole proprietary information from their firms and sold it to competitors. Vi and Di had been assigned by the agency to take possession of the one penny orange for a client. The task was not in the agency's usual line of work but the agency was assured that the stamp had been stolen and the owner, the client, wished to have it recovered. The client was a regular customer and, although the agency was not altogether comfortable with the assignment, the fee more than compensated for the risk involved.

"Di," said Violet, sitting up on the sofa, "we know where he is staying so we could go after him again."

"No, Vi," replied Diane, quite dejected. "The stamp is most certainly in the bank so hitting on him in the hotel won't work. Let's wait and see if the agency has another plan."

"I did not see another stamp in his case that fit the description," Diane continued. "Perhaps, I should have checked out the brief case more carefully. I must say, he certainly was good-looking and the military type, but I did not think I was distracted."

They sat quietly, contemplating their failure, and drinking, not sipping, their martinis while staring at the telephone as though it were about to ring. The beaker on the bar containing the martinis emptied before their phone rang.

* * *

News, of course, had spread in London about the discovery of the rare stamp and Edward soon received calls from the philatelic press and collectors. He refused interviews, informing reporters they would have to wait until he disposed of the stamp. One caller was Stanley Roulette, a famous collector known internationally for his British collection.

Roulette implored Edward to visit his home in London to view his collection. Roulette wanted to make an offer for Edward's stamp. Edward insisted he would not sell it privately. Roulette persisted and Edward, a bit annoyed by Roulette's arrogance, agreed to meet with him but not at Roulette's home. He arranged to meet Roulette in the hotel lounge where he was staying. Perhaps, thought Edward, he might glean more information about the value of that stamp. Edward also decided to call Dr. Seebeck, for more information about Roulette. Luckily, Seebeck was available for his call and knew Roulette's reputation well.

"Major, he is a very aggressive operator. Your stamp is one of the few missing from his Mauritius collection and he would do almost anything to obtain it. Mr. Roulette will push hard to negotiate but he will offer you more than any dealer would."

"Would his offer likely meet the auction price?"

"There are no guarantees, Major. In my opinion, a classic stamp will command the highest price at the auction. Stand your ground because Mr. Roulette can be very insistent."

Edward thanked him and rang off.

* * *

Meanwhile, Edward was enjoying his evenings with Penny

who stayed with friends while visiting London. This evening they went to dinner, then the theater and dancing were on the agenda. Tonight she looked particularly alluring in a simple black dress that hugged her figure and set off her face like a cameo. Maturity became her like a vintage portrait. *I should have paid more attention to her back in our younger days in Mauritius.* Each time he saw her his feelings intensified, despite Penny's constant reminder that he had a rival, a friend of her former husband whom she was seeing.

Undaunted, Edward enjoyed their evenings together which became more intimate with each encounter. However, his passions were barricaded because she declined his invitations to his hotel room.

"Penny," said Edward one late evening, "I am dismayed that I am one of two suitors for your charms. You have known me for quite some time; why can you not be more forthcoming with your feelings?"

"Believe me, Edward," replied Penny, "I am overwhelmed by your attention. I am not trying to complicate our friendship but I just did not expect two friends courting me! These past weeks have been filled with dining and dancing. I've felt almost as if I were part of a fairy tale but I do need some time to work things out."

Edward agreed to wait, to give her the time she needed, not wanting to spoil their evenings.

*   *   *

The time was fast approaching for Edward to leave for the United States and the day arrived for his meeting with Stanley Roulette. Promptly before tea time, Roulette entered the lounge in the hotel where Edward was staying. They sat in the smoking section where Stanley lit a cigar and offered his selection to Edward. Edward, already at ease with this meeting, declined.

Multiplex Man 61

The decor of the room was elaborate, much like the gaslight era of the turn of the century. Electric lamps simulated gas jets of that period and the tinkling sounds of glasses were subdued by the deep carpeting. Smoke rising within the room had the not-unpleasant aroma of cigars mixed with an occasional whiff of sweet tobacco from pipes. It was an ambience conducive to do business but Edward remained uncomfortable.

Roulette entertained Edward with drinks and a tea laid on with delicious scones and crumpets. Roulette began the meeting by stating he was the president of Roulette Traders Ltd., a major import/export company headquartered in London. He then told Edward about his fabulous stamp collection representing Great Britain and her former colonies. He candidly admitted that the stamp he sought from Edward would enhance his collection of Mauritius and earn him international acclaim.

"Edward, I have built my collection since World War II. I grew up when the British Empire was at its peak so I do relate to the classic era of stamps, 1840 to 1940. Stamps broadened my knowledge of many countries and helped me in my business. Besides, I have very strong feelings for the Empire which we shall never see again."

Roulette was in his soft sell mode and even hinted that he would pay the best price for the one penny orange. Edward countered that an auction sale would set the best price, unknown until after the actual sale. After an hour of discussion, Roulette began to lose his patience and all but threatened Edward with violence. Edward was not fazed, having faced violence in his army career, and in turn refused further discussion. He arose from his seat to leave but Roulette also stood up and grabbed Edward's arm.

"Consider, Edward, I may not win the auction!"

"You will have to risk it."

"Now look at the other side of the coin, "continued Stanley, "it is also possible and perhaps likely that the stamp will not command a good price so you are also taking a risk. I can eliminate that risk by offering you a substantial sum now."

Roulette struggled to contain himself as Edward pushed his arm away.

"I am prepared to offer you US$250,000 cash, more than 20% of the catalog value!".

Edward paused. He was tempted because he could not be certain that the stamp would actually sell for more than that amount. He sensed he could negotiate a higher price now and be done with it because Roulette certainly had the resources. Instead, he decided to stick to his plan to sell it at auction. Roulette put his chewed-up cigar in the ash tray, thanked Edward for his time and left the lounge. Roulette appeared emotionally spent but he was seething. So close, he thought! He knew he must have that stamp!

The tea and pastries were untouched.

* * *

Edward finished his business and prepared to leave London. On the night before his departure, he picked up Penny at her lodging for a quiet dinner and an early evening. Penny wore a spectacular, strapless black dress, short enough to highlight her long shapely legs. Dangling pearl earrings, a long pearl necklace and black high-heeled shoes completed her outfit. Her hair was cut in a lengthwise bob which perfectly framed her face. Edward was indeed attracted to Penny and regretted his imminent departure. He helped Penny into her coat and once in the cab, suggested a nearby restaurant, but he quickly discovered Penny had other plans.

"I know you have to catch a plane tomorrow morning, so let's have dinner at your hotel."

Edward was pleasantly surprised. At the hotel they walked into the dining room and were promptly seated. Heads turned to admire the handsome couple. The dining room was heavily carpeted and decorated almost entirely in red. The walls were adorned with oil paintings, each in a gilded frame with its own shielded light above it to cast a glow on the canvas. The noises of people talking, clinking glasses and cutlery were muted by the carpet. The aroma of roast beef and freshly made horseradish wafted through the room.

They dined quietly as Edward attempted to understand her feelings about him and their future. Edward had decided not to mention the stamp to Penny. As they finished their coffee and dessert, Edward held her hand.

"Penny, as you know, I must leave for the U.S. to take care of some important business. I will then return to London to see you. Perhaps when I return you will have made some decision about your future."

"Edward, I have noticed that you seem changed from the last time I saw you in Mauritius. You seem nervous which is out of character for you. Is there something connected with your trip?"

"Why, yes. I am in a rather unique situation that I have never encountered before which is making me a bit edgy. It will be resolved on this trip and I shall explain when I return."

Penny withdrew her hand and opened her compact to check her hair as a distraction. She did not want to expose her true feelings about this dilemma. She liked both men very much but neither had made an offer of marriage.

Following dinner, Edward prepared to return her to her lodging, after which he would finish packing and retire early. But before he could hail a cab, Penny suggested a nightcap in Edward's room.

"We will say goodnight there for a change."

Riding up in the elevator, Edward was bewildered and disconcerted at the change in plans. At his door, he fumbled for the key. Finally, he entered the room but before he could reach the light switch, Penny had her arms around his waist and her lips planted firmly on his. Edward was startled but reacted quickly. He brushed aside the why's and wherefore's in his mind and kissed her passionately.

With Penny still clinging to him, Edward maneuvered his way to the sofa. He tried to untangle himself but she would not let him go. He was having difficultly breathing. She clawed at his clothes and he slipped off her dress. There were no undergarments, only Penny's sensuous body. His mind was beyond thinking and completely overcome with emotion. Penny was a tigress; she was animated and seemed to be all around him. Their pulsations accelerated while she gripped like a vise with her legs and arms. Edward pushed hard against her body and the climax came in a sudden, sodden explosion.

Penny reluctantly released him and they parted. Edward was speechless. Penny excused herself. Edward slowly dressed, poured the nightcap they had not yet had and sat down on the sofa where they had just made love. *Was that the Penelope I remembered? No, I did not recall her being so passionate; but that was long ago.*

Penny returned with her dress on and sat in his lap.

"I do have a dilemma to resolve," cried Penny.

Her cheek was damp against Edward's face and he held her closely.

"I am afraid to make a decision because of the failure of my first marriage. A second failure is more than I can handle."

They finished their drinks, Penny dried her eyes and Edward led Penny from his room to the hotel lobby. Edward quickly hailed a taxi and escorted Penny home. Edward tried to reassure Penny as they parted at the front door.

"To say the least, it has been a delightful evening!" said Edward.

They said good-bye with one more embrace and one more kiss. With the excitement of the evening lingering, Edward almost proposed marriage to her; and Penny almost, but not quite, agreed to delay her decision until his return to London.

* * *

Edward checked out of the hotel the next morning and, in the lobby, met the security guard that he had hired from an agency to get him safely aboard his plane. The guard was half his age and sturdily built. Edward felt confident that the guard would be more than a match for the woman who had accosted him in the bank, should she show up again. As an added precaution, he had purchased an attache case identical to his other one. He thought he might need another decoy.

Edward and his guard took a taxi directly to the bank where Edward retrieved the one penny orange from the safe deposit box. He carefully hid it in a small pocket of the attache case and left the bank with his guard in tow. Edward noticed a woman waiting outside the bank. As Edward and the guard climbed into the waiting cab, the woman made a call on her cellular phone as she hailed a taxi. She climbed in and instructed the driver to follow Edward's cab. Before he arrived at the airport, Edward gave his case, containing the packet of stamps and the rare stamp, to the guard. Edward carried the new case.

At Heathrow Airport, Edward immediately spotted the lady again. How, he wondered, did she get here before he did? He instructed the driver to continue on to the airport exit and circle back to the terminal. Perhaps, he thought, he could elude her by not going directly to the gate. Once in the terminal, he sent the guard, with his ticket and luggage, to check in for him and then meet him at the baggage carousel in the lower level.

The guard returned with Edward's tickets and the attache case. Edward still had the decoy case. Edward checked the time, waiting until the last minute to dash for the security checkpoint and the departure gate. Suddenly, he was confronted by two identically dressed women who were obviously twins! He was on a red alert but before he could act, one of the twins roughly pushed him onto the moving baggage carousal and grabbed his case. Simultaneously, Edward's guard dropped his attache case onto the carousal and tried to grab the woman who had seized the decoy attache case but the woman's twin blocked him sending him sprawling.

Edward's head hit the edge of the baggage carousal during the melee. He fell onto the moving platform which carried him around to the outside like a piece of luggage. A surprised baggage handler helped him to his feet up but he was dizzy and unable to stand. Edward's guard had seen Edward fall onto the carousal and jumped on the platform himself in search of Edward.

"Quick! " cried Edward, attempting to stand up, "get the attache case off the carousal!"

The guard lay back down on the moving platform to reenter the baggage claim area where he looked for the case. He quickly found it and waited for Edward who was entering the passenger area through a door marked "Authorized Personnel Only."

The guard advised Edward to go to the hospital as he seemed quite dizzy still. The guard then found a wheelchair and pushed Edward to the airport passenger area. He hailed a taxi and proceeded to the nearest hospital. Edward's plans had abruptly changed but he still had the stamp.

*   *   *

While Edward was transported to a nearby hospital, Diane and Violet, who had gone to the nearest restroom following the confrontation, dismantled the attache case looking for the rare stamp.

"Dash it!" screamed Di, "he did it again! There are no stamps here! I know which flight he is on; let's catch him before he boards."

They returned to the ticket counter where they had seen

Edward's guard check in. Di approached the ticket attendant, flashed her private detective's ID card, identifying herself as a policewoman, and asked if Edward Postmark had boarded his flight. The attendant looked at her screen and said he had not. Di and Vi split up and placed themselves in strategic locations waiting for Edward. Within minutes, the flight was called and Edward did not show. The gate was closed and the twins faced having to report yet another bungling of their assignment.

"He may be planning to board another flight to sidetrack us," said Vi, "so you start checking all of the flights out of here. I will go back to the baggage area to find out where they went."

* * *

At the hospital, Edward seemed to have survived the altercation but his doctor insisted he remain a day or two for observation. He was still dizzy but his mind was clear. He was moved to a small room where he called for a nurse to find his guard. The guard had been standing by and arrived within minutes.

"I cannot keep the stamp here," said Edward. "Those two women are obviously going to pursue me until they get the stamp. They will quickly find out what happened at the airport and track me down. Since you cannot access my box, you will contact your agency and secure my attache case and the stamp in their safe until I get out of here and reschedule my flight."

The guard left to contact his supervisor and quickly returned with the news that the agency would keep the case and stamp in their vault.

"One more thing," said Edward. "Call this number when you get to the agency. Talk to the director of the London Gallery in Washington, D.C. and tell him that I will be delayed a few days and explain why. I will call him as soon as I get out of here."

The guard took the attache case and left Edward with his

paging number in case he needed any help. Edward decided not to call Penny. He felt all right and was anxious to get to the U.S. without any further complications.

As he finally fell into a medicinal asleep, his last thoughts were of the twins and his stamp on its way to a safe place.

Edward need not have worried about the twins. After Di reported the failed attempt to claim the stamp, the client aborted the assignment. He told their supervisor he would have to work out a solution in the U.S. He said he was afraid that too many attempts could lead back to him.

* * *

Edward remained in the hospital for two days, then returned to his hotel to prepare for his trip. He assumed his adversary knew where he was and would follow him when he tried again to get to the airport. He of course did not know that the twins were told to drop the case.

Early Monday morning, Edward met his security guard at the airport gate, took the attache case with the stamp in it from him and boarded the aircraft bound for the U.S. He looked for the twins or any suspicious persons but saw none. He had planned his trip to arrive at the London Gallery in Washington, D.C. the same day. Once seated on the plane, Edward nervously opened and closed his attache case.

For the twentieth time he took the packet of postage stamps out of the attache case and looked at the ten small cards with various sets of stamps in the acetate slots. Each card was in a plastic envelope for protection. In the middle of the packet was the rare stamp he had discovered in Mauritius. Edward did not notice the flight attendant staring at the open case.

"May I get you a drink, sir?" she asked.

"Er... no thank you," he replied. Startled, he quickly shut the case, reflexively inserting the packet into his coat pocket.

This was Edward's first trip to Washington. Once he delivered the stamp to the gallery it would be safe and he could do some sight-seeing. It was time for the in-flight meal so Edward sat back and tried to get his mind off of the mission. He hoped for anonymity when he arrived in the states but he realized that he would be approached by many collectors and the press which would leave little time for sight-seeing.

As the airliner soared toward the United States, he thought about the trip and wished to be done with it. He anxiously awaited the landing. He would take a cab directly to the London Gallery in downtown Washington. He had the legal documents ready to be signed by the director of the gallery. The responsibility for the stamp would then be transferred to the Gallery. What a relief that would be; he could then concentrate on the auction and acquiring a large sum of money.

But Edward was still apprehensive. The events of the past two days: the twins who had attacked him and the meeting with Stanley Roulette, were vividly replaying in his mind. He was relieved that he had not lost the stamp. Penny had told him he was nervous; he had to admit the stamp added a dimension to his life that he was not trained for. It was unlike the adventures he had faced during his army service. Perhaps, Edward wondered, that was the connection with the cobra in the attic: both the snake and the stamp were dangerous.

The in-flight meal completed, Edward sipped a second cup of tea, and again chided himself for not hiring a security agency to protect him in the U.S. He rationalized that he had not done so because he did not fully comprehend the value of the stamp. Until the auction took place he would not really believe it. He remained uneasy.

Although he had not espied any suspicious activity or persons, he was determined to avoid an overnight stop and deliberately planned to transfer the stamp from London to Washington within the same day.

The pilot was now turning the airplane into the approach pattern to Dulles International Airport. *Soon, soon, I shall reach the end of this journey and deliver the one-penny orange in time for the auction.* The airport was located in the countryside of Virginia not far from the foothills of the Blue Ridge mountains. As he looked out of the window he could see the hills ablaze in typical fall colors. Washington was truly the city of trees. Edward had been told that Washington's climate was tropical in the summer and Arctic in the winter, but the spring and fall were delightful and he looked forward to the welcome change in climate.

Edward resisted another peek look at the stamp. He tried to turn his attention to the landing, recalling again the old satchel guarded by the cobra. The thought made him uneasy again. He wondered if he had missed something in the suitcase besides the stamps and letters. *How did the snake get into the attic and survive? Poppycock! I must dismiss the idea that something ominous will happen because of the snake's presence.*

The aircraft was now in its final approach. After touchdown, he eventually disembarked, collected his luggage and went through customs. As he walked toward the front of the terminal, he noticed the flight attendant behind him. She smiled at Edward and he smiled back. *Is she following me? She watched me too obviously during the flight.*

He entered a cab and headed for downtown Washington. In the cab he once more looked at the stamp amidst the packet to make sure it was still there. The cab left the terminal and headed east on the Dulles Access Road. The road and its surrounding area were uncrowded and rural in appearance with miles and miles of trees and shrubs. The colorful trees were very unlike those in Mauritius. The green foliage was turning into an array of floral-like hues. Against the green grass, which was everywhere, the trees were splotched with a multitude of colors: green leaves turning to crimson, claret and vermillion.

The driver diverted to a route which crossed over the Potomac River into Washington. The London Gallery occupied a four-story renovated townhouse near a group of high rise buildings not far from Georgetown, Washington's oldest urban area. The taxi pulled up to the gallery entrance and Edward asked the driver to put his luggage inside the front door. Edward would ask the director to store it until he went to the hotel. The cab driver got out and pulled the luggage from the trunk.

"Are you alright, mister?" asked the cabby. "You don't look so good."

"Yes, yes," replied Edward, looking furtively around the area, "I'm fine."

"Is someone following you?"

"No. Bring the bags inside."

As Edward followed the cabby toward the entrance, someone brushed past him, grabbed the attache case, shoved Edward against a stone column in front of the London Gallery door and dashed off. Edward slouched over, with the air knocked out of him and his hopes for riches seemingly lost in one brief moment.

Chapter 4

"She dwelt among the untrodden ways
Beside the springs of Dove,
A maid whom there were none to praise
And very few to love;"

- A Poem by William Wordsworth

The cruise ship, Sea Wind, left the port of Nassau, Bahamas, and headed back to Miami after a week in the Caribbean. Previously, it had visited ports in the Cayman Islands and Jamaica.

Virginia Couvert, one of the ship's many passengers, was enjoying a week's vacation from her job, Marketing Manager for Dockside International, an import/export company. She had chosen a cruise for her vacation to relax and be pampered by the ship's amenities and perhaps meet some interesting people. The cruise worked wonders to get her mind off her problems, but after a week, she had found little companionship.

Watching the aquamarine-colored water as she stood at the railing of the ship, Virginia marvelled at what a perfect vacation the cruise was, sailing on the serene Caribbean sea. Life aboard the Sea Wind was far removed from the demands of her daily life. Sumptuous food tempted the passengers all day and half the night; amusements prevailed all day; dancing and entertainment began after dinner; gambling at the casino; ship's parties every other night; and a handsome crew saw to their every need. She liked the idea that the ship was her hotel at each port they visited. Why, thought Virginia, didn't everyone take a cruise? Cruises used to be prescribed by doctors as rest cures in the days when they were very expensive.

Before leaving Nassau, Virginia had experienced the "straw market," one of Nassau's famous sights, where thousands of objects made out of straw and rattan were sold. Besides the usual hats and handbags, there were many unique dolls made out of straw and brightly colored fabrics. The hot climate in Nassau contrasted with the air-conditioned ship so she bought a straw fan to cool her face as she wandered along the main street shopping and taking in the sights and sounds of the city. At the end of the busy street was the hotel that she read to have once been an emblem of British rule when the Bahamas were a colony. It looked like the typical tropical hotel with its cane furniture and hand-operated fans. Virginia cooled off in the lounge with a fruity-tasting gin drink before walking back toward the ship.

After departing the hotel, she noticed a stamp shop just off the main street. Stamp collecting was her one passion, although some days she felt like collecting men was also a hobby. Being in the import/export business, she travelled extensively for her company looking for new sources or renegotiating terms with established sources. The search for new products was an ongoing process; the trick was to find new ones that would sell. Seeing the stamp shop, she remembered that it was on one of those business trips that her first serious stamp acquisition had occurred.

She had already made several trips to India, the source of a many exotic products sold by DI. It was during a visit to the city of Bangadore that she purchased her first stamps. Mr. Sirkha, who had escorted her to his production plants, took her to the local stamp shop to pick up some new issues. She was grateful for his company, well aware that a woman travelling alone was a target. While waiting for Mr. Sirkha, Virginia took an interest in the colorful stamps, captivated by the historic scenes on the stamps. As a souvenir she bought a large packet of stamps from India and the India States that once issued their own postage.

The India States recalled the days of the British Empire romanticized by Kipling and others. Much literature was conceived about the life of the British soldier in the remote parts of the country. In those days, Pakistan and Burma were still part of India. She learned through her travels that there were six states in India: Chamba, Faridkot, Gwalior, Jind, Nabha and Patiala. Other feudal states such as Cochin, located in the southern region, also issued their own postage stamps.

Later, back in her home in Arlington, a suburb of the Washington, D.C. area, Virginia opened the packet containing the stamps and was once again fascinated by them. Her interest continued to grow and she built an impressive collection of stamps from India and Indian Ocean countries which included Mauritius. Once involved she was amazed at the volume of activity in the field; it was a whole new world of information and diversion, like an Internet of its own. It helped too, that most stamps were not expensive.

As she entered the shop in Nassau, she was reminded that the hobby seemed to be still dominated by men although more women were taking a serious interest. Looking through the stock books, she was surprised to find several early issues from Mauritius that she needed. She spent a lot more than she had planned but decided the money was well spent. Putting them in her purse, she made her way back to the ship to prepare for a party that night, the last night at sea.

After a sumptuous dinner, Virginia started dressing for the party. She admired her reflection in the full length mirror. Yes, she thought, she had curves in all the right places and tonight she was determined to abandon her usual conservative attire. Her slim white skirt ended above her knees but the white blouse fit snugly with a long v-neck. She decided not to wear a bra and again studied her reflection. She completed her outfit with white pumps and amber beads. Finally, she put a small orchid in her dark hair, something she had always wanted to do.

It was an exciting evening for the passengers, almost like New Year's Eve. Virginia got attention from some of the male passengers and crew. Some wanted to dance and flirt, others tried to coax her to their rooms but she evaded their approaches and decided instead to explore the upper deck where the magnificent midnight buffet was laid out, complete with ice statues of flying geese. While she nibbled on a tasty pineapple tart, she was joined by a man who had occasionally invited her to be a fourth at bridge.

"Well, hello there, Virginia. Are you enjoying the trip?"

"Yes, of course. It's just what I need before going back to work."

Virginia had only briefly talked to the gentleman in between bridge hands. He seemed decent enough and was actually quite handsome with his shiny, grayish hair and sun-baked complexion. He had told her he was a lawyer and he looked the part of a senior partner. She noticed that he always had a handkerchief flowing out of his blazer's breast pocket.

"As pretty as you are, I guessed you had a date every night of the cruise and now I find you dining alone."

"Oh, I've had some attention but nothing serious. What about you? Are you having a good time?" asked Virginia.

"No, I'm afraid not. I came here with my wife and I'll leave alone!"

"What happened to her? Is she ill?"

"No, no, not at all. In fact *she* couldn't be better. I suppose I got carried away on this cruise by playing bridge every night and day. It's my passion, you know, but my wife is not a player. She became angry about my ignoring her on the cruise and apparently began to seek the company of other men. She told me tonight she'd met a charming man and was leaving me for him after we dock. She's already moved into his stateroom!"

Virginia listened intently. What a nightmare, she thought

and tried to console him. After awhile, she said goodnight and retired to her room to pack and put her luggage outside her door so the crew could move all luggage to the ship's hold during the night. She was exhausted and fell asleep as soon as she went to bed.

The ship sailed on through the night towards the mainland, the glittering lights eventually turning off all over the ship, leaving only the ship's running lights on. A moonlit night over a calm sea could not have better suited the last evening of a romantic cruise. The passengers on the Sea Wind slumbered as the night turned to dawn. The crew began picking up luggage from outside the cabins and stowing them in the lower hold for removal to the pier when the ship docked at eight o'clock in the morning.

Just before 5 a.m., an urgent knock at Virginia's door awoke her; the crewman simply said to get up to the deck. It was just after 5 a.m. when she learned that there had been an explosion in the engine room and fire at sea! There were no lights except in the main stairwell. She put the minimum of clothes on in the dark and felt her way along the corridor for the stairs to the deck. Dawn was just beginning to creep along the eastern sky. She went to the lifeboat station she was assigned to during the drill that had been held at the beginning of the cruise. *I can't believe this is real! It must be a drill. How am I going to get into a lifeboat?*

There had been no alarms because, she learned later, the electrical cables were severely burned which rendered the ship systems inoperable. Because of the electrical failure, the toilets and sinks did not work. The crew had some emergency power and began passing out coffee, water and doughnuts. A crew member who would handle the lifeboat told the group to stand by. By 6 a.m., the fire was contained because the hatches had closed automatically. With the engine room closed off there would be no power to get to port. The ship was dead in the water. The ever-present vibration of the engine was gone; it was ominously quiet.

Soon the word spread that the ship's lifeboats would not be used; rather, a sister ship from Miami would be dispatched and her lifeboats would be used to transfer the stranded passengers. Swell. I am carrying a packet of mint stamps and I am about to get soaked trying to get into a small lifeboat! The cloudless, blue-steel sky allowed the blazing sun to beat down on the passengers. The once cool, blue water seemed to turn yellow-green and uninvitingly warm. They had to remain on deck because there no lights below. As the citron-colored sun rose higher in the sky, there was less and less shade for the passengers.

As the day wore on, the seagulls deserted the ship because food scraps were not available. The passengers grew more and more uncomfortable for lack of facilities, despite the crew's attempt to maintain a light mood. The steel band played on but the music did little to boost morale. Virginia remained fairly calm but others grew upset and even hysterical. The ship's doctor and his nurses frantically tried to help those in need.

Sitting next to Virginia was the bridge fanatic who recently lost his wife. He nervously fiddled with the zipper on his ditty bag. Virginia decided not to move from her half-shaded spot so she made polite conversation.

"It's a pity this happened. The cruise was so relaxing. I guess that's not so for you. Did your wife return last night?"

"No, she did not. And we've been married for fifteen years!"

"You had no inkling she was unhappy?"

"To be honest, I guess I did. Back home, she did not like being alone when I played golf at our club nearly every day and cards every other night. I thought the cruise would make up for my ignoring her but instead I only made matters worse."

Abruptly, he left her to talk to some other people but soon came back to Virginia.

"This will be a long day. How about playing some bridge?"

Virginia stared at him for a moment, wide-eyed, and then

declined. *I can see why his wife left him!* The noon sun became hotter and without food, people began to show the effects of deprivation. A priest she had seen earlier was tried to calm everyone. At least, thought Virginia, the fire was out and they would not have to abandon ship! They could have been bobbing around in the lifeboats, waiting for rescue.

To the cheers of the passengers, the sister ship sent to rescue them appeared on the horizon. She anchored just off the stricken ship and soon lifeboats appeared around the Sea Wind. By then, word of the incident had reached the mainland and a helicopter from a Miami TV station circled overhead to video tape the evacuation. Virginia made her way down to the hold and climbed down a rope ladder into the lifeboat which caused a lot of spray as it bounced gainst the ship's ladder. Virginia clutched her purse above her head to avoid getting it soaked. Even in the boat the spray occasionally wet the passengers. When the lifeboat was filled, it pulled away and chugged over to the sister ship. The crew helped the passengers up the ladder and directed them to staterooms they would use until they reached Miami.

Just as the sun began to set the rescue ship docked in Miami where buses were waiting to transport the passengers to motels for the night. After Virginia awoke the next morning feeling she had just about had enough excitement to last her until her next vacation, she left early to return to Washington. Work sounded good to her now!

Virginia slept most of Sunday. When she woke up and dressed, she checked her laptop computer for her schedule the next day. It showed a weekly staff meeting, a lunch date and then a visit to the London Gallery. She wondered if she could afford to take Monday off but decided not to call her office in the morning or discuss her disastrous last day of the cruise. After she had some dinner and finished unpacking, she spent some time examining her Mauritius stamps and then called it a night.

*   *   *

Virginia awoke on Monday morning to music from her radio. Her first thought was: am I still on the cruise ship? *I don't want to miss the first seating for the ship's breakfast.* She shut off the music alarm and, with one foot out of bed, intended to arise. Instead she fell back on the bed asleep. A half hour later, she suddenly sat up.

"Damn," she said to the radio, "I'm going to be late."

The announcer began his bad news about the traffic conditions, "...and on the Capital Beltway, traffic is heavy but moving along..." Translated, thought Virginia on the way to the bathroom, that meant cars were bumper to bumper. "...and on the ramp to the Wilson Bridge, watch for an incident which may slow you down..." Translated, thought Virginia in the bathroom, that meant traffic was stalled and the backup was horrendous.

She rushed through her toilette, dressed and prepared to leave her apartment. She admired her reflection in the full size mirror on her bathroom door. *Not bad for the ripe old age of 35 that I admit to,* she thought. She felt comfortable in her business suit but already missed the fun clothes she wore while on vacation.

She dressed in a pin-striped, dark blue suit with a light blue blouse and dark blue shoes, adding a pearl necklace which picked up the white of the pin stripes. Her chest was too full to be hidden by the suit. She believed in dressing the part of a business executive and spared no expense when it came to her wardrobe. *Well, I can't stay here and admire myself.* As she rushed out of the flat she recited to herself:

"Mirror, mirror, on the wall, why can't I get someone to fall - for me."

Virginia owned a condominium unit in Pentagon City, almost walking distance to the Pentagon. Her company, Dockside International, an import/export firm, occupied the 5th through the 9th floors in the Twin Towers Center, located in Rosslyn just minutes by Metro from her condo. The tall, white building had sun-proof windows that looked black, like the windows of those stretch limos. Her office was on the 9th floor with a view of the nearby historic monuments of Washington, D.C. Virginia was the Manager of Marketing. Her company separated marketing and sales into two separate departments.

 The company she worked for had been founded by three individuals who imported unusual foreign items into the U.S. market. Their first store was located right on the Potomac River. As business grew they began selling U.S. products to foreign markets. The company expanded when it located its own outlet stores on the waterfronts of major cities.

 Each store featured a large bulletin board listing by name the various products which were arriving on ships. This gave the stores an adventurous aura and the customers often bought up a whole shipment of a popular item in a matter of days. The original owners switched the mission of the company to a national operation and moved their headquarters to Rosslyn.

 After college, Virginia had started to work for Dockside as a salesperson in the Georgetown store. The variety of household merchandise never failed to interest her. Her enthusiasm carried over to her dealings with the public and thus she advanced steadily. She eventually was promoted to Marketing Manager, reporting to a vice president. It was her department's job to buy the right products; those that sold easily and quickly. Virginia's staff analyzed the movement of all imports in her area and to recommend action to get rid of those items which did not sell without losing money on the deal. Her business instinct lead to many successful deals where the company gained a foothold in major markets, bringing her to the attention of senior management. She liked the challenge and prestige of being one of the managers and, of course, the pay.

 As she entered her building, one of the company's finance managers stepped right behind her on the escalator. Virginia knew the manager's reputation with women and she usually steered clear of him.

"Hello, Virginia. Is it too early to ask for a date?"

"Now, now, sir," replied Virginia, as they got off the escalator. "How can you date when your family and dog are anxiously awaiting your return home every evening?"

"Ah, yes, I'm afraid you have a point but I am in love!"

Virginia stifled a grin.

"By the way, I saw a TV news bulletin last night about a cruise ship on fire. Weren't you on a cruise?"

"Yes, I was and that was my ship! I can't believe what happened but I would go again. The crew handled the emergency competently and no one was seriously injured."

"Well! I'm glad you survived. Don't forget to check your schedule anyway and let me know when you are free for a date!"

Virginia shook her head, smiled and went to the coffee shop for a bagel and coffee. She entered her office and turned on her computer. Pulling up her schedule, she noted that only the staff meeting was on for that morning. She had looked forward to visiting the London Gallery's stamp auction. She was a serious collector and was not about to miss an auction there.

The computer monitor also confirmed that she had a lunch scheduled with a single male who had responded to her ad in a singles magazine. He had called and they agreed to meet for a quick lunch at a nearby hotel coffee shop. These first meetings seldom took long; one either clicked with the other or one did not. She would meet him and then go on to the gallery.

Although Virginia's professional life was successful, her personal life was not particularly active. She realized in recent years that she should have married while in college or soon thereafter. As she got older, it seemed the men she met were divorced or, if single, not at all interested in a sincere relationship. The men tended to be abrupt, critical and rude; and yet, confused, uncertain of what they expected of a woman. She recalled again her parent's concern that she was raised for a world that no longer existed. Her parent's world disappeared with the sixties revolution.

These singles meetings became rituals with their own set of rules. The meeting was an occasion to check each other out; to see if there was enough interest to continue on to the next step which was usually a date for dinner or the movies. The male often could not wait for a second date to suggest they go to bed and she usually ended the dating there.

Somewhat regretfully, she thought, she was more interested in seeing the auction material at the London Gallery than she was in the lunch date. But for now she had a meeting to attend and she did not want to be late.

For this meeting she had to recommend how to unload 500 hundred sets of wicker furniture which were not selling because the manufacturer in Malaysia had painted the furniture yellow-green. Had they been painted white or beige they would have sold promptly. Did the purchase order to the Malaysian company list the color? She called up the order on her computer and read the first page. No, it did not specify the color; a mistake by the buyer and by her staff for not checking the order.

She gathered her papers and went to the conference room. Most of the staff were men and, as usual, were discussing their weekend golf scores and the football games. Her colleagues welcomed her back from vacation and, before she could mention the ship's fire, the vice president came in to start the meeting. He was somewhat rotund and dressed well to offset the plumpness of his frame. The thinning hair was combed strategically to hide the scalp. He was not as tall as Virginia which seemed to bother him when they conversed.

"Welcome back, Virginia. I saw a cruise ship's rescue operation on the news. I knew you were on a cruise but I didn't know which ship you were on. Were you on that one?"

"Oh, yes. I couldn't miss it! Chalk it up to my many travel

experiences."

She went on to explain what had happened. The audience was acutely concerned; just the thought of abandoning ship and ending up in the water was frightening.

"Aren't there sharks in those waters?" asked one.

"Virginia, did you see any sharks when you were in the lifeboat?" asked another.

"No, but I did meet some sharks aboard the ship!"

The vice president of marketing interrupted the laughter and began the meeting with her problem first on the agenda. She gave a short summary of her recommendations, backed up by calculations. Other opinions were offered by the staff. The vice president liked that because it meant all bases would be covered and he could be assured of making the right decision. He liked the "team concept" wherein everyone got involved.

"Let's see," said the vice president, "this is your problem, Virginia, so you take this action. It appears the best course to take here is to have the furniture repainted white and put back in stock."

"No," replied Virginia, "that is the most costly approach because it keeps the inventory around too long. My numbers showed that less money would be lost if we unloaded them to a discount outlet and let them worry about repainting them."

Virginia persisted in debating the issue.

"The calculations show a bigger loss," insisted Virginia, "if we do it the way you suggest. What good are the calculations if we don't believe the numbers?"

"I'm not ignoring your figures, " replied the vice president, "but I am changing the premise. I believe repainting the furniture and keeping it will work because the demand for wicker furniture is increasing and we can increase the price."

"If you increase the price," countered Virginia, "sales will be slow, again increasing the loss or reducing the profit, no matter how you look at it."

The vice president would not back off so Virginia dropped the subject and let him go on to other problems. Interestingly, he did not go into who was responsible for ordering that color. Her review of the purchase order to the manufacturer disclosed the color was inadvertently omitted and she had signed the order. Instead of phoning her, the vendor had gone ahead and used his own color.

As the meeting droned on, she thought back about her career. She stood up, got a cup of coffee and sat down. The freshly brewed coffee had a nice aroma. As she savored the taste of mocha, her thoughts drifted away from the meeting.

She heard her name mentioned which jarred her attention back to the meeting. The vice president was talking about the success of the mother-of-pearl objects they were importing from the Philippines through a company in London, and was acknowledging Virginia as the source of the original recommendation to buy those products.

"How did you arrive at that idea?" he asked.

"I once saw a bolo knife encased in an inlaid mother-of-pearl scabbard at a friend's house which had been brought back from the Philippine Islands after World War II. My friend said it came from Mactan Island which is across the bay from Cebu City. It seemed to me that other objects with mother-of-pearl might exist. I spoke to the marketing vp at Roulette Traders in London, who is one of our sources for that part of the world, and suggested they investigate. They found a number of such products."

"The repeat orders sold quickly," said the vice president. "On your next trip to Europe, Virginia, please stop by Roulette Traders and see what else they can develop in this line."

"Okay," replied Virginia, "I plan to go over next month."

The meeting continued on, reviewing other problems. By comparison, her goof was minor. Perhaps that was why the vice president did not explore who was responsible for the error.

"The last item on my agenda," he went on, "is the reengineering effort which has been going on for the past 3 months. I believe you all have been interviewed and consulted by the company that is doing the analysis."

Virginia had spent a lot of time with the people running around reviewing the company's processes so she listened more attentively.

"I don't know the outcome yet," he continued, "so keep in touch with these people. The company is trying to streamline procedures and reduce costs. That's all I have this morning."

The "flattening of the organization" had started as a suggestion by a member of the board of directors to "improve the operation and profitability" of Dockside International. That was the standard language presented to the Wall Street analysts and the news media. But that really was not the reason to spend over $1 million to save an ephemeral $5 million. The real impetus behind such projects was to give the analysts a reason to recommend the stock and thus raise its value. The Board was not looking for more profit; they wanted the stock price up which would enhance the value of their incentives and stock options. Virginia knew that was the corporate game and she expected to get into it by eventually being promoted to upper management. She expected to eventually break through the "glass curtain" which kept women out of upper management.

Virginia had her suspicions when she first got involved with the company that was hired to do business process reengineering (BPR). She recalled the meeting wherein the reengineering Project Manager was introduced. He spoke in glittering generalities. The BPR company brought many of the employees into their procedure to get them to explain how the everyday business was conducted. Employees also had many ideas on how to improve operations and were only too glad to have someone - anyone - listen to them. It was paradoxical that the management could not implement them unless an outside company - which knew little of DI's functions - was brought in. Ultimately the BPR company picked up many of the employees ideas and implemented them. True, some of the BPR company's ideas were gleaned from other companies but most of the changes came from DI personnel.

At the end of the analysis, the BPR company would confirm that it was going to reduce the cost of operating substantially. The cost reduction estimate always exceeded the amount which was originally proposed in order to win the contract. Since the DI management would not measure the impact of the changes, the estimates soon became hard facts.

Virginia went along as required but she knew that the board of directors knew it was all fiction because no one in management intended to actually measure the impact of the changes. The Wall Street analysts went along because it was "the thing to do" in today's business world and it gave them something to talk about to the media.

As she left the conference room, one of the managers came over to her and put his arm around her shoulder. She gently twisted away from his arm; he was one of those people who had to touch you when speaking.

"Glad to see you survived the ship's fire, Virginia."

"Thanks. It could've been a disaster."

Virginia lingered in the conference room. Several of her colleagues also lingered, obviously worried.

"I'm not worried about BPR," said one of the managers. "This is just another 'efficiency expert' exercise."

"Yeah. Big companies do it every few years."

"Do you remember when the management introduced "TQM?"

"Sure; 'TQM - Total Quality Management'. But this BPR is more sinister because jobs will be more directly affected, unlike the TQM exercise, which involved mostly slogans, posters and meetings."

"That's what worries me. See you at the next BPR meeting."

"From TQM to BPR," said one of the managers. "If I could come up with the next management fad, I would be rich!".

She returned to her office and began identifying companies in her computer listing who could refinish the wicker furniture. She then sent faxes directly from her PC requesting quotations from three of the companies. By afternoon she would have replies and then, by videophone, she could clarify the bids, if she had questions, directly with the bidders. The videophone was the latest hi-tech item added to her desk. Sometimes when she was replying to a singles ad, she would call the male from her videophone and they could see each other's face before they agreed to meet. In a few cases it was all they needed to agree not to meet!

Virginia then faxed the company in Malaysia to ask why they did not call her about the missing color note on the purchase order. It was a loose end and she had to pin it down to avoid a repetition. It also occurred to her that she should seek some competition to keep the price down. She decided to check out other sources in Malaysia and other countries. She believed wicker furniture would remain popular. If she ever bought a house it would have a porch with such furniture and the brightly-colored cushions that went with it. She might plan her trip to Europe so that she could return by way of the Far East.

Lunch hour was approaching and she decided to prepare for the date. She left the building and walked the few blocks to the hotel where they planned to meet. On the way, she thought about her social life. Although Virginia was seldom at a loss for a date, she could not seem to commit herself to a long-term relationship. When she had started working she assumed she would meet someone at the office, have a prolonged engagement and then marry. She had met a few single men in the company but there was no mutual interest. On the other hand, she got plenty of attention from the married men but she refused to date them.

She arrived at the coffee shop a bit early. Part of the drill was to arrange beforehand how to recognize each other. She looked around but did not see her date so she sat down in a booth and ordered a diet coke. The restaurant was crowded and noisy. The pungent smell of the day's blue plate special - Salisbury Steak - drifted across the room. She sipped her drink and stared vacantly at the frosted drops of water on the outside of the glass. She thought about a young man she had fallen for in college, a grad student who had offered marriage but expected Virginia to sacrifice her career in the bargain. She still remembered their parting. It was in his dorm the evening after graduation when she saw him last.

"Gil," Virginia had said, "why're you packed? Where are you going?"

"Virginia, I'm going to a Western state where I can relax for a year or two and then maybe decide on a career. I want you to come with me."

Virginia was startled and confused. What would she do there? Where would she work? She had had definite plans about her career and they did not fit that pattern.

"I don't know, Gil. Where'll we work?"

"We won't have to for a few years! The state we are going to will give us unemployment compensation, food stamps and other benefits which will add up to about $9000 a year!"

That was a goodly sum in those days, thought Virginia. Why did she not go? She painfully remembered turning him down.

"I can't do it, Gil. I have made up my mind on a job with a one of several companies here on the East coast."

Her reminisce was interrupted by her date, standing beside the booth. They introduced themselves and he reminded her he was a lawyer. That did not impress Virginia as Washington was loaded with lawyers. There was polite chit-chat as they ordered lunch. Virginia ordered a diet coke and a club sandwich; he ordered a beer and a club sandwich.

"Being a lawyer," ventured Virginia, "I suppose you're working long hours?"

"Yes, indeed," he replied. "I average about 70 hours a week to make my billings quota."

"You have a quota imposed on you?"

"Not exactly. I set it myself knowing what it takes to advance. There's a lot of competition within the firm. How many hours do you put in a week?"

"Usually about 50 hours. Sometimes when there is a problem I work even longer. I travel quite a bit which consumes many hours especially when I have to travel over weekends."

They began to eat and talked between bites. He wore the lawyers' uniform: a 3-piece suit, dull necktie on a gray-blue button-down, cotton shirt, complemented by unshined tasseled loafers. Virginia thought he was nice looking enough to go on a date. When Virginia mentioned the London Gallery and her interest in stamps, she noticed his eyes glaze over, then an abrupt change of subject.

"Well," the lawyer said, "I better get back. It was nice meeting you. May I have your phone number?"

Virginia handed him her business card. He got up and left. Suddenly Virginia realized he had not mentioned the check. She got up and called after him.

"You forgot the check!"

"No, I didn't!" he replied, walking swiftly to the door. "It's all yours!"

Virginia stood there composing herself. That pretty well cinched it. She would not be seeing him again! She was still somewhat old-fashioned when it came to these matters. It wasn't the money it was the manners. She paid the check, left the restaurant and looked for a cab to take her to the London Gallery. As she waited she thought: *I know what I'm going to do. I'll send a bill to the lawyer for half the check. He'd mentioned his law firm so I'll send the bill to his secretary!*

She was glad she had some place to go to get her mind off the subject of men and on to the subject of stamps. She really looked forward to this interlude at the stamp gallery. Waiting for a taxi, the autumn breeze cooled her hot brow. A hint of soon-to-come frost was in the air. A taxi pulled up.

"London Gallery, please," she said to the cabby.

The taxi crossed Key Bridge heading for K Street. She admired the view of the Potomac River. Passing near the fashionable Georgetown area, she decided that, of all the big cities that she had visited, none was as attractive as Washington. When American tourists visited foreign cities they raved about the buildings and the churches. If one wanted to see churches just ride up Sixteenth Street or visit the National Cathedral or the Shrine at Catholic University. There were numerous embassies and government buildings one could visit. She had lived here many years and yet had not seen all the tourist attractions. She had tried to visit some of these places with dates but most were not interested. Her dates were willing to go into Georgetown on a Saturday night but would not go with her to visit the National Gallery of Art on a Sunday afternoon.

Washington overflowed with culture but not with men who were interested in partaking of it. She could not figure it; either she was meeting the wrong type of male or attending the wrong activities.

The taxi pulled up suddenly. She paid the driver, got out of the cab and entered the London Gallery.

Chapter 5

> *"To collect stamps not only appeals to one's esthetic sensibilities, but to finesse and curiosity, to care, to sense the quest, to embark on an endless journey without a guaranteed ending..."*
>
> - *"The Test of Time" by Mathias B. Freese*

Stanley Roulette, a well-known stamp collector from London, was on a flight from Singapore to the Philippine Islands. It was the last leg of a business trip for his company, Roulette Traders, Ltd. From the Philippines he would fly to Japan and then return to London.

Following his honorable discharge from the Royal Air Force, after World War II, he started a trading company. Initial contacts were with friends in China, Burma, Singapore and Malaysia which allowed his company to supply exotic merchandise from the Far East to England.

Roulette Traders, Ltd. was enormously successful and expanded when he began to export English products, such as fine china, to other countries. The company grew so big that eventually Roulette reorganized and delegated more authority and responsibility, allowing him time to travel and establish additional sources.

He began to collect stamps in the early years of his business when he travelled extensively. In the years that had passed, he built a first-class collection from the former British colonies. He concentrated on the so-called "classic" era: stamps issued between 1840 and 1940. He amassed stamps from every British colony and, for many colonies, he owned a copy of every stamp issued.

His visit to the Philippines was for business and pleasure. The business part entailed contracting with a source of mother-of-pearl products. The pleasure part was to chase down a rare stamp. The hunt was one of the real pleasures of stamp collecting. It was challenging, exhilarating and euphoric, feelings universally shared by collectors and dealers in objects d'art. And it was a deviation from work stress.

The stamp he sought in the Philippines was a classic from the British Straits Settlements. In 1884, one of the five-cent Queen Victoria stamps was surcharged "4 cents" and then overprinted with a large number "4", perhaps because the first overprint was so faint. Only seven copies were known to exist and each one catalogued at $15,000 in used condition. Stanley had not been able to find a copy in England but one had surfaced recently at a dealer in Cebu City, Philippines. Roulette had heard about the stamp and had immediately contacted the dealer, convincing him to hold the rare issue until he arrived in Cebu.

When he arrived, he went straight to the dealer, even before checking in at a hotel. Stanley, with his somewhat bearish frame, towered over the diminutive dealer and his expression signalled that the negotiations were going to be prolonged. If he could intimidate his adversary with his body size and bellowing, he would do so. But in this instance, the dealer was not overly impressed and informed Stanley that he planned to auction it off rather than sell it privately. Stanley countered that because of the lack of provenance and proof of ownership, it would not bring a big price. They verbally parried back and forth; the dealer insisting the auction would give him the true market price, Stanley countering that someone could claim it was stolen which would result in removal from the auction and a legal hassle. The dealer admitted he had purchased it from a source without proof of ownership. He finally submitted to Stanley's logic and agreed to sell it for a tidy sum. It was more than Stanley had wanted to pay but he agreed. He knew he would not regret the purchase; the stamp's catalog value was bound to increase.

Stanley also purchased a number of Malaya stamps which had been overprinted by Japan during their World War II occupation. Stanley was missing some of this elusive issue which had greatly increased in value because the stamps had been printed in small quantities and many were destroyed when the war ended.

Now he could begin to complete the business part of his trip. The marketing vice president at Roulette Traders, Ltd. had advised Stanley to visit Mactan Island to check out the mother-of-pearl products. He told Stanley that Dockside International in the U.S. had placed a large order. One of their managers had urged Roulette Traders to find additional sources for this highly successful product.

Cebu, the second largest city in the Philippines, was teeming with people. He was glad he could pass through and not have to stay. Stanley took a rickshaw to the Cebu docks where he boarded an overcrowded ferry boat to Mactan Island. Riding in an old taxicab to the manufacturer, he was surprised to find a major historic monument: the grave of Ferdinand Magellan, the Portuguese navigator whose fleet, sailing under the Spanish flag, made the first trip around the globe. Magellan was killed on Mactan in a fight with its natives during that journey. His fleet continued, but in the end, only one ship made it back to Spain four years after departure.

More then two hundred years later, Stanley, following Magellan's lead, was also seeking trade opportunities. Of course he did not expect to fight the natives. He found the unique item originally suggested by the Dockside International manager: a bolo knife in a sheath in-laid with mother-of-pearl. He arranged to buy the knife in large quantities along with other objects with beautiful in-lays, such as combs and brushes. Stanley established a contract with the new source, confident of the workmanship and the sale of the merchandise. He made a note to visit Dockside International at the next opportunity to commend the manager who had suggested the bolo knives.

Stanley took the ferry boat back to Cebu City, and before leaving the Philippine Islands, he visited other stamp dealers in Cebu to seek other rare stamps of the World War II era. One dealer showed him stamps issued when General MacArthur had returned to the islands. The post office had had to use prewar issues overprinted with the word "VICTORY." However, Stanley did not purchase them; his interest was confined to the British area.

The last dealer he visited gave him exciting news. A mint copy of the Mauritius one penny orange had been discovered and the owner was now in London to have it expertised. Stanley was excited; it was one of the few stamps missing from his collection. One of the rarest stamps in the world was in London! He immediately called his office and instructed his administrative assistant to locate the owner and keep him in London, no matter what it took. He also gave her instructions to forward to a security agency he often used. Then he rushed to the airport and booked the most direct flight to London.

* * *

Stanley Roulette was undoubtedly the most famous philatelist in all Britain. His collection of British colonial stamps was second only to the Queen of England's collection in terms of quality and completeness. Her collection had been inherited from its originator, King George V. If Stanley could get his stamp tongs on the Mauritius stamp he knew he would own something that even the Queen would want to see. He fantasized that the Queen would send for him just to examine the stamp.

Although he was now a noted collector, owning the one penny orange would make him world-famous. He decided he would have that stamp no matter what the obstacles. And Stanley Roulette always got what he wanted.

Stanley arrived in London and devoted all of his energy to preparing for the meeting with the owner of the one penny orange, Edward Postmark. Stanley knew he had to develop a strategy to convince Postmark to part with the rare stamp. But the meeting had not been successful and Stanley, forced to retreat, was wholly dismayed. Postmark was adamant that he would sell the one penny orange at auction. Once it got on the auction block, the stamp would sell for the maximum market value. Stanley was prepared to bid high but he did not want to risk being outbid. Stanley had to devise a way to acquire that stamp before it was auctioned and thus pay a much lower price as well as reduce the risk of losing it.

Stanley's mood reflected his recent encounter with Edward Postmark. *Dash it! The owner should have been happy to sell it to me! If Postmark were a collector he would not have been reluctant to do so. If I could have seen the stamp I would have wrenched it away and replaced it with a check!*

He returned to his fashionable home, an old Victorian style house located in an exclusive part of London. For a moment, as he entered, Stanley's troubled thoughts subsided as he admired his meticulously adorned home. The interior featured the wide curving staircase to the upper floors so popular many years ago. On the walls surrounding the large entrance hall hung oil paintings illuminated by subdued spotlights in the ceiling. On one wall was a large portrait of Queen Victoria, portrayed in her middle years.

Stanley's long-time companion, Olivia, appeared at the top of the staircase. Although Stanley forced a smile, she could see that her lover was unhappy.

"The owner would not budge," Stanley said after embracing

her. He then related what had happened at the meeting.

"I have somehow missed an opportunity to obtain that stamp. He would not budge even at my immediate cash offer."

"Is he a collector?" asked Olivia.

"No, he is not. Can you believe he called me an anachronism because I specialize in British Colony stamps! He said my collection is symbolic of what was and what will never be again. Certainly the stamps of Queen Victoria's reign through those of King George V's reign represented the mighty British Empire."

"I think `anachronism' is a bit strong, Stanley, but I noticed you have often lamented to your fellow collectors that the stamps are always a reminder of the British Empire."

"Well, I suppose you are right. When I look at the King George V Silver Jubilee issue, I must say it is a reminder of the world I grew up in."

"If the auction of his stamp is scheduled for next week, why is he still in London?" asked Olivia.

"I believe he is about to leave for the States, as are we," replied Stanley. "I assume that the stamp is already in the vault of the London Gallery in Washington. Come to think of it, that is only an assumption; suppose he has the stamp on him and is about to deliver it?"

"You can still catch up with him before he delivers it."

"Quite! P'r'aps I can intercept him at the London Gallery before the auction takes place. But I must be ready for this move. First, I will call Joe Coil to arrange for him to meet us at the Gallery. Coil's sinister appearance alone will help persuade the owner to sell the stamp to me!"

Joe Coil was a trusted member of the security agency often employed by Roulette Traders for business in the U.S.

Olivia went to pack while Stanley reached Joe Coil at his apartment in the States and told Joe to meet him in Washington, DC. He briefly explained the mission and instructed Joe that the rare stamp must be acquired and protected.

On Monday morning, Stanley and Olivia departed on Flight 111 from London to Dulles International Airport in Virginia, U.S.A. They were sitting in first class seats enjoying drinks and trying to relax after rushing to the airport.

Glancing at Olivia who appeared to be napping, his mind turned to thoughts about her. *I don't know which I am more fond of: Olivia or my collection.*

Stanley was over 60 years old, healthy as a lifeguard and a widower the past ten years. He had met Olivia about five years ago and since then they had settled into a pattern. She was ten years younger than he, but looked even twenty years his junior.

Her figure still turned the heads of younger men which Stanley noted wryly. Olivia was a statuesque titian blond with a wide, beguiling smile and amber, flashing eyes. He was envied by friends and colleagues, not just because she was a beauty, but because she was a bright sensitive companion. She had that combination of a smile, good looks and disposition that invited strangers to be friendly. Men much younger than Olivia would often engage her in conversation.

When Stanley was not travelling, she spent weekends with him at his home, returning on Monday morning to her flat in Knightsbridge. Stanley's weekdays were consumed by business; he often traveled then so he could be home on weekends. Stanley's relationship with his late wife had been near perfect and he had no inclination to marry again. Olivia, thus far, had not hinted that she wished to remarry, but he sensed lately that she desired a closer relationship.

Yes, Stanley thought, with or without that stamp, he was a lucky man. He clasped Olivia's hand and closed his eyes to nap.

*   *   *

Olivia was not asleep. Rather, she was thinking hard about her situation with Stanley. The perfect lover; that's how Olivia saw herself. Until recently, she believed that neither of them wanted to marry again nor change their pleasant arrangement. She could even see other men when Stanley was away but she rarely did; Stanley was enough male for her.

Olivia knew she was still attractive but was not consumed with her looks. Her natural curly hair and the white slacks and navy blue blazer over a red and white print blouse made her look even younger than her age. Blue, high-heeled shoes over light stockings completed her outfit. Her simple accessories were a gold choker with matching gold bracelets.

Stanley once told her that it was Olivia's hair that first drew his attention; those golden, tight curls that framed the pale pink skin of her face. Once, in a tender moment - for which he seldom had time - Stanley found a quote from Alexander Pope's "The Rape of the Lock" which he had read to her:

"This nymph, to the destruction of mankind,
Nourished two locks, which graceful hung behind
In equal curls, and well conspir'd to deck
With shining ringlets the smooth iv'ry neck."

Her reaction, she recalled, was surprisingly passionate.

Born and bred in London, Olivia Block came from an established family in the banking business. She had married a banker but divorced him some years later. They had two grown daughters, one married and one not, who lived outside London.

Lately, though, she had started to wonder about her feelings. Each time he went away, she missed him more. Perhaps, she thought, she was simply anxious about growing old alone. She was worried that Stanley might meet a younger woman. Perhaps, she thought, she was just worried about being lonely as she got older, or that Stanley might meet someone younger. She recently saw a play called, "Leave After Love," which had made her very uncomfortable. The theme of the play was based on the notion that female beauty fades with age while men appear to remain attractive. She began to fantasize that Stanley would want to marry again and felt she should develop a strategy to make sure he married her. The trip would be an opportunity to formulate that plan.

She gave up trying to sleep, opened her eyes and realized Stanley's hand was holding hers.

* * *

Stanley's thoughts drifted to his collection. The hobby was perfect for Stanley. He was constantly travelling for his business; stamps forced him to slow down and enjoy the scenes on the stamps and stories behind them. His stamps were neatly mounted in albums with small, folded paper hinges. If the stamp was removed from the album, the hinge left a small blemish on the gum of an unused stamp. It made no difference on a used stamp because the gum was already removed when it was moistened and applied to an envelope for postage. For unused stamps, condition was subject for serious debate in the philatelic world. Those unused stamps were identified as "hinged" or "never hinged." A premium was charged by dealers for never hinged, mint condition stamps. In fact, the new catalogs cited higher prices for never hinged stamps. In the era that Stanley collected, most stamps were hinged; the never hinged craze began during or after World War II. Lately, Stanley had to admit the craze was here to stay. In a way, he had already acknowledged the never hinged trend because he kept his most valuable stamps separate from his albums and did not hinge them. He displayed those stamps in cards with clear polypropylene sheets where the stamps could be secured and yet remain visible.

Many collectors have followed the never-hinged trend by acquiring those albums that hold stamps without the use of hinges. Someday, Stanley thought, he might convert to the hingeless albums but the logic of doing that bothered him. For one thing, a collection displayed the face of the stamp, not the gum side.

While some albums make both sides of a stamp observable, interest in a stamp's subject matter lay in the face, not the gum. For another thing, unused stamps can easily be re-gummed, to the extent that it would take an expert to tell the difference. Right or wrong, Stanley avoided buying never-hinged mint stamps unless there was no choice. He always sought stamps in near perfect condition except, of course, for the gum. This meant the stamp had to be perfectly centered with no perforations missing, no stains or other blemishes, and with bright, unfaded colors.

Stanley thoroughly enjoyed reviewing his collection, carefully turning each page. The sweep of time and history allowed him to imagine events that occurred during the reigns of Queen Victoria, King Edward VII and King George V. Events such as the coronation of George VI in 1937 were commemorated on stamps. One set of stamps was issued showing Edward VIII even though he abdicated the throne.

The British presence in other countries was reflected in their stamps used during occupations: China, Morocco, Turkey and others. Stanley reflected that today almost every event or popular personality is reflected in a stamp issue.

It was time to enjoy the meal. He finished his drink and took out his briefcase to jot down some reminders.

"Stanley," said Olivia, finishing her drink, "you seemed so absorbed I did not want to disturb you. Are you going to eat with me?"

"Of course, Olivia. By the way, what do you plan to do while we are in the states?"

"I want to visit the art galleries. I wish you could go with me.

"Yes, indeed. Once I obtain that stamp, we can spend the rest of the week seeing the sights. I do have one business visit to make. I want to see Dockside International's outlet. P'r'aps you will join me. You will enjoy shopping in Georgetown."

Stanley's mind stayed on one track.

"You know, Olivia, I had an amusing thought. If I can somehow obtain that Mauritius one penny orange stamp I could become truly famous."

"You are already well-known for your collection," offered Olivia. "What else can you achieve even if you acquire that stamp?"

"For one thing," enthused Stanley, warming up to his subject, "I would certainly get an audience with the Queen. I am not aware that she has that stamp but even if she did have it, I am sure she would want to compare copies. I would certainly want to compare some of the rare issues that we both own."

"There other ways to get an audience with the Queen. Your business is one of the largest in England; surely you will be recognized eventually for that."

"Yes, but, that is so common! If she really wanted to view the stamp, that would be a special audience."

"Dream on," laughed Olivia, "First you have to land that stamp."

"For another thing, Olivia," continued Stanley, "there is another honor that I could claim. Would you not be impressed if, after I am gone, the British Government issued a stamp in my honor for my collection?"

"Really!" said Olivia. "You are getting carried away with your pursuit of this stamp!"

"Not at all," said Stanley, excitedly. "I will have you know that a set of postage stamps was issued recently by Nicaragua in honor of three prominent stamp collectors! Why not me?"

"Well," replied Olivia, "you have a point there. Perhaps it could happen as you say."

"In fact," said Stanley, "while you are at the gallery, I want you to buy me a set of the Nicaragua stamps. Also, I shall give you a list of Mauritius stamps to buy if they are available."

"Will do" said Olivia.

As the flight approached the U.S. coastline, Stanley grew

restless. The only idea Stanley had so far to acquire that stamp was to use Joe Coil and his less subtle methods to convince the owner of the stamp to sell before the auction. Having just seen Postmark in London, he assumed the stamp was not yet at the gallery. He did not know when Postmark was scheduled to arrive in the States but knew he should go straight to the gallery to meet Joe Coil as soon as his flight landed.

Stanley was prepared to offer Postmark an additional $100,000 for a total of $350,000. If Postmark still refused he must find a way to take the stamp from Postmark and then negotiate a price with him. Of course, that would foul up the auction and the director of the London Gallery would probably never invite him to bid again. But that was too bad; it would be worth it to get the stamp. If he could possess the stamp, Stanley reasoned, Postmark, not being a collector, would be willing to take his offer rather than wait for another auction. If he could get it for $350,000 Stanley was sure that would be less than half of what it would sell for at auction. He could not imagine the price exceeding the catalog value of $1,100,000, but he conceded he could be surprised in which case he would not be able to win by bidding. That thought made him even more determined to wrest the stamp away from the owner.

He turned his thoughts away from the stamp to Olivia. He told her he had seldom visited Washington so he wanted to take advantage of the trip. As a former Royal Air Force pilot he must visit the Smithsonian Air and Space Museum. The World War II exhibits there would be of great interest. He could show Olivia the type of plane he had flown during the war. Also on his list was a trip to the Postal Museum. He was anxious to see if their collection of British Colonials was as complete as his. He was very curious about the condition of the earlier issues. In return for her indulgence he would go to the art galleries.

The aircraft was over the east coast nearing the airport. Stanley finally put his thoughts and papers away, happier now that the flight was almost over. He turned to look at Olivia with satisfaction. Olivia responded with a big smile.

"Stanley, I cannot help thinking about your portrait appearing on a British stamp as a famous collector. Well, strange things are happening. Some countries have issued stamps showing movie stars, singers and even cartoon characters."

Stanley smiled at her and caressed her hand.

"Just think." he said, enthusiastically, "if I am successful we will have a lot more entertaining to do. We will have more visitors than ever."

"That's fine," replied Olivia, looking straight at Stanley as if to deliver a message. "If you luck out I may need to spend more time at your place."

Stanley did not appear to have received her message.

"Well, we shall soon find out. By the way, after we land and clear customs would you mind going straight to the hotel with the luggage? I must go directly to the gallery."

"Quite alright," replied Olivia. "I will welcome the chance to shower and change."

The aircraft was slowly losing altitude; the air noise in the cabin changed from the loud whine to a lower decibel count. Stanley went over once more his plan to capture the one penny orange before it reached the auction. The key to his plan, he thought, was Joe Coil. Joe had proved to be very reliable and resourceful; Joe would have his own ideas to capture the stamp. With that optimistic thought he got up and went to the lavatory. I must get to the London Gallery!

Chapter 6

> *"Like doric temples, stamps support an entablature that is classic: order, repose, thought, symmetry dialectic, choice and balance."*
>
> - *"The Test of Time" by Mathias B. Freese*

Andre Setenant and his wife, Marie, were seated in the rear of the first class section. Andre could see Stanley Roulette seated up front near the bulkhead. Yes, he thought, Stanley would be very surprised to learn that he was on this flight. Andre glanced at Marie who had fallen asleep as soon as the plane took off.

Andre was not the famous collector that Stanley Roulette was and that irked him. It was not a question of resources because Andre commanded a large salary and bonuses with which he was able to finance his collection. In addition, his wife was quite wealthy in her own right and had even helped him fund the purchase of rare issues. Andre did not directly use her money; instead, he borrowed a large sum when needed, repaying her after the purchase. Marie had begun her own collection with Andre's guidance.

Andre gazed at Marie asleep, and reclined his seat thinking he also might fall asleep during the long flight. His eyes closed but memories of his recent trip to Africa occupied his mind. As an executive for a successful French architectural engineering firm, Andre travelled extensively on business. His firm was involved in a multitude of large-scale projects throughout the world: dams, bridges, power plant facilities and similar structures. Being a French company, business was especially good in the former French colonies where contacts were well established. He and his engineering team were meeting with a client in Brazzaville to review an invitation to bid for a new dam project. After a busy day with the client, Andre visited a stamp dealer with whom he had a long acquaintance. The dealer, Monsieur Fronde, told him he had heard about a collection of very early French Colony stamps held by a retired French postal employee, named Marat who lived in a remote village. Coincidentally, the village was not far from the dam site which Andre and his engineers had to reach by boat.

It took the group four hours on the river to get to the village which they used as their base while inspecting the dam site, about two miles away by boat. This worked out well for Andre because he could meet the postal employee and look at his stamps after he completed his review of the dam site. On the last day at the dam site, after resting at the hotel, he went into the jungle to find Marat. Locals who knew of Marat's whereabouts pointed him to a well-traveled path through the overgrown foliage and underbrush of the green jungle. Once on the path, deep in the foliage, Andre wished he had gotten better instructions.

He passed women dressed in bright clothes carrying fruits on their heads, who were surprised to see a foreigner so far from the village. Surrounded by animals he could hear but not see, Andre fervently hoped they would not cross his path. He did not mind the heat and insects in the dense growth because he had made similar trips many times in the course of his business and he kept himself in excellent physical condition. Now, not sure of his direction, he began to worry as the path narrowed and almost disappeared.

"Quelle horreur!" he exclaimed out loud.

His foot landed on a large ant hill. An army of ants immediately swarmed from their home to attack the invader.

Andre pushed himself through the dank, dark green foliage which all but covered the narrow path from the main road.

Suddenly, he was free of the jungle growth and found himself in a clearing of sorts around a thatched-roof hut. A wooden post on the path held a plank with the letters "M. Marat" burned into it. The hut was once a native abode but windows and doors had been added. As if awaiting him, Marat met him at the door.

"Bonjour, Monsieur Marat. I am Andre Setenant and wish to see the stamps you recently showed Monsieur Fronde in Brazzaville."

"Bonjour. Come in and sit. I am surprised to meet someone here interested in my stamps, but I must tell you that I am not anxious to part with them. The dealer wanted very much to buy them but I sensed that the stamps have much more value than I would have been paid."

Inside Marat's untidy hut, Andre was reluctant to sit on the offered ragged chair. He was quite uncomfortable from perspiring through his shirt. A strong odor of fish added to Andre's discomfort. Marat was obviously unaffected by his dishevelled abode. Andre hoped the stamps were in better shape than Marat's living quarters, picturing food and drink spilled on the stamps.

Marat had just finished a meal and was enjoying a brandy and a cigar. He offered both to Andre who accepted the brandy but not the cigar. Marat took the cigar over to a gadget designed to neatly clip off one end. The mechanism was a small guillotine. Marat seemed to enjoy watching the blade drop down neatly lopping off the cigar end.

After lighting up and puffing the cigar to a red glow, Marat handed Andre a cigar box which contained his stamps. Andre spread them out on a clean towel on the table and was amazed at what he saw.

Marie roused herself from sleep, interrupting Andre's reminisce.

"Were you asleep, Andre?" asked Marie.

"No, cheri, I was thinking about my last trip."

"We rushed so to follow your friend Roulette on this flight, you never did tell me about it."

"No, I did not. After we finished the study of the dam for the Brazzaville agency, I met a man in the jungle with a collection of old French colonies stamps. These were unused postage stamps issued in the 1800's by the French Post Office for general use in those colonies that had not yet issued their own stamps. These particular issues were soon replaced by postage stamps from each of the French colonies. There were several copies of about a dozen different sets. Not having a catalog with me, I recalled that the stamps with the bust of Napoleon III were worth in the neighborhood of hundreds of dollars. I looked at another group of stamps from the French Congo, as this area was referred to in the early days of the colony. This territory, incidentally, became part of French Equatorial Africa which was eventually split up into four Republics. Included were several sets of the famous leopard issue which were not worth a lot but are very hard to find as a complete set.

"Ah, Andre, I can use one set in my collection."

"You may have it. Without a catalog I could not ascertain market value on which to base an offer. I asked Marat how much he wanted for them but Marat hesitated and asked how much I would offer. Most of the stamps were quite cheap, so I separated those from the ones of higher catalog value. I counted the higher value stamps, then estimated an average value to come up with a percentage of the retail value. To my surprise, Marat accepted the offer, no doubt because it was much more than what the dealer had offered. I thought I probably paid too much for the stamps but, because some of the issues contained errors, I could end up with a bargain."

"Sounds like you had a successful trip."

"But wait. There is more; I nearly did not return. I was so engrossed in the stamps that I lost track of the hour. It was dusk by the time I left the hut. I had to move quickly to make it back to the village before night fell. Twilight had nearly set in and I realized I should not have gone alone. There was just enough light, though, to see the nearby trees and hanging vines. Suddenly one of the hanging vines moved. I froze. I was staring into the open mouth of a viper hanging from a tree! I knew enough to stand stark still while the snake slowly slithered down the tree, crossing the path. I backed up as the snake watched my every move. Sweating profusely, I inched away all the while eying the deadly serpent. When it was safe, I turned and ran to the village."

"Andre! You could have died alone in the jungle!"

"Yes, it was a close call. Would you have missed me?"

"But, of course! How can you think that?"

"When I returned to my room at the hotel, I gulped some brandy while I stripped off my clothes in the shower. About that time, a dealer in Paris telephoned me about the discovery of a copy of the Mauritius Post Office issue, the one penny orange. The owner, he said, was is in London to expertise the stamp in anticipation of an auction at the London Gallery in Washington, D.C."

"And here we are, Andre, chasing after another stamp."

"The dealer in Paris also told me that Stanley Roulette had met with the owner and planned to go the U.S. to bid for the stamp at the auction."

"Andre, let's have another drink. The risk you took has unnerved me! But, I am glad you invited me to come with you. I have some friends in Washington I plan to see."

Marie sipped her cocktail while Andre tried once more to nap. Now that the children were grown and on their own, he and his wife had time to spend on their hobbies. Andre had long believed that their shared interest had helped keep their marriage intact. He pushed his seat back again but his thoughts turned to the one penny orange.

Restless but half-asleep, he thought about his early interest in stamps which had started when he first began to travel for his company. He learned much from the stamps of the countries he had visited. The knowledge helped him understand other cultures which, in turn, helped in business negotiations. While in other countries, he visited historic sites depicted on the stamps he collected. Gaining knowledge in this fashion had another dimension. Not only were his contract negotiations more profitable, but when he reported back to management, Andre was able to talk about his customers in a manner which got their attention and ultimately several promotions.

Andre was soon viewed by his colleagues as very erudite, not aware that he had gleaned much of his information from postage stamps.

* * *

Marie roused from her nap and looked at Andre who was restlessly trying to nap. She had agreed to accompany him on this particular trip ostensibly because a truly rare stamp was being auctioned. Marie had other plans.

Marie Setenant grew up in Paris with the understanding that it was almost a tradition for French men, sooner or later in their marriages, to engage a mistress. She perceived her marriage to Andre with some irony: Andre never had a mistress to her knowledge (women know). Instead, Marie had entertained a lover for many years. Andre, of course, had no knowledge of the affair. She loved the irony of it all. Perhaps it was a trend toward equal rights; French women more confidently taking on paramours and all that.

But Marie also loved her husband, she reminded herself as she glanced at him. He was still very attractive; his body not yet giving in to portliness. His dark hair and thin mustache were just starting to turn gray, giving him that mature and distinguished look. She had to admit his looks compared well with the various lovers she had had.

Because Andre travelled so much, Marie had free time to spend with her boyfriend. Yet she enjoyed being with Andre when he was available. She came with him on this trip knowing he would be busy, leaving her ample time to shop her favorite up-scale stores in downtown Washington. She especially liked the service. Their personnel truly pampered their customers with attention and the merchandise was from the best designers. After shopping the many floors for women's clothes she would relax in their tea rooms. She could select Paris fashions or American ones, whichever she was in the mood for.

Marie was five years junior to Andre but looked much younger. She had grown up thin but not anorexic. Her complexion was not clear and rosy colored, nor was it pockmarked; nothing a little rouge could not fix. Her legs were thin but shapely and her bust was not full but neither was she flat-chested. Her green eyes were too large for her face but mascara adjusted the proportion. The black hair was cropped but not too short. Marie was one of those persons whose individual features were not beautiful by today's standards but the sum of the features was striking.

Her clothes complemented her figure; above-the-knee skirts and high heels were her style. If long skirts and ankle-length dresses were in style, she did not wear them; they would have made her look too thin, like a pencil. She wore only those styles that enhanced her appearance. Marie was noticed wherever she went by both men and women. Her lover adored her (so did her husband) and had proposed to marry her but she did not believe him and anyway she enjoyed her life with Andre.

For the flight, Marie wore black slacks and a white blouse covered by a jacket with a black and white print. She did not often wear slacks but they were practical for a long trip. A single strand of pearls adorned the blouse. She wore several rings on her fingers; emerald, ruby and amethyst. A diamond bracelet completed the jewelry. To Marie, her look was not finished without appropriate jewelry. She appeared stunning as usual even in a simple outfit.

Gazing at the other passengers around her she wondered why the women did not dress these days. Most wore an assortment of jeans, overalls, sweatsuits, shorts, - anything to make them look unappealing. The men were just as badly dressed.

Marie looked at Andre. Yes, she cared for her husband and had even taken up an interest in philately, not just to please Andre but because she became truly interested in the collection that Andre had assembled. She had developed an interest in the French Colonies because Andre kept bringing home those attractive issues from his trips. Who could resist owning the 22-stamp set of colorful stamps from the Middle Congo? Issued in 1907, they depicted native scenes of that period. While visiting the London Gallery to see the famous one penny orange, she would try to buy more of the French colonial sets, which, although not expensive, were hard to find in complete sets. For example, she had been unsuccessful in locating the set of French Guiana which showed a Carib archer, Maroni Rapids and the Cayenne government building. The set of forty-three was issued between 1929 and 1940 and was very hard to find complete even though it catalogued under twenty dollars. Most of the stamps were printed in bright, two-color combinations which caught the eye. The scenes and the colors fascinated her and the difficulty in locating a complete set stimulated her interest. She often realized she had missed a lot of fun and knowledge because she had not collected stamps in her youth.

Her thoughts turned once more to her itinerary for the trip. While Andre was tied up at the auction she planned to call her friend, Adrienne, who living near the French Embassy. Perhaps she would find a long distance lover; a change from her boyfriend in Paris. He had wanted to meet her in Washington but she said no; it was asking for trouble. Besides, who knew what new romantic adventures she might find?

*   *   *

Awakening from his nap, Andre looked at Marie who smiled at him.

"Would you care for a drink, cheri?" asked Andre as he rang for the flight attendant.

"Yes, Andre, I would."

"Why were you smiling?"

"I was thinking about you!"

"Well, ma chere, I must confess I was thinking about my trip to Africa. He shuddered slightly as he ordered two martinis from the flight attendant.

"I forgot to tell you about more of Marat's stamps. The prettiest set was the one issued in 1907 which showed a leopard, a native woman and a coconut grove. There were three complete sets in perfect condition. There were twenty French Colony stamps including the "Ceres" stamp issue number 17 which retailed for $300. Overall, I did very well because the stamps with errors were worth more than I had paid for the whole lot."

"I could use that 1907 set from Middle Congo," said Marie.

"It is yours, Marie. Put it in your collection. I was fortunate that Marat's stamps were not glued together from the humidity. I remember when I was in the navy, one of my shipmates was a collector. He was stationed on a cruiser in World War II and whenever the ship stopped in port, he went ashore and bought stamps. The cruiser was sunk by a German U-boat during a battle. He ended up in the water with the stamps in a plastic bag tied around his waist. Luckily, he was rescued, but the stamps were soaked by the salt water and they could no longer be considered 'mint'."

Andre mused about his hobby as Marie checked her makeup. He wondered how many other people were lucky enough to travel on business and enjoy their hobby at the same time. His trips took him to remote parts of different countries where old stamps might still exist undiscovered. When he heard about the circumstances surrounding the finding of the Mauritius stamp he began to think he should spend more time in some of those countries uncovering rare stamps. His next trip to Africa would give him that opportunity.

What a find the Mauritius stamp was! If only he could find a way to obtain this rarity, he would certainly join the ranks of Stanley Roulette and the growing circle of world renowned collectors. He would be invited everywhere; the most famous collectors in the world would want to see the one penny orange and he in turn would be invited to see their collections. The Premier of France was also a collector. Imagine being invited to a state dinner! His wife would forever adore him for that honor alone.

Andre knew that if Stanley Roulette was hotly pursuing the Mauritius stamp then he too should pool all of his resources to get that stamp.

As a collector, Andre specialized only in postage stamps with errors. His favorite, a complete set of the United States Pan American Exposition issue of 1901, including the three stamps with inverted centers, was in perfect condition; mint and never hinged, a rare thing in itself for issues of that period.

He settled back in his seat and had a glass of wine served while he thought about the one penny orange to be auctioned off. He had to consider that he might not, even with his wife's help, be able to make a winning bid at the auction. The Mauritius stamp could sell for much more than a million dollars. He wondered if he should try to negotiate with the owner through the gallery's director. That was not a likely scenario for success. Why should the owner take a lot less than what the auction would provide? He needed another solution. Once again, he was lost in thought as he sipped his cool, dry wine.

Andre was in his early fifties and believed he had time to build a collection comparable to Roulette's. While he was not yet as famous as Stanley in philatelic circles, he was well-known and often received media attention. Whenever he travelled, he contacted dealers for the latest tips about rarities. It was in this fashion that he was often in the right place at the right time to buy an unusual, sought after stamp.

"Marie, while I am at the auction, will you be able to amuse yourself?"

"Oh, yes, Andre, I plan to visit a friend from Paris. I would also like to do some shopping if we have time."

"Do I know your friend?"

"You do not remember Adrienne? She moved here a few years ago."

Marie opened her purse and removed her makeup kit, busying her hands to cover the rising blush.

Andre stirred in his seat. It was time to seek out Stanley Roulette for information on the Mauritius stamp. He didn't think Stanley knew he was on board so he looked forward to the surprise.

"Come, Marie, let us go see Stanley."

Flight 111 was still reducing altitude. Andre and Marie approached Stanley Roulette.

"I have been following you," said Andre to the tall, hefty man.

"Well, well," exclaimed Stanley. "Olivia, I want you to meet Andre Setenant, a noted stamp collector from Paris, and his lovely wife."

"Enchante," said Andre, as he kissed Olivia's hand.

Andre then turned back to Roulette.

"I understand you are in pursuit of a rare stamp to be auctioned at the London Gallery."

"Since you have been following me, I will not spoil your fun by so easily responding to your query."

"Yes. We must return to our seats as the plane is preparing to land but I shall see you at the London Gallery."

"Perhaps," said Marie to Olivia, "we can meet at the gallery as well."

"Delightful idea," replied Olivia. "I shall call you when we are settled."

"We cross paths occasionally," explained Stanley after Andre and Marie left. "He is indeed a renowned philatelist in France. His success is in no small measure due to his practice of keeping up with the activities of other collectors. He is as aggressive as I am and I respect him for it. I understand his wife is also a collector. You will enjoy talking to her, I dare say."

Andre and Marie returned to their seats.

"Andre, are you going straight to the gallery when we land?"

"No, I shall go to the hotel with you first. I must make an important phone call and possibly meet someone. Then I shall go to the London Gallery."

Chapter 7

> "If Paris is the city of lights, then Washington is the city of trees."
>
> - Anonymous

The Director of the London Gallery, Winston Watermark, was on a flight from Washington, D.C. to Long Island, N.Y. He had taken the day off from his busy schedule to meet with the chief executive officer of a large aerospace company who wanted to auction off his stamp collection. To compete with other firms, Winston often travelled to bid for large consignments.

The business executive wanted to sell a portion of his U.S. collection in order to build a collection of China which he felt would be interesting and a good investment. Expecting his company to enter the Chinese market, he wanted to learn about their culture, history and politics and knew that their stamps would be a productive part of his education. The meeting was scheduled to be held in his office where he would show Winston his inventory along with photocopies and certificates of his rarer items.

Winston's flight landed at LaGuardia Airport where he grabbed a taxi to the sprawling manufacturing plant for his 11:00 a.m. appointment. He marvelled at the size of the aircraft plant and after he was cleared and badged at the security office, the escort took him through one of the plants to the executive's office. On the second floor, the aisle was enclosed in glass so that one could see the long production line of aircraft in various stages of completion. Workers were crawling all over the structures.

Winston loved to watch people work with their hands. The noise from the riveters was deafening despite the enclosure.

After what seemed a long walk, they arrived at the executive's outer office where Winston was introduced to the secretary. Standing near her desk were a woman and a man. The man wore a picture badge indicating he was an employee, but Winston's attention was diverted to the woman. His first impression was that she was not exceptionally pretty as her face seemed rather large for her body, but he liked her profile.

"I have an appointment," announced Winston forcing his eyes away from the woman. Suddenly she moved next to him.

"Wait one minute," said the lady sharply to the secretary, "I've an appointment at eleven."

"I don't know how this happened," said the secretary quite flustered. "Just a moment; I'll go in and straighten this out."

Within a minute the executive emerged from his office and apologized.

"Hang on for a bit, Winston," he said. "I'd better take care of business before pleasure. Please come in, Ms. Serrate."

Ms. Serrate and the badged man with her quickly followed the executive into the inner office.

Thirty minutes later, their business concluded, Ms. Serrate departed the office. As she left, Winston was struck by her poise. Dressed in a charcoal gray, pin-striped suit and a light orange blouse, her chestnut hair was attractively contrasted. Seeing Winston stare at her, she flashed him a brief glance and left.

It did not take long to evaluate the collection. Winston noted some items he had not seen in years that would significantly enhance his next quarterly auction. One of the prizes was a complete set of the Columbian Exposition issue of 1893 in pristine mint condition. The inventory also turned up a surprising collection of U.S. coil stamps issued in 1908. These stamps were perforated horizontally with straight edges on the vertical sides. One of the coil pairs catalogued seventy-five thousand dollars. He had no doubt the auction price would exceed that value. Another rarely seen item was a set of complete sheets of the Jamestown Exposition Issue of 1907. The stamps were in perfect, never-hinged condition. That set of three commemorated the founding of the first English settlement in Jamestown, Virginia in 1607. It portrayed pictures of Captain John Smith and the Indian princess, Pocahontas, dressed in English attire.

Winston negotiated a fee and left a contract for the executive to review, sign and mail back. Within the hour he was in a taxi heading for the airport.

At LaGuardia Airport, waiting for the shuttle back to Washington, Winston noticed the same woman waiting for the same flight. He got a warm feeling as he stared at her. She was writing in a notebook when he came over and interrupted her.

"Hello," he said, smiling. "Did you ever find out why we both had the same appointment at the plant?"

"Oh, hello," she said, after she recognized him and closed her notebook. "No, I never asked. I had too many problems to discuss with him and his program manager."

After introducing themselves, they chatted for a while until the flight was called. They realized they were on the same flight bound for Washington, D.C. With the unreserved seating on the shuttle, he sat next to her on the plane. By the time they arrived at Washington National Airport, she had agreed, somewhat hesitantly, to meet for lunch the next day.

* * *

They met for lunch at a small bistro in Georgetown. Peggy removed her coat and avoided sitting next to Winston, taking the opposite chair instead. Winston sensed Peggy was uncomfortable, assuming her reticence was due to him being considerably older. Winston was dressed in his usual dapper fashion. He admired Peggy's business suit chosen to be appropriate for the office and yet emphasize her figure. A light orange blouse set off her brunette hair which, Winston did not fail to notice, glowed with a sheen.

The room featured a gay-nineties type of bar with lights in large globes and Tiffany lamp shades. Gold spittoons sat near the long, brass floor rail. The bartenders displayed long moustaches and garters around their upper sleeves. Tables for dining surrounding the bar. The entire room was packed with chattering people.

The noise level forced them to speak louder than normal. Winston ordered an ale, Peggy a diet coke. Conversation did not come easily at first.

"I find it interesting," said Winston, "that these places are so noisy here in Washington. In Los Angeles, the restaurants are darker but quieter."

"People here seem to like the noisier places. Perhaps it gives them a feeling of camaraderie," replied Peggy.

Winston and Peggy both ordered the French onion soup a shrimp cocktail, a dish of cole slaw and French rolls. While waiting for the lunch to be served, Winston suddenly realized he was doing all of the talking. He stopped abruptly and asked Peggy about her occupation.

Peggy told Winston about her career with the federal government. She worked for the Department of Defense as a senior contract administrator for the Navy. She said she met a lot of contractors, was well paid and liked her work as long as she was able to keep contract problems under control. Occasionally, one would get out of hand and eventually the dispute would have to be resolved by the department's legal office.

Lunch was served and the sharp aroma of the soup seemed to arouse Peggy from her reticence. She commented on the delicious cole slaw, almost like a pepper slaw without excessive mayonnaise. As they ate, Winston felt a desire to sit next to her.

They had coffee after they finished eating and Winston essayed a personal question.

"Peggy, are you, were you married?"

"No, Winston, I'm not."

The way she expressed it, Winston realized the subject was sensitive to her.

"I've been too busy working at my career. I assume you're not married, or is that a wrong assumption?"

"No. I have also been busy with my business."

"Tell me a little about your business, Winston. I am totally unfamiliar with the stamp hobby."

He told her about the London Gallery which he had founded. She appeared interested but, not being a collector, was puzzled at some of Winston's terminology. Winston went on to explain what many people collected as "topicals." There were over a hundred categories such as religion, ships, flags, architecture, mathematics, and so on. One of the most popular topicals of recent times were the stamps depicting the many Walt Disney cartoon characters. Sometimes Winston wondered if these were really stamps, yet they were in demand by collectors. Even the U.S. Post Office joined in the fun by issuing stamps with movie and music personalities on them. A big seller was the stamp with the picture of Elvis Presley.

"Is there a potential for investment in stamps?"

"Yes, there is potential, but you have to know your stamps. Some stamps do appreciate in value, especially the rare ones. As investments go it's somewhat akin to the stock market. If you pick a good growth stock and hold on to it you will do very well, but then a stock might not grow and even decline. Stamps do not often decline but any given issue may only appreciate slowly."

"Are stamps expensive?"

"On the contrary. Most of my auction lots are very reasonably priced. The rare, high priced stamps are a small percentage of the total lots. Also, there are so many facets to stamp collecting, one can spend very little by collecting used stamps from mixtures. Some people even collect postmarks."

"I'll have to study this market. I'm interested in any investment that might pay off."

"In that case," offered Winston, "I can put you in touch with an investment service and you can judge for yourself. The service will send you a monthly selection of stamps they think will appreciate in value. I remember an investment company that provided this service with such confidence that they would buy the stamps back with a ten percent profit after a three years. I am not sure that could happen in today's market but you might check it out."

While Winston spoke animatedly about his business, Peggy looked at him, eyebrows raised, expectant, as though she wanted Winston to invite her to his gallery. But the invitation was not forthcoming. Winston did not feel that she would see him again but, by the end of lunch, he felt he had nothing to lose by asking her out. She hesitated but said yes.

"How about dinner and a play at the Kennedy Center?" Winston asked.

"Good, I haven't seen a play in a long time."

"Then you have missed some fine plays. However, I must admit I prefer plays that have curtains. Most plays were staged without curtains between the acts. I think showing the scenery without a curtain and having the actors moving the stage props between the scenes, impacted negatively on my imagination. A play was supposed to be make-believe and carry the mind away with the action but moving scenery around in front of the audience introduced reality and attenuated the make-believe."

"Winston, you've got to get used to plays without curtains."

"I cannot. I remember one play vividly. There was no curtain, only various pieces of furniture arranged on the stage. A person in overalls came on the stage and swept the stage with a broom.

We assumed it was a stage hand cleaning up the set, but it was the first act of the curtainless play!

Winston paid the check and helped her into her coat. Being near her for the first time during lunch, he admired her fragrant perfume. He looked forward to being with her, closer to her. As they departed for their respective offices, Winston felt the lunch had gone very well, indeed.

*   *   *

They met again the following Sunday evening. Winston picked Peggy up at her apartment in Virginia, drove back to the Watergate complex and parked his car in the garage. A short walk later, across the street, they settled into the Kennedy Center restaurant. Peggy was wearing a black dress, a yellow blouse with puffy cuffs topped by a string of pearls. Dark hose on her long legs and black pumps completed the outfit. Winston admired her figure, visualizing her wearing only the string of pearls.

"...my contractors," Peggy was saying, "keep offering to take me to dinner but none has ever suggested this restaurant. I'm impressed!"

They both ordered roast beef and although Winston preferred the English version, the dinner was delicious. The special horseradish aroma opened the sinuses and complemented the beef. As they ate, Winston learned more about Peggy's job, a strange world of contracts and litigation. She got somewhat carried away explaining the complex procurement system used by the government.

"Why does not the government buy equipment from commercial vendors, right off the shelf?" asked Winston at one point.

"There's a trend toward that practice," replied Peggy, "but it will take a while. There is a whole bureaucracy that gets involved with specifications, stock numbers and logistics. It will take a generation to change that process."

The conversation drifted comfortably on until Winston realized they were late for the theater.

"Well, its time to go, Peggy. We are already late."

* * *

After the play, Winston took Peggy to his apartment. She appeared somewhat tense as she wandered around the apartment admiring his furnishings and the view of the river. They sat on the sofa, offered her a brandy and explained more about his business. Peggy thought, as he spoke in his mild British accent, *I like this man even though he is much older. I hope he will ask me out again though I imagine he has a lot of female friends.*

He leaned back on the sofa and put his arm around Peggy and related the tale. Peggy leaned back against his arm, sipping her brandy. But then she wondered what he was doing as his fingers touched her throat and removed the scarf. Peggy took a larger sip of brandy.

"Peggy, remember the parrot in the play?" Winston was saying.

"Oh, yes," replied Peggy, putting her scarf in her purse.

"It reminded me of a stamp story," said Winston.

"A stamp collector who was a retired ship's officer owned a parrot from South America. He collected the stamps of Great Britain and concentrated on the first issues, the so-called, 'penny blacks.' In time, the parrot picked up on it and would chirp out the words, 'penny black, penny black!' One night, the retired officer went to bed but forgot to cover the parrot's cage. On that particular night, a burglar entered the house through the back door. He snooped around shining his flashlight and came across the stamp albums. The parrot, alerted by the flash of light, began to chirp, 'penny black, penny black!' The thief dropped the album and ran toward the back door. The noise woke up the officer who went in to see why the bird was talking. He saw someone leaving the back door and feared for his collection. But his albums were intact. His parrot had saved his collection. He realized the thief must have thought the parrot was saying, 'put it back, put it back!'"

"That's fascinating! Is it a true story?"

"As far as I know, it is," said Winston.

With that, he removed his arm from Peggy's shoulders and stood up.

"Come, I shall take you home. I have an auction this week and I usually take it easy on Sunday evening, but I did want to see you."

"Okay. I've a busy week also. I enjoyed the dinner and play. Thank you."

Peggy wondered if Winston was interested in seeing her again. Winston got their coats from the closet and while he helped her into hers, he gave her a kiss on the cheek. Then he held her and gave her a warm kiss on her lips.

"Peggy, I shall call you after the auction and invite you out again."

Oh my, she thought, *he is nice. No rush to the bedroom.*

"Please do, Winston. I would like that."

"If you get a chance, come by and see the exhibit at the gallery."

"I will put it on my schedule."

Winston drove her to her apartment and, although they were both eager to retire early, they lingered in the car, not quite ready to part company.

*   *   *

On Monday morning, the week the auction was to be held, Winston hurried through his morning routine. His nights were beginning to take their toll, but in one more week he would be through with the quarterly auction for which his store was noted.

Today was to be especially exciting because Winston expected to receive the classic stamp, the centerpiece of this auction. Winston was worried. He had planned to exhibit the stamp for one day prior to the auction. There was fervent interest in the one penny orange from collectors throughout the world and Winston expected a record breaking turnout.

As he showered, Winston reviewed his agenda. Number one item was to meet Edward Postmark at the gallery as soon as he arrived from the airport. Winston had offered guards to and accompany him to the city but Edward had thought it safer to keep his flight plan to himself, and would only tell Winston that he would arrive sometime today. Winston chastised himself for not insisting the stamp be delivered much earlier.

Winston's thoughts alternated between his agenda and Peggy. He had enjoyed the evening and looked forward to seeing her again. He found her physically exciting, picturing her in his bedroom. He was glad he had not suggested it despite his constant desire since meeting her for lunch. He would soon find out if she felt the chemistry as strongly as he did. Just the recollection of the perfumed smell of her body stimulated him.

As he began to dress, Winston thought he heard a noise at the door. He went to the door, opened it and peered into the hall. A tall, hefty man Winston did not recognize was walking toward the elevators.

Winston hurriedly dressed. In British style he put on a gray suit with a vest. A conservative gray and red necktie was tied in a Windsor knot on a pin-striped white shirt. His black shoes were shined to a gloss. The lapel of his suit begged for a carnation but instead he wore in his pocket a smart red and gray handkerchief. The clothes added the right touch to the looks of a distinguished older gentlemen. His outfit complemented his pepper mustache. He finished off this ritual with an approving look in the mirror. He wondered briefly if Peggy would like his outfit and then went to the kitchen for breakfast.

While eating, he wrote down his list of must-do things for the day of the exhibit. Before he puts the stamp on the exhibit he will have experts and noted collectors who were in attendance view the stamp first-hand in his office. He got on the telephone to invite local dealers to attend the preview. It was early in the business day so he left messages on their answering machines.

The Watergate Complex where he resided was about a mile from his store. In good weather he would walk in the morning and in the evening take a cab back. But today he would take a cab; he needed to conserve his energy.

After establishing his business in Washington, Winston was wise enough to buy a condominium in the city not far from his gallery. He had hunted for the right location for about a year, concentrating on the historic downtown part of Washington. The Watergate complex was located not far from the west end of the Mall, not far from the Lincoln Memorial and Memorial Bridge which spanned the Potomac River into Virginia. He bought a condominium at the Watergate with a magnificent view of the river.

Near his condo complex was an entrance to the Rock Creek Parkway, a winding road that went all the way to Maryland through a small forest. The road followed the Rock Creek, a small rill full of large rocks. Winston was astounded when he first took a drive through the park. Here was a scenic drive through a variety of trees that ran the length of the city. In the middle of the park is the National Zoo. He marvelled that a virgin area of land had been kept out of the hands of building developers all these years. Whenever he wanted to drive north of the city he used the Parkway. From his entrance to the Parkway to the Maryland line there were only two traffic lights. The sights in the park were a balm to the eyes and a comfort to the soul. Winston had never seen anything like it.

On his days off, Winston often walked through the park. He

especially liked the park in September when the summer colors were at their deepest; every shade of green was visible. Dark green from the dogwoods which would soon turn into deep reds merged with yellow green in the maples. Deep green from the tall oak trees provided a dappled effect against the birch trees. Within a month, sometime in October and before Halloween, the dogwood leaves would change from green to a crimson which, combined with the remaining green leaves, provided the holiday colors of red and green two months too early. The maple leaves would evolve from green to cadmium yellow and vermillion. The oak leaves would turn from their green to a mottled green and yellow then into ocher and yellow. The canopy of colors lured Winston into the woods to enjoy nature. Being an expert on colors of stamps he liked to compare their colors with nature's colors.

Winston had never married. The reason was very simple; he was totally absorbed in his work, even before he established his gallery. The world of stamps fascinated him, day and night. It was not that he worked that hard; it was just that all of his time was spent at the Gallery or on business trips. He had women friends along the way but each soon tired of his extended hours and long periods between dates.

* * *

Winston left his hotel to take a taxi to the gallery. As he left the building he noticed someone waiting at the door. Winston's mind flashed back to the hallway when he was dressing. *He looks like the man I saw in the hall. Is he following me?* The cool fall air was gentle on his face and the bright sunshine warmed body. There was a cool, sweet smell to the air blowing through the park that was unique to this time of the year, reminding him of his days long ago in England. *I can't just stand here and smell the flowers. I must get to the store and meet Postmark and the stamp. Will he be there?*

The man was still there apparently watching him as a taxi pulled up.

"London Gallery," he said to the driver.

When Winston arrived at the London Gallery, people were already waiting. The taxi drove through an alley behind the store so that he could enter through the back door. At ten o'clock he opened the front door to let in the patrons.

Whenever Winston opened his gallery he stood back and smiled with entrepreneurial satisfaction. He walked around to check with his staff and chat with some of his regular customers. Most of the conversation centered around the upcoming auction of the famous stamp and Winston became restless each time he was reminded the stamp was not yet here. Not knowing which flight Edward Postmark was on, he could not even check the airline schedules to see if the plane had arrived. He could only wait.

As Winston wandered he realized he was fortunate to have established the London Gallery on K Street in Washington, D.C. He had had an opportunity to locate on Nassau Street in New York City's lower Manhattan in the financial district near Wall Street. This locale once flourished with legendary stamp dealers who thrived there in the years preceding World War II. Nassau Street was to stamp dealers what Tin Pan Alley was to songwriters and music publishers. Their enthusiasm created a market for the hobby. It was a time when many stamp publications, clubs and auctions began to flourish. Following the war, the dealers slowly dispersed. The historical aura of Nassau Street had appealed to Winston; who in philately had not heard of Nassau Street? But he did not like the fact that most stamp dealers had moved elsewhere so he decided not to set up business there. Instead, he considered a novel approach; he visited Washington, D.C. Although the city did not have a large number of dealers, he perceived Washington as the center of the western world. It took only one visit to the "city of trees" to make his decision. He established the London Gallery on K Street, the center of financial and legal power. It was the largest stamp store in the area and held major international auctions four times a year.

On the first floor of the store were several rooms with cases designed to display stamps from all over the world. On the second floor, where the auctions were held, there were three rooms. One room was a library containing the latest publications and reference material. The library drew a considerable crowd because of its scope of reference books. A second room was utilized for the quarterly auction and contained a display area for the most valuable stamps to be auctioned. The third room was Winston's office which was also used for private, direct sales.

Winston's office was uniquely designed around the vault. In his business, a large vault was essential to house a myriad of stockbooks containing stamps as well as the items assembled for each auction sale. Winston had the office cleverly decorated to conceal the walk-in vault. Two large Japanese print screens diverted one's attention from the steel door. Two majestic Chinese vases were placed in front of these screens. Several lush plants in oriental urns blocked the direct view and yet left adequate space for the daily transfer of the merchandise. A large rosewood table was used for meetings and private sales. Japanese dolls - geishas, warlords - in fantastic costumes were placed around the office. Winston had fashioned his opulent office to appear as if a sea captain sailing the seven seas had delivered each object. The decor befitted his business of selling stamps from all over the world.

While Winston conceived the London Gallery in terms of a business, its patrons viewed it as a magical land of opportunity, a unique place where good things happened. It transcended Winston's original objectives. Collectors spoke of it in awe as the temple of their hobby; a place to seek and find satisfaction.

Perhaps the two classic ionic columns framing the entrance gave the visitor the impression of entering a temple of antiquity. Once inside, one could discover a rare stamp or envelope buried in its troves. The driving, insatiable desire of collectors to find rare items was satisfied by participating in the auctions. The chance of a "find" existed in every sale; an overlooked stamp or stamped envelope. As an example, a philatelist recently discovered letters written by Mark Twain.

Fortunately, the stamp hobby did not depend only on people who could afford rare, costly stamps. Most stamps were not expensive, permitting people of all incomes to participate; from children who spent pennies to the super rich who could afford the rarest of stamps.

He had learned that stamps were a unique collectible. They were highly transportable, unlike antiques, large paintings or even coins. In times of stress, such as World War II, people were able to leave Europe by converting their cash and belongings into classic stamps which they could easily hide during travel. Once they arrived in the U.S., for example, they would quickly convert the stamps into cash. There was a steady stream of people in the gallery to sell stamps bought in their homelands.

Valuable stamps tended to appreciate over time so when the stamp was sold under distressed conditions it brought a good price to immigrants who lived on the money until they found work. Many obtained sufficient funds to start a small business and prospered after the War. But one had to be knowledgable about stamps in order to know which stamps were worth buying and keeping. As with many collectibles one had to know where to go to certify authenticity, especially if large sums of money were involved.

Many who visited the gallery did their own business within its confines. They carried philatelic items in their brief cases and bought and sold directly to each other. Others crowded the gallery because they were lonesome. Instead of staying home alone, they could meet peers and stir up conversation. The gossip about well-known collectors and new discoveries assuaged the lonely thoughts.

Of course, where there were such huge sum of money involved, there was chicanery. Collectors must always be on the lookout for forgeries and modified stamps. As an example, a counterfeiter might take a perforated stamp and trim the off the perforations to create an "imperforate" stamp worth far more than the original. Fortunately, most rare stamps can be authenticated by an expert for a small fee.

With stamps, as with paintings, the provenance was very important. To the extent possible, a provenance provided proof of ownership, origin and authenticity. In the case of the one penny orange, the history was credible with witnesses supporting the discovery and with a certificate of genuineness from a well-known expert. The offering of stolen or counterfeit merchandise was carefully watched in public sales.

Bidding for quality material was always fierce. Quality was the most important factor in the price of the stamps. A well-centered, unhinged, mint (unused), undamaged stamp brought the best price. Winston recalled one auction in which a superb copy of a U.S. stamp, Scott catalog number 434 sold for seventeen times the catalog price. Older stamps were not necessarily the most valuable. Many stamps over a hundred years old hardly appreciated in value compared to inflation.

Winston had had a few experiences with forgeries, a major problem in this business and, for that matter, in any business selling collectibles. The temptations were great and so were the opportunities. He remembered one forgery in particular, an attempted sale of a stamp that was expertised to be genuine but turned out to be a counterfeit. The stamp was issued by Dominica, a former British colony located in the West Indies. The fake was discovered before the auction by a collector who specialized in British Colonies. Winston had to withdraw the stamp from the auction. The so-called expert was taken to task but he would not agree that the stamp was counterfeit. In fact, for a short period, the incident became a small scandal in the trade media. Winston never used the expert again but it made him more diligent in determining the provenance of rare stamps.

On the day before an auction, Winston would exhibit famous stamps. A special stand was set up holding two thick panes of glass at about a 45-degree angle. Centered in between the two panes would be the showpiece. A sheet of paper on the bottom of the top pane would describe its history and provenance. A black felt cloth would be placed over the glass so that he could unveil the display at the appropriate time. Two strong spotlights would shine on the face of the glass. The exhibit would be available only one day with two armed guards posted to protect it. After closing the exhibit, the stamp would be returned to the safe until the successful bidder took possession.

Winston went downstairs to the front entrance. With the red carpet on the stairs and on the second floor, a newcomer might expect to see gaming tables, but in the world of high stakes philately, gambling was not the game. Instead, careful, methodical research was needed.

Winston stood outside the entrance in hopes of seeing Edward Postmark arrive. He waited at the door for a short time and, as he reentered the building, he noticed the same man he had seen at the Watergate standing inside the door. He was obviously waiting for someone. Winston had a sudden, sinking feeling, that he was also waiting for Postmark. He returned to his office to complete preparations for the exhibit on Tuesday and the auction on Wednesday. He was uneasy, worried that Postmark might be delayed again or worse, that someone might steal the stamp from him. Winston felt the weight of concern, in stark contrast to the cheerful patrons within the walls of his gallery.

Chapter 8

> *"There's no art*
> *To find the mind's construction in the face;*
> *He was a gentleman on whom I built*
> *An absolute trust."*
>
> - *"Macbeth" by William Shakespeare*

    Virginia Couvert got out of her taxi in front of the London Gallery. She stopped for a moment to admire the full size, light bronze sculptures of a lion, one on each side of the imposing columns. The lions resembled the one depicted on the 1924 British Empire Exhibition stamps. The entrance was designed to entice visitors inside to see the exhibits from far off places. As Virginia entered the London Gallery, she noticed a stranger staring at her as though surprised to see a female collector. She was used to this having often noted the customers at the gallery were predominantly male. She glared at the man briefly, turned and went toward the stairs.
    She had never seen the gallery so crowded. People were everywhere; coming and going, up and down the stairs. It reminded her of a convention; in this case, collectors, who had not seen each other since the last auction or stamp show, chatting about the latest philatelic gossip. Here and there, brief cases were opened and stamps or albums were removed to show off an unusual item. It was a jolly atmosphere, induced by the ambiance of the layout.

Virginia walked up the plush carpet stairs to view the displays of stamps included in the auction. The aroma of freshly brewed coffee reminded her of the library room where refreshments were being served. At the top of the landing, she saw an easel holding a large poster which read:

ANNOUNCEMENT

NEW LOT ADDED TO THIS AUCTION

A MAURITIUS ISSUE NO. 1, THE ONE PENNY ORANGE, WAS RECENTLY DISCOVERED AND WILL BE ADDED TO THIS AUCTION. THIS RARE STAMP WILL BE DISPLAYED TUESDAY, 4 TO 8 P.M. AND AUCTIONED OFF ON WEDNESDAY.

She suddenly felt excited because Mauritius was one of the countries she collected. At the thought of being able to see that stamp, she felt a surge of warmth. *If only I could bid on the one penny orange. I can just see it in my album. I would become the most famous female collector!*

Suddenly, she realized someone was staring at her. It was the same man she had seen earlier. She ignored him and moved off to find a catalog describing the contents of the upcoming auction. In it she saw some hard-to-find issues even thought they were inexpensive. She decided she would leave reserve bids on them. Reserve bids were honored by the auctioneer even though you were not present; however, someone who was present could then outbid you. Since she could not spend the whole day there, leaving a reserve bid at least gave her a chance to win some.

As Virginia studied the catalog, the man who had stared at her was back. This time he spoke.

"I noticed you were studying the catalog," said Roger Essay.

"Are you planning to bid?"

"Yes, I am," said Virginia, coolly and a bit uncertain. "Some of my countries are listed."

"It's unusual to see a woman interested in stamps," said Roger, too quickly, "so I'm afraid I was staring at you."

Oh, my! Another macho male. Should I give him what for or just walk away? He's too nice looking to ignore so I will give him what for! Unconsciously, she moved her hand to arrange her hair.

"Yes, you were staring at me," she exclaimed calmly, tossing her hair back, and then blurted out, "Are you afraid women are going to take over another male-dominated bastion?"

"Well," said Roger, a little embarrassed, "I didn't mean to be rude."

"You know," retorted Virginia, now ready for full battle, "I bet you collect male chauvinists on stamps!"

I must not smile but that was a good remark! Virginia turned away. Roger stood there as he watched her leave, seemingly enthralled by a young female collector.

Virginia went downstairs to one of the counters and purchased sets that she needed for her Mauritius collection. She bought the King George VI set commemorating the centennial of the first Mauritius postage stamp: a "stamp-on-stamp" set showing the one penny orange. She examined a mint copy of the 1924 50-rupee Coat of Arms issue colored lilac and green, a copy of which was included in the auction. She would put in a reserve bid.

Virginia moved over to another counter to look at stamps of India. She now understood the gallery was so crowded because of the one penny orange to be auction off on Wednesday. She gazed idly around her looking for the nice-looking stranger who had spoken to her.

*   *   *

The cab Stanley Roulette rode in was on its way to the gallery. He expected to intercept the owner of the one penny orange before Setenant showed up to try to make a deal. Now that he was off the aircraft, his mind sought with renewed vigor a strategy to acquire the stamp. He was too engrossed to enjoy the lovely country landscape of trees and shrubs decked out in full autumn colors. Nor did he notice the racing Potomac River as the taxi sped over Key bridge and turned onto the Whitehurst Freeway into the District of Columbia.

Ignoring the scenes around him, he had formulated a plan. He could see only one possibility and that was to take the stamp away from the owner and then negotiate a price. He regretted he had not accomplished that when he was in London, but he had assumed incorrectly that the owner, as a noncollector, would have been happy to sell it for cash. He had figured wrong but he did not dwell on it. He would try again with Joe Coil's help. If he could get his hands on the stamp, Stanley thought, perhaps wishfully, the owner would accept his original offer.

Satisfied that he had a solution he now wondered if the stamp was already in the vault of the gallery. If so, how could he obtain it before the auction? Now he had to mull over that contingency and come up with a another strategy if that turned out to be so. He would, he thought, go over his plan with Joe and then devise another plan if the director had the stamp.

The taxi was now on K Street and would soon be at the gallery. Stanley sighed with relief as the taxi slowed down. The director of the London Gallery, Winston Watermark, knew him from previous sales and would tell him if he had the stamp. With that piece of information, he would move into Plan A or Plan B.

The cab pulled up and Stanley greeted Joe Coil at the door. While Joe chatted about their last project together, Stanley felt reassured that Joe was the right person to help him. Joe was dressed in a black silk suit - a sign that he was prospering - with a dark blue shirt and navy blue tie. Joe's height of over six feet, his solid body and his grim face gave the impression of sinister strength. With his coat buttoned, the revolver Stanley knew he carried was not obvious.

Stanley pulled Joe away from the streaming crowd and described his Plan A. He would discuss the other plan after he saw Winston and learned the location of the stamp.

"Joe," said Stanley, "I want you to watch out for the arrival of the stamp's owner, Edward Postmark. He is a retired British soldier; tall, trim, a gray mustache and a close-cut haircut. Let him come in but do not let him go out until I see him. I will be in the director's office; I'll let you know if he had already arrived."

"Okay," replied Joe. "I'll stay near the door and wait."

As Joe waited for Edward to arrive, he watched the activities on the first floor. The crowd swarmed around Joe as he shifted around the entrance to keep his gaze on the street. Stanley marched up the stairs into the director's office.

"Good morning," announced Stanley, barging in. "You remember me, Stanley Roulette of London."

"Of course," replied Winston. "I assumed you would be here to enter the bidding."

"I would prefer to acquire the stamp without the auction. Has the owner arrived yet with the stamp?"

"No, he has not, but he is due here any minute."

"Jolly good! I wish to wait and try to negotiate a sale with him."

"That will be difficult; I have a contract with him for the sale through the auction."

"If I can make a deal with him, I will pay you more than the commission you would receive from the auction."

"No." replied Winston, staring intently at Stanley. "I do not believe he would sell it to you."

There was no point arguing the matter, thought Stanley, so he let it drop. Winston excused himself and left the office. Stanley could guess that he went to the entrance to intercept Postmark but Stanley was confident Joe Coil would not let that happen. Stanley stayed in the office, determined to wait for Postmark. He picked up the phone to check in with Olivia at the hotel.

"Hello, Olivia. I just wanted to make sure you checked in alright. I am in the director's office."

"No problem checking in and we have a nice suite. Has the stamp arrived yet?"

"No, we're in luck. It is not yet in the vault."

Stanley could not sit still; he kept looking at the door for Coil and Postmark.

"I called some friends. Stanley, you remember Cynthia? She's going to have a beautiful wedding after so many years!

"Yes, I do remember her but I must get off the phone. I will see you later."

Stanley paused and wondered; *that's strange. Olivia sounded odd, as though she wished to go to the wedding. I shall tell the hotel to deliver some flowers to Olivia.*

* * *

Back in his office, Winston ignored Stanley and made a phone call to find out if the flights from London had arrived. He was not sure which flight Postmark was on but, at least, all flights were on schedule.

But Winston was still uneasy. Where was Postmark? The one penny orange would hold the limelight of his auction. If Roulette should intercept the stamp it would ruin his auction even though he would receive, as Roulette had suggested, the full commission. He needed a word with Postmark before he got to his office but Stanley was camped there and there was no way to get him out of there. Winston was now convinced the surly man standing at the entrance was also waiting for Postmark and was somehow connected with Roulette.

He stared once more at his door, patted his brow with his

handkerchief and sat down silently in front of Roulette.

* * *

Because of the constantly moving people, Joe Coil, still waiting inside the entrance, did not notice the attack on Postmark when he got out of the taxi. Edward's assailant had run off with his attache case, knocking Edward against the column in front of the gallery. As he caught his breath, he knew he was not injured nor was he surprised at another attempt to steal his stamp. For an awful moment he thought he had lost the rare stamp but remembered, as he quickly reached inside his coat, he had removed the packet from the attache case before deplaining. He pulled the packet from his coat pocket and checked for the one penny orange. It was there.

He paid the driver and entered the gallery. At the door there was someone he did not recognize staring at him. Joe Coil said nothing but watched Postmark closely to make sure he went up to the director's office. Roulette had told him about his frustrating encounter with Postmark in London, so Joe thought it best not to forewarn him. Edward moved in with the crowd, pleasantly surprised at the layout.

He was amazed at the large number of customers who seemed to be everywhere. As a non-collector, the world of stamp collecting grew more interesting the more he learned about it. He had no idea so many people enjoyed the hobby. Yet he was still skeptical that his stamp could be worth as much money as indicated by the catalog. Well, he thought, he would soon have the stamp in the Winston's hands and he would know its value by Wednesday afternoon. He approached the director's office and stopped suddenly.

Through the glass window he saw Stanley Roulette speaking heatedly to a man he assumed was the director. Edward backed up a step, not wanting to be seen. *Why was Roulette here if not to intercept the delivery? He knows me and would correctly assume I have the stamp with me. I had better slip out and come back later.* He walked quickly to the head of the stairs and hurried toward the entrance. Joe Coil immediately stepped in front of him and blocked the door.

"Mr. Postmark, did you see Mr. Roulette?" asked Joe. "He doesn't want you to leave until he's spoken to you."

Now it was clear to Edward that Roulette intended to take the stamp from him and this man would help him do so.

"I saw him," said Edward, stretching the point, "and now I must go."

"Hold on a minute," said Joe, "until he comes down."

"Never mind, I will go get him," replied Edward, heading for the stairs.

Edward, ever the experienced army officer, knew instinctively that this was a situation he needed to avoid. If he were spotted, Roulette would search him outright and remove the stamp. *I noticed the man at the door carried a gun. I cannot trust Roulette; I suspect he was the one who hired the twins to grab the stamp in London and now someone tried again here.* Caught between Roulette in the director's office and Roulette's companion guarding the door, Edward moved quickly away from both areas.

A number of customers were at the displays but who could he trust to help him? He moved next to a neatly dressed man wearing a dark blue suit and who appeared to be studying the lots. Edward hoped he could blend into the crowd but he could see the sinister man coming up the stairs looking for him. Edward looked around for another exit and then spotted Joe approaching through the crowd. There was now no time to ascertain that the man next to him had an honest face. Quickly, Edward handed the man in the blue suit the packet of stamps.

"Hold this for me while I get a catalog," said Edward. The man did not have time to react and automatically held the packet, waiting for the stranger to return. Edward moved toward the stairs but then Joe Coil intercepted him. He opened his jacket to show his gun.

"You can't leave, Mr. Postmark." said Joe. "Move to the office. My client is anxious to speak to you."

He had no choice but to walk with Joe Coil to the office hoping the man he gave the packet to would wait for him. Still at the counter, the man kept looking around and then looked at his watch.

Edward, prodded by Joe Coil, entered the director's office.

"I am Edward Postmark. I met Mr Roulette so you must be Mr. Watermark."

Winston Watermark, the director of the gallery joyfully stood up and shook his hand.

"Delighted to meet you, Mr. Postmark," said Winston. "I trust you have the stamp with you?"

"Ah, hello again, Mr. Postmark," interrupted Stanley. "I must talk to you again before you dispose of the stamp."

Edward paled but remained stalwart.

"Now," said Stanley, taking over the meeting, "let me see the stamp so we can make a deal here and now. Once the stamp is in my possession I am sure you will accept my last offer. You know what they say: 'Possession is nine-tenths of the law.' I have always loved that expression."

"Sorry, I do not have the stamp with me," said Edward.

Hearing that, Winston crumpled in his chair and turned ashen.

"Well," replied Stanley, moving on, "I tend to believe you but let us make a search to be sure."

"Wait!" shouted Winston, raising out of his chair. "You cannot do this on my premises! This is highway robbery! I will have my guards stop this!"

Winston rushed from the office to call his guards as Joe Coil took over. Edward emptied his pockets as Joe made a rapid search and found nothing.

"The transfer papers are here," said Joe, "but no stamp."

"Alright." exclaimed Stanley, trying to remain calm with his face red and his fists clenched. "We will have to keep you away from the gallery. When you realize the mission has failed you will be more willing to sell it to me."

Edward, seemingly indifferent, put his things back in his pockets. *I'm not afraid of Coil. I've hunted tigers in India but he has a gun and I do not!* Winston returned with two guards but it was too late.

"I am shocked! In all of my years in this business I have never seen strong-arm tactics used to obtain a stamp."

"P'r'aps your auction will be delayed," said Stanley, addressing Winston. "We shall leave with Mr. Postmark and go to his hotel."

Edward stood calmly, almost at attention.

"I may as well leave these papers with you," said Edward to Winston. "They are of no use without the stamp. Also, I will leave you my hotel phone number."

As Stanley and Joe prepared to leave, Edward wrote on the back of one of the Director's business cards and handed it to him. The three left together while Winston numbly stared at the card. Under the hotel phone number was written:

"1st floor man in blue suit loud tie"

Winston, dabbing his face with his handkerchief, rushed downstairs and searched through the crowd for a blue suit and loud tie. Winston recognized the wearer standing at a counter.

"Hello, Mr. Essay. May I have a word with you?"

"Yes, of course." said Roger, following him to the office.

"Did you happen to speak to a Mr. Postmark?"

"No, the name is not familiar," replied Roger.

"Has anyone spoken to you recently?" persisted Winston.

"Yes, a man asked me to hold some stamps for him and left," responded Roger. "Perhaps he was Mr. Postmark. He said he wanted to get a catalog but he never returned."

"May I see the stamps?" requested Winston.

"Well," said Roger, hesitating, "I'd rather return them to that person."

"I understand, " said Winston. "I will contact Mr. Postmark and we will call on you to retrieve the stamps he gave you. Are you returning to your office?"

"Yes," said Roger, "I must get back. Here's my card."

As Roger descended the stairs, Winston tried to reach Edward at his hotel. Edward did not answer the phone. Winston called the hotel back and left an urgent message for Edward to call him and then sat down to wait. Obviously distraught, Winston expressed his frustration out loud.

"Would Edward hand the stamp to a total stranger? Perhaps he only gave Essay a clue as to where the stamp was." Winston got up and paced his office, waiting for Edward's call.

* * *

Andre Setenant arrived at the Gallery after checking in at the hotel and getting Marie settled. This was his first visit to the London Gallery so he needed to become acclimated as he looked for Stanley. Unlike Stanley Roulette, Andre had assumed the one penny orange was in the gallery's vault. Later, after he determined what Stanley was doing, he would talk to the director.

Moving around the various display counters he was amazed at what people collected. Topicals continued to be the rage. At one counter, the stamps were set up in stockbooks under all of the topical subjects; dogs, cats, religion, ships, trains, birds, fish, butterflies and on and on. Andre noted many Walt Disney issues, one of the most popular topicals of all time. He remembered when collecting airmail stamps was the most popular topical. Another counters was devoted to albums and accessories where people were actively buying.

Another counter was set up with stamps organized by country. The ever-changing geography of the world resulted in a constant flow of new issues. Every time a new country was formed it issued sets of stamps. The latest demand was for new issues of countries that once were part of the U.S.S.R. Some countries subsisted on revenue from selling stamps to collectors. One example was the country of San Marino, a small, independent state in the northern part of Italy.

Andre was not only impressed with the gallery's ambience but with the scope and quality of the material to be auctioned. He decided to sit at one of the counters to look at the stockbooks. He sat next to Virginia Couvert who was examining a book of stamps from some of the former states of India: Gwalior, Cochin and others.

"I see you are interested in India," ventured Andre. "I have one of the rarest stamps from there, the 4 pie gray green stamp from Cochin with the picture of Ravi Varma on it."

"Yes," replied Virginia, "I know about that stamp. It's a vacant space in my album because it's so hard to find."

"It is rare," said Andre, "and I paid more than the catalog value for it."

Virginia got up to leave and Andre automatically and politely rose with her.

"I suppose you're also surprised to see a female collector," blurted out Virginia.

"Of course not," replied Andre, a bit confused by her statement. "As a matter of fact, my wife is a dedicated collector."

"Well, goodbye," said Virginia, sheepishly as she got up from her seat and walked toward the stairs to go back up to the second floor exhibits.

Andre admired her as she left. He was glad he did not have the urge to chase women. He continued examining some issues and then decided to purchase them.

As he went upstairs, he turned his thoughts again to the Mauritius stamp and went over to where the exhibit was to be set up. He tried to picture the exhibit with the one penny orange in it. It certainly would be a dramatic display.

Andre went over to the library room as an unfamiliar figure approached him.

"Mr. Setenant. I am Dr. Seebeck of the Philatelic Society of England."

"Ah, yes. I am pleased to meet you." replied Andre, shaking hands. "I have heard of your position."

"I recognized you as a well known collector of errors so I assume you are here to bid at this auction. I had the privilege of examining the one penny orange and certifying it."

"Yes, I am impressed. How much do you think the one penny orange will sell for."

"Well, I have no doubt it will sell for at least the catalog value. When you see the stamp tomorrow, what excellent condition it is in, you will understand. The stamp was protected in an envelope in a file cabinet all those years and remained in its original, almost untouched state, what I call pristine condition. It looks like the owner had just purchased it from the post office."

"Does the stamp have any flaws?"

"None that I could observe. That issue came out without perforations and yet the margins around the stamp are clear, resulting in a well-centered picture of Queen Victoria; very unusual for those early issues. The color is a very bright orange and the unwatermarked paper is unsoiled and not marred in any way."

Andre sat still, nervously fingering the auction catalog as Dr. Seebeck spoke.

"Also, Mr. Setenant, the stamp is a classic error. The engraver etched 'POST OFFICE' instead of 'POST PAID' on the plate which is why the issue was quickly replaced with new stamps.

"Dr. Seebeck, have you seen any forgeries of the stamp?"

"I have not seen any. The stamp is so rare that any counterfeits would be quickly exposed. I can see you are intensely interested!"

"Thank you for the information, Dr. Seebeck. Perhaps I will see you at the auction?"

"Yes. Good day to you."

* * *

Roger left the Director's office and headed for the stairs on his way back to work. He noticed the woman he had spoken to leaving so he followed her out to the street. Virginia didn't notice that Roger was standing near her a she hailed a cab.

"Twin Towers Center," she said as she entered a yellow cab.

"I work there, too," Roger shouted from the sidewalk. "May I share the ride with you?"

She nodded, looked at him, then turned her attention to the busy streets.

"By the way," said Roger, tentatively, "my name is Roger Essay and I work for Power Engineering in the same building?"

Virginia nodded but continued to look at the traffic as the cab pulled up in front of their building.

"Allow me to pay the fare," offered Roger. "I'd have to anyway if I were alone."

"No, thanks, I'll pay my half."

"Well, goodbye," said Roger, as he opened the door and paid the driver. "Perhaps I'll see you at the auction."

"Goodbye. Perhaps you will."

Roger quickly departed and went into the building.

Virginia got out of the cab to pay the driver, noticed that he had left his copy of the catalog. He was already in the building so she took it with her thinking vaguely that she would return it to him later in his office. *Well,* she thought, *it was the stamp chauvinist! He kept looking at me as though he knew me. He was good looking. I can feel him still staring at me. Maybe he was just impressed to find a female philatelist.*

A pity, she thought, that she had to get back to work. It was a perfect autumn day. The trees in front of the many office buildings displayed their bright green and dark red colors in the sunshine. The last butterflies of the season with their yellow and black wings fluttered about the bushes.

As she headed for the elevator she thought about Roger Essay. He was definitely attractive and although he stared at her at the gallery, he wasn't obnoxious and oppressive like so many frustrating men she had met.

This was the first time she had met someone from her building who might be interesting. One question after another went through her mind. Was he married? Was he committed to another woman? What was he really like? At least, they had a hobby in common which could be a good start. Guarding against too much hope, she admitted to being a little excited and looked forward to possibly meeting him tomorrow.

Virginia reached her office and closed her door as if to shut out thoughts about men. She refused to become optimistic about her encounter at the gallery. Look what happened at her lunch meeting with the lawyer. Oh, yes! She was going to send that invoice to his secretary. She turned on her computer, called up her word processor and typed an invoice for half of the cost of lunch with the lawyer. Instead of mailing it, she faxed it over to the lawyer's office so that more people might see it!

Then she returned to work on the wicker problem which had to be straightened out before the next staff meeting. But the one penny orange kept intruding on her thoughts. She visualized the brightly colored stamp in her Mauritius album's number one slot, radiating an orange aura across the page.

Chapter 9

> *"The chase is on! The neighing and yelping, the wind and the mane, the blare of the horn and the anticipation; all after the fox!"*
>
> *- Stanley to Olivia on the pursuit of a stamp*

Stanley, Joe and Edward climbed into a cab and headed for Edward's hotel. In the cab, Stanley continued to press Edward to produce the one penny orange, his frustration mounting. Stanley sensed he was close to the stamp and did not want to waste anymore time pursuing it. What he did not know was that the stamp was in the hands of Roger Essay.

"I do not have the stamp" said Edward, with stiff upper lip. "I decided to deliver it at another time."

"Well," said Stanley, "this is indeed a problem now, is it not? Someone must deliver that stamp to the gallery. If you will not tell me where the stamp is, we will have to intercept it. Since the stamp is to be on exhibit tomorrow, you or your messenger must make a move soon."

Edward said nothing as the cab arrived at the hotel.

"Joe," Stanley said, turning to his cohort, "you take this cab back to the gallery and watch out for anyone delivering the stamp. I will get out here with Mr. Postmark and meet you later in the director's office."

Edward got out of the taxi as Stanley followed him into the busy lobby.

"Wait one minute, Edward," said Stanley. "Let's sit down. I have an offer to make to you."

"I will listen, replied Edward, testily, as they sat in the lobby, "but I must say again that I am committed to selling the stamp at auction."

Stanley realized that Postmark's military background could make negotiations difficult. This man would not be intimidated; he had to change his tactics.

"Look, Edward, you are not a collector, so you may not understand how important this find is to me," offered Stanley. "It is one of the few stamps missing in my Mauritius collection. If I acquire it, both of us will gain publicity because I intend to exhibit it.

"Yes, I understand your need, Roulette, but I have a contract with Mr. Watermark and I do not intend to abrogate it."

"Edward, if you will agree, I can take care of the contract. I will see to it that Mr. Watermark gets whatever fee he would have gotten from the auction."

"But the fee depends on the bids," persisted Edward, "and you are offering me much less than what might be bid."

"Alright," said Stanley, encouraged. "I will raise the offer I made you in London to $350,000. Then you won't have to worry about the auction price. The auction is a risk; the final bid may be higher and then again it could end up lower. This way you will have no risk."

Stanley continued his gentle persuasion but Edward was adamant and finally stood up, said goodbye and left the lobby for the elevator. Stanley's face turned a mottled red as he clenched and unclenched his fists. He went outside and found a taxi.

"The London Gallery and hurry!"

By the time Stanley reached the gallery, he was furious and even more determined to have that stamp. Joe Coil was waiting for him in the director's office. Winston Watermark had not yet returned.

"Mr. Roulette, look what I found in the office."

Joe handed Stanley the papers he had found. On top of the transfer papers lay a business card with Edward's writing which had alerted the director to the "man in blue suit." Underneath the card was a Rolodex card with a name and telephone number.

"I think," said Joe, "it's a good guess that this is the name of a customer, the man in the blue suit."

Stanley immediately grabbed the telephone on Watermark's desk and dialed the number on the card. Roger Essay answered.

"Mr. Essay," said Stanley, "I am the owner of the stamp in your possession and I wish to get it back."

"You'll have to be more specific," replied Roger. "You don't sound like the owner."

Stanley paused.

"I will be right over to see you," said Stanley, gruffly, "and I expect you to return my stamp!"

* * *

Roger was suspicious as he mulled over the brief conversation. The voice did not sound like the voice of the man who had left him the packet; it was deeper with a much stronger British accent. Also, the caller mentioned "stamp" and not "packet".

Roger did not need this interruption at work, but now he knew he had a problem. The caller was not the person who had given him the packet. Of course, he could give it to the caller and forget all about it, but he refused to be bullied. Obviously the stamps inside the packet were valuable. Roger reached into his briefcase to take a closer look at the packet and see what was so important. He opened the packet and found a number of Mauritius sets; nothing unusual until he reached the middle of the packet. There, in a plastic envelope on a black stock card was a Mauritius one penny orange!

Roger was thunderstruck! Why, he wondered, did someone

put this in the hands of a stranger? Did someone steal the one penny orange from the gallery and he was holding a stolen packet? Who was the real owner? He was expecting the director to bring the real owner but he did not know how soon they would arrive.

Roger decided not give up this prize to the strange caller. Instead, he grabbed his laptop computer and dashed over to the publications department. There, he found an optical character reader and scanned the stamp into the laptop's memory. Back at his office, he transferred the picture from his laptop to the PC on his desk. He called up the graphics mode and proceeded to enlarge the image and then darken the lines and fill in the gaps. The original engraver of the stamp had put his initials, "JB" on the bust of Queen Victoria engraved on the face of the stamp. Roger, on a whim, changed the engraver's initials to his own, "RE."

After Roger completed the picture on the screen, he colored it orange around the white lettering. He then produced a picture on his color printer and took it back to the publications department where, using a large color printer, he reduced it to roughly the size of the stamp. Back in his office, Roger realized there was still a problem: what about the gum, the adhesive on the back of the stamp? The real stamp appeared to have no gum on the back but he dared not wet it to find out. Not having a catalog handy, Roger decided to put some gum on the fake. He found several U.S. postage stamps in his desk drawer, licked the gum and put the back side of the copy on the wet gum. He slid the copy off of the wet gum and let it dry. It did not look like the original stamp and he did not like the feel of it, but with no time to experiment, he went ahead with it. At least the paper did not wrinkle. He trimmed the copy, put it in the plastic envelope on the same card, and slipped the card into his coat pocket. If the stranger who had called was a collector, Roger knew he still had a problem. He put the original Mauritius stamp into one of the remaining plastic envelopes and put the packet in his desk drawer.

Roger tried to work while waiting for the caller. He did not have to wait long as two large men quietly appeared at his office and closed the door. Roger did not recognize either of them. If they should tell him that the packet had been stolen, then Roger would have a dilemma; who stole it from whom? They both loomed over him.

"Alright, Mr Essay, let's see the stamp. I am Stanley Roulette and this is Joe Coil, my security guard."

"Pleased to meet you but neither of you own the stamp," replied Roger, "so you'll understand why I can't comply with your request."

Joe Coil faced Roger, letting him see his gun.

"Never mind, Mr. Essay. Hand over the stamp and be quick about it. I can get rough!"

Seeing the gun was a shock. Roger's mind could not absorb the possibility of a someone using a gun to further one's hobby! He tried to remain resolute but his stomach began to feel queasy.

"I don't know who you are," said Roger, "but I'm waiting for the director of the London Gallery and the owner of the stamp. Until they arrive, I can't turn it over to you."

"Joe," said Stanley, now red in the face and towering over Roger. "I am standing within an arm's reach of the classic stamp! We have to get out of there before Watermark shows up. Let's search him. I cannot wait any longer!"

"Never mind," said Roger, as he quickly handed over the forged stamp to Roulette.

Stanley quickly looked at the stamp in the plastic envelope, grinned broadly and hurried out of Roger's office with Joe right behind him. To Roger's relief, Roulette had not closely examined the stamp. His trick had bought him some time but he knew Roulette would soon recognize the forgery. Roger was shaken. He stood in front of the window, wiping his brow with his handkerchief. He went back to his desk, called the director to find out if he had left but the line was busy.

At that moment, Winston was on the telephone talking to Edward.

"I spoke to the person in the blue suit," said Winston hurriedly, "but he will only return it to you personally. Let us go immediately to his office!"

"Thank goodness, Winston, "said Edward. "I have been totally devastated, second-guessing my decision to give the stamp to a stranger..."

"I will meet you in the lobby of his building," Winston interrupted.

He quickly gave Edward the name and address, rang off and rushed out of his office to the front door.

Winston and Edward arrived in taxis at almost the same time in front of the Twin Towers Center in Rosslyn. They walked quickly to the building, talking breathlessly and trying to calm their nerves.

"The man in the blue suit was Roger Essay." said Winston. "He seemed to be honest and reasonable so we should not have a problem."

"I hope not. He may not know what is in that packet."

The elevator took them to Roger's floor and in a few moments they were in Roger's office.

"Mr. Essay," said Winston. "This is Mr. Edward Postmark, the owner of the packet of stamps given to you earlier today."

"How do you do?" said Roger and Edward, shaking hands.

"Yes, he is the person who gave me the packet," said Roger, "but I'm depending on you, Mr. Watermark, to identify him as the true owner. I've already been confronted by a Stanley Roulette, who also claimed the stamps were his."

"Yes," replied Winston, "I can verify that he is the owner. We have a contract to auction the Mauritius stamp."

Roger told them the story of what had transpired earlier in his office, emphasizing that Roulette was in possession of a forgery and would surely return for the original. Then he produced the packet of stamps containing the one penny orange and returned it to Edward. Winston and Edward visibly sagged with relief now that the stamp was in their hands. Roger also showed them the blow-up copy he had created on the computer.

"What a relief!" said Winston. "I think we cut the delivery a little too close. Another day would have ruined the auction."

"I must say," said Edward, "I did not expect this intrigue."

"May I keep this large copy?" asked Winston.

"Certainly, but you'd better leave," said Roger. "I don't know how long that forgery will fool Roulette. He could return at any minute."

Winston and Edward quickly left his office for the gallery where Winston would complete the transfer papers and deposit the stamp in his vault.

Roger returned to his chair and tried unsuccessfully to enjoy the thought that he had seen the rare stamp. He could not imagine that collectors would resort to threats to obtain a stamp. He had felt threatened when Coil exposed his gun and he expected Roulette to return after he discovers the forgery. He wondered if he should contact the police. No, he had given nothing but a forgery to Roulette; the matter was now in Watermark's hands.

Roger wasn't shaking but he needed to calm down. He went to the pantry and made a strong cup of coffee. He returned to his desk and tried to focus on sorting out the actions taken by his staff on the Project 006 problem before his meeting with the technical director.

*   *   *

Andre returned to the hotel suite. He made several calls to stamp dealers he knew in New York City, explaining the situation at the London Gallery regarding the one penny orange. They were all awaiting the outcome of the auction, and expected a record sale, which meant the final bid would exceed the catalog value. This did not please Andre. He probed the dealers for ways to circumvent the sale and explained how Stanley had tried to negotiate with the owner without success. None of the dealers offered any suggestions.

Andre made a drink, stretched out his long body across the living room sofa and pondered his dilemma. By now, he assumed the owner of the one penny orange stamp had delivered it to the London Gallery where it would remain in the vault until the exhibit tomorrow. He tried to think of some drastic solution to capture that stamp; there was little time left.

While Andre was cogitating, Marie took a shower and changed into a new outfit. She went into the living room, said hello to Andre who hardly noticed her, made herself a drink, picked up the phone and dialed a number.

"'allo," she said, softly. "I am in Washington. Andre has already been to the gallery. I think he is becoming obsessed with that rare stamp. He will be busy the next few days so I shall meet you."

Marie paused to sip her drink while listening and watching Andre.

"Have you heard from our friend?" asked Marie.

As the other party replied, Marie smiled and opened two top buttons on her blouse as if to cool off.

"Tres bien, I shall be there tomorrow!"

Andre got up to gaze out the window, apparently not listening to Marie's conversation.

* * *

In his hotel suite, Stanley was celebrating the capture of the original one penny orange. Olivia was still in the bedroom, resting from the trip.

"Ah! The chase is over," Stanley exclaimed. "I shall negotiate a price well below the auction price, and have something to show the Royal Family in the bargain!"

"I'd no idea," said Joe, "that a stamp could be worth so much."

Stanley looked tolerantly at Joe, the way a seasoned collector might react to a novice collector. Stanley picked up the telephone to reach Edward so that he could negotiate a price for the stamp but there was no answer. He then called the hotel operator and left a message for Edward to call him immediately. By now, surely Edward would know that Stanley had the stamp. Stanley placed another call.

"Andre," he bellowed, "come up to my room. I have something to show you!"

Stanley went back again and again to view the stamp. The bright light of the lamp exposed the blush of excitement on his face. He mopped his brow with his handkerchief. He had never been so elated over adding a stamp to his collection.

A knock on the door; Joe got up to let Andre in.

"I have won the chase, Andre!" crowed Stanley. "I have the one penny orange! Look for yourself and then I shall lock it up. I am about to buy it from the previous owner. The auction will have to proceed without it."

"How in the world did you get it!?" cried Andre, his eyebrows raised in genuine surprise.

"Good detective work by my associate here, Joe Coil," replied Stanley. "It's a long story and I shall enjoy telling it as we drink a few toasts. But first, allow me to introduce you to an original one penny orange! I will put the stamp away after you look at it."

Stanley showed Andre the stock card and gently positioned it on the table under a lamp.

"There it is," Stanley exulted. "The greatest philatelic find in the past decade!"

"I am both excited and disappointed at the same time," said Andre. "The realization that I am in the same room with this classic stamp is simply awesome! A once-in-a-lifetime experience."

Andre sat down at the table and looked at the stamp secured in a stock card under a transparent acetate sheet. He simply stared at it, afraid to touch it while Stanley hovered over him, beaming at the prize. Andre picked up the card and examined the face of the stamp. There was the usual profile view of Queen Victoria's head. The stamp was not perforated as most stamps were. As Andre he studied the stamp, he spoke out loud.

"I recall the paper was unwatermarked and, for an unused stamp, the color should be very bright. Also, I remember there are supposed to be initials of the engraver on the Queen's bust."

Andre prepared to touch the orange stamp in the card. Even Stanley was suddenly quiet. Joe watched the two collectors huddle, still not sure why the fuss over a stamp. All was tense and still. One could hear voices of passer-bys in the outside hall; it was so quiet, the air coming out of the heat duct was audible.

Andre bent down closer to the stamp.

"Here is a pair of tongs," said Andre. "Please remove it from the card to take a closer look."

Stanley gingerly removed the stamp from its slot on the card and held it closer to the lamp. Andre examined the stamp from all aspects.

"The color appears flat and the paper is too thin. Get your auction catalog. The description mentioned the engraver's initials on the stamp."

Stanley gave Andre the catalog and then grabbed the magnifier and frantically studied the stamp. Andre looked up the description and read it.

"The catalog says the engraver's initials, `JB' are on the bust. Look through your magnifier and see if there are any initials."

"Yes!" exclaimed Stanley. "There are initials here. Wait! The letters are 'RE'. Was there another engraver?"

"Not according to the catalog," Andre replied. "Stanley, let me call Dr. Seebeck. He is the one who expertised it and he happens to be staying in a nearby hotel."

"Good idea! I own several stamps which he certified."

Stanley began pacing back and forth, returning to look at the stamp again and again. The possibility of a forgery is unacceptable, he said to himself.

"The stamp looked so fresh in the clear plastic envelope; I should have taken it out and scrutinized it earlier."

As they waited for Dr. Seebeck to arrive, the silence gradually created an aura of apprehension. After a seemingly long time, there was a knock on the door. Joe opened it to let Dr. Seebeck in. Andre made the introductions and Dr. Seebeck sat down at the table to examine the stamp with his special magnifier. Stanley perspired from the heat of the lamp and the mounting tension. Now, all three men bent over the table to watch as the expert picked up the stamp with his tongs.

"Well, well," said Dr. Seebeck. "This won't take long. This stamp is a forgery! The paper and color are incorrect. This has gum on the back whereas the original I saw had no gum. The reproduction is very good but whoever did this put the wrong initials on the bust of Queen Victoria!"

"Was there another engraver?" asked Andre.

"No, there was only J. Bernard. This is definitely a counterfeit!"

"Bother!" shouted Stanley. "I've been duped. But by whom? Did the owner carry a fake or did Essay give us a forgery?"

Stanley was trying to control himself. He kept staring at the stamp as if he could transform it back into the original.

"Thanks for your help, Dr. Seebeck," said Andre.

"Yes, you're quite welcome. I shall see you at the auction."

Stanley sat and clenched his fists. He could not look Andre in the eye.

"I just thought of something," said Joe Coil. "The engineer's name was Roger Essay; his initials would be 'RE,' the same that are on your stamp. Maybe he faked it. Let's go back to see him before he leaves the office."

"Yes," said Stanley, jumping up from the chair, "let us go over there immediately and catch him off-guard!"

* * *

Olivia took her shower, changed and relaxed in the living room. Since Stanley would be tied up all afternoon at the gallery, she thought she would like some dinner - although it was lunchtime here - and then a visit to the art gallery. She called the room of Andre Setenant to see if his wife was there.

"'Allo," Marie answered.

"Hello, is this Ms. Setenant?" asked Olivia.

"Yes, it is." replied Marie in her smooth French accent. "Who is this?"

"This is Olivia Block. I am travelling with Stanley Roulette and we met on the flight. I wondered if you are free for dinner? Stanley is at the London Gallery."

"Delightful idea. I need to make some phone calls, but I will meet you in the lobby in thirty minutes."

They rang off. Olivia had in mind taking a cab over to Chinatown where, she had been told in London, she could find her favorite Chinese cuisine. She went down to the lobby and waited for Marie. Coming out of the elevator was the thin and stylish looking woman that Olivia recognized from the flight. Marie warmly greeted Olivia with a hug which made her suddenly feel grateful for female company.

Their taxi entered Chinatown under the massive and elaborate arch that was provided by the Peoples' Republic of China. They got out and strolled the three block area. Walking past at least twenty different restaurants, they picked one that had southern Chinese cooking. As they entered, the door brushed the tinkling wind chimes and out of the dim light a Chinese hostess materialized. She wore an ornate, colorful long gown with a slit on one side, and taking small, quick steps, showed them to a booth. The pungent smells of sharp spices hung in the air. A waiter promptly took their orders for martinis and General Tso's spicy chicken dish.

"I know you are aware of the auction," said Olivia, "of the classic Mauritius stamp. I wish I could help Stanley acquire it. The one penny orange is Stanley's fox, the object of the hunt."

"Yes. Andre is also after that stamp and I hope that he can successfully bid for it. I have tried to help him with financing a bid. Honestly, Andre would trek through the jungle to capture a rare stamp!"

"You and Andre seem very compatible. Do you share the hobby with him?"

"Yes, but we collect different items. We are close but I am naughty at times. Are you and Stanley close?"

"Yes, quite, but I must say, I would like to be closer."

"Marriage?" asked Marie.

"Yes, but I have to convince him. Stanley is happy with the status quo."

"Ah, ma cher, but it may not last for the female. Men look to younger women as they grow older; women must look for security! You must do something!"

"I am thinking about it, which is a beginning."

Waiting for their food, they chatted about their families.

Olivia felt Marie could be a good friend. She would visit her in Paris sometime. She liked Marie's candidness; Olivia tended to be less outspoken.

They were both silent as the food was served. As they ate, Olivia thought about Marie's nonchalant attitude toward her own marriage. Perhaps Olivia's attitude about Stanley was too cavalier. Marie's comment about younger women had stung a bit and hardened her resolve to marry Stanley.

"I must admit, Marie, you have made me worry a bit more about my future with Stanley. You are right: he is a virile male and could be tempted by a younger female. Usually he is absorbed in his business or hobby, leaving time for me. It has worked well for me but now I fear he could change."

"Does Stanley have, as you say, a wandering eye?"

"No, not that I noticed but he meets many women in his business; he could easily be swayed. I am beginning to worry; the odds are against me!"

Following the meal, Olivia convinced Marie to go with her to the Corcoran Art Gallery where they had no trouble finding John Singer Sargent's "The Oyster Gatherers," one of her favorite paintings. She and Marie sat in front of it and enjoyed its serene view. Olivia could almost smell the salty sea air and feel the cool morning sand washed over by the receding tide. Her feet actually tingled at the imagined feeling of the sand between her toes! What a joy!

"I am so glad you came with me, Marie. It's double the pleasure when you share it."

"This is a beautiful edifice, Olivia. It is not the Louvre but it is a magnificent housing for the art."

As they walked across the marble floors from one salon to another, some of the paintings displaying passion between a man and a woman reminded Olivia of her designs on Stanley. What had started out on this trip as a vague concern about her future with Stanley was now a nagging notion. Marie's comments over lunch further hardened her notion into a worry. A sense of urgency added a further disturbing dimension. She had to think it through; find a way to marry Stanley upon their return to England.

They went outside to find a taxi.

"I am glad you called, Olivia. I enjoyed the afternoon but I am not going straight back to the hotel. I have to meet someone to plan some mischief. See you at the gallery tomorrow."

She gave Olivia a hug and got into a taxi.

"Yes, tomorrow," Olivia replied. She waited for another taxi as she wondered what mischief Marie was referring to. Marie had mentioned a friend at lunch or was it connected to Andre's pursuit of the stamp?

* * *

Roger was still unsettled, wondering if he should call the police. But what could he tell them; Roulette stole a forgery? And he couldn't prove that he was held at gunpoint. He forced himself to face the problem of Project 006. He invited the technical director, Dr. Arthur Newton, to his office.

Dr. Newton listened to Roger's explanation of the problem and made some notes.

"Roger, did the symptoms of the Project 006 problem change?"

"No, Arthur. When the plant was producing 100% power, the turbine bearing temperature instrument reading was correct. But when the plant was running at 95% or less power, the reading dropped to near zero. It's as though the meter was turned off."

"What tests did you run at the site?"

"We checked the power on the system and it checked out."

"What about the software."

"That was also checked. The software code was completely tested in a static mode."

Dr. Newton went to the blackboard; he liked to talk from the blackboard as if he were teaching a class. First, he wrote on the board his version of the problem to make sure both he and Roger agreed on what the problem was. The technical director explained that, upon analysis, sometimes a problem presented often was not the real problem. Sometimes an engineer's preconceived notions would deflect him from understanding the true issue. As a result, he liked to play back a problem definition to make sure both parties had it right.

Having agreed on the statement of the problem, the technical director wrote down all possible solutions, however far-fetched they might appear. After some discussion they narrowed the list.

"Roger, It looks to me like we have four possible solutions. One, retest the code when the power changes from 100% to 95%; two, check all of the interconnecting cables; three, switch indicators; and four, measure the strength of the signal output."

After the technical director left, Roger got right on the telephone to Pamela at the power plant site.

"Hi, Pamela, this is Roger. I need some more information. How are the tests coming?"

"So far, Roger, we are making progress through the test plan except, of course, the turbine bearing temperature mode. That horse's ass foreman is talking delaying the schedule."

Just what I don't need, thought Roger.

"We are still looking for a solution. By the way, did you ever replace the instrument with a new one?"

"Yes. I did that when the malfunction first appeared. It made no difference."

"Okay, Pamela, here's what I need. Recheck the cables in the instrument loop and get me the value of the instrument signal at the output of the computer."

"Okay. I'll have it for you late today."

He sorted out the notes on his computer in anticipation of a meeting with his engineers. Roger was absorbed in his notes when Stanley and his entourage barged into his office.

"Where is the stamp?" bellowed Stanley, barging through the door. "You kept the original and passed off this fake!"

He threw the card with the counterfeit into Roger's open brief case on the desk.

"Now, give me the stamp or else!" yelled Stanley, face-to-face with Roger.

"I can't," Roger yelled back. "It's back with the owner. It

wasn't mine to begin with."

"I don't believe you," yelled Stanley. "Joe, let's search him and the office!"

"I'm calling Security" said Roger, picking up the telephone.

"Wait," interjected Andre. "Stanley, he may be telling the truth. Call the gallery director who can confirm or deny that he has the stamp. Watermark has no reason to mislead you."

Andre quickly got the director on the line. Stanley grabbed the phone.

"Watermark," bellowed Stanley, "this is Stanley Roulette. I have been duped out of the one penny orange. Where is it? Does the owner have it?"

"Mr. Roulette, I am pleased to tell you that the one penny orange is safely stored in my vault. The transfer was completed and the auction will continue on schedule."

"I have been swindled!" screamed Stanley into the phone while glaring at Roger. "Is the owner there?"

"No."

Stanley slowly hung up the telephone.

"I thought I had it and now I do not," said Stanley, lowering his voice, "Let us go back to the hotel; I must find another way to get that stamp back."

"Stanley," said Andre, quietly. "you never really had it." " I know, but it felt for awhile like I did."

They left Roger half-collapsed in his chair, wondering again why the fates chose him to hold the packet that contained the rare stamp. He was amazed at the vehemence of Roulette's behavior in his desire to acquire that stamp but perhaps the worst was over. He still planned to return tomorrow to see the famous stamp on exhibition. Roger got up, paced his office and tried to calm down so that he could continue with his work.

* * *

Virginia Couvert took a break from her computer, picked up her cup of coffee and went to the elevators. She got off at the 20th floor and located Roger's office. Seeing he was working alone, she knocked and entered his office.

"Hello." said Virginia, quietly. "You left this catalog in the cab. I thought you might want it back."

Surprised, Roger looked up at Virginia. She looked even prettier than before.

"Oh, yes, thank you. I do need it. I may want to bid on some items. Please have a seat."

"By the way, I'm Virginia Couvert and I work for Dockside International. Have I interrupted your work?"

"No, no, not at all. I just had a strange experience which involved the Mauritius classic to be auctioned off tomorrow."

Roger proceeded to tell her the highlights of his encounters at the London Gallery and at his office. Facing Roger across his desk, Virginia listened intently to his story, with eyebrows raised.

"They left before you came, so that's why I am uptight..."

As Roger continued talking, Virginia couldn't help wondering if he was exaggerating. After all, she hardly knew him. Roger stood up and went to his door as if he expected to see Roulette again. He returned to his desk.

"... and I couldn't believe those two were so threatening. I can still see Coil's sinister face and his gun. You know, the director of the gallery told me that Coil often worked with Roulette. I wonder if Roulette always used Coil to put together his collection?"

"Maybe he needed protection carrying valuable stamps."

"The director told me that the owner was attacked in London and when he arrived here but was able to hang on to the stamp. I wonder if Roulette was behind those attempts?"

"Why didn't you call security or the police?"

"I admit I should have. It happened so quickly I was just

glad to see them leave."

"My company does business with Roulette Traders in England. I wonder if it's the same Roulette?"

"It could be; he certainly had a distinct British accent."

"Well, I must get back to work," Virginia said as she looked at her watch and got up to leave.

Roger thought quickly: *She's leaving; I must make my move and ask her out!*

"Since we have this stamp thing in common," offered Roger, "may I suggest dinner sometime? That is, if you're not married or committed."

"No, I don't think so," replied Virginia, seeming to dash Roger's hopes, "but I would agree to a snack after work in the coffee shop here in the building. I'm planning to go the gallery late tomorrow afternoon."

"Fine," agreed Roger, too quickly. "I'll meet you in the lobby. Let's share a taxi again."

As Roger walked her to the elevator he watched her body move in ways that excited him. Perhaps he had found a much needed distraction to this work. Maybe, he thought, she'll be a friend, forcing me to spend more time on my hobby and less time on work. That would be synergy!

Before leaving the office, Roger thought about the auction. He had not spent as much time as he had wanted at the gallery, but he had a solution to that. He called up the Internet on his computer screen then, after working his way through the gates, he reached the display of the stamps to be auctioned off that week. Hundreds of photographs of the major items were there on the screen and he could study each as he clicked with his mouse. Even the catalog descriptions were under each picture.

The bars over each tableau permitted the viewer to enter his name and customer number (assigned previously) and submit a bid through a modem over a phone line to the London Gallery. The bid could be increased later or even removed before the auction occurred. Roger studied a number of stamps needed for his Middle East collection and entered several bids.

There was one in particular he was anxious to get, a lovely set was issued by Palestine when it was a British mandate. It depicted scenes of Rachel's Tomb, the Dome of the Rock, the Citadel and the sea of Galilee. Roger seldom saw that particular issue available as a complete, mint set, so he entered a bid that was fifty percent higher than the catalog value.

Realizing that he had diverted from his Project 006 problem, he called up the project data into an inset box so that he could look at both the data and the auction graphics. The telephone rang and it was Pamela at the site. She reported she had checked the cables and saw no change in the reading on the instrument.

She read off the computer voltage values that Roger had asked for and they both agreed the voltage was within tolerance. While he quizzed her about some of the test data in the insert box, Roger continued to scan the auction material. As she replied he typed in notes on his laptop. Satisfied with her answers, he rang off the telephone, added more notes, changed some of the data on the screen and took one last look at the auction graphics. Finally, he turned everything off.

He turned his thoughts away from work and instead thought about seeing Virginia tomorrow. As he closed his briefcase, Roger remembered that Roulette had tossed the forged stamp into it. He looked for it among the papers but it was gone.

Chapter 10

"Opportunity makes a thief."

- Letter to Earl of Essex by Francis Bacon

Winston Watermark was still tired when he awoke on Tuesday. He hadn't slept well; thoughts of Stanley Roulette and his gun-toting comrade, Joe Coil, pierced his subconscious. He tossed all night, recalling nervously how he had almost lost the centerpiece of his auction. And had Roulette gotten away with it, his business would have been ruined. He certainly owed Essay a debt of gratitude. Over the years, Winston had dealt with emotional collectors and a few petty thieves but none so brazen and bold as Roulette. In hindsight, he should have called the police when Roulette threatened Postmark in his office but there was no evidence at that point.

He took a quick shower, and, tired as he was, he became energized by thoughts of the exhibit. Today was the day for the exhibit and he expected a mob scene. By the time he arrived at the gallery before 10 a.m., people were already waiting to get in even though the exhibit was not scheduled until 4 p.m. The largest crowd would come after 5 p.m. He had engaged six guards to handle the crowd and protect the exhibit, but now he wondered if six would be enough.

On the second floor, in the room where the auction would be held, an easel displayed a large card providing the visitor with salient information about the stamp. If he put that information on the glass below the stamp people would have to take more time to read the story. In this way, he could expect the line to move more quickly. The card on the easel read:

MAURITIUS NO. 1 ISSUE

* FIRST STAMP ISSUED BY A BRITISH COLONY IN 1847.
* ERRONEOUSLY INSCRIBED "POST OFFICE" INSTEAD OF "POST PAID."
* REPLACED BY NO. 3 "POST PAID" ISSUE IN 1848.
* ONE UNUSED COPY SOLD IN 1993 FOR $1,079,000.

Despite the thick carpet on the entire floor, the loud humming increased as more people scurried about, reading the sign and examining selected auction lots on display. Anticipation pervaded the atmosphere: people kept looking about as they brushed against each other. Satisfied with the exhibit arrangement, Winston returned to his office to await the hour for the exhibit to begin. He was still uneasy, remembering the attempt by Roulette to circumvent the auction.

* * *

Stanley and Olivia were having a late breakfast in the hotel restaurant. Stanley was dressed in one of his many dark blue Italian silk suits, which covered a white shirt and well complemented his orange necktie with blue stripes. He wore a dark suit to business meetings so he referred to it as his "negotiating suit." The necktie particularly appealed to him this morning because the color matched the one penny orange.

When Olivia saw his outfit, she tried not to clash with it by dressing in a pale blue suit. She tied a blue bandanna around her golden tresses. Turquoise beads, matching her shoes, hung across her white blouse.

"I would have liked breakfast in bed for a change," said Olivia, "but I know you are anxious to get to the gallery."

"I would like to get there by 3 o'clock," said Stanley, "before the exhibit opens. I have to visit the bank this morning to confirm my resources for the bidding."

"I am going to the Corcoran Art Gallery so I shall meet you later at the gallery."

"I hope you will forgive my distraction, Olivia, but it will be over with tomorrow once the auction is done."

"That's alright, Stanley. I only wish I could help you."

"Well, I have a plan but I need to check some things when I get to the gallery."

The restaurant offered a sumptuous spread for breakfast or lunch. While Stanley waited for his toast and coffee, Olivia sampled various morsels from the buffet before settling on a freshly-made waffle with hot maple syrup. She resisted the potatoes and onions despite the tempting aroma. The savory smells did nothing for Stanley's appetite as he pecked at his toast. A waiter hovered nearby and filled their glasses with champagne. Stanley tasted it while Olivia imbibed freely, pursing her lips at the dryness.

As Stanley was signing the check, Olivia drained her glass and, looking up, saw Marie and Andre approaching their table.

"Ah, good morning," said Olivia. "Please sit down."

"Merci," replied Andre, bowing slightly. "I presume you will both visit the gallery today?"

"Righto. We would not miss it," said Stanley. "You must excuse me; I have some business to take care of."

Stanley got up and left, leaving Olivia at the table.

"You're nervous as a cat, Andre," said Marie. "You may as well sit down. What ever will be will be."

"I cannot calm down," retorted Andre. "I have to bid on for one penny orange, knowing that Stanley will outbid me."

"Cher ami, if only I could help you. Do you want to increase your bid limit?"

"Perhaps."

Andre finished his breakfast quickly because he ate very little.

Marie had her usual croissant and coffee.

"I am going to meet some dealers," said Andre as he signed the check. "I will meet you in our room after lunch so we can be at the gallery by three o'clock. Au revoir, Olivia."

"I will see you then," replied Marie. "I plan to shop and visit friends so I should be back in time. Au revoir."

Andre hurried out of the restaurant. Marie ignored the champagne and poured another cup of coffee while Olivia toyed with her empty glass. Marie confided in Olivia about her plan for an indiscretion.

"My twinge of guilt is somewhat assuaged by my offer to help Andre finance his bid."

"Marie, doesn't Andre suspect?"

"No, Olivia, he is totally absorbed with the one penny orange, just as Stanley is."

"Well, while Stanley is diverted, I have the opportunity to find a way to marry him. Before returning to England, I must have a plan.

"Olivia, why don't you take him on a real vacation? No business, no stamps, just a romantic holiday."

"I have tried that with Stanley but he always found reasons to call the office or look for new products. No, I need a more subtle plan."

"Dear Olivia, I wish I could help. I have never been in your situation so I cannot offer my experience."

"You made a painful point yesterday, Marie. My charms will not last and Stanley will find a younger companion. It's not fair!"

Olivia took a last sip of champagne but it did not help her mood; she was still at a loss how to approach Stanley regarding matrimony.

*   *   *

Virginia stared out of the window of her office, gazing absently at the heavy traffic near some of the monuments of Washington. It was not yet rush hour but the streets were already crowded with tourists. She was thinking about her late afternoon date with Roger Essay. Virginia had given Roger a lot of thought after meeting him in his office yesterday. She was excited that he had asked her to go out with him. Perhaps she should have agreed to his suggestion of dinner but she was satisfied with this kind of "half-date." She also wondered about Roger's story about copying the one penny orange. Would a collector really threaten him like Roger said?

She had intended to wear slacks to work but decided on a skirt instead for the date with Roger. She wore a flattering business ensemble - a "sincere suit" - gray pin-striped jacket over a trim skirt. A light blue blouse was adorned with her largest string of pearls. Her long legs, thin but shapely, symmetrically filled the gap between the gray pumps and the skirt's hemline just above her knees.

She wondered if she and Roger would get past the first meeting. He seemed rather a studious type so she thought talking about stamps would be a safe subject. There was no way she could predict the outcome; her previous experiences did not auger well for this one. She was not optimistic.

She had to get to work. She looked up her notes on the wicker problem and checked her computer to see what the status was of replies from the companies she had called yesterday. The manufacturer confirmed that her purchase order had not specified a color. Would she please specify color on her orders?

Her phone rang; it was the vice president.

"Virginia, please come up to my office. We have a visitor I'd like you to meet."

Virginia reported to the vp's office and saw a tall, heavy-set, impressive looking man stand up as she was greeted.

"I wish to introduce Mr. Stanley Roulette, owner of Roulette Import/Export Co. in London. You visited the company before but I don't believe the two of you had met."

"Pleased to meet you," they both said at the same time.

She recalled that Roulette was the name of the man that Roger had told her tried to filch the one penny orange! Could he be the same person?

"Were you at the London Gallery recently?"

"Why, yes," Stanley said in his strong British accent. "I was there. Are you a collector?"

"Yes, I am," said Virginia as they sat down.

"Perhaps we can have lunch this week while I am in town and compare philatelic notes?"

"Certainly, and we can also discuss some business!"

The two men smiled at the rejoinder. Stanley recounted his trip to the Philippines in search of the mother-of-pearl products and complimented Virginia for her idea. He talked to them about some new products and then the meeting broke.

"I will call you to arrange a date for lunch," Stanley said to Virginia as they left the office.

On the way back to her office, Virginia could not help wondering about Roger's story. Roulette seemed harmless.

* * *

Around 1 p.m. Winston sent one of the staff out for sandwiches. The crowd was building and he dared not leave the premises for lunch. When he finished he asked his staff to come in one at a time to report on sales or problems. Sales were reported as brisk, better than they had been in a long time. The only problem was keeping up with the customers demands and watching the handling of the stamps.

"Do the best you can," Winston told each of them as they sought help. If he were not so keyed up about the Mauritius stamp exhibit he would have personally helped to sell but he did not want any further distractions.

Unfortunately, surmised Winston, he could not call up a temporary agency and quickly hire a knowledgeable person who can sell stamps. However, he did call the agency right downtown for clerical help. At least they could assist the staff and watch the books. Within the hour, Winston was surprised to find two women and two men from the agency enter his office. He gave them instructions and went out and placed them with members of his staff. Winston returned to his office to find Edward Postmark.

"I just thought I would come early to share the excitement," said Edward. "I am constantly amazed at the interest in this hobby. Look at the crowd out there!"

"Frankly," said Winston, "I have seldom seen such a crowd and they are buying. By the way, I am showing your stamp to a number of experts here in my office about half past three so why not join us?"

"Alright, but please do not tell them I am the owner. I had someone chasing me for the stamp, and now I worry that someone will think I own other rare stamps."

"No problem, sellers are generally kept anonymous. But the press will certainly want to find out and unfortunately they could do so from Roulette."

Edward left the office and went to the counters on the first floor to look through the books containing stamps from Mauritius. He scanned the many themes on the stamps, smiling in recognition of many of the scenes and portraits of people. There was the long set showing King George VI in various scenic settings. Similar scenes appeared on the Queen Elizabeth II set. There was even a stamp issued in 1991 commemorating Joseph Bernard, the engraver of the one penny orange!

One of the stamps in another set issued in 1978 showed a letter posted by Lady Gomm, wife of the Lt. Governor of Mauritius, which contained an invitation to a ball. The letter was franked with a one penny orange. He bought those sets.

Stanley and Olivia arrived at the gallery at the same time as Andre and Marie. The women decided to go look at the counters while Andre and Stanley went to see the director.

"I have got to get that stamp," bellowed Stanley to no one in particular.

"And so do I," said Andre. "I see some noted collectors here and also some agents. It appears the stamp will draw some high bids."

In Winston's office, Stanley engaged Winston in another heated discussion about the Mauritius stamp.

"Did the owner put a minimum price on the stamp?" asked Stanley.

"No," said Winston. "He wants no reserve on it; we will let the price fall where it will."

"Perhaps," said Stanley, looking more cheerful, "I will be the successful bidder after all. I must have that stamp!"

Winston was of a mind to bar Stanley from the auction but decided not to. Stanley was along time customer and his attempted theft did fail.

"Come back about half past three," said Winston, despite his misgivings. "I will have a private showing of the Mauritius then."

The two collectors then left the office. Stanley went to the first floor counters and purchased some unusual British colonial issues. Andre stayed upstairs to study the displays of the auction stamps and the setup for the forthcoming exhibit. Joe Coil arrived and joined Stanley at the counters.

"Joe," said Stanley. "It looks like I will have to bid tomorrow so I won't need you until then."

"That's okay," replied Joe. "I'm going to stick around here for a while, though: it's an interesting setup and unfamiliar to me. I'd no idea that so much commerce was transacted for these bits of paper. It's like the jewelry or art business; large sums of money spent for collectibles."

"Joe, what do you think of the security here?"

"Exposing a valuable object to a large number of people is very risky. The director does have guards including some that are not in uniform. Off hand, I think he needs more guards to protect the exhibit. I'm going upstairs to take another look at the exhibit area."

"I will go with you. It is almost time for the private showing."

Just before the Mauritius exhibit was to be unveiled, Winston conducted a pre-exhibit showing in his office for a small group of experts, renowned collectors and important colleagues. This was a courtesy he provided whenever he auctioned a truly rare item at the gallery. He carefully checked the credentials of each person if he did not personally know them. His office was filled to capacity, more than he ever accommodated for an advance display. Winston dimmed the lights except for the bright lamp on the table where the stamp would be shown. Winston propped up against the lamp the blow-up copy Roger had given him, its bright orange color vivid in the dimness.

Soon, the guards brought in the frame holding the two glass sheets and magnifier from the exhibit stand into Winston's office. Winston removed the stamp from the vault, and placed the card and the stamp in between the two glass sheets within the frame. Placing the frame on the table he allowed each expert to carefully examine the stamp in front of his watchful eye. The volume of the conversation rose as excited collectors gazed upon the stamp. Except for Dr. Seebeck, none had ever seen a one penny orange.

Dr. Seebeck received considerable attention because he had expertised the stamp.

"This is only the third unused copy known to exist," expounded Dr. Seebeck, enjoying the opportunity to lecture. "It is now one of the rarest stamps in world. Only 500 copies were printed but quickly replaced by a new issue with the correct 'POST PAID' engraving."

"Were you able to compare the paper with another one penny orange?" asked one collector.

"I did not have access to another one, but I did have an enlarged photograph for analysis. Also, I compared the paper with several other issues around that time period. Microscope analysis showed the paper to be typical of that period. I did not want to use chemicals on the stamp."

"I'm surprised the stamp is in such good condition." exclaimed another collector.

"Considering the stamp is almost 150 years old, the condition is remarkable!" replied Dr. Seebeck. "At first, I had to suspect that only a forgery would be that crisp. Somehow, the stamp was stored under the right conditions. Fortunately, Mauritius is not near the equator."

People were shoulder to shoulder, constantly moving in to see the stamp and then leave the crowded office. Winston was anxious to conclude this phase of the exhibit and prodded people along as politely as he could.

By 4 p.m., the ceremony was concluded and the guards carried the glass to the exhibit area. The gallery was full and people were beginning to line up outside. Winston began to worry that he did not have enough guards. Two guards would now have to control the entry of people. Winston and the guards brought the stamp to the exhibit stand where Winston carefully mounted the glass on the stand. The stand was draped in black felt to cover the display while Winston arranged the frame holding the stamp. After he was satisfied, he stepped in front and parted the felt curtains. With the stamp now in full view, those in front of the line applauded and cheered appreciatively.

On into the late afternoon came the crowds. Winston could now see that he needed two more guards and instructed one of his managers to call the security agency. Winston lingered near the exhibit to make sure the line moved along, then wandered around the gallery noting how busy the counters were. Winston finally began to relax knowing the rare stamp was in his hands and that the auction could proceed as planned. He was more confident that the bidding tomorrow was going to break records. He had sold many rare stamps but the Mauritius one penny orange was certainly the rarest. Once the stamp was back in his vault he reminded himself to make sure to brief the three guards that he had hired to stay overnight at the gallery, as an added protection.

* * *

Roger was busy with his projects but kept thinking about his upcoming date with Virginia and congratulated himself on speaking up and inviting her out. He thought they already had something to talk about - stamps - so he felt comfortable already that they were off to good start. The Mauritius exhibit would be an exciting attraction for both of them and would serve to enhance their first date. Finally, he was able to concentrate on his project problems.

The engineers working on that project assembled in his office and he briefed them on his meeting with the technical director. They reviewed the notes on the blackboard. It was not really a blackboard but it served the same purpose with a new wrinkle; at the push of a button, the notes on the board were copied onto paper within a few seconds and the board was erased.

The team went over each of the possible solutions and either added to or subtracted from the odds of a correct solution. With this information Roger was able to prioritize the list and get his team working in that order. To Roger's disappointment none of the avenues listed appeared to be a likely solution. Each one had obstacles to a quick resolution. Roger called it the "peeling the onion" phase. Each layer of a problem had to be peeled back before the solution could be identified. Sometimes a new layer revealed a new problem requiring a complete reevaluation. So he made his assignments anticipating that the layers would be clearer at their next meeting.

Late that afternoon, Roger met Virginia in the lobby of their office building as planned and together they went to the coffee shop in the building. Roger commented on her attire. They each ordered a sandwich and coffee.

"What do you collect, Virginia? Countries, topicals or covers?"

"I collect a few countries that I've visited during business trips. One of the places I often visited was India, because many of our imports come from there. As a result, I was very interested in their stamps and those of nearby countries like Ceylon, which is now Sri Lanka, Mauritius and other Indian Ocean countries. What do you collect?"

"I collect the Middle East where I've often visited on business," replied Roger, warming to the subject. "As a kid, the stamps from foreign lands had travel appeal; places you would like to visit but were not likely to."

The conversation about philately went on. While Virginia spoke, Roger felt she was not only attractive but quite knowledgeable about stamps. The subject matter reminded him of yesterday's encounter with Roulette and Coil.

"What are you thinking," asked Virginia, frowning at Roger.

"I guess I was thinking about Roulette and his security guard, Coil."

He could still see Coil's cold face and his steely gun.

"That was quite an experience."

"Yes, it was. The director told me Coil goes almost everywhere with Roulette. Doesn't that strike you as a bit odd?"

"Well, Roger, perhaps he is always carrying valuable stamps."

"Maybe. It just seems like there is more going on than meets the eye."

"This is quite a coincidence. I met Mr. Roulette yesterday at the office. He seemed to be a gentleman. I couldn't imagine him threatening you."

Virginia went on to explain the relationship between her

company and Roulette Traders.

"Well, he's probably a normal businessman but when he's pursuing a rare stamp, he's like another person."

The meal and conversation ended. They went outside, hailed a taxi and headed for the gallery. Roger thought to himself that he should ask her for a date after the auction tomorrow since this was kind of a half-date. He kept glancing at Virginia throughout the ride. Once their eyes met and she smiled but turned away. The taxi stopped at the entrance and they went in.

"Are you planning to attend the auction tomorrow?"

"Yes. I am," replied Roger. "I want to be there when the Mauritius stamp is up for sale. Are you going to be there?"

"Absolutely. Mauritius is one of the countries that I collect."

"Why don't we meet in the lobby about 3 o'clock so we can share a taxi again?"

"Okay." said Virginia. "See you tomorrow."

On impulse, Roger shook her hand, holding it a bit longer than a handshake. She pulled her hand away, smiled and walked over to the counters on the first floor.

* * *

Winston watched the crowd grow. He was satisfied that many of the people went on to look at other merchandise and that sales were brisk. He was aware that not everyone came to prepare for the auction. Just seeing a rarity such as the Mauritius stamp sparked enthusiasm in collectors, compelling them to buy. Winston was a savvy businessman who had learned early in his career the importance of publicity. He wandered around speaking to the customers he knew.

Meanwhile Dr. Seebeck was enjoying attention everywhere he went as visitors learned that he had certified the one penny orange. He was unusually dapper, dressed in a plaid gray sport coat with a red handkerchief in his lapel pocket. Instead of a necktie, he wore a blue silk kerchief around his neck under the open shirt collar. He was a long way from his academic environment and had made sure he would be properly attired for the event.

Winston saw Roger Essay nearby and went over to pull Dr. Seebeck away from the small group around him.

"Dr. Seebeck, I want you to meet Mr. Essay," said Winston beckoning to Roger.

They shook hands and exchanged greetings.

"Dr. Seebeck is an expert on British stamps and collects those of the former British Empire. He certified the one penny orange. Mr. Essay is the gentleman who made the copy I told you about yesterday. Fortunately, his quick thinking thwarted Roulette's attempt to hold the stamp as ransom, so to speak, while he negotiated with the owner."

"I saw the forgery in Mr. Roulette's room. How did you get such a good reproduction?"

"Well, I wanted it to look better than a straight copy so I enlarged a copy and enhanced it on my computer even though the paper and color were not suitable."

"That was devilishly clever. If you had had a heavier paper and brighter color, it could have fooled most people. However the initials were a giveaway. If I may ask, why did you put your initials on the copy?"

"It was just a whim. It was only later that I realized how important the initials were."

"Well, jolly good to meet you, Mr. Essay," said Dr. Seebeck, turning and heading for the stairs.

Winston also left to welcome Peggy Serrate who had just arrived. Winston sent Peggy upstairs to look at the exhibit and continued talking to customers. He stopped to talk to Virginia who was shopping the counters on the first floor. She found some unusual early issues which were missing from her Mauritius collection.

"Hello. I'm the director, Winston Watermark, and I know you come here often. You are Ms.-?"

"Virginia Couvert. Pleased to meet you."

"Ah, yes! You are a collector of Mauritius stamps. I hope you are going to bid on the one penny orange!"

"I'm afraid not, but I appreciate the opportunity to see it. I've one big empty space for it in my album."

"I noticed you came in with Mr. Essay. He is a gentleman; a fine, clever fellow. Do you work with him?"

"No, but we work in the same building."

"Well, I hope to see you at the auction. Perhaps you will change your mind and bid!"

Winston moved away to his office as Virginia went upstairs to the end of the line for the main attraction. She would be one of the last to see the exhibit.

*   *   *

Olivia went over to the counters so as not to interfere with Stanley's fierce pursuit of the rare stamp. Stanley, she thought, was now totally obsessed with it. She worried that he would do something foolish. She had heard the rumors that the bids would be very high; high rollers were expected who could outbid anyone. Collecting was fun Stanley had told her more than once but his pursuit of rare stamps bordered on anatocism.

She strolled slowly by the stamp counters on the first floor, admiring the exquisite carpet and the ambience of the gallery. Olivia sat at a counter and sought the stamp sets that Stanley had asked her to buy. She found the Nicaragua set and bought two of them along with two Mauritius sets that were on Stanley's list.

On the same counter was a display of old envelopes adorned with stamps from all over the world. Some were identified as having letters inside the envelopes. That piqued her interested.

To peek into a private correspondence that was more than one hundred years old intrigued her. She decided to buy one "cover" - as it was called - that was mailed from Halifax, Nova Scotia to London in 1863.

With her purchase, Olivia went upstairs to the lounge, sat in a comfortable chair and read the letter inside the cover. The handwriting and style were not easy to read but she persisted. How exciting, she thought! A woman had written to her sister about the difficult hard life she was having in the cold climate. She gave details of her clothes and how the house was heated. She gossiped about some neighbors. Nothing historical was contained in the letter but she loved the personal aspect about things that took place so long ago. Perhaps, Olivia thought, she would make a hobby of it. So she went back to the box on the counter and pored over other covers containing letters.

Meanwhile, Marie had gone upstairs to view the exhibit. After she saw the stamp she lingered near the stand, looking for Andre. Not finding him but seeing Olivia in the lounge, she went to meet her.

"Hello again," said Marie. "Have you seen the great exhibit?"

"Oh, hello, Marie. No, I haven't yet. I will go up when the line gets shorter."

"I see you purchased some items."

"Yes, I took a fancy to these old envelopes which contain actual letters. I bought one that is over a hundred years old and the letter fascinated me. Listen to this."

She proceeded to read some of the more interesting passages.

"I never thought of that," said Marie. "I collect French colonial issues, but never covers."

"Well," said Olivia, "I had better go upstairs and get in line. I assume the men are still afoot."

"Perhaps we can have lunch again before flying back. Are you attending the auction tomorrow?"

"I will be here but not at the auction. Stanley is so busy I would only be in the way."

"I had better find Andre. I shall see you tomorrow."

Marie went to look for her husband while Olivia went over to get in the dwindling line.

* * *

As the hour approached to close the exhibit the crowd began to thin out but the excitement continued. Some milled about, talked in groups; others went downstairs to the display counters. Winston's strategy to work the auction publicity to his advantage had worked; sales were high and he was still one day away from the auction. Winston circulated through the room talking to his customers and the press while checking the time. The exhibit was still being viewed by the thinning line.

At exactly 8 o'clock, Winston strode over to the display case containing the one penny orange and closed the felt curtains. He instructed one of the guards to shut off the spotlights, leaving the rear of the exhibit in semi-darkness. Winston and the guards went behind the stand to lift the frame holding the glass panels. The frame was then transported to his office table. Winston carefully removed the orange colored stamp from between the glass sheets and placed it in his vault. He closed the heavy door with an audible sigh of relief.

Joe Coil moved away from the front of the exhibit after the director and the guards dismantled the display. He saw Roulette near the exhibit and went over to say goodnight.

Stanley said goodnight and looked around for Olivia. Across the room, Andre found Marie in the lounge looking at the purchases that she had made.

"Come, Andre, I made reservations at a nearby restaurant just for the two of us. I expected you to be too keyed up to enjoy any other company."

Her thin eyebrows suddenly rose in surprise at seeing someone familiar standing at the exhibit.

"Wait Andre, there is a friend of ours, Pierre Inverte," Marie said, hoping her blush did not show through her scant makeup.

"Bon Soir, Marie and Andre. Welcome to America!"

"Hello, Pierre," said Andre. "Are you still with the Foreign Service?"

"Yes, I am with the French Embassy here in Washington."

They chatted briefly until Marie suggested she and Andre should leave, firmly pulling his arm toward the entrance.

Olivia found Stanley standing near the exhibit stand.

"Let us leave," said Stanley, gruffly, "I have done all I can and I must get out of here."

"I am ready," replied Olivia. "I suggest we have a quiet dinner at the hotel."

"Sounds perfect to me. Let us go; I do not want to talk to Andre any more tonight. I believe he just left."

They departed the gallery along with the thinning crowd moving out into the night. Roger and Edward were standing near the exhibit chatting after the exhibit closed.

"I am relieved," said Edward, "that the stamp is in the good hands of Mr. Watermark, and, of course, I have you to thank for saving the stamp."

"Well, most anyone would probably have lent you a hand in that situation," replied Roger.

"It is fortunate that I gave you the packet. You must have an honest face!"

By nine o'clock all was quiet at the gallery as the staff, guards and Winston closed up for the evening. Guards were posted at the vault in Winston's office for the night. With the crowd gone, an innocent quiet descended on the floor like the end of a dance; the dancers were gone and the band packed up.

Winston checked the vault lock again and left his office thinking about all the trouble stirred up as a result of one stamp. In the quiet rooms, he began to feel somewhat relieved from the day's events. He locked the front door and walked to his home as the cool evening breeze picked up, wafting the fall still on K Street as it usually was in downtown Washington after out; Act I was over and Act II would begin tomorrow.

Chapter 11

The crying of the lots...

- The Auctioneer's Song

All along K Street on Wednesday morning the city awakened with its typical noisy beginning - belching buses, honking automobiles, occasional tire screeches and thousands of people walking. Pigeons, crows and other birds added their sounds as well. As the morning brightened, the raucous rush hour traffic increased and the day's work began. But today, there was an added chorus to the usual sounds as hundreds of vociferous protesters marched toward the London Gallery. When the group reached its destination, the chanting soon drowned out the sound of local traffic.

Placards were everywhere; some said "STOP SELLING DUCK STAMPS - THEY KILL DUCKS." Others stated "WE WANT SEMIPOSTALS TO SAVE THE TIGERS." Many signs protested against various individuals on commemorative stamps. The crowd was splashed with brightly-colored banners, placards and hats. They were armed with petitions and stopped passersby to get signatures in support of their causes. The police soon arrived to control the traffic.

When Edward arrived at the gallery for his big day, a day that would make him wealthier, he got out of the taxi and stood stark still, gaping at at the horde of people. He then pushed through the crowd and entered the building to find Winston at the door, keenly watching the rotestors. They greeted each other and stood together observing the mass of people; those coming in and those on the street waving signs.

"This scene reminds me of the riots in Mauritius many years ago." said Edward. "Of course, these folks are not likely to change the government!"

"We get these demonstrations from time to time. This one is quite large, very organized and timed to coincide with the auction."

"One of the placards reads `semi-postals.' What are they?" "Those are stamps with a tax added which is used by a government for a specific purpose. For example, Switzerland issued many semi-postals. A ten centime stamp was sold for twenty centimes; the extra ten centimes were used to help needy mothers."

Winston excused himself to check on the frenzy of activity required to set up the auction. On the second floor, the large meeting room was arranged to handle a capacity crowd. The exhibit stand, which would display the Mauritius one penny orange, was placed near the auctioneer's podium. When the time came to auction the stamp, Winston would remove it from the vault and place it under the glass for all the bidders to see. He had checked the stamp more than once that morning to make sure the stamp was in its place in the vault. The philatelic press would turn out, creating even more excitement and anticipation among the bidders. Perhaps, Winston thought, he should have had a television news crew here to get this event into the main news stream. Philately still lacked the glamour of antiques or paintings and generally received little national attention from the press, despite its growing popularity.

The auction would begin at noon as cheduled, but many people had already arrived given the early hour. At the English auction houses where he had worked so many years, the crowds were usually small and consisted of the same network of people. He acknowledged most of the people present. Wandering the room he said hello to a number of judges who were customers. He shook hands with military officers and congressmen that he knew. Some had retired and were very active bidders. Many dealers attended his auctions because they needed a constant influx of material to sell.

Making his rounds, Winston met an unusually large number of visitors from the Far East and Europe. The visitors from the Far East were all new to him so he took the time to introduce himself. Winston always made it a point to meet each bidder; this took time because of the large congregation of bidders and collectors. Winston felt vindicated for establishing his business in the nation's capital. It had enabled him to meet many high level persons from government agencies and congress. These were people who travelled extensively and taken to stamps as a hobby. Winston carefully planned each auction to be a gala event and this one would be talked about for many years. Many of the "stars" - those who were well-known in philately - were in attendance. He needed to convince the philatelic press to devote more columns on famous stamp collectors. This would not be easy because collectors of valuable stamps often were reclusive. Anyway, he filed the thought in his mind for future action.

For a hobby that received little attention in the large newspapers and magazines, Winston was amazed at the interest of the customers in some of the big names in philately. It was like an opening night at a theater where people ogled the stars as they arrived for the performance.

"Look," said one collector, "that's Stanley Roulette. His collection of British colonials rivals the Queen's! Let's get his autograph!"

Two collectors were looking for the owner of the one penny orange.

"There's Mr. Watermark, the director of this gallery. Let's ask him which person is the owner of the rare stamp. He might tell us how he discovered it!"

"Look!" said another collector, "there's General Perforate. I read that he created quite a collection of stamps from the Gulf War."

A small crowd had surrounded one individual. It was Madame Gumme, one of the popular talk show hosts in the area. Her presence in any gathering could not be missed because she always wore a fancy hat. This one was a wide-brimmed, white bonnet with three red and blue ostrich-like feathers waving above it. A young woman, apparently her assistant, stood close to her with a open steno pad making notes.

Madame Gumme was telling the crowd about a recent show devoted to stamps. She also was looking for the owner of the Mauritius stamp to get him on her show. If she could not locate him, she said she would entice the director to talk about this fabulous event.

"I was once linked with Winston Watermark as having an affair," she whispered in an aside to her assistant. "Neither of us denied it at the time."

"Will he appear on your show?" asked the assistant.

"I think so. If not, I shall repeat the old gossip about the two of us!"

Turning back to her audience, which was increasing in numbers, she continued her discussion of the hobby.

"We must do more for the hobby. Look about you; there are too few women enjoying this. This 'King of Hobbies' should also be the 'Queen of Hobbies!'"

The serious bidders were slowly taking their seats while the others moved to the back or out of the room. There would be standing room only.

Winston had to admire the ambience for the auction. This multipurpose room was rearranged specifically for that purpose. The comfortable chairs on the plush red carpet were arranged in a circle so that the auctioneer could easily spot those bidding. Registration was set up outside of the room at the entrance so that the noise was attenuated. An open bar with a large array of light potions also was set up there, supervised by a bartender. Next to the bar was a long table with coffee and tea samovars, surrounded by trays of tempting, bite-size Danish pastries. The many partakers of the food and drinks expressed delight, licking their lips at the satisfying taste of the fresh pastries.

Besides the ambience, he encouraged his auctioneers to be instructive; that is, to highlight special items when they were up for bids. Comments on the provenance, history or the owner were entertaining and educational to the audience.

By noon the room was packed. The registration continued wherein the bidders received cards emblazoned with large numbers to raise when they made a bid. There would be constant turnover in the audience because different bidders came for different sections of the auction. Out of long habit in the trade, the auctioneer began with the sale of United States stamps, followed by stamps of the British Commonwealth and concluding with general foreign countries. Many nations were still grouped with the former colonial powers of France, Britain, Germany, Portugal and Spain. However, this was slowly changing as most of their colonies were now independent.

While the auctioneer was crying the lots, Winston nervously moved around watching the auctioneer hammer down one lot after another. After the first hour, Winston could tell if the bids were high enough by marking in his catalog the knock-down bids.

United States stamps always did well. This auction contained the always popular Zeppelin sets and an early U.S. stamp with an inverted center. In 1901, a set of six stamps was issued in connection with the Pan-American Exposition held in Buffalo, N.Y., which was organized to celebrate nineteenth century advancements. Three of the stamps were noted in the catalog as having inverted centers. The auction highlighted the two-cent stamp which showed the "Empire State" express train upside down.

Winston watched the hammer go down for lot after lot. Bidding was frenetic, like betting at the racetrack. Some of the unusual lots sold for well over catalog value, a good omen. Winston had by now met all or most of the bidders. He was struck by the increased number of women in the audience. He thought about his new friend, Peggy, and how pleased she would be with this trend.

Edward stood near the exhibit even though the rare stamp would not be auctioned until about 4 o'clock. Winston noticed Edward and went over to him.

"This is your big day," said Winston. "We almost missed it."

"Look at this crowd," said Edward. "I am beginning to believe that my stamp may indeed bring me a small fortune but will they bid more than Roulette offered me?"

"Auctions are hard to predict, Edward, but I have a good feeling about this one."

"When I discovered that stamp," said Edward quietly as the auctioneer continued through the catalog, "I had absolutely no idea there was such commerce and interest in stamps. I reckoned a stamp that old could not even be used for postage, much less be worth a large sum of money!"

"Edward, last year an uncancelled Hawaiian Missionary stamp was auctioned off at $660,000 and your stamp is considered to be rarer. So it is not unrealistic for your stamp to sell for much more."

The bidding continued throughout the afternoon while the audience changed constantly. Bidding for U.S. stamps wasextremely active even though many lots were inexpensive. Those issues that came out before 1940 and in exceptional condition - mint, centered and unhinged - were selling above catalog value. People were bidding on all sorts of philatelic material: covers, revenues and airmails.

The bidding was so animated for certain U.S. stamps, there was almost a fight between two collectors! When the dollar value Candleholder stamp with the brown color omitted came up for bids, three bidders jumped up with their placards, one after another until the bid approached three times catalog value. It looked like a puppet show with the three characters hopping up and down. The final bid closed at $1200, four times catalog value!

The auctioneer then began the section of Confederate States. These postmarks and stamps were issued in 1861 and 1862 and were very popular. Prices for them were very high and much of the material was expertized with certificates. Following these issues the U.S. section covered the Canal Zone when it was a U.S. reservation, Guam, and Hawaii when it was a territory. This, the last part of the U.S. section, took up more time than had been planned because of the unusually active bidding.

About three o'clock, the sale of U.S. lots was completed. Winston had planned a half-hour break at this point to allow the audience the opportunity to change seats. Since it was running late he decided to start the British section after only a ten minute pause. A new auctioneer took over.

* * *

While Andre was sweating out the auction, his wife, Marie, was in the French Quarter of the city, an enclave not far from the French Embassy. The day before, after she had left Olivia at the Corcoran, she met some of her female friends from Paris. Her intent was to locate a former lover she had known in Paris and who was now in Washington. To her surprise, the lover, Pierre Inverte, showed up at the gallery last night. The tryst was to take place in her friend's apartment, which had been loaned to Marie for the afternoon.

Pierre arrived at the apartment not long after Marie had settled in and they embraced warmly.

"You are still debonair, Pierre," said Marie, already a little flushed.

"And you, Marie, look as exciting as ever!"

"I could not comment last night in front of Andre. In fact I was surprised to see you at the gallery. Are you a collector?"

"No, I am not, but the Embassy pushes French issues and we follow the general philatelic scene. I will be reporting on this exceptional auction."

Pierre was not as tall as Andre but leaner and more physical looking with his broad shoulders. He worked out constantly at a gym to maintain his no-fat body. Marie could not help being drawn to his muscular body, knowing how he looked in the nude. He had a gaunt face under the long, black hair now flecked with gray. The sight of his muscles stirring under his shirt was too much for Marie. She removed her blouse.

Pierre poured the Pinot Noir Wine but it was hardly needed to stimulate the two lovers. They kissed passionately on the sofa as they whispered sweet words into each other's ears. Their hands were soon in all places of each other's body as they shed clothes, ending in a tangle of hands and legs across the sofa. Passion, like a curtain, descended upon them, shutting out the reality of their lives. Too soon, the stormy passion was spent, the curtain lifted and they were back to reality.

"Pierre, you are still the lover I remember."

"That was my pleasure, cheri, just like old times with you. A pity you had to run off with Andre."

"I do not regret it. You would have kept me in the bedroom and locked me in a chastity belt!"

"Avec plaisir!"

As they dressed, they spoke of earlier times in Paris.

"You are still unmarried, Pierre, why do you avoid it?"

"I did marry but it did not last. Since you are not available, perhaps I shall remarry. Adrienne has a friend she pushes at me, but I think only of you!"

"Vous plaisantez! You are joking with me, Pierre. But before we leave I must ask you a question on another subject."

"Yes, Marie, what is it," Pierre said as he admiringly checked his attire in the mirror.

"Pierre," Marie continued, "you said the Embassy follows the market for postage stamps. I wondered if you have an opinion on what the famous Mauritius stamp might sell for today."

"Well, my guess is that the bids will reach the catalog value which is over $1 million. It could go well beyond that. Why do you ask?"

"I want to help Andre get that stamp. We can outbid most collectors but I had hoped it would not reach catalog value."

"No, cher Marie," replied Pierre, "I am afraid it will not go for the 'half-catalog' price that stamps used to sell for."

They rose to leave, embraced and kissed. In no time they were back on the sofa. The curtain of passion descended again enclosing them in their togetherness as the afternoon waned.

* * *

The Auctioneer moved quickly through the stamps of Great Britain. The former British Colonies followed starting with Aden and on through the alphabet. Bidding was also enthusiastic for these countries. Winston tried to stay calm by pacing around the room which was now overflowing with standees. All major bidders that he knew were in the room and obviously as tense as he, waiting for the highlight of the day. The Auctioneer was now nearing the countries that began with the letter "M."

* * *

Olivia returned to the hotel after spending the morning at the National Gallery of Art. She had to admit she was curious to find out where Marie had been, especially if it had to do with the rare stamp. She called Marie's room but there was no answer.

What else could she find out to help Stanley? He had sufficient funds to make a large bid but he had told her he did not want to bid much more than the catalog value. Japanese collectors were paying record prices for art masterpieces and now for stamps. She prepared to leave for the gallery.

Olivia arrived at the gallery and went immediately to the auction room. She spotted Stanley; his ruddy complexion showed his excitement. He already had caused a stir among the press and collectors by informing them he would be a major bidder. He loved entertaining the philatelic press and knew their articles in the newspapers would precede him back to London.

Stanley was sitting near the exhibit to be close to the one penny orange, his philatelic dream. Olivia waved at Staley to let him known she was there. Olivia went to the lounge where she would wait for the one penny orange bid. She was beginning to worry that the quest for the stamp was taking its toll on Stanley. She had never seen him this keyed up over a stamp or anything, it seems.

* * *

About that time, Roger appeared in the lobby of his building and waited for Virginia to appear. She emerged from the elevator looking very feminine in a royal blue dress under her topcoat, instead of her usual business suit.

"Hello, Virginia. I'm glad you made it."

"Hello, Roger. I could hardly miss this sale. I hope we can get into the room when they get to the Mauritius stamp."

"Are you still planning to bid on anything?"

"If we get there in time, I'll bid on some India and Mauritius. There are some very reasonably priced lots available."

In the cab, Virginia wondered if Roger would ask her for a another date but he appeared to be preoccupied. He briefly mentioned the problems with one of his projects and that he had left his office despite them. They shortly arrived and hurried out of the cab. Roger put his arm around Virginia's shoulders to guide her through the noisy protesters who were still parading around in a circle. The auction room was completely filled. The one penny orange had not yet been sold so they had time to find a place to stand.

*   *   *

The auctioneer was now calling out the bids for the "M" countries beginning with Malawi, once known as the Nyassaland Protectorate. Then he called the country of Malaya. This would take some time because a large number of stamps were listed. Malaya was originally part of the Straits Settlements and each area or island had its own stamps. Malaya became part of the Federation of Malaya which is now part of Malaysia.

Andre Setenant had closely followed Stanley throughout the auction, wryly noting his popularity with the collectors and the press. Now he was seated, nervously moving his card from one hand to the other. These auctions were full of surprises and one could not tell who would win the prize offerings. Often the new owner remained anonymous until years later by bidding through an agent. Earlier, in their suite, Andre had told Marie he fantasized about owning the stamp. He would be elevated to the highest levels within philatelic circles. He would be known throughout Paris and finally, he would achieve a life-long dream - to be famous. He would be famous and for a while, more famous than Stanley Roulette. He could taste the renown and that would be his crowning achievement in the hobby. Marie had laughed when he pictured himself riding in a motorcade down the Champs d'Elysee. He would display the stamp in the Louvre with himself photographed along with the exhibit and, no doubt, the Premier of France!

Andre saw Marie standing near his aisle. He waved; she

blew him a kiss and pointed to the lounge. Andre turned back to stare at the exhibit where the one penny orange would soon be mounted.

It was time. Winston, with two guards in tow, removed the main attraction from the vault. He took it to the exhibit just as the auctioneer announced "Mauritius." After he set the card with the stamp in it under the glass, he moved the black felt cloth aside and the crowd applauded. The auctioneer took up his chant and reminded the audience of the salient features of the rare stamp which everyone in the audience surely already knew.

He began the sale, "crying the lots," as some auctioneers call it. The auctioneer started the bidding at $200,000. Hands holding their pre-assigned customer number cards quickly shot up as the bidding progressed. The auctioneer barely kept ahead of the moving cards - resembling the "wave" at the ballpark - so that the price moved up rapidly. At $350,000, the auctioneer increased the bidding increment but the number of cards in the air did not subside. Both Stanley and Andre had expected to go well beyond that number.

The bids kept coming and soon the price was at $500,000. Winston paced excitedly; he had told Edward this could be a record breaker for his auctions. Edward stood at attention, as if remote from the reality that he would soon have a large windfall. Edward had a passing feeling of guilt. Why was he lucky enough to discover the stamp in the first place? Roger and Virginia silently watched the proceedings from the rear of the room as the action continued at $700,000. He kept glancing at her; her face alit with the excitement of watching the historic sale of a stamp she could only dream of seeing in her Mauritius album. The number of bidders began to decrease; the bidding pace slowed. The room grew silent as the bidding reached $900,000. The auctioneer geared his pitch accordingly, exhorting the remaining bidders to continue.

Edward Postmark no longer stood at attention, now somewhat animated by the action. The bids were now approaching catalog value. The auctioneer paused, as though needing to catch his own breath, and then continued as the few cards left continued to flash, carrying the bidding to $1 million. The auctioneer continued on, sensing a historic bid level. Stanley and Andre raised their cards at the $1.1 million level and even stood, expecting their bid to be the last. The auctioneer continued his chant.

"Going, going..."

Stanley and Andre sat down stunned as cards flashed at $1.2 million. Stanley sat quietly. One could not tell whether he was in shock or whether he was simply relieved that it was over for him. Andre got up and fidgeted near the exhibit. Meanwhile, the bidding continued to $1.3 million and yet a few cards continued to flash unabated. The auctioneer paused again as if to allow the few remaining bidders time to regroup their resources. He continued at $1.4 million at which time two cards still flashed. At $1.5 million, only one card was visible.

"Going, going, gone for one million five hundred thousand dollars to bidder number 45!" exclaimed the auctioneer, slamming down the hammer.

The excitement of the crowd reached a crescendo which went on for a while, interrupting the auction sale. People crowded around bidder number 45 who was trying to extricate himself, explaining he was an agent and could not divulge the name of the new owner. But he did announce that he represented a Japanese collector. With that he finally made his way to the director's office to complete the transfer of funds. Stanley quickly elbowed his way through the crowd to catch up with the agent. Before he went into the office they had a short conversation and then Stanley left. The tumult began to abate and the auctioneer prepared to complete the rest of the British section, and then the general foreign.

* * *

Stanley walked quickly to the lounge where he met Olivia.

"I hope you are not too disappointed, Stanley," said Olivia gently. "You gave it a good distance run."

"Well," replied Stanley, "I have not yet given up. I still have a card to play. Let's get back to the hotel; we can dine there and then I need to make some phone calls."

Joe Coil came by for instructions.

"Joe, I will call your pager later. I hope I will need some help."

"O.K. I'll hang around here for a while and then get something to eat. My pager will be on."

On the way out Stanley and Olivia saw Andre and Marie rushing through the crowd and out the door into a taxi.

"I wanted to talk to Marie, Stanley, but I guess it will have to wait."

"Andre seems in a hurry," replied Stanley, "and I am anxious to get back. We can call them before we leave the city."

Virginia was in the lounge and came out looking for Roger to say goodbye. She did not see him so she drifted out with the crowd.

* * *

Once the one penny orange was hammered down by the auctioneer, Edward Postmark made his way through the crowd and took a taxi back to his hotel. He was euphoric but anxious to leave the gallery. He did not want to be identified as the former owner of the classic stamp and endure attention by reporters. He wanted to relax, plan the rest of his stay in Washington and then return to London to see Penny. He could now face the fact that he was going to be, if not rich, well-to-do. This was the climax of his last trip to Mauritius.

* * *

The crowd calmed and the auctioneer began to call out the remaining lots. Winston quickly moved to the exhibit stand to move the one penny orange to his vault. Joe Coil hovered, watching him. Roger stared at the stamp through the magnifier just before Winston gently removed the card and stamp from under the glass.

Roger suddenly gasped. It looked like the forgery that he had made two days ago!

Chapter 12

"Sir, will your questions never end?"

- *"An English Padlock"* by Matthew Prior

Winston carefully removed the card and stamp from the glass as the auction sale continued. After following Winston and the guards into the office and closing the door, Roger pulled him aside and whispered in his ear. Suddenly, Winston paled, dropped his tongs, then quickly retrieved them. At his desk, he removed the stamp from the card with his tongs and examined it under the light. He touched the stamp lightly with his fingers to feel the paper. Under the magnifier Roger pointed out the initials on the bust of Queen Victoria. Winston's hand shook ever so slightly as he read "RE," the initials that were on the forgery.

Slowly, he sat in the chair and shook his head.

"It was guarded all the time it was here!" cried Winston. "How could this happen?"

The guards, looking askance at each other, then leaned over the desk to look at the stamp. Not being collectors they clearly had no idea as to the difference between Roger's forgery and the real Mauritius one penny orange.

"That stamp was monitored the whole time it was on display," cried Winston, hysterically. "When could it have been switched?"

Roger tried to calm Winston, reminding him that the police must be called. Winston, in a weak voice, immediately instructed the guards to call the police.

"And tell them to hurry," he called after them.

As they waited, Winston attempted to squelch a small,

gnawing fear in his mind. Only he had handled the original. His fear was well-founded; the police could place him at the top of their list of suspects. He turned toward Roger.

"I thoroughly inspected the stamp at your office, "said Winston. "It had the correct initials and it was in fact the one penny orange."

"Yes," said Roger, "the stamp I handed you definitely had the 'J.B.' initials on it."

"Come to think of it," said Winston as he got up from his chair, "I had a number of experts see the stamp in my office. It was the original!"

And the thought that he was the only one who handled that stamp came back again and again. Winston slumped back in his chair and stared at the forgery.

Meanwhile, the auctioneer completed the final section of the sale as the crowd continued to thin. Most bids would be settled by mail because many bids were made by mail, phone, fax or E-mail. Those who wanted their properties immediately waited in another area to pay. One customer was the agent for the Japanese collector who had won the bidding. Realizing the agent was waiting, Winston excused himself, called him in and explained what had happened.

"We have called the police and I am confident they will find the stamp," said Winston. "As soon as the stamp is recovered we will honor your bid. Please reassure your principal that we will do everything possible to retrieve that stamp. The thief will find it difficult to sell such a famous stamp."

Winston waited while the agent called his principal in Japan where it was early morning. Winston was perspiring as he wondered what made him speak so confidently. Following the telephone call, he gave the agent a copy of the bidding record to use at a later date. The agent reluctantly left, quite disconcerted at the shocking turn of events. Once the door was closed, Winston continued his discussion with Roger, going over and over the scene.

"I am completely baffled," said Winston, mopping his furrowed brow. "How could anyone have gotten to that stamp?"

"It's possible that someone took it yesterday from the exhibit," said Roger.

Winston did not respond. He knew he had to call Edward Postmark to inform him of the loss of his stamp but, instead, he kept gazing at the stamp and then at the door, awaiting the arrival of the police.

* * *

Edward was enjoying a leisurely dinner at his hotel, smiling occasionally as he realized the record sale of the stamp would bring him a small fortune. He had been enjoying his early retirement, but he must be careful, he told himself, not to let this new found windfall complicate his life. After a third cup of coffee he paid his check and went to his room.

As he entered the dark room, he recalled the episode with the king size cobra that nearly kept him from reclaiming the stamp. The hairs on the back of his neck bristled as he remembered the other cobra on the day of the riots in Mauritius. It was because of the riots that he had taken the files containing the rare stamp. He turned on the lamps and sat own, switching his thoughts to his plan to return to England. He wondered, would Penny be waiting for him?

* * *

The silence in Winston's office was so intense, the knock on the door was startling. Two men entered, one of whom announced they were from the police station. Both were wet from the cool, autumn rain that had begun to fall, as if to add a chill to the gloomy scene in the office. They shook the water and wet leaves off of their raincoats and took in the solemn aura of the room.

Detective Lieutenant Theodore T. Beche and his assistant, Detective Sergeant Anthony A. Parcel, introduced themselves by displaying their identification badges.

Winston took a few moments to introduce the guards and Roger Essay.

The detective worked out of the Fraud and Bunko Division in Washington, DC, for the past ten years. He had once thought he had seen every type of theft and scam in the book but lately he realized there was always a case that he had never seen before. This, he thought, is one of them.

At first glance, one had the impression of viewing Basil Rathbone as Sherlock Holmes but Detective Beche did not wear a hawkshaw hat or the famous unique coat. Although fairly tall, he was a bit gaunt. He looked to be over fifty but was actually still in his forties. He appeared to be fit and trim, someone who took care of himself. Light gray and intense, his eyes contrasted with his dark hair and mustache. The eyes, set somewhat close to his long nose, were one of the tools of his trade. They seemed to connect to your eyes whenever he looked at you, as though he created an instant telecommunication link to your mind.

His mustache it had an ever so slight curl at each end. Between the mustache and the eyes, he could hold one's attention like an asp mesmerizing a bird.

Younger then Beche, Sergeant Parcel was not as tall, rather stocky with a scarred face. If this were New York, one would say he came from a tough neighborhood. Actually, he grew up in a tough, ethnically mixed D.C. neighborhood. He wore a crewcut hairdo. He had a ruddy complexion implying a heavy drinker, but he was a teetotaler; he had stayed away from drink and drugs for most of his life.

Winston explained, too rapidly, what had happened. While Winston was talking, Roger idly noticed the detectives' attire.

He was smartly dressed in a dark gray suit with a gray, red and blue tie against a white shirt. Like Roger, he wore a pair of shiny moccasins. Parcel, in contrast, did not have Beche's trim figure and wore a rather baggy, brown plaid sports jacket. Its pockets seemed to bulge with papers. His plain brown tie was loosened at the collar. He wore brown, scruffy loafers.

Detective Beche admired Winston's British accent. He wished his speech sounded like that; instead, it had a slight southern drawl. Despite the crisp enunciation, he had trouble following Winston's exposition. He asked Roger to repeat the story since he was identified as the one who actually discovered the theft. Roger's comments were punctuated with Winston's explanations about the exhibit, the auction and just how much was at stake.

"Okay," said Beche, crisply, "let's start again at the beginning so I can get a complete chronology."

Winston sounded tired as he told of the arrival of the stamp's owner and Roulette's subsequent attempt to prevent the delivery of the stamp to the gallery. He then brought Roger into the picture who explained how he happened to obtain the original stamp in the first place.

"...if I understand you," interrupted the detective, "the owner, a complete stranger, just handed you a valuable stamp and left?"

"Yes," replied Roger. "I learned later that he was being pursued by Roulette."

Roger continued with his story, explaining how he had made a forgery and gave it to Roulette until he returned the original to the owner.

"Were you threatened by Coil's gun? In other words, were you actually held up at gun point? You should have called the police."

Knowing the detective was right, Roger got red in the face, finished his story and sat down quietly.

"If Roulette held you up, it sounds like he would be desperate enough to steal the stamp. To go on, you made the forgery, and you also spotted it after the sale."

"Yes," said Roger, "this forgery has my initials so it must be the one I made. If someone else had copied the original, they would likely have left the original 'JB' initials there."

"I get the picture now, " said the detective, turning to Winston. "When do you think the stamp was stolen?"

"I do not see how it could have happened during the auction," replied Winston. "The stamp was exhibited before a full house and under guard. It must have happened yesterday or the day before, after I received the stamp from the owner."

"Anyone in that crowd could be suspect." said Beche. I can't hold on to the audience since most have left. But you must have the names and addresses of those who attended the auction."

"Actually," said Winston, "I can do better than that. I have the names and addresses of everyone I sent a catalog to in addition to those who signed up to bid. Of course, not everyone who received a catalog came to the gallery."

"I'll review that list tomorrow and see if I can get any clues from it. Also, give me the names, addresses and telephone numbers of those in this room as well as your staff. I'll have to take the forgery as evidence so put it in something protective and seal it so that I can mark it for identification."

The detective then dismissed everyone but Winston and Roger.

"I'll need both of you to sign statements at the station. You'll come with me when I'm through here. Now, let's examine the vault and the exhibit to see where the theft may have occurred."

Since only the director could open the vault and there were no indications of forced entry on the door, Beche concluded for the moment that the theft occurred elsewhere. He could not rule out Winston as a suspect but filed that thought away for later.

They moved outside the office to the exhibit area. Detective Beche and Sergeant Parcel examined it carefully. The glass did not appear easy to lift and the stamp had been guarded in full view of the audience, so how could it have been done? The detective instructed his assistant to call in the lab technicians for fingerprints and other clues.

"What's behind the exhibit stand?" asked the detective. "Is there a door or window there?"

"No," replied Winston. "There is just a wall."

Beche pictured where the two guards had stood, then he and the sergeant moved behind the stand. There was not much room between the stand and the wall. He could see nothing in front of the structure because the black curtains were drawn. "Look at these scratches on the top of the panels. Get the lab people to check everything back here. There appears to be enough room to maneuver the glass plates apart. Just a minute; I see something on the floor under the frame."

Beche leaned down and gingerly picked up a glassine envelope with a single stamp in it. He did not want to smudge any fingerprints that might be there. He returned to the front of the exhibit and showed it to Winston and Roger.

"I found this on the floor behind the stand. What kind of stamp is it?"

Both Winston and Roger recognized it immediately as an early issue of Mauritius. Winston went to get a catalog from his office. He opened it to the country and showed the detective a photograph of the stamp.

"Well," said the detective, "it's possible that the thief dropped it while stealing the rare stamp but we still don't know when or how the stamp was stolen. But, for now, it's the only lead we have so let's check with your staff on who might've made the purchase."

"I will check," replied Winston. "Unfortunately, it is a low value, so the customer probably paid cash."

"I'll hold this for the lab people and for possible evidence for now," said the detective. "To get back to the theft, how do you know you had the original? Did you ever see it and the forgery together?"

"No," replied, Winston, pondering his answer. "I never had the two at the same time. However, just before the stamp was displayed yesterday, I did show it privately in my office to a number of experts. The stamp appeared to them to be the original as well; some even commented on the initials, 'JB.' Also, after I had accepted the stamp from the owner, it certainly did not look like a fake; the paper was heavier and the color brighter than the counterfeit."

"So the original appeared to be here before the exhibit opened to the public," mused the detective. "Now, did you check the stamp again after the exhibit closed?"

"No," replied Winston, thinking back. "I recall that I took it out of the display case and put it right in the vault. I did not remove it from its card."

The detective grunted as he made some notes.

"I did have the two together," said Roger. "The differences were like the director said; the paper was noticeably thicker and the color definitely brighter."

"Okay, tell me about motive. What can the thief do with a stamp worth that much. Can he sell it right away?"

"The thief could sell it to a collector who might hide it away for many years," replied Winston. "A reputable dealer would not handle stolen property. However, I suspect that a dealer could be found who was willing to make a profit from stolen merchandise. Yes, there are ways of disposing of it."

"Right. The motive could be he wanted to sell it for a tidy sum. If the thief were a collector you're saying he'd hide it and not expose it for many years."

"Possibly," replied Winston, "but I cannot imagine a collector doing that because he would want to show the stamp, not hide it."

"Couldn't I assume that a collector took it? To make a switch like that would take someone knowledgeable, wouldn't it? Someone like Mr. Essay here."

"Certainly that person would have to know that this stamp had a high catalog value, but someone could learn that from the catalog or the exhibit. Everyone here for the auction knew the value of that stamp. It is possible that someone was here who was not a collector and saw a chance to make some money. But how would that person also know about the fake?"

Before Winston's question could be answered, the lab technicians arrived and Detective Beche interrupted the questioning. After briefing the technicians he returned to Winston and Roger. Both had begun to show the strain of the last few hours but the detective appeared not to notice.

When Roger explained how and why he had created a forgery, Beche looked at him suspiciously, wondering why anyone would go to that much trouble to protect the possession of a complete stranger. What the detective could not appreciate at the time was the impact on a collector of just seeing such a rare stamp.

While Sergeant Parcel continued to check the crime scene, Beche paused to consider the theft. This was his first time investigating a rare stamp theft. The director had explained the value, showed him the Standard Postage Stamp Catalog, and told him why this was not any common postage stamp. He explained the value of stamps to the detective who listened patiently and slowly came to realize there was a large market here. Off hand, the motive seemed to be money. His many years on the force had honed his ability to figure out a crime. He suspected that this crime demanded a well thought-out plan.

The counterfeit stamp, which Beche now held with a pair of tongs, looked exactly like the picture in the catalog except the catalog photo was not in color. If not for the wrong initials, he would not have been able to tell that he was holding a forgery. The paper was thinner than U.S. postage stamps but the catalog said nothing about paper so that was hardly a conclusive factor. Winston had pointed out the catalog did not list perforations or a paper watermark which might have helped. The catalog listed the retail value as $1.1 million so this was not a petty theft. To solve the case, Beche realized he had to learn about the philatelic world. But he didn't have to learn more about the criminal mind. He already knew about that.

They left the exhibit area for the first floor of the gallery. On the way downstairs, the director explained how the counters and stockbooks were set up for customers. Detective Beche looked around for exits. After touring the first floor, the small group returned to the second floor. Most of the lots had been picked up by the successful bidders and the remainder would be put in the vault to await mailing. The detective again examined the exhibit where the theft could have occurred and pondered the possibilities. This could have been an inside or outside job. The detective figured the time of the theft could have been yesterday or today. It was not clear how someone could have lifted the glass without being spotted. Who was closest to the stamp? The two guards, of course.

Sergeant Parcel had interviewed the guards who were hired for the sale. Nothing unusual or suspicious was noted. They said they were all too busy watching counter books and stamps. None admitted to being stamp collectors. After reporting his findings to Detective Beche, he indicated he would check the records of the guards through the employment company.

Beche walked back to Winston's office with Sergeant Parcel.

"Sergeant, do you know anything about stamps? Are you a collector?"

"No, sir, I thought this was a kid's hobby."

"Well, I guess I'd better talk to some dealers who can educate me. Those two, Watermark and Essay, are suspects. Why would Essay expose his own theft?"

"Could be a clever move to throw off suspicion from himself."

"Maybe. Get a warrant to search his home but I doubt we'll find the stamp there."

In the office, Beche and Parcel went over to the desk and

again examined the stamp.

"Sergeant, without having the two stamps side-by-side, one could easily assume this was the genuine article. Perhaps the thief had access to the fake in order to make the switch; or he was like Essay, clever enough to make a copy."

"Essay said he copied the original but couldn't someone copy the picture in the catalog?"

"But that copy would have the original "JB" initials on it if the counterfeiter knew nothing of Essay's copy."

Beche stared at Roger while processing this information through his mind. Then he turned his attention back to Parcel.

"Essay is the only one who had both the original and the forgery together. But why hand over the original to the owner? He fooled that guy Roulette for a bit with the copy. He could've done the same with the director."

Beche and Parcel walked over to speak to the lab personnel and then went back to face Winston and Roger.

"Well," said the detective, "I guess we've enough to get started, so let's go to the station and do the paperwork. I'll keep the forgery with me; the lab people are through with it."

As Winston locked up, the tired party moved out of the gallery into a cool, drizzling rain and headed for their cars.

*   *   *

Stanley and Olivia were back in their suite after a quiet dinner in the hotel. Stanley was on the phone while Olivia undressed and made herself comfortable. Stanley finished his call and walked to the window in the living room. He stood there staring at the night view of the city. He peered out at the slow moving traffic, headlights and tail lights amplified by the rain drops on the window pane pretending. Also in his view were several federal buildings, glistening in the glare of floodlights. Stanley turned from the window as Olivia came out of the bedroom dressed in white silk pajamas that clearly outlined her figure. Stanley stared at the sheen of her pajamas, brightened by the glow of the lamps.

"What are your plans, Stanley, now that the auction is over and the stamp has been sold?"

"I am still working on this project, my dear Olivia. I spoke to the agent for the Japanese collector, trying to work something out."

"How do you know he will sell you the stamp? It could even be on its way overseas as we speak."

"He will get offers. The wealthier dealers will be after him now that a price has been set. I need to make some more calls and then I may have a solution. However, if not, we should leave for London on the weekend."

Stanley picked up the telephone while Olivia frowned at him momentarily, sighed, and went into the bedroom.

* * *

In another suite in the same hotel, Andre and Marie finished a light supper delivered by room service. Marie excused herself from the table to watch television. Andre began pacing back and forth in front of the living room window, stopping occasionally to peer out at the city lights, magnified on the window by the rain drops. He went over to the phone, dialed a number but then hung up. He resumed pacing.

"It is interesting to see television in the U.S.," said Marie. "It is not as risque as it is in France."

Andre did not reply, obviously lost in thought.

"Andre, why are you pacing? The stamp was sold so why worry now about it?"

"I am worried," replied Andre, stopping and looking at her, "because...yes, perhaps you are correct; why worry about it?"

"Cherie," said Marie, trying to calm him, "let it go. Pierre said it would sell for more than one million dollars."

"Pierre? When did he tell you that?"

"Oh, when he met us at the Gallery," replied Marie, quickly. "He spoke of it briefly as we were leaving."

"Well, I do not recall it. I did not think he was even interested."

He stopped pacing and turned to stare at Marie.

"It has been an exciting day. I shall retire," said Marie as she yawned, stretched and went to the bedroom.

Andre went back to stare out of the window. After a while, he turned on the TV and sat down to watch the late news.

* * *

Peggy Serrate sloshed along the rain-soaked sidewalks and entered her apartment about 9 p.m. Anxious to speak to Winston, she immediately went to the telephone. She knew he'd had a long day but expected he would be at his apartment by now. She wanted to know how the auction went, but there was no answer at the apartment. She took off her clothes, put on something more comfortable and then made a snack while she waited to reach Winston.

After eating quickly and watching the news on television she tried again to reach Winston at the Watergate, then called the gallery after getting no answer. No answer there either. She began to wonder where he was; perhaps he had gone out for dinner. Something made her wonder if anything was wrong. She would have to wait and try again later.

Finally, she went to bed and then the telephone rang. It was Winston calling from his apartment.

"I just got back from the police station," said Winston, his English accent more clipped than usual. "You will not believe what happened!"

He related the highlights of the theft and then, obviously exhausted, said he would fill in the details the next day. Peggy was astonished but allowed Winston to continue without too much comment. She had never heard his voice so tense before.

"As it stands now," concluded Winston, "I am probably the prime suspect. With that, I had better say goodnight and try to get some sleep. I have a lot of calls to make early tomorrow."

"Goodnight and don't worry," said Peggy. "Everything'll be alright, you'll see. I'll call you tomorrow."

Peggy hung up the phone, uncertain if things would ever be all right.

* * *

Virginia was in her condominium, drying off from the rain she had encountered walking home. She quickly prepared dinner. She seemed to rush through her meal, watched TV, then turned it off. She was very edgy. She took out her stamp collection and looked over the Indian Ocean countries. She turned the album pages to Mauritius and felt somehow empowered having seen the original of the one penny orange at the gallery. So near and yet so far. She wished she could share her feelings with Roger but she didn't know if he would even ask her out again. She closed her album and prepared for bed.

* * *

Roger finally returned home after a grueling session at the police station, his clothes and his spirit soggy. Why him, he kept asking himself? Surely it was just fate that caused him to be there at the moment the owner of the one penny orange had handed him the packet. Perhaps he had an honest face. Well, he thought, he was stuck with it. So much for trying to help a fellow collector, he thought. He could have just given the stamp to Roulette instead of making a forgery. Right. Detective Beche had made no secret of the fact that he was high on the suspect list.

Roger mused quietly at his desk. His home was almost an extension of his office but he was able to relax here. His computer was always on so he put on his favorite relaxation compact disk and leaned back in his chair. He tried to concentrate on the sound which relaxed his body and his breathing, but other thoughts intruded like the opening and closing of a door. *What a stew I am in! My hobby has trapped me in a sinister plot and the detective sees me as a suspect!*

He pushed these troubling thoughts from his mind as the disk continued. He thought about when he was a kid starting a stamp collection. He stopped while in college but began again after he joined the company. Still recalling his teens, which were most pleasant, he remembered the Saturday mornings walking to the local stamp stores where he spent hours in search of new acquisitions. There were a half dozen stores then in the downtown area that catered to collectors and he usually visited each one. He even recalled some of his purchases like the nickel packet of 100 German post World War I stamps inscribed with millions of inflated marks. Imagine a stamp costing one million marks! They were not worth a lot today but he could never get them again for a nickel.

Most dealers were friendly even though he spent no more than the equivalent of pocket change on each visit. There was one dealer who discouraged him from sitting at his counter and looking through the books. Even then, Roger wondered why this dealer didn't realize that kid collectors usually grow up to be adult collectors and spend money?

His musings were interrupted once again with his immediate problems. He was exhausted and needed sleep, so he locked up, prepared a snack and turned in for the night.

In bed, he did his usual nightly routine. While he ate his snack, he listened to some favorite music on a radio station, read the paper and occasionally tapped some thoughts about work into his laptop. The problem of Project 006 was still bothering him. He needed to talk to someone so he entered a note to remind him to call Virginia. Then he went to the bathroom to brush his teeth and called it a night, leaving the music and his laptop on.

The rain spattered on the empty streets and against his windows, at times drowning out the music. Wet leaves, from nearby trees, brushed across the windows, some sticking to the glass as if to peek inside. The steady sputter soon lulled him to sleep, overcoming his apprehension of tomorrow's interrogation by the detectives.

Chapter 13

"Your suspicion is not without wit and judgement."

- "The Tempest" by William Shakespeare

It was still raining the next morning when Winston arose after a night of restlessness. He hurried through his morning routine and arrived at his office before the gallery was due to open. He had much to do but first prepared a list. At the top of the list was a call to the insurance agent. Then he would publicize the theft and offer a reward in the philatelic press. This would help spread the word and prevent an illegal sale. Winston was prepared to do everything he could to retrieve the stamp. He wondered if a guard or a staff member might have been involved. He could still see Detective Beche's eyes on him because he was the only one who had handled the original stamp.

A soon as he got to the office, he called the insurance agent who promised to come right over. Within the hour, the insurance agent knocked on the door and walked in.

J. MacPherson Pane, had a demeanor that made a client feel comfortable; that he would immediately eliminate the problem and write out a check. Even his name was arranged so that people could address him as "Mac." He was muscular, like the college football player everyone on campus knew and cheered. His appearance and manner of speech made one feel protected. "Not to worry" was one of his standard expressions.

"Hello, Winston. I brought the file with me including a faxed police report so we can expedite your claim."

"Good morning, Mac. I am too depressed to think about it.

Where do you wish to start?"

"Begin with what you told the detective and his reactions. By the way, who's on this case?"

"Detective Beche is in charge of the investigation."

"Well, you've got the best man. I've worked with him on several grand theft cases. He is highly competent; likes to theorize and it usually works out that way. Not to worry; he will either solve the case within the week or he will know that it is unsolvable."

"That is only half encouraging," replied Winston, forcing a smile. Winston recounted the events of the past evening, pausing here and there as he realized how desperate the situation was. The agent opened his laptop and began to question Winston. The forms were re-programmed into the memory of his computer and he only had to fill in the blanks as they appeared on the screen; just like tax return software.

"Winston," said the agent, "the problem here is the stamp was insured for the catalog value of $1.1 million. Since it sold for $1.5 million the difference will be your problem. The owner of the stamp might settle for less but, if not, you could have a lawsuit on your hands."

"Bloody bad news!" Winston responded, looking weary even though it was still early.

Winston quickly made some calculations. From the auction price of $1.5 million, Edward, as owner, would owe him the percentage fee in the contract. Even if Winston swallowed the loss of his fee, he would still owe Edward substantially more than the $1.1 million insurance money.

After the agent left, Winston picked up the telephone, which suddenly felt heavy in his hand, and placed a call to Edward Postmark.

"Hello, Edward," said Winston. "I am sorry to have to tell you this but the one penny orange was stolen."

There was sputtering noise and then silence.

"Edward! Are you there?"

"What are you telling me?" exclaimed Edward. "How could this happen?!"

While Winston repeated yesterday's events, Edward interrupted with questions, the tone of which alternated between disbelief and rage.

"The bottom line," continued Winston, trying desperately to sound positive, "is that for now you are entitled to the insurance money but it only covered $1.1 million. The police are already working on the case and we hope the culprit and the stamp will be found quickly."

Winston could feel the tension, that Edward was trying hard to control himself.

"I do not know what to say. I will be over to see you directly!" replied Edward and abruptly rang off.

Winston's positive attitude began to sag as he faced the next item on his list; the press. First he called the three leading philatelic magazines. Then he called the two local papers. Stamp collecting usually did not get much space in the press, but a theft of this magnitude would get prominent space. One last call was made to the local news bureau of a national paper. Once the story was published, the news would spread quickly to the stamp dealers.

Winston then turned his attention to his business and went over the previous day's receipts with his staff. As he expected from the bidding, he had reached a record auction for the gallery - the only good news he'd had since learning of the stolen stamp. He prepared the deposit for the bank. It was short the $1.5 million yet to be paid by the Japanese collector's agent.

He looked around his office as if for the first time. Reputation was paramount in the collectible community and his was indeed going to suffer from this incident. Collectors would be leery of an establishment whose rare stamp was stolen. There might even be some collectors who would want their material withdrawn from the next quarterly auction. He grimly returned to his work.

*   *   *

Detective Beche sat at his desk reading his notes from the night before. He had retrieved the forgery and was again examining the catalog. The director of the gallery had loaned him a copy with a marker on the page listing the Mauritius stamp. He noted the price of $1.1 million and also the prices of the next issues. He pulled at his mustache as he pondered the surprisingly large prices. He found it hard to believe that small pieces of paper could be worth so much, but were they any different then other collectibles? How about a piece of canvas with oil on it that sold for $20 million?

In his many years of experience he never failed to recognize that there was always some new angle on theft. He had a good record of solving such cases because he was tenacious. Parcel occasionally reminded Beche that he never let anything go but Beche wasn't sure that was a compliment. He had to admit that the thought of this stamp being worth one million dollars distracted him. To get the right perspective, he decided to think of the stamp as a flawless diamond worth $1 million.

He went over his notes again to establish firmly in his mind the exhibit scene. He drew a sketch of the doors and walls near the exhibit. Next, he outlined a script of events which surrounded the exhibit. Then he reviewed Winston's list of auction bidders. He set the lists aside and stared at the wall. He needed a starting point to develop a list of suspects. His first step would be to start with Roger Essay, the person who made the fake, and then talk to the three persons who accosted Essay in his office, especially Stanley Roulette. With that notion he telephoned Roger Essay to let him know he would be at Essay's office in about an hour.

Leaving his office, Beche called Coil's pager from his car. Before he crossed over Key Bridge to Rosslyn, he received a call from Coil who agreed to meet at the Key Bridge Hotel and how to recognize him. Arriving in the lobby, Beche spotted Coil immediately. They sat in the oversize chairs in the lobby.

"Mr. Coil, I understand you have been engaged by Mr. Roulette to protect him and the Mauritius stamp if acquired by him at the auction."

"Yes, that's true."

"Mr. Essay informed me you exposed your gun to him in your attempt to get the stamp which, at the time, he was holding for the owner. A bit unorthodox means, I would say. Wouldn't that have been the same as a theft?"

"Mr. Roulette was prepared to pay the owner for the stamp if he'd gotten his hands on the original. We weren't doing anything illegal."

"Mr. Coil, I want you to recount for me the sequence of events that involved Mr. Essay and the facsimile."

Joe Coil explained the series of meetings with Roger Essay.

"So you never saw the original except at the exhibit but you did see the forgery which Roulette held and then returned to Essay the same day."

"Yes, that's correct."

Beche made notes, then continued his questions.

"You spent a fair amount of time at the gallery. How do you think, as a professional, the thief pulled it off?"

Coil thought for a moment.

"I studied the exhibit area but I don't have a clue as to how it was done. My guess would be that the theft occurred when the stamp was moved back and forth."

"That makes sense. My problem is that those who did the moving did not have access to the fake, unless one of them made a second fake and put Essay's initials on it. By the way, Mr. Coil, are you a stamp collector?"

"No."

"Here's my card. I'm sure you understand that you will not leave the area until further notice."

They both departed without further words.

* * *

Stanley and Olivia had finished their breakfast in the hotel restaurant and had returned to their suite. Stanley opened his briefcase and took out his schedule book. After looking it over he picked up the telephone and called Virginia Couvert at Dockside International to set up lunch.

"Ms. Couvert? This is Stanley Roulette. I called to arrange lunch with you as we discussed the other day. Is tomorrow noon a good time?"

"Yes, that's fine, Mr. Roulette," replied Virginia.

"Good. I will meet you at the Rose and Crown restaurant near your office. Do you know the restaurant?"

"Yes, of course. See you then."

Olivia, overhearing Stanley's call, wondered about Ms. Couvert. She knew Stanley met many female buyers and managers yet it never bothered her until now. She knew she could not say anything for fear she would upset Stanley.

The telephone began ringing. It was Andre Setenant and he was so excited he could hardly speak.

"I just heard some news from a dealer" he choked. "The one penny orange that we bid on was a forgery! Someone has stolen the real one!"

"What!" yelled Stanley. "How did it happen?

"I do not know but I am on my way to the gallery to find out what they know. You have not heard about it?"

"I had better see the director," said Stanley, ignoring Andre's question and abruptly hanging up the telephone.

Stanley called to Olivia, relayed the news as he put on his

coat and left.

* * *

When Detective Beche arrived at his office, Roger quickly closed his door, hoping his staff would not be overly curious. Outside the office, the soft clatter of computer keyboards and conversation created a steady hum. The air carried the aroma of chicory coffee and warm pastries.

The detective wandered about the office as if to acclimate himself to the suspect as much as to his surroundings. He stood for a few minutes at the window looking at the view.

"You have a good view of high rise buildings. How come your office doesn't overlook the river and the Mall?"

"Those views are reserved for the upper echelon. I'll get there one day."

"That's okay; my office doesn't have a good view either."

Detective Beche could tell Roger was uneasy, waiting for him to get down to business. Finally, Beche sat down and began questioning Roger about the circumstances surrounding the forgery. Roger repeated his story beginning with receiving the packet from Postmark, Roulette's threats and the copy made to divert Roulette and Coil from taking the original.

"When the stranger shoved the packet of stamps in your hand, didn't you wonder what he was doing? Did it occur to you that the packet might have been stolen?"

"Yes, I did wonder and I was upset when he didn't show up. At that point, I didn't know the packet contained a rare stamp but, when Mr. Watermark asked me about the stamps, I began to worry that there was something valuable there."

Detective Beche scribbled his notes as Roger spoke. Then, he made him go over the sequence of events again, adding and changing his notes.

"You said Coil had a gun. Did he pull the gun on you?"

"Not exactly. He made sure I saw his gun but he didn't draw it from the holster."

"Why the devil didn't you call the police?"

"I don't know. Had they returned I would have called Security. I can only say that I was concentrating on hanging on to that rare stamp."

The detective got up from his chair, went over to the window and stared out at the scene below him. Roger offered to get him some coffee which he accepted. He was still looking out the window when Roger returned with two cups, spilling some of the liquid on his desk.

"I can see I'll get an education in philately whether I want it or not," said the detective.

"I don't know what I can do," said Roger, "but I'll help in any way I can."

"Well, Mr. Essay," said the detective with a grim smile, "you were certainly in the wrong place at the wrong time, as they say. Postmark was lucky you returned the packet. Now, as I recall, you copied the stamp from the original. I have to consider that anyone who handled the original could have done what you did. That would be the owner, Edward Postmark, and the director of the London Gallery, Winston Watermark. Can you think of anyone else who had the original stamp in their possession?"

"No, those are the only ones," replied Roger. "Either one could have put the stamp into a color copier and ended up with a fair reproduction. However, I doubt that a collector would do that because the hot light could affect the stamp. I copied the stamp using a low-level light source."

"Well, this is some progress." said the detective. "Of course, someone could've made a copy from the catalog illustration."

Roger, obviously nervous, sipped his coffee, spilling some on his shirt.

"If someone copied the original stamp on a copier," Roger explained, "it would have the original initials on the fake. So I think I have made a case which says that the thief did not simply copy the original stamp. And it makes no sense for someone to make a copy of my copy. Why have two fakes?"

The Lieutenant consulted his notes and then continued.

"Now, we've covered who actually handled the original. Let's now identify who knew of the fake. According to you, those who knew of your substitute were Postmark, Watermark, two collectors, Roulette and Setenant; and a man with Roulette named Coil. They probably mentioned it to others, like their wives, friends or families. And then you mentioned your friend, Virginia Couvert."

The detective paused to read his notes, humming some notes from a familiar blues song, which added to Roger's discomfort.

"Okay. Now, you said Roulette and Coil returned to your office after they learned the stamp you gave them was a fake. You said Setenant was with them. Roulette, mad as hell at you, threw the forgery into your brief case. Where is the forgery?"

"I don't know. I searched my brief; it wasn't there."

"So any of those three or any other visitor to your office could've taken it.

"I had people come in that afternoon but I don't know if any of them took the copy. Oh, wait. I did have a brief visit from Virginia Couvert who returned a catalog I had left in the taxi."

"Write down the names of your visitors, where I can find them and whether they came before or after Roulette's crowd."

Roger began writing the names while Beche continued.

"If you switched the stamps, why would you hang around and expose it?" asked the detective, as his eyes, under his raised eyebrows, held Roger's for a moment.

"I wouldn't hang around and I didn't make the switch," Roger retorted. "Besides, I had the original in my hand. If I'd wanted to steal it I could've done it at any time."

Roger handed Beche the list of visitors which he immediately read and put it in his notebook.

"I see you had a number of visitors that day but only one after Roulette came back the second time and left the forgery. That visitor was Virginia Couvert and she works in this building."

Detective Beche got up, put away his notebook and headed for the door.

"Mr. Essay, do not discuss this with anyone and do not leave the city. Here is my card and I'll be in touch."

As he got in the elevator to visit Ms. Couvert at the Dockside International Company, he pondered the new information from Essay. Five people could have seen the forgery in Essay's office: Roulette, Coil, Setenant, Essay and now, Ms. Couvert. Any one of them could have taken it. He allowed himself a smile; he now had a workable list of suspects.

* * *

Virginia was staring intently at her computer screen when she became aware that someone had entered her office.

"Ms. Couvert? I'm Detective Beche. I need to ask you a few questions regarding the theft of a rare stamp."

Detective Beche proceeded to recount his interview with Roger Essay. Virginia shifted nervously in her chair.

"Were you in Mr Essay's office on this Monday past?"

Virginia hesitated, very apprehensive.

"Yes, I believe it was on Monday."

"Did you know the Mauritius stamp had been stolen?"

"Yes, there was an article in the paper."

"What happened during your visit to Mr. Essay's office?"

She paused again, thinking the more she said the more involved she would be.

"I remember him telling me about getting the original and returning it to the owner. He also told me what happened with some collectors who tried to take it away from him."

"Did you see the Mauritius stamp copy that Essay had made?"

She tossed her hair back as she began to redden a bit. Why did Roger involve her in this, she wondered? She wanted no part of a policeman's visit. What would the vice president think? "No."

Beche's eyebrows raised as he pulled at his mustache, watching her reaction. He got up to leave.

"Here's my card, Mrs. Couvert. Call me if you recall any other information."

Virginia stood up but did not reply. She looked at the card a long time.

* * *

Back in his car, Beche picked up the telephone, consulted his notes and called Winston Watermark at the Gallery.

"Mr. Watermark, I'm on my way over to see you. I assume you know two collectors by the names of Roulette and Setenant?"

"Yes, I do," replied Winston. "As a matter of fact they are here with me right now."

"Good!" exclaimed the Lieutenant. "Tell them to stay with you so I can talk to them."

"By the way," said Winston, "that stamp you found last night was purchased here but it was a cash transaction. The salesman could not recall the buyer."

Detective Beche continued on his way to the gallery.

* * *

As it turned out, the gravity of Roger's situation struck him full force around lunch time that same day. Sergeant Parcel called to tell him he had a search warrant for his home. They wanted him there to assist the police. Roger was obviously upset particularly since Beche had not mentioned the search earlier.

As Parcel and two policemen searched his home and

personal possessions. It was not a tidy operation; beds were unmade, drawers spilled out their contents on the floor and his stamp albums were rifled. Roger wandered impatiently from room to room, feeling violated. After Parcel's search was concluded with no results, Roger was still unsettled because of Beche's questions. He was too upset to eat lunch so he drove to the subway station. He had to visit the local electric utility company's simulator where he had an engineer running tests in connection with the problem on Project 006.

Nearly every utility in the U.S. had a training device that simulated their nuclear power plants in appearance and operation. Only a few utilities bought devices for their fossil fuel power plants. Nuclear plants were so hazardous in comparison to fossil fuel plants that the companies needed simulators to train their plant operators to properly operate the plant and to handle emergency procedures. After the Three Mile Island nuclear plant accident, it became obvious to the Nuclear Regulatory Commission and the utility companies that plant operators needed more training on emergency plant shutdowns in a simulator.

It was not possible to train personnel in emergency conditions on a real live nuclear plant; some other way had to be developed. For example, one could not deliberately break open a steam line because of the extreme hazard that could follow. Besides the cost of repair, the consequences were not always obvious or controllable. And the Commission would not permit it. But the simulator which reflected the operation of the plant could be used to repeatedly simulate the opening of a steam line. The consequences of a steam line rupture were readily produced by the device, and corrective action could be taken in a safe environment. In fact, the simulator often was used to confirm the results of a malfunction. Any malfunction could be repeated as often as necessary for crew training in recovery techniques.

Roger, however, was only dealing with fossil plants and the local utility had bought a simulator for their largest plant. The training it provided for shutting down and overhauling a plant was worth more than the cost of the device. And the fossil simulator had other applications. It could be used to test new instruments and controls to see the effects on operation and on the crew before the changes were installed into the real plant. This is where Roger took advantage of its existence.

The beauty of the simulator was its ability to predict the future. It was neat to be able to set up a simulator for everyday conditions and predict what could happen before it happened. Some called this "virtual reality." All kinds of hypothetical conditions could be set up in the software and the device would reproduce sensory effects: visual, aural, tactile and motion. Another approach was the "what if" scenario wherein math models of a process were solved by the simulator. Results from changes in a variable were then readily analyzed.

A vivid example "what if" prediction in a simulator occurred during the space flight of Apollo 13. The spacecraft's service module had been crippled by an explosion which greatly reduced its power output. The mission was cancelled but the problem of getting the astronauts safely home from the moon remained. The malfunction was set up in the Apollo simulator and all possible scenarios were explored through the night. By morning a plan was derived from the simulator that was used by Mission Control to bring the crew back safely.

A reverse of this was the "what happened" scenario. This was utilized in commercial and military aircraft flight simulators. In order to confirm what may have caused a plane crash, the simulator for that aircraft was set up to reproduce the conditions that had occurred based on the salvaged flight recorder and/or eyewitnesses. The simulator was then "flown" to play out what likely happened.

The fidelity of the fossil simulator - that is, how well it acted like the real plant - was outstanding. Thus Roger used it to test new instruments for upgrading old plants, or for installation in new ones. While instruments are thoroughly tested on the bench, the simulator provides easier access for dynamic testing. After going over the tests for an hour, Roger instructed his engineer to fax the results to him. He left for the office with the problem unsolved.

* * *

After struggling with the downtown traffic, which was worse than ever because of the rain, Detective Beche arrived at the gallery and headed straight for the director's office.

"Come in, detective," said Winston. "Let me introduce you to Messrs. Roulette and Setenant."

"How do you do. If I may use your office, Mr. Watermark, I would like to chat first with Mr. Roulette."

Beche removed his wet raincoat and looked around for a place to hang it. Once again he looked at the objects d'art, comparing Winston's elaborate office with his own. At the detective's request, Stanley Roulette gave him a brief biography, describing his background as a collector and why he was after the rare stamp.

"I need it to nearly complete my collection of Mauritius," explained Stanley. "This issue seldom gets to the market so when one shows up I have to go after it. I have never seen a mint one penny orange."

"By `mint' you mean an unused stamp?" asked Beche.

"Yes," replied Stanley. "It was never used for postage and therefore does not carry a cancellation."

"You were more than an active bidder, I'm told, Mr. Roulette. I suppose you'll argue that you didn't steal it or you wouldn't have tried so hard to outbid the winner."

"As I recall," said Stanley, his face reddening, "I was quite busy with the bidding. Then I left after the winning bid was made. On the day before, I did visit the exhibit."

"And where was your wife?" asked the detective. "Was she at the gallery with you?"

"She happens to be a friend, not a wife," replied Stanley, obviously trying to sit still and remain calm. "She came during the bidding for the one penny orange and left later with me. In fact, she was in the auction room for a brief moment."

"Did she see the forgery before it was put on exhibit?"

"No," replied Stanley. "I did mention my experience with Essay after he gave me the fake stamp, but she never saw it."

"On Tuesday," said the Lieutenant, "the stamp was on exhibit from 4 to 8 p.m. When were you and your friend there?"

"I recall," replied Stanley, "that we came around 3 p.m. and left after eight. I attended the private showing in Watermark's office just before he opened the exhibit. We went straight back to the hotel and had dinner."

Beche make some quick notes, then continued.

"I understand the stamp was out of the vault say 20 or 30 minutes before it was put on display.

"Yes, there were a dozen experts or noted collectors like myself there."

"Did you and others handle the stamp?"

"There was no way to touch the stamp," replied Stanley, his British accent becoming more clipped as he became more restless. "It was already mounted between the heavy glass sheets."

"Mr. Roulette, I want you to go back and restate your meetings with Mr. Essay."

Beche, who normally maintained a poker face during interviews, raised his eyebrows as Stanley recapped the visits.

"Your man Coil showed his gun to threaten Essay. You realize he can press charges against you?"

"Yes, but I did not take the original, only a forgery. And Coil did not pull his gun on Essay: he gave up the fake willingly."

"I wouldn't put it that way, Mr. Roulette. You certainly had a strong motive to commit the theft."

"No. I did not steal it. Remember, I made a large bid at the auction. Why bother if I had stolen it? In fact, I returned the forgery and left it in Essay's office."

"Okay, Mr. Roulette, you may go but do not leave the city until further notice. I will talk to you again. Here is my card."

Stanley brusquely left as Beche called Andre into the office.

"As you know, Mr. Setenant," began the detective, "I'm conducting the investigation of the theft of the rare stamp from the gallery. Tell me about yourself as a collector."

"Why are you talking to me?" asked Andre, testily. "Am I suspect?"

"For now I am talking to those who saw or handled the counterfeit," replied the Lieutenant.

Still ruffled, Andre explained his collecting interests and why he wanted to bid and win the one penny orange.

"Mr. Setenant, tell me what you did here at the gallery on the day of the exhibit."

Andre proceeded to describe his activities that day.

"Do you recall anything that might give me a hint as to what happened at the gallery?" asked the detective. "Any theories that might give me some insight on the thief, I'd welcome them."

He thought for a moment, his breathing audible.

"I recall," said Andre, "at the end of the auction I was talking to Stanley Roulette and commiserating with him because we dropped out of the bidding. The day before, my wife and I saw the exhibit but I noticed nothing unusual."

"Was your wife with you all the time you were there?"

"Marie was with me the day before the auction and she saw the display. She came to meet me at the auction."

"Did she see the forgery?"

"No. She heard about it from me."

"You were also at the meeting with the experts." said the detective. "Do you recall anything unusual there?"

"No," replied Andre. "The stamp was under glass the whole

time. Only the director touched the card with the stamp on it."

"Okay," said Beche. "That concludes my questions for now.

"Did you take the forgery from Essay after Roulette returned it?"

"No."

"Do not leave the city until further notice. I hope to complete the investigation within a week. Here is my card."

Andre glared at the detective and left in a huff.

Beche sat quietly for several minutes reviewing his notes. When he called in the director who advised him that the owner of the stamp had just arrived.

"Good. Tell him to come in and then I'll have a few more questions for you."

Edward Postmark walked into the office and introduced himself to Beche in rather formal English. They shook hands, then Edward sat stiffly across from him.

"I'm handling this investigation which I'm sure you would like to see completed as soon as possible. Tell me why you were at the gallery."

Edward stirred restlessly in his chair while he related his background, how he had discovered the stamp and then decided to sell it at auction.

"While I was in London," Edward continued, "there were several unsuccessful attempts to steal the stamp from me. Perhaps that was an omen of things to come."

Edward elaborated on the attempts to wrest the stamp from him, adding the last attempt after he had arrived in the U.S. While Edward spoke, Beche pulled at his mustache. Suddenly, his eyebrows arched and he began flipping pages in his notebook.

"I noted that Roulette and Setenant were in London at that time. Did they have anything to do with those attempts?"

"I do not know. Roulette tried to buy the stamp from me but I refused his offer."

"So Roulette or Setenant could've engaged someone to steal

the stamp directly from you. Sure would've been cheaper than buying the stamp at the auction!"

Edward managed a thin smile.

"Did you know Roger Essay before you handed him the packet?"

"No. There was no time to strike up an acquaintance!"

Edward went on to explain that Winston had told him Essay had his packet and they went to his office to retrieve it.

"So, whoever tried earlier to steal the stamp could've done it with Essay's forgery. We have Roulette, Setenant and you with the stamp in London and in the U.S. at the same. Roulette and Setenant both had access to the forgery, since you said you never saw the forgery in Essay's office."

Lt. Beche stood up to stretch.

"I'm concentrating on those parties who saw the copy made by Mr. Essay. Knowing how Essay copied the stamp, you or the director could've made a copied the original."

"No. We brought the stamp directly here and placed it into the vault. There was no time to go through that process."

"Mr. Postmark. Do you use a computer?"

"No. When I worked at the British Office in Mauritius computers had not yet replaced typewriters."

"Well, since you are the owner of the stamp, I must admit I can't see a motive for your stealing your own property. As I understand this business so far, a stolen stamp is hard to sell and would result in much less money than was bid. I may need to talk to you again so here is my card. Call me if you can recall anything unusual that happened while you were at the gallery. And do not leave the city until further notice."

Edward slowly got up, said goodbye and left. Beche called in the director who appeared visibly tired.

"Mr. Watermark, I've a few more questions and then I shall leave. You showed the stamp to a group of experts. Tell me more about it."

"Yes. I did take the stamp from the vault about 3:30 p.m. to let some experts and noted collectors view it first hand. However, no one touched it. I took the stamp from the vault and put it and the card under the glass. They could each see it but no one could pick it up."

"I'll need a list of those people who attended that showing," said the detective, as he got up and stretched again.

Winston sat at his desk staring.

"What about your wife, Mr. Watermark? Did she see the fake?"

"I am not married, but my companion, Peggy Serrate, did see the exhibit on Tuesday."

"Did she see the original or the fake outside of the exhibit?"

"No, only whatever was under the glass."

"Now," continued Beche, "after you and the owner got the original from Essay, you had time to make a copy like Essay did."

"No, there was no time; I put the original in the vault as soon as I could. You can confirm that with Mr. Postmark. I could not make a copy the way Essay did because I do not have his know-how. Besides, if I were to make a copy why would I put Essay's initials on it instead of the original initials?"

Beche thought for a moment, his eyes locked on to Winston's face.

"Okay, Mr. Watermark, fax me the names of the experts and I'll let you get back to work," he said abruptly.

Detective Beche left the office to once again examine the exhibit area. As he headed towards the exhibit stand which still had the yellow police ribbons in front of it, he noticed someone emerging from behind the curtains!

"Stop!" he yelled, as he tried to get through the small crowd of patrons in front of him. The intruder, wearing a large trenchcoat and hat, was already out the front door as Beche got to the stairs. He raced out of the building and almost lost the trenchcoat but then saw it moving rapidly down the opposite street apparently heading for the Metro subway station.

The detective started running, huffing and straining as he saw the person go into the stairs leading down to the subway escalators. Once inside the station, the intruder took off his hat and coat, tossed them under the stairwell and rushed down the "UP" escalator, dodging the people coming up from the subway platform. Just as Beche rushed in and half-jumped down the stairs, the intruder turned around and faced the "UP" direction. The detective jumped on the "DOWN" escalator and hopped down the steps not recognizing the intruder in sunglasses passing him on the other escalator.

When Beche got to the platform, a train was pulling out. He stopped to catch his breath, cursing at losing his quarry. He went back to the escalator and out of the Metro station thinking the thief must have returned to the recover the stamp that he had found under the stand. Why else would the thief return? On the plus side, this could mean the thief was still in town and that the stamp was also here. He headed back to his office.

* * *

Stanley and Olivia were sitting in their hotel suite following a light, but late, lunch in the coffee shop. Olivia was prodding him to finish his business so they could return to England.

"Stanley, you have interrupted my sightseeing with all this fuss about the theft of the stamp."

"Well, I cannot do much about it. I came here to win it and I still may have a way to work something out with the owner."

"First they have to find it, do they not?"

"Yes, but I may know who has it."

Stanley appeared uncomfortable. He got up and paced in front of the window.

"Stanley, are you through with the detective?"

"I do not know. I did want to return to London but the detective insisted I not leave yet. He may want to talk to me again and he will probably want to talk to you."

"I cannot imagine why. I know almost nothing about the stamp."

Stanley went to the telephone and made some phone calls. Olivia got up and stared out the window. When Stanley was through he told her about his schedule tomorrow.

"I am meeting one of the managers from Dockside International, Ms. Virginia Couvert, for lunch tomorrow so you will have time to continue your tour of the art galleries."

Olivia wondered: how old is Ms. Couvert? She had a twinge of jealousy. The light through the window suddenly had a tinge of green. She suspected she felt this way because she now desired a permanent arrangement with Stanley. She had to be careful, she reminded herself, not to let her desire to marry Stanley become obvious.

The telephone rang and Stanley answered. It was Detective Beche who said he would be over to see Olivia tomorrow at 9 a.m. Stanley gave her the message and then sat. Olivia stared at him.

*   *   *

After a late lunch, Detective Beche was back at his desk reviewing his notes. He called for Sergeant Parcel.

"I'm still working on the premise that someone took the fake from Essay's office and replaced the original with it on either Tuesday or Wednesday, the two occasions the rare stamp was out of the vault. I want to wrap up this approach by tomorrow in case it turns out to be the wrong avenue. Anything new for me?"

The sergeant opened his notebook.

"We're still waiting for the lab report. Should be here this afternoon. I found nothing suspicious talking to the guards and staff at the gallery. None of the guards collect stamps nor did they see anything unusual around the exhibit. They never handled the stamp itself; only the director did that."

Beche looked again at his suspect list.

"That point keeps coming up, but I can't pin a motive on him. If he were caught stealing a rare stamp it could cost him his business. What else do you have?"

"I had a talk with Joe Coil, the security guard that Roulette brought with him. He was noticed hanging around the exhibit when the stamp was removed during the auction. He is retired military and has a private investigator's license. I checked his record and he's clean. However, in view of his being there at a crucial time I think you should speak to him again."

Beche opened his notebook and wrote something down.

"To go on," continued the sergeant, "Essay was at the exhibit when it was shut down after the bidding for the Mauritius stamp ended. As you know, that was when he spotted the copy under the glass. Also, we found nothing from the search of his house. He does not even collect Mauritius stamps, judging from his albums."

Sergeant Parcel closed his notebook.

"And that's all I have so far."

"Okay, Sergeant, I have one for you."

Beche told him about his encounter with the unknown person he had chased to the subway station, quoting from his notes.

"I want you to check on the whereabouts of each suspect at those times. This could point to the culprit."

"Okay, I'll get right on it."

As the afternoon wore on, Beche read his notes again wondering if his assumption would hold up. Was there a second forgery made by someone other than Essay? But why put Essay's initials on it? Who was the person he chased from the gallery?

* * *

Andre and Marie had just arrived in their suite from a long lunch at the Chez. The phone rang as they entered the room and Andre answered. It was Detective Beche. Andre listened, said "yes" and hung up.

"That was Detective Beche, the officer in charge of investigating the missing Mauritius. He wants to speak with you tomorrow about 9:30 a.m. I do not see that there is any choice."

"Why speak to me? I know little about the stamp or theft."

"Apparently he is talking to everyone who knew or heard about the copy given to Stanley. You never saw it; you only heard about it from me. That's all you have to tell him."

"I was hoping, Andre, that we could return to Paris, but you told me we must remain until this mystery is solved."

"That is so. But at least you can continue your visits."

Marie stared at Andre and wondered if he was referring to her visits to Pierre? Andre paced back and forth at the window, his body tense, his mind obviously engaged.

"I have to make some calls."

Marie sat quietly and thought about their extended stay in Washington and decided to make the best of it. She would see Pierre again, of course, being careful not to alert Andre to her indiscretion. *Laissez les bons temps rouler; let the good times roll! Meanwhile, how shall I dress for the detective's visit?*

Chapter 14

"Ask me no questions and I'll tell you no fibs."

- *"She Stoops to Conquer"* by Oliver Goldsmith

The next morning, a bright, cool autumn day, Detective Beche entered his office carrying a cup of coffee and sat at his desk. He looked around the drab, gray-green furnishings, recalling the well-appointed office of the London Gallery's director. Perhaps he would attempt to spruce up the place with some artwork.

He shrugged, drank some coffee and picked up the report submitted by the crime lab. There appeared to be no surprises. The glass in the exhibit showed no fingerprints, probably because the director carefully cleaned it off each time he set it up. It appeared from the scratches on the glass that a tool was used to lift the glass. There were so many fingerprints on the card that held the forged stamp that a clear impression could not be made. The lab reported no other evidence at the crime scene.

Beche wrote down his agenda. Joe Coil was first on his list. He would visit Roulette's girlfriend and Setenant's wife at their hotel. Then he would spend the morning talking to some well known dealers to learn how someone would dispose of a valuable, but stolen, stamp. While he did that, he would have Sergeant Parcel interview the director's girlfriend.

Beche called Sergeant Parcel into his office.

"Sergeant, how does the case look to you this morning?"

"Nothing new to add, sir. I can't say I have a clue as to who might have done it."

"I have a hunch that the director did not purloin the stamp although he had plenty of opportunity. There doesn't seem to be a clear motive. Roulette and Setenant appear to have the strongest motive, but why bid for the stamp if one of them already owned it? Essay had the most opportunity but his motive is debatable. He said he did not collect that country but he could've done it for the money. But if it was for the money, he could simply have kept the original without being discovered."

Detective Beche stood up and walked slowly around the office, looking at the furniture and walls.

"Sergeant, remember Watermark's office, how well furnished it was? Look at my office; it's plain as can be. I need something to spruce it up."

"You could hang Essay's large picture of the one penny orange," Parcel replied with a rare smile.

"Maybe I'll do that after the case is solved."

Beche left the office to pursue his agenda.

* * *

Roger held a meeting with his engineers on Project 006 in the local electric utility's building which housed a fossil fuel plant simulator. After finishing the meeting and before returning to his office, Roger went to another part of the building where a new device was recently installed. It was a virtual reality simulator called "Cyberplant," designed to train nuclear power plant maintenance personnel to walk through a nuclear facility and physically locate malfunctioning components, especially. By wearing the virtual image helmet, a person could see the simulated full-scale interior of the buildings and "walk" down the aisles through hatches and other access points to locate and correct a component failure, broken pipe or electrical circuit. It was often necessary to move around in tight spaces to avoid exposure to radiation.

In an emergency, the plant team could quickly evaluate and practice implementing a plan of action. The simulator would speedily answer the immediate questions: where is the problem located and how best to get to it safely? If a steam pipe ruptured on a live plant - usually a very serious malfunction - the crew could run the Cyberplant simulator to determine the location of the break and how best to get to the problem without hazard. A ruptured pipe could result in a major shutdown if radioactive steam or water contaminated the area. In the Three Mile Island accident, time was lost just trying to understand what was happening while radioactive steam was escaping.

A loss of coolant accident was not unlike an automobile situation in which a hose filled with radiator coolant breaks and leaks. The engine would overheat and the coolant in the radiator would turn to steam; in one's car, one does not have to deal with radioactive contamination, only a big bill to repair the engine.

Based on computer-aided design (CAD) technology, the virtual reality (VR) helmet was connected to two powerful personal computers which solved equations (the model) derived to simulate the architecture of the buildings which house the power plant. Each person wore a helmet and walked on a treadmill with eight possible directions. A sensor on the treadmill detected the speed and direction of movement by the individual. This information fed into the computers which made the simulated dynamic scene in the helmet move relative to the person.

Besides the helmet, the subject wore gloves which were instrumented to simulate the "feel" of any object. For example, the person could shut off a large valve by moving his gloves onto the picture of the valve and the valve wheel would be hard or easy to turn, as in the real plant.

Roger experienced some of the action himself but had to get back to his office. He thought how neat it would be if the VR device were coupled to the power plant simulator in the other room. Malfunctions which appeared in the simulator could be introduced to the VR device and the crew could then physically "walk or run" to the location of the simulated malfunction!

Roger's mind swirled with the possibilities of simulation technology, but he had to head back to his office. The air was cooler following yesterday's rain and it helped to buoy his spirits as he reminded himself he still had to face the Project 006 problem and the stamp theft. The exciting thoughts he had of the simulator were replaced by the image of Detective Beche pointing him out as a suspect. Irritated at that thought, he kicked at fallen acorns as he walked to the Metro.

* * *

"Detective, this is my friend, Olivia Block," Stanley said when Detective Beche came to their hotel suite.

"Pleased to meet you, Ms. Block. As I informed Mr. Roulette yesterday, I've a few questions to ask you."

The Lieutenant removed his coat and sat down. Olivia wore a royal blue robe pulled tightly against her svelte figure. Lt. Beche tried to avoid staring at her but could not help but notice her beautiful golden hair.

"You've heard about the theft. Did you see the copy of the Mauritius one penny orange?"

"No, I never saw it. All I know about it is what Stanley told me."

"Okay. Recount for me where you and Mr. Roulette were when the stamp was exhibited and auctioned."

Olivia explained where she was and what she was doing both days. Beche took notes and, as casually as he could, watched Stanley as Olivia went through her chronology.

"By the way, Mr. Roulette, I understand from Mr. Postmark there were attempts to steal the stamp while he was in London.

There was another attempt here in D.C. Do you have any knowledge of who might've been behind them?"

"No, I do not."

"You can see the parallel to your encounter with Essay."

Stanley reddened and shook his head.

"No, detective, I do not see the parallel. I was prepared to pay Postmark for the stamp."

"That's all for now. As I mentioned before, do not leave the city until I give you the word."

"I have to get back to England, Detective. How long will we have to stay?"

"I can't say for sure, Mr. Roulette, but I expect to solve this case within the week. If I don't, I would suspect the stamp would be long gone. In fact, it may've already been sold."

The detective left for the suite of the Setenants where Andre let him in. Marie was still in the bedroom.

"Are you making any progress, Detective?" asked Andre.

"Some, but we've not recovered the stamp. Which reminds me, I understand you were with Mr. Roulette and Mr. Coil when Mr. Roulette tried to get the original one penny orange from Mr. Essay but ended up with the forgery."

"Not precisely. I was not with them when they first saw Essay. They returned to Roulette's suite with the forgery thinking they had the original. Stanley called me to his room to show me the stamp. I thought it was suspect and called in an expert, Dr. Seebeck, to verify that it was indeed a forgery."

Beche listened attentively. He liked the way Setenant pronounced English words.

"By the way, what do you know about attempts in London and D.C. to hoist the stamp from Mr. Postmark?"

Andre hesitated.

"I am not sure I understand. What attempts?"

Beche pulled out his notebook but before he could record Andre's comments, Marie glided into the room wearing a black sheath which ended above the knees. A single strand of pearls adorned her dress.

Detective Beche intended to ask the same questions of Marie that he had asked Olivia, but before he could get the words out, she sat down next to him and mesmerized him with her charms.

"I am so pleased to meet you, mon gendarme. Please ask anything you wish. First, would you care for a coffee?"

"Er, no, thank you" stammered the detective.

He caught himself staring at this striking woman. Somewhere in his mind his memory vaguely visualized that all French women looked like Marie. A whiff of authentic French perfume wafted through the room. What was it: a rose or lilac scent? He hesitated; it was as though the fragrance rendered him motionless, like being in a mist with zero visibility. He stammered as he began to ask his questions and, although he hung on to every word that Marie uttered, he forgot to take notes. He also forgot to pay attention to Andre, who stood by the window. Finally he reminded himself to pay attention and tried to repeat some of his questions.

She enthralled him with her French accent and the way she accentuated her speech with fluttering hands. Occasionally she fluffed her hair. When she put her hand on his arm to emphasize a point he could not remember the point, only her touch. After completing his questioning, he got up abruptly, said goodbye and left.

Later, Beche sat in his car as though hypnotized. He realized he must make some sense out the meeting with Marie Setenant. *How did she overwhelm me? I'm a professional and not supposed to let that happen! I can't read my notes because I forgot to take any. It's a good thing the sergeant wasn't with me. I can still smell the perfume.* Ms. Setenant was charming, indeed, but he was disappointed with his reaction to her, considering the serious nature of his visit. He'd acted like a schoolboy on his first date and what was worse, he wanted to see this enchantress again!

He shook his head as if to erase Ms. Setenant from his mind. He started the engine and careened into the busy street, tires squealing and headed for the stamp dealers.

* * *

In her office, Virginia finished up some paperwork and prepared to meet Stanley Roulette for lunch. She wondered why her boss wasn't invited. She hoped it would be strictly a business lunch and not a thrust and parry meeting with another male, especially one so influential. He was not young but neither was he unattractive. He could certainly help her career so she tried to keep an open mind about the meeting.

As she left, Virginia passed by a pile of express envelopes already overflowing the overnight express package bin in the lobby of DI's office floor. With the capability of seeing the big picture, she wondered why companies spent so much money for unnecessary overnight shipments. Virginia believed as a manager She would do something about it when she became a company officer.

Fads come and go in the corporate world just as in the private world. Corporations have their hoola hoops. Many fads, Virginia had observed, disappeared quickly but some never went away. The overnight express delivery of documents to corporate headquarters in New York had started innocently enough.

Throughout the fiscal year the accountants in New York obtained data from their many divisions such as: monthly actual costs month, overhead costs, quarterly forecasts and so forth. The chief financial officer had set up a schedule and, if a division missed a date, the accountant requested it be sent by overnight delivery. That was a reasonable enough request. But, in time, the accountants began to insist on overnight delivery to make sure the paperwork arrived on or ahead of schedule. It did not stop there. After a while, division personnel began to send all paperwork by overnight delivery whether it was due or not!

Leaving the building, Virginia walked to the restaurant to meet Stanley Roulette, glad to be outside in the bright sunshine and swirling leaves. She assumed he wanted to talk about the nacre objects she had recommended.

Stanley was already at their table, sipping a martini. She sat down as he stood to meet her, then ordered a diet coke. She looked around as Stanley read from the menu. The room was designed to look like a British pub with a long bar, which was crowded and noisy. A buffet was set up on one end of the bar for those who desired a light lunch with their pints of ale. When Virginia pointed out the large tabby dozing on the end of the bar, the waitress commented that the cat was a good "mouser."

After they ordered lunch, Stanley got right down to business.

"I spoke to your vice president about some very exotic products that I came across in the Far East. I intend to let your company have the first opportunity to sell. In about a month from now, you will visit my company to see them. Then you will assess the marketability of the merchandise before I invest.

"That's great!" said Virginia, excitedly, "I'll make plans."

"Also, while you are there I would like to show you my stamp collection," he added. "Beyond finding you attractive, I have no ulterior motives."

"All men," replied Virginia boldly, "have ulterior motives, but I look forward to seeing your collection."

Now, she realized, this gentleman must be the same Roulette that Roger had confronted. She couldn't picture him stealing a stamp. It made her wonder about Roger's story.

"Now that we have finished our business, let me tell you about my collection," said Stanley without modesty. "You know I am an authority on classic British Colonies. I have many complete country collections, both mint and used. I had hoped to fill a gap in my Mauritius album by outbidding everyone at the auction, but as you probably saw in the papers, the stamp has been stolen."

"The newspaper stated a copy was found in its place."

Virginia talked about her collection and commented on some of the rare stamps she was missing.

"As a result of my countless trips to Asia, I began collecting India. The many Indian states that used to issue stamps intrigued me. I also collect the Indian Ocean countries, like the Seychelles."

"So you are collecting some of the same countries I am," said Stanley, "because they were all colonies at one time."

"It appears we both need the one penny orange for our collections!"

Both were momentarily quiet as their lunches were served. Virginia visualized the one penny orange in her album. She wondered again how this charming man could have threatened Roger.

"I'm going beyond the classic issues and collecting the new issues as well," Virginia said. "I've a hingeless albums for the later issues to keep the stamps in the mint, never-hinged condition. I'm also trying another approach to handle never-hinged stamps. I arrange the sets in catalog order in a stockbook with transparent pockets on black pages until I receive the yearly update to the album."

They finished their lunch and parted. Stanley took a cab to his hotel and Virginia walked back to her office. She needed time to think about the trip and her role in Stanley Roulette's business proposal.

*　　*　　*

Detective Beche drove to a hotel in suburban Maryland just outside of Washington. Watermark had told him there was a large stamp show going on there and it was a good place to meet some of the high level dealers from different parts of the country. At the show, there were dozens of dealer's stands exhibiting their wares to customers who lolled about from one display to the next. A particularly large display attracted Beche's interest. It was a topical collection showing policemen and related subject matter on stamps from various countries.

Winston Watermark had said that this show was similar to the well known Paris stamp bourse which was held outside.

Watermark also had told him this business was a small community of dealers and he might learn something that could point to one of the suspects. Beche approached a dealer who appeared to have one of the largest counters, identified himself and explained why he was there. The dealer was well acquainted with the theft of the rare stamp. Beche asked how he reacted when someone brought him stamps to sell that the dealer suspected or knew were stolen. The dealer said he would call the police while the person was in the store. That way, he maintained, there was a chance the stamps would be returned to the owner. The detective continued his questions.

"If someone should come to a dealer with that stolen one penny orange and if the dealer was a fence, how much would the dealer pay?"

"For a stamp that catalogs over $1 million the thief might get $50,000, possibly more. That dealer would be taking a big risk to try to sell it. He might not sell it for years or he might want to dump it, in which case he could get $200,000 from an anonymous overseas collector. The quicker he sold it the less he could make."

Had the dealer been approached by anyone regarding the one-penny orange stamp, Beche asked? The dealer said no. Beche then wondered if the thief would likely go to the nearest stamp dealer in Washington. The dealer suggested a shop close to the gallery on F Street. Beche thanked the dealer and then drove to the stamp store on F Street. Many stamps were on display.

The dealer, as Beche expected, denied any fencing activity. Asked how a stolen rare stamp could be disposed of, the dealer was convinced that the stamp would be held a long time or sold overseas. If the stamp was in the possession of a collector, it would be kept in his or her collection. If the thief needed money he would try to sell it overseas where he might get between 10 and 15 percent of the catalog value, or well over $100,000. Not a bad day's work.

Beche sat in his car and mulled over what he had learned. Either scenario made it difficult to track the stamp, particularly if it was sold immediately overseas. He already had suspects who were visiting from overseas. He needed to make sure they did not leave the country. Would the thief fly over himself or peddle it through a local fence or agent? And he had to find some way to expose the thief before the stamp was sold.

The detective started up his engine as he saw a familiar person going into the dealer's store. It was Joe Coil. Beche, suspicious, quickly cut his engine. *Maybe this is a break! I'll talk to the dealer and then confront them separately on what he was doing there.*

He got on the radio and reached Sergeant Parcel, told him to get over to this address and instructed him to follow Joe as soon as he left the store. Beche would flash his lights when Coil left the store.

A short time later, Joe came out and walked in the direction of the Metro as Parcel walked some distance behind him. Beche returned to the store to confront the dealer, who showed surprise to see Beche so soon again. Beche fired his questions at the dealer.

"Did Mr. Coil suggest in any way that he knew where the stolen stamp was."

"No," said the dealer. "He too wanted to know if someone had tried to sell it here."

Beche thought it over, asked a few more questions and left. Later, he would talk to Joe himself.

Back in his office, Beche appeared much calmer after his encounter with Marie Setenant. Parcel was waiting and immediately began his report as Beche brushed the demons of desire and the cobwebs of confusion from his mind.

"...I spoke to Penny Serrate, Watermark's friend," Parcel was saying. "She was at the gallery the day of the exhibit but she wasn't there the day of the auction. She saw the exhibit but knew nothing of the theft until Watermark called her the night he was at the police station. And she is not a collector."

"That fits the timetable. He did leave the station late, probably around 10 p.m."

"Next, I spoke to Virginia Couvert who works for Dockside International in the Twin Towers Center, the same building that Roger Essay works in. Seemed like a very smart person, has a big job and is quite a looker. She confirmed she was at the gallery both days with Roger Essay. She only met him briefly on Monday at the gallery and did not consider him a boyfriend. She wasn't sure she would see him again. Regarding the theft she said she saw a piece about it in this morning's paper."

Beche made some notes.

"Did Essay tell her he was a suspect?"

"She gave no indication of it. She didn't really know much about him."

"Okay. Anything else?"

"Yes. Ms. Couvert *is* a collector and" - Parcel paused for emphasis - "what's interesting is she collects the country of Mauritius. In fact, she bought some Mauritius stamps at the gallery."

"Now, that *is* interesting. She collects Mauritius, knows about that stamp and the copy and she's computer literate. I'll move her name up on my list of suspects."

"I spoke to the technical director at Essay's company. He said he was unaware of any stamps in Roger's office. He was concerned about what was going on but stated he was not a collector."

Beche added to his notes.

"I also interviewed the three engineers who were in his office. None were collectors. Finally, I followed Joe Coil on the Metro and he ended up at a computer company. I left him there. That's it for now."

"You say he went to a computer company? So, he could've made a copy there. I think it's time to talk to Coil again."

Detective Beche relayed to Sergeant Parcel the information from the dealers. After the Sergeant left, Beche sat at his desk to look over the reports again and review his notes. Then he left to visit Joe Coil at the computer company.

Joe Coil was just hanging up on a telephone call to Roulette when Detective Beche arrived.

"Well, I have to tell you, I saw you leave a dealer's store the other day. He confirmed that you visited him, asking questions about selling the Mauritius stamp. I could conclude you were there to arrange a sale."

"No. I don't have the stamp. Without breaking confidence with my client, Mr. Roulette, I'll say I was just trying to get information for him."

"I'd better talk to your client again. That's very suspicious activity. By the way, did you take the forgery after Roulette left it in Essay's office?"

"No."

Beche stood up, shook hands and left. On the drive back to the station, he wondered about Joe Coil. Joe is not a collector so his motive would be money. He was exposed to the forged stamp and could have made the switch more easily than the others.

* * *

Roger was hard at work on the Project 006 problem. On and near his desk was a computer with keyboard and mouse, telephone, fax machine, printer and videophone, the latest communication device. It had a 12" TV screen and sat atop a speaker phone so that one could see the person at the other end.

Roger was engaged in a conference call with the technical director, addressing the suggestions made previously. At the same time, Roger cradled a telephone against his shoulder listening to one of his engineers talking about progress on the problem. Roger was typing notes into his laptop as he reacted to both parties. This went on for about twenty minutes. Then he hung up the phone, switched off the videophone and hit some keys on the laptop that would automatically transfer data into his desktop computer.

He stood up and admired the action. The printer began making copies of his notes to send to the technical director and the engineers. The fax machine reproduced information on the instruments from the manufacturers. Satisfied that he knew what just took place, he relaxed with a cup of coffee. He smiled even though he did not as yet have the solution to the 006 problem.

Roger loved complexity as long as it was orderly, not chaotic. The theft of the one penny orange and his role as suspect intruded on his thoughts. The whole series of events had introduced disorder into his life even though he was initially an innocent bystander. The detective's parting words to him that he wanted to see him again crowded his mind. He did not want to think about Beche right then so he thought instead about Virginia. He picked up the phone and reached her extension.

"Hello, Virginia, this is Roger Essay from the 20th floor and the big view. I lost you at the auction."

"Oh, hello, Roger. I looked for you but you were not around. You know, the detective came to my office to question me about the theft of the Mauritius stamp."

"No, I didn't know."

"Why did you tell him about me?" Virginia said a bit curtly.

Virginia was silent and Roger was apprehensive.

"I called to ask if you would consider a dinner date."

"Well," she hesitated, "you appear to be an upright citizen, although appearances can be deceiving. Yes, I'll consider dinner in a public place."

"Good. How about Saturday night? I thought we might go to the Nightingale Casino. They're bringing back big band music. How does that sound?"

"I'm not familiar with big band music but I'm interested." She proceeded to give Roger her address and directions. "I'll pick you up at 7 p.m. See you on Saturday."

* * *

Despite Winston's problem with the theft of the one penny orange, daily business had to go on. He recently had appraised an estate collection that he included in the next quarterly auction. A meeting with the two lawyers had been previously scheduled and he did not want to delay the meeting for fear of losing the lot. Unless they happened to be collectors, heirs usually did not know what to do with stamp collections. Most of the collections presented to Winston, while they had great interest for the original owner, had little monetary value.

Yet, every now and then, a valuable aggregation of stamps like this one would surface. Prior to this meeting with lawyers, one of the heirs had sent Winston an inventory of a U.S. collection and a check for an appraisal. It seemed there were five heirs who disagreed over what to do with the stamp collection. Two of the heirs wanted to keep the stamps. One of the other heirs insisted on an appraisal while the remaining two wanted them split five ways and used for postage!

Winston completed his review and met with the two estate lawyers to discuss his evaluation. He pointed out that the collection was very valuable. It was rich in turn-of-the-century U.S. issues and even included partial sheets of the 1893 Columbian Exposition issue. One set of this issue cataloged $16,450 in never hinged condition. It was unusual to even see one complete set and the owner had at least twenty!

"My appraisal," said Winston, "indicates the inventory is worth at auction between five and six hundred thousand dollars."

Both lawyers blanched.

"I thought it was worthless," said one.

"I can't believe this," said the other. "It was only a hobby for the owner!"

"Well, he certainly picked the right stamps," said Winston. "Are you interested in entering it in the next auction?"

What followed was a heated argument between the two lawyers. Finally they contacted their respective clients for instructions. Once the value of the collection was relayed to them, the heirs, who could never agree on anything, agreed to sell.

Winston had a contract prepared and the lawyers promised to have it signed and returned quickly. Although he welcomed this diversion, he knew he now had to get back to the biggest problem ever, the theft.

* * *

Detective Beche returned to his office and immediately called Stanley Roulette.

"Mr. Roulette, your man, Joe Coil, was spotted coming out of a stamp dealer's shop. I could easily conclude that you sent him there to find a buyer for the stolen stamp. You certainly have motive because you want that stamp badly. Now you've provided the opportunity to unload it."

"Joe went there at my request to see if anyone was trying to sell it," Stanley replied in his brusque English accent. "I hate to blow your theory apart but if I had that stamp I certainly would not sell it. As I informed you before, I need the one penny orange for my collection."

"Nevertheless, Mr. Roulette, you have a strong motive and

you will remain on my list of suspects."

"As you wish, Detective, but I did not steal the stamp."

Detective Beche hung up the telephone, called Sergeant Parcel into his office and began reviewing his notes. Beche related Joe Coil's version of the visits to Essay's office in the attempt by Roulette to obtain the original one penny orange. He also related his conversation with Roulette.

"I checked on the whereabouts of the suspects at the time you chased someone from the gallery to the Metro," Parcel said, reading from his notebook. "Roulette, Setenant, Coil, Essay and Couvert. You were with Watermark so I didn't talk to him. Nor did I speak to Postmark, the stamp's owner."

Parcel described where each one was at the time. None had a witness who could verify where they were.

"Any one of them could've been at the gallery," Parcel said. "Virginia Couvert in particular was very reluctant to talk."

"The person who ran from the gallery wore a very large trench coat with a wide-brimmed hat covering the face. Could've been any one of them under that coat and hat."

"Too bad. That was our best lead so far," Parcel said.

Beche stretched back in his seat and looked around his drab office. It was unusually quiet in the precinct as the morning shift prepared to leave for Friday afternoon "happy hour." It was the pause before the typical weekend frenzy of arrests. Beche felt he had reached a milestone in the investigation and was ready to take action. He sat up, opening his notebook.

"Sergeant, here's where we are. I've made a summary of each suspect and come up with odds on who stole the stamp. Roulette and Setenant, as collectors, were highly motivated, were in the gallery at crucial times but, since they both bid at the auction, I put medium odds on them."

"But," Parcel added, "Roulette tried unsuccessfully to steal the stamp from Essay. He could have tried a second time and been successful."

"Agreed. But I reduced the odds because he bid for the stamp, which tells me he doesn't have it. Now, Watermark had the best opportunity but his motivation was low. Postmark, had opportunity but low motivation. Besides, they did not see the forgery in Essay's office. I gave both of them low odds."

"Sounds reasonable," Parcel added. "Watermark would've ruined his business and Postmark would've lost the opportunity for getting the most money by way of the auction."

"Now," Beche continued, "Coil had high motivation because he might've stolen it for the money. But I gave Coil low odds because he is not a collector and not aware of what to do with a valuable stamp."

Beche rose out of his chair and began pacing, still reading from his notes.

"Essay had a strong motive if he went after the money coupled with the fact that he is very knowledgeable about stamps. He certainly had opportunity, having access to the fake and being at the gallery at the right time. The way he made that forgery tells me he has a very orderly mind. I believe he cleverly clouded his motive which was likely money. He even discovered the fake in the exhibit. Could've made a switch under the director's nose! I gave him high odds."

Beche sat down and put his notebook on the desk.

"Now we come to Virginia Couvert. She had access to the forgery, was at the gallery with Essay and is an ardent collector of Mauritius stamps. I gave her high odds also."

"Do you think, Lieutenant, they might be in cahoots?"

"Could be, Sergeant. Tell you what. I'll give this scenario the weekend and then, if nothing turns up, I'll arrest Roger Essay and Virginia Couvert on suspicion of grand theft.

"Sounds reasonable," replied Parcel. "When we get them to the station, maybe one of them will admit to the theft. What if the stamp was sold overseas?"

"I'll have to deal with possibility later. I got the impression from the dealers that a stamp that well-known would be hard to hide even if it were sold."

Both sat silent amid the sounds of the next shift reporting for duty. Beche looked at his notebook with satisfaction. He had made a momentous decision; the case was about to be solved.

The afternoon sun was low on the horizon as Beche and Parcel called it a day and left the police station.

Chapter 15

> *"And the night shall be filled with music,*
> *And the cares, that infest the day,*
> *Shall fold their tents, like the Arabs,*
> *And as silently steal away."*

- *"The Day is Done" by Henry Wadsworth Longfellow*

    Lt. Beche repeated a ritual every Saturday morning when he was home and not at a crime scene. He could not seem to sleep late so he rose early while his wife was still asleep. He would make some breakfast and enjoy it without rushing as he usually did, then would read the paper and do the acrostic puzzle. This morning he went into the same routine with enthusiasm to get his mind off of the stamp theft. He knew he needed to solve the case but it would have to wait until Sunday. Sometimes, he thought, a solution appeared through serendipity. He would watch football this afternoon, have dinner with his wife, then play bridge in the evening.

    But, by half-time he was so relaxed he decided to review his notes on the theft. Perhaps some answers would tug at his mind. He studied the growing list of suspects. All those on the list had been exposed to or had heard of the forgery, according to all of their interviews. Parcel had told him Ms. Couvert was a collector and she had met Mr. Essay on the two crucial days. She was in his office and had heard about the fake from him. She was capable of making a copy from the catalog so she had opportunity and motive. Beche wondered if they were possibly in cahoots.

The detective looked again at his notes. The gap in his notes reminded him of Marie Setenant and his mind went suddenly into a free fall of desire. Not for him he thought, so he turned her off immediately. He was a married man and if he wasn't careful his wife would pick up a clue from his behavior. She would probably read his mind if he kept thinking about Marie. No, Marie was an exotic and hypnotizing creature, but he would have to resist temptation.

Just before Marie had entered the room, he remembered asking Setenant about the attempted thefts in London and D.C. His reply was negative. He recalled the D.C. attempt occurred at the entrance to the gallery. He picked up the telephone and called the London Gallery.

"Good afternoon, Mr. Watermark. This is Lt. Beche. I have a question. Tell me what you know about the attempted theft of the Mauritius stamp from Postmark. I understood it took place at your door."

Winston repeated what Edward had already told the detective. He could add no new information.

"I will be at the gallery all day, Lieutenant, if you have more questions. This is the busiest day of the week for me."

Beche hung up the telephone thinking about Watermark. He was still the suspect with the most opportunity but with the least motive. Beche turned his attention to the game.

*   *   *

Stanley Roulette and Olivia Bloch were lounging in the living room of their suite deciding how to spend the day. Olivia wanted to visit the Corcoran again but Stanley declined, offering instead to take her to the Kennedy Center to see a performance of a new British play.

"Are you expecting information regarding the theft?"

"I am not sure, Olivia. I am expecting a call that could change my plans."

"In that case I will call Marie and see if she would like to join me for lunch and a visit to the Corcoran."

Olivia telephoned Marie who said she would be delighted to have lunch again. Olivia eventually dressed and blew Stanley a kiss as she left to meet Marie in the lobby. After Olivia departed, Stanley placed a call to Joe Coil's apartment.

"Joe, you remember the engineer who hoodwinked me with that forgery? I have a theory that he did it again; this time he fooled the owner and the gallery director. I believe he did give the real stamp back to the owner and the director did verify the stamp was an original when the experts studied it just before it went on exhibit. So the exhibit did contain the original. Remember, I left the forgery in his office. That means the engineer switched the two stamps that evening or before the exhibit was set up again the day of the auction."

"Sounds like a good theory, Mr. Roulette. I've a feeling you might be right."

"Do you know where he lives?"

"I can find out."

"Can you get into his house without a fuss?"

"When he leaves I can get in. I assume I'm looking for the original stamp?"

"Yes. Keep in touch."

There was nothing more Stanley could do now except avoid Detective Beche.

*   *   *

Edward Postmark was desperately trying to free his mind of the theft. The director of the gallery had assured him the insurance company would pay $1 million of the $1.5 million that was bid. But he was not comfortable. The insurance payment would take a long time; the company would wait to make sure the stamp was not retrievable.

Since he could do no better than the police, he left the hotel and half-heartedly started sightseeing, taking a taxi to 10th Street. He stopped at Ford's Theater to view memorabilia of Abraham Lincoln on display. He wandered through the hushed area and read some of the featured letters. Lincoln was revered in Mauritius because the island at one time was tilled by slave labor. He then went across the street to the house where Lincoln was taken after being shot, then died without ever returning to the White House. Seeing the bedroom where he had succumbed was depressing so he did not stay long.

Edward then walked toward the city's Chinatown to visit Mrs. Surrat's Boarding House where Booth and his co-conspirators lived while plotting Lincoln's demise. Only a plaque indicated it was the boarding house; there was no museum in the building. Passing the many restaurants apparently awakened his appetite and he entered one nearby.

Olivia and Marie returned to the same restaurant in Chinatown where they had dined before. As they were led to their booth, they could not help but notice the rugged looking gentleman smiling at them. Both quickly scanned the menu trying to avoid staring at him. Olivia ordered General Tso's Chicken while Marie ordered Shrimp and Scallop Imperial. It reminded her, she said, of a French dish.

"Marie, would you go again with me to the Corcoran Art Gallery after lunch? Stanley is in a funk and won't leave the hotel until tonight. He wants to see a British play at the Kennedy center."

"No, thank you, Olivia. I have an appointment with a friend. But perhaps we can join you for dinner. Call me before you leave the suite.

As they continued their conversation, they could not help noticing the glances of the dapper gentleman in the booth across the narrow aisle. Their food was served and while they spoke in between bites the gentleman seemed to be listening to them as he drank his tea.

"Marie, if you do not mind my asking, who are you meeting after lunch?"

"Ah, cherie, it is an old friend from Paris who works at the French Embassy."

"That sounds like a rendezvous!"

"Yes! If he shows up!"

Suddenly they looked up and there was the gentleman from across the aisle standing at their booth.

"I beg your pardon, ladies, but one of you speaks with a British accent and I wondered if you are from London."

"Ah," said Marie, "we both speak with accents. Can you tell the difference?"

"Of course! Your's is not the one so it must be the other lady's."

"Yes, you are correct; I am from London. Perhaps you would like to join us for tea?"

"Yes, I would. Thank you."

They introduced themselves and he chatted a bit about London as Olivia thought his name was familiar but she could not place it.

"Pardonez-moi, Olivia, but I must leave. I will call you later."

Marie left and Olivia was faced with what to do; take her leave also or...

"I am going to visit the Corcoran Art Gallery. Would you care to join me?"

"I would be delighted. I have never been there."

They left the restaurant, got into a taxi and headed for the Corcoran. Edward thought, this is better than taking in the sights of Washington alone, as he gazed appreciatively at his lovely companion.

* * *

Andre sat alone in his hotel suite agonizing over the missing stamp. He wondered if he should call Stanley to see what he knew. No, he thought, Stanley would only evade his questions. Stanley had hinted that he knew who had the stamp and Andre was desperate to know what Stanley knew. He had another thought; he would call Joe Coil to see if he could pry something from him.

Late that afternoon, when Marie returned to the hotel suite, Andre was still out of sorts so she went to the bedroom, changed into more comfortable clothes and dialed Olivia's room.

"Cherie, I am back in the hotel and I had promised to call."

"And did you make your appointment with your Parisian friend?"

"Oh, yes! It was a fun afternoon! And what did you do with your afternoon? I suspect you did not see many paintings!"

"Oh, but I did," replied Olivia, glancing at Stanley who stopped staring out the window and went into the bedroom. "I think I heard his name mentioned somewhere."

"Where could it have been? In London?"

"I am not sure and I can hardly ask Stanley about him!"

"May we join you for dinner? You can tell me more about your handsome friend. Perhaps you will see him again in London."

*　　*　　*

Roger left his house to pick up Virginia for their date at the Nightingale Casino. He whisked off the red and green colored leaves from his windshield as they fell steadily from the trees in front of his house. The leaves, now changed to darker hues of brown and chestnut, danced in the wind. In contrast, the leaves on the maple trees were turning into brilliant yellow hues, tinged with copper and crimson. The night was young and the cool autumn air sharpened Roger's anticipation, as he sped off.

On the way through the city, Roger thought about the big band music. Roger was not a musician but he had an ear for music. Although he grew up on rock and roll, he had also spent many hours absorbing the big band music and jazz of the thirties.

He had read a lot about the big band era; it struck him that the music, introduced in the thirties, was not accepted at first and was often vilified by the general public. By World War II it was quite acceptable although many of the jazz groups were still ignored. In fact, the World War II media campaign included the big bands, the music and song lyrics that were important to the servicemen.

Similarly, rock and roll was not at first accepted by the general public. He remembered the early treatment of Elvis Presley when television at first refused to show his gyrating hips. Here, thought Roger, the similarities ended. Whereas big band music and jazz offered many lyrics about love and romance and some politics, rock and roll went way beyond that. It became a major social influence probably aided by the frustrating Vietnam War. The song lyrics of that era preached anti-patriotism, the use of drugs, infidelity and free sex. The music of that era did not just reflect the times; it molded the culture of a whole generation. Lyrics were often whining and depressing. Roger listened to some of the new rap and heavy metal styles but the lyrics which tended to preach violence against police, violent behavior toward women and use of weapons turned him off.

The more the new music progressed the more Roger turned to the big band jazz era music. He would never stop listening to the Beattles but he was more comfortable with the big band sound. For the most part, the main themes of the music and lyrics were of a gentle and romantic nature. It was "happy" music, often unrealistic, but friendly to the soul. That music may have signalled the end of remaining fragments of the Victorian culture. Lyrics about sex were mostly implicit, never openly crude. What went on in the bedroom was hinted at, seldom bared in the lyrics. Sex was considered a private matter; not something you heard day and night from radio stations and records.

Driving on the Rock Creek Parkway, Roger was excited about his date with Virginia; it gave him a break from his obsessive schedule. He pulled out of the traffic pattern in front of her apartment building. The area was fairly deserted but there were a few people coming in and out of the lobby. When he saw her coming he got out and opened the door for her.

Virginia outfit was stunning. A large pearl choker smartly topped a dusty red blouse, modestly unbuttoned. A bumble bee pin covered with small rubies and diamonds was attached to her dark blue coat collar. White pumps matched her white skirt.

"My, you look lovely tonight," said Roger.

"Why, thank you," said Virginia, smiling broadly.

Roger hesitated, not sure how much to say. He liked the way her hair shone in the evening lights and there was a light in her eyes that he found alluring.

"I hope I'm not late."

"No, not at all," replied Roger. "Make yourself comfortable. We have a bit of a ride to the Nightingale Casino."

Virginia did not hesitate to steer the conversation abruptly to more personal matters. She was a excited about this date and, thankfully, she didn't have to go through a singles meeting routine.

"I gather you are, as they say, unattached?" asked Virginia. "Were you married?"

"Yes and no. I'm available, and no, I've never been married. I guess I've been too busy trying to carve out a career. I also was travelling a lot before I got promoted. And I suppose the right one didn't come along. Were you married?"

"No. I also do a lot of travelling and it never seemed the right time. I was all but married to a grad student once. Like you, I seem to be concentrating on my career."

Traffic began to pick up as they approached the Nightingale Casino. It was a unique place, created in the 1930's during the rise of the big dance bands. Such buildings multiplied all over the country following the success of the Benny Goodman band's engagement at the Palladium Ballroom in Los Angeles. Five hundred people could crowd into the Casino. Small tables and chairs around the large dance floor were used for meals and lots of drinks. When it was built out in the country, the road leading to it was a two lane highway. Now it was surrounded by motels and businesses on a four lane divided highway. The place was packed on Friday and Saturday nights and good crowds showed up during the week. It was a romantic meeting place for dancers. Music filled the night air; in the thirties and forties, it was the place to go for dancing.

*   *   *

At the power plant on Chesapeake Bay, the second shift was winding down. In a few hours they would turn the problems over to the graveyard shift. Roger's crew was testing more of the instrumentation but the Project 006 problem with the Turbine Bearing Temperature Indicator was still not solved.

During one of the combined test runs, the turbine was up and running and the digital meter showed the temperature to be in the normal range. The engineer, Pamela, went over to the turbine room with her walkie-talkie to check on the sensors on the bearing housing. She looked at the signals on her oscilloscope which indicated a temperature far above normal. She called the engineer at the console to compare readings. The meter continued to show a normal temperature while Pamela's readings showed it to be 50% higher. She wrote down her data and started back to the console but stopped suddenly when she sniffed an odor that came from friction caused by metal rubbing against metal. It was coming from the area of the bearing housings. She called the foreman.

"Hey, Bart, there's a burning smell coming from the turbine. Get someone to shut it down!"

"Can't be, but I'll be right over!"

Within seconds, the turbine began to slow down as the foreman and his crew ran toward Pamela.

"Where's the smell coming from?" asked the foreman as he approached her.

"Right here at this bearing. The temperature reading is way above normal!"

"Wow!" said the foreman, looking under the housing, "the bearings are almost red hot!"

He turned to the crew.

"Get your trouble shooting manual up on the screen and start through it."

The crew dashed over to a nearby maintenance room and called up the manuals on the computer screen, checking off each item as it appeared.

The use of bulky maintenance manuals was disappearing. All maintenance data and drawings were stored in computer memory, cross-indexed for rapid retrieval. In this case, merely entering the word "GENERATOR" brought up an overall illustration on the screen. A top-down structure allowed the crew to quickly find the bearing part number, location, manufacturer and all maintenance data.

As the crew scanned the screen, the foreman began to undo the housing to check the part number of the bearing. He called out the part number to the crew and then turned to Pamela.

"It's a good thing you were checking the signals, Pamela, or we would have lost the bearings and blown the schedule! Makes up for that transformer you blew last week!"

"Transformer, my ass! It was an accident! And, by the way, why are you running the turbine before the instruments are completely checked out?"

"Okay, okay, you have a point. I will alert the turbine crew. I'll call the test manager to rearrange the daily schedule. But if you can't solve that problem it will screw up the delivery schedule!"

On her way back to the console, Pamela thought she had better call Roger and give him a heads-up about this latest development resulting from with the turbine bearing temperature meter problem.

* * *

Roger drove on now hitting the Saturday night traffic as the car neared the casino. Many of the famous band names were still around: Tommy Dorsey, Jimmy Dorsey, Count Basie, Artie Shaw, Woody Herman, Stan Kenton, Glenn Miller, Duke Ellington and others. But the original leaders were gone. Roger remembered coming here a few years ago when the Stan Kenton's band was featured. The band really jumped with young musicians just out of college. Roger's favorite was Artie Shaw whose band at its height played memorable big band jazz, not to mention his small combo. Roger could imagine that era when every large night club had a band. Between night club dates, the bands played the college proms and five shows a day at movie theaters.

The car pulled into the crowded parking area. Roger escorted Virginia to the front door as the lush sound of the music got louder.

"That sure sounds great!" exclaimed Roger. "Listen to the brass section coming through the air!"

They went into the crowd and were seated not too far from the bandstand.

"What a sound!" said Roger again.

The waitress came and Roger ordered a vodka gimblet. Virginia ordered a Perrier with lime, which sent the message that she was not going to succumb to alcohol on a first date. Roger proceeded to order dinner.

"How about the special, Virginia?"

"Okay. Sounds delicious."

Through drinks and dinner the conversation became a little more personal. Virginia told him of her roots and upbringing and where she went to college. Roger did likewise. They both skipped dessert. Roger was anxious to get in front of the bandstand. He took Virginia's hand and walked to the front and just stood there listening intently.

The sound of music flowed while they watched the orchestra. Big band music or "swing" as it used to be called, was a gentler form of jazz. The arrangements were melodic with a steady beat. The songs that came out of the swing era were also gentle and one could understand the lyrics because the singers enunciated clearly. Those who were repelled by the harsh guitar noises and heavy metal sound of rock and roll were surprised to find a library of songs and jazz which was easier on the nerves. Even though not part of the original swing generation, Roger found the big band sound very appealing. Maybe he was just getting older. Virginia appeared to find the music pleasant. Maybe she would succumb to the lyrics. Who can resist poetry set to music that sings; "I'll build a dream on your kiss...?"

The band began to play a slow tune and Roger asked Virginia to dance. He danced very closely even though Virginia seemed a bit awkward with it at first. The set closed and they went back to their table.

"I grew up with rock and roll," explained Roger, "but I've come to like the old big band music especially the dancing that goes along with it. What do you think of it?"

"It's fun but it's new to me. It wasn't easy to keep up with you. Let's try some more when the next set begins; I'm sure I'll do better."

"Swing and sway" was another description of these dances.

Roger hoped Virginia had a similar reaction. He certainly enjoyed dancing with her; she was an armful! This kind of dancing was obviously new to her but she seemed to catch on quickly.

Between sets, Roger and Virginia were talking about their respective careers when Roger's pager suddenly beeped, startling both of them. Roger's first thought was that Detective Beche was calling, but the digits on the pager flashed a familiar telephone number. He excused himself and called his engineer, Pamela, at the power plant site. She gave him the heads-up on the potential delay to the master schedule. He thanked her and tried to put his mind back on the dance and Virginia.

* * *

At that moment, Detective Beche was at home. Following dinner out with another couple, the foursome sat down to an evening of bridge. Like his grand theft case, the cards were not going well for him. When he did get a biddable hand it did not match with his wife's hand. Once, he opened with two spades and his wife had a bust. The cards went downhill from there; he had no more opening bids that evening. The other couple won all the rubbers and completely swamped the Beches' scores.

When his hand was the dummy, his thoughts turned to the case. He wondered what Essay was doing? Was he disposing of the stamp which he probably hid somewhere? Beche had a miserable time at the bridge table, in contrast to Roger's good time Saturday night. After the guests left, he picked up the telephone. He had more questions for Essay about the forgery. The telephone rang but only the answering machine responded.

* * *

While Roger was on the telephone, Virginia relaxed and thought about how she was enjoying the music and the casino.

She wasn't used to dancing so close but Roger seemed to like it. The evening was very romantic; was she getting carried away?

As she grew more comfortable dancing with Roger, she listened more closely to the music and songs. Roger was quiet and obviously listening also. Her first impression of him was that he seemed more restrained than other men. Did the music have that effect on him, she wondered?

* * *

After Roger returned to their table, the band played another set and it was time to go. He paid the check and, still listening to the music, took her willing hand and walked slowly out to the car. The cool breeze off the Potomac River and the bright, harvest moon enhanced the mood.

Roger kept stealing glances at her as he drove, watching the way her shoulders moved beneath the silky fabric. The drive back to her apartment seemed short. She invited him to come up.

"If you like, I can show you some of my collection."

"This is a switch; men used to invite girls up to see their etchings. I would like to see it."

Getting out of the car, Roger took his laptop computer from the back seat, explaining that he needed to add information from the call he made at the Casino. In her apartment, Virginia went into the kitchen, while Roger tapped on his laptop.

"I certainly enjoyed the dancing. I thought that kind of dancing was passe," she remarked as she began to brew the coffee.

"It was, but it is enjoying a revival."

They sat on the sofa drinking coffee. Virginia had her India album in her lap.

"Typically, I don't have too many of the early issues, but I do have this early set with Queen Victoria on it. Hard to believe this set was issued in the late 1800's. I also have the set with

King Edward VII on the stamps which are becoming quite valuable."

"These are in nice condition," said Roger. "I see you use a hingeless album."

"Yes, I do. I prefer hinges but the later issues seem to be worth more if they are unhinged. Many of the early issues were hinged so it makes no difference if you hinge them."

As they drank coffee and looked through the album, the glow of the evening hung over them. He enjoyed looking at the stamps but, by the time they got to the issues of the sixties, Roger was admiring her legs as well as the stamps. He could contain himself no longer. The music of the night was still in his ears. He looked less at the stamps of India and more at her. Then he slowly leaned over and kissed her.

Though unprepared, Virginia did not resist. The album slipped from her lap, replaced by Roger's hands. She was receptive to his kisses and another.

"Roger...wait," she said, uncertainly. "It's too soon...this is only our first date, so..."

"No, Virginia," Roger replied, as he nuzzled her neck, "it's really our second date, maybe our third, counting first meeting at the gallery..."

"... we should wait for another date, Roger." she said, all the while warming to his embrace.

They undressed as they stretched across the long sofa, suddenly aflame with emotion and energy. Her nearness was overwhelming as he stroked her and cuddled up close to her receptive body. They soon joined together and were enjoying every pant of it. Roger was gliding along when he abruptly stopped and reached for his laptop. Virginia went stiff.

"What are you doing!?"

"Sorry, I just thought of something I must put in my laptop."

"While you're loving me!?" gasped Virginia.

Roger quickly stopped hitting the keys and went back to

caressing her and to enjoy the climax.

Virginia lay back and could not believe what happened. She was thrilled by his caresses but shocked by his interruption.

"Sorry," said Roger again. "I have this habit of doing two things at once if they occur to me."

Virginia stomped into the bedroom and soon came out in her robe.

"I think we should call it a night. I am a bit startled."

"I had a great time," said Roger as he finished dressing and collected his belongings. "I hope you will go out again with me."

"I don't know," whispered Virginia, having difficulty with words. "We'll see."

Roger headed for the door and left her in a silent daze.

Virginia sat in a chair staring at the sofa. A few moments of ecstasy and then a pang of despair. She had thought of Roger as a gentleman and now he added a disturbing dimension. He was a multiplex man; like a computer which processed many tasks at the same time. But he wanted to see her again; did she want to see him?

She got up from the chair and walked out on her balcony. It was a cool night, full of moonlight.

Chapter 16

> *"When lovely woman stoops to folly,*
> *And finds too late that men betray,*
> *What charm can soothe her melancholy?*
> *What art can wash her guilt away?"*
>
> - *"Song" by Oliver Goldsmith*

Virginia awoke late Sunday morning with an emotional hangover; that "I shouldn't-have-oughta-done-it" feeling. She slowly put on her jogging outfit for her usual two-mile walk.

The day was chilly but the sun gradually warmed the still-bright foliage. As she walked along the trail, she thought about another problem that she had tried to ignore: the interview with the police. She was quizzed about the missing Mauritius stamp. Why her, she had wondered? Because she knew Roger Essay, who had created a forged stamp, and because she was a collector of Mauritius issues. Roger was in her life just because she went with him to the gallery. Between Roger and the detectives, her spirits were blue even though her body felt good.

On top of that, the detective had told her not to leave town until further notice. Now, what was she going to tell her superiors at the office? What about the trip to visit Roulette Traders? How could she explain to the vice president why she is under suspicion by the police?

She started to walk fast. As she walked, she kicked through random piles of leaves and acorns. Squirrels darted past her to store them for the winter. She felt better after kicking something, even a little acorn.

When she returned to her condo, she checked her schedule on the computer. She would visit the Dockside store in Georgetown this afternoon to see how the wicker furniture was selling.

* * *

Stanley Roulette was having breakfast alone in the hotel coffee shop when Joe Coil walked in.

"Have some breakfast, Joe, and tell me about your investigation."

"Thanks. Just some coffee. I had trouble getting into Essay's house last night because he has quite a surveillance setup. I didn't find the stamp. If you think he took it I'd guess that he put it away in a bank vault. He has stamp albums but he didn't have an album for Mauritius stamps."

"Well, I am still convinced that he is the culprit. I am sure the detective also thinks so. Setenant was just here; the dealers he had spoken to had not heard from anyone about disposing of the stamp."

Stanley signed the check and they rose to leave.

Stanley left while Joe settled down, apparently enjoying the ambience. He buttered one of the pastries and poured more coffee. After finishing the coffee and pastry, Joe got ready to leave just as Andre came in and sat down in the same booth.

"Mr. Coil, I am glad I caught you. I wondered if I may ask you a hypothetical question. I hope you will not mind. If you had taken that stamp how would you dispose of it?"

Joe watched Andre closely as he responded.

"I don't know. I know very little about stamps, only what I learned on this assignment. In fact I was amazed to find out that stamp collecting was so popular."

Andre tried another tact.

"Stanley Roulette told me he knew who had the stamp. Do you know who has it as well?"

Joe Coil smiled at Andre.

"Even if I knew I couldn't tell you. Mr. Roulette is my client and I follow a strict confidentiality code for clients."

"Let me put it another way," persisted Andre. "Suppose you were asked for advice on how to sell it?"

"I don't get involved with stolen merchandise so I'd stay away from such a party."

"But, if someone were to contact you," asked Andre, "would you let me know. I would like to buy it if it were available and you would be paid well for your assistance."

"Well," Coil hesitated, "I'd give that some thought, but bear in mind this case is still open."

"Yes, well, this was just an academic discussion. Let it go at that. By the way, how do you figure the stamp was stolen?"

"I've thought about that," replied Joe. "and I don't have an answer. Whoever did it had to have access to the forgery and that's why a number of us are suspects. But I don't see how anyone could have switched the stamp under the noses of the guards. I'd suspect the director."

Andre nodded, said goodbye and they both left from the restaurant.

*   *   *

In his hotel room, Edward Postmark was restless. He understood the insurance would pay for his stamp but it would be a long drawn out process and he would not be paid the same amount that was bid. He could do no more until tomorrow. He expected to be back in London by now, instead he had to wait around until the detective gave him permission to leave. He was still baffled by how the stamp could have been stolen from under the gallery staff in the first place. He could no longer wait in his hotel room for word from the police or Watermark so he decided to visit the city. He thought of the pleasant time he had had at the Corcoran Art Gallery with that delightful lady, Olivia Block. She would not give him her phone number, but so be it; she said she would be leaving soon for London so perhaps she was gone.

* * *

Detective Beche had gotten up early. He called Sergeant Parcel who was on duty. Parcel had nothing new to report.

"I'm still working on the theory that we'd discussed Friday; that the robber had access to the forgery," said Beche. "For now, I'm ignoring the notion that someone created a second copy but left Essay's initials on it to implicate him. There's just no evidence to support it."

"There's no way to tell if the forgery is the one Essay made?" asked the sergeant.

"No, I explored that possibility with Essay." replied Beche.

"With the evidence of the forgery, I will question Essay and Couvert again. Essay is still my number one suspect."

"We've got three clues." Parcel said. "The Mauritius stamp that was dropped at the exhibit, the scratches on the glass and the forgery. But why would Essay drop the stamp since he doesn't collect Mauritius? Couvert could've dropped the stamp."

"Good point. But I have to go with what we have. I'll go see them now. I'll call you when I get more answers."

"Okay, I'll be here at the station."

No rest for the dreary, Beche thought, as he rang off.

* * *

From her suite, Marie placed a call to Olivia's room.

"Olivia, this is Marie. Have you time to chat? Andre has an appointment to meet someone. I thought we might have some coffee in the lounge. I want to be here when Andre returns."

"Sounds like a good idea. Stanley is in rather a dark mood. He must get back to his business in London but he cannot leave because of the detective."

"Andre cannot leave either and he is as nervous as a cat. We shall commiserate together. See you there."

They arrived at the lounge within a few minutes of each other and chose a table near the lobby.

"Marie, are you visiting your Embassy friend today?"

"But, no! Andre needs care today; perhaps another day."

"Is it not risky to keep seeing him while Andre is around?"

"Yes, Olivia, I suppose so. I do love Andre but I cannot resist Pierre!"

Olivia loved to hear Marie's French accent.

"Since Stanley will be busy with work on the phone tomorrow perhaps we can have lunch again. Maybe our British friend will reappear. I did not give him a telephone number."

"Cherie, he was true British military. You should have told him where you were staying."

"No, Marie, I think I did the right thing."

"Au contraire! But, perhaps you will think of a better way before you return to England. By the way, Andre believes we can leave by Wednesday, if the stamp is not recovered by then. If not, Andre will appeal to the French Embassy to intervene."

"Good. I shall tell Stanley."

The afternoon wore on and the ladies eventually retired to their suites to console their mates.

* * *

Roger awoke late on Sunday. As he lay in bed he thought about last night at the Nightingale; about the music, about Virginia. He felt a tremor through his body as he remembered holding her close when they danced. He thought the night had been perfect. Not only had he shared the evening with a beautiful, intelligent, interesting woman, he also had the genesis of a solution to Project 006. Of course, Virginia wasn't that enthusiastic about his interrupting their love making to record his thoughts. He wanted to talk to her but thought maybe she wouldn't be too friendly. He'd call her at the office tomorrow.

Roger put on his sweatsuit and went outside for his morning walk. As he walked through the neighborhood, his thoughts turned from Virginia to his two immediate problems; Project 006 and the stamp theft. After breakfast, he would get right to work on the project but thoughts of Detective Beche lay on his mind like heavy dew in the morning mist. He sensed he was still a suspect but he didn't know what to do about it. Just as he'd had no control over receiving the stamp, he felt powerless to overcome Beche's suspicions.

Roger dressed for his jog; perhaps the exercise would divert his mind from the detective. A half-mile from Roger's house was a small shopping center of seven stores and a gasoline station. Its location in the middle of the neighborhood was a factor in Roger's choosing to buy his home there. As usual, Roger did his jogging past the shopping center. The sun was just appearing on the horizon, not yet dispelling the chilly mist.

Trees were everywhere. The tall oak trees somehow survived the winter gales and the encroaching buildings. Colorful leaves and fat acorns were falling constantly. Squirrels scurried everywhere to hoard acorns for the coming winter. Ignoring the people, some sat still while eating acorns; others were burying them for another day's meal.

Despite the early hour, there were cars parked there, their drivers buying pastries and coffee at the bakery. The aroma of freshly baked bread drifted across the parking area. The intra-county bus chugging up the hill belched its exhaust gases, completely overcoming the sweet bakery smells.

Coming toward Roger as he started to jog were two young

women wearing very brief shorts, despite the cool air. Roger offered a good morning as he approached them. The women answered with a hello, smiled and tittered to each other after they passed Roger. Here and there, people were walking their dogs, some picked up after the dogs evacuated, some did not. Dogs were not Roger's favorite pet but he knew he could not walk a cat.

The gas station was already busy with Sunday drivers. The gas station was an anachronism; rarely did one find one in a residential neighborhood. Most stations were much larger and located where they could do a volume business. The other stores were not closed. When Roger shopped there after work, he admired the women coming out of the beauty salon with their dazzling coiffures.

Roger stopped to admire a large, white dog of unknown pedigree. He also admired the dog's owner, a woman who appeared to be his age wearing shorts. Roger remarked on the dog's clean fur but both the woman and the dog ignored him and continued on their way.

The sun was now over the horizon warming up the air and dispersing the morning mist. Walking under the canopy of maple trees with their brilliant yellow leaves, Roger headed back to his house for a shower and breakfast. He jogged back to his house without noticing the yellow and orange colored leaves still on the maple trees or sniffing the turpentine-like scent of the pines.

After a light breakfast, Roger went right to work on Project 006. Pamela's call to him at the casino had stirred his subconscious and may have triggered the idea that came to him on Virginia's sofa. The idea needed further development. He did not want to be caught short at the Monday morning staff meeting, so he started working on it before he watched the football game.

Roger went back to his laptop computer and pored over the notes he had made last night. Every now and then, thoughts of

Virginia and how delicious she smelled invaded his mind. He got a warm feeling at just the quick thought of Virginia, but then forced himself back to his work. He was beginning to see a solution. He worked right through the morning, made a snack for lunch and sat down to watch he game.

The way Roger watched a game was not relaxing. He multiplexed. When a commercial came on he worked on his bank statement and paid bills. He would do other routine work such as read his mail. Sometimes he listened to a game on the radio as he watched a different one on television. When two games were on two different TV stations, he would switch between the games at each commercial. He thought he soon would get a large screen, mosaic type of TV where he could see four networks at the same time. Then he could watch two games without switching. The commercials were so frequent he could still do some extracurricular work.

He also multiplexed during commercials when he listened to baseball on the radio. A few years ago when commercials occurred only between innings, Roger predicted that the stations would eventually present advertisements between pitches. It was not too many years later before it began to happen. Not after every pitch but enough to start the trend. On the radio where the announcer's comments were important to the continuity of the game, this trend had a negative impact on the listener. Baseball was a slow game anyway and the commercials only made it seem slower.

The telephone rang. He had a fleeting wish that it was Virginia calling, but it was Detective Beche.

"Sorry to bother you on a Sunday, but I need to question you again."

"Sure, come on over or do you want to meet somewhere?"

"No, I will come to your house."

Detective Beche arrived shortly.

"Pretty nice location. Any problem commuting to work?"

"No. The Metro train station is five minutes from here and conveniently stops right underneath my building."

Beche stared out the windows.

"But what is this all about," asked Roger, apprehensively.

"I want you to review the whole situation beginning with Postmark handing you the packet of stamps. There are some loose ends I need to clear up."

Roger blanched and was momentarily speechless.

"You know I have no motive to switch stamps!"

"Did you drop a Mauritius stamp at the gallery's exhibit and then return to pick it up? You fit the size of the person I chased to the Metro station. That was last Thursday."

"Of course not! I don't even collect Mauritius stamps. I wasn't in the gallery Thursday."

"According to Sergeant Parcel," Beche said, looking up his notes, "you were at the utility company not far from the gallery."

Roger was a bit startled at what these detectives knew about his whereabouts.

"No, I was busy at the simulator the whole time and then went right back to my office."

"Let's move on. Tell me about your meetings with Virginia Couvert. You know she collects Mauritius stamps and she was exposed to your forgery."

Roger stared out the window at the billowing leaves. His mind was racing, like the leaves being chased down the street by the wind. *I've got to get out of this predicament. I must come up with some ideas to get me off his list. What if this were an engineering problem? And how do I avoid involving Virginia?*

Roger repeated the sequence of events, answering Beche's questions and trying to come up with some reason to dissuade the detective.

"With all these possibilities," offered Roger, "it helps in my business to make up a matrix. Let's start with your list and see if we can conclude anything from it."

Roger opened his laptop and typed the list as Beche read off the names.

"These are the people who had access to your forgery; Winston Watermark, director of the gallery; Stanley Roulette, collector; Andre Setenant, collector; Joe Coil, Roulette's security guard; Edward Postmark, owner of the one penny orange; Roger Essay, collector; and Virginia Couvert, collector."

Roger winced at the mention of Virginia's name.

"How did she get on your list?"

"I added her name because she was with you both days, collects Mauritius stamps and could have taken the copy from your office."

Roger was stunned at the thought that she could even be a suspect. He forced his attention back to the matrix and added a column describing what each person collected based on information given to Beche from Watermark. It now looked like this:

    W. Watermark: doesn't collect but sees all issues
    S. Roulette: British Area
    J. Coil: not a collector
    A. Setenant: all countries' errors
    E. Postmark: not a collector
    R. Essay: Middle East
    V. Couvert: Indian Ocean countries including Mauritius

"Now," said Roger, "I'll add more columns on the chart and check those who fit under each:

    Column 1 - Those who saw the original.
    Column 2 - Those who saw the fake.
    Column 3 - Those who had heard of the fake.

As soon as Roger finished the chart, Beche checked the information on the computer screen.

"The original was seen by you, Postmark and Watermark in your office. Postmark, Watermark, Roulette and Setenant saw the original at the experts' meeting in the director's office. Those who saw the fake include yourself, Roulette, Setenant and Coil. Ms. Couvert was in your office after the counterfeit was returned to you."

Roger listened intently.

"So," continued the Beche, "everyone on that list plus their wives and girlfriends knew of the copy and could have made another copy. Anyone could make a Xerox copy from the catalog or an illustration in the media and color it. Your matrix has expanded the list instead of reducing it!"

Roger began to see where he was heading, as Beche showed him he forgery he had brought from the precinct.

"What's missing," said the detective, "is some way to analyze this fake to determine if it is indeed your forgery or a second copy. If I knew for a fact that this copy was the one you made, that would eliminate Column 3, the longest one."

"I can enlarge the copy to match the size of my original artwork and then compare the two."

"Lets do it!" Beche replied.

Roger and the detective drove to a nearby office service store open seven days a week where Roger had the forgery scanned into their computer. From the memory, a large copy was produced without color. They drove back to Roger's house where his printer made a large copy from the original data in his laptop.

"What's it look like?" Beche asked, staring at the copy.

"The lines are almost identical. This looks like the one I made. It would be a rare coincidence for someone to precisely duplicate my enhancements."

Detective Beche paced the living room, occasionally stopping to stare at the blow-up of the stamp.

"One more thing," Beche continued, "I saw your original blow-up in the director's office. This forgery could've been copied from that."

"But we can't prove there was only one copy."

Beche narrowed his eyes as though he did not want to hear

that answer.

"Great! All my suspects and more had access to that copy in his office!"

Beche started pacing again but his eyes were on Roger.

"Since the forgery you'd made disappeared from your office I'm going to assume you or someone else took it from your office. For now, I can eliminate the girlfriends, wives, except for Ms. Couvert who said she is not your girlfriend."

Roger was getting more upset; he got up and moved around.

"Tell me, from a collector's point of view, which one would be the most motivated to steal it?"

"That's easy," said Roger. "The collectors on your list would be highly motivated because they want it for their collections. The non-collectors would want it for money, but I don't know how that stamp could be sold."

"I spoke to a well known dealer," said Beche, "and he told me the stamp could not be easily sold because of publicity in the trade. The robber could get more if it were disposed of overseas and, if it's on the way there, my case never will be solved. I'm counting on the stamp still being here with one of our suspects."

"Your mentioning the dealers brings up a thought," said Roger. "If the thief is trying to sell the stamp in this country or overseas, I can contact a number of collectors on the chance that they might hear something."

"Interesting. How can you do that?"

"Watch this," replied Roger as he pulled his laptop computer over in front of the detective.

"I'm going to connect with the Internet which has an on-going stamp collectors' network. Then, we call up the code numbers to connect with the collectors' panel. Here we are."

The detective watched with fascination. He used a computer at work but only for word processing. He had not yet ventured into cyberspace territory.

"Now," continued Roger, "I will send the following message

to all the collectors who are listed as callers to the panel:

> Re Mauritius No. 1 issue. An unauthorized person may be trying to sell it in U.S. or overseas. Send E-mail immediately if you hear anything.

"Wow!" exclaimed Beche. "You mean all those people overseas will see this message?"

"Yes. Not only that but I can send it several more times during the day to make sure the word is out. This network of communication is almost infinite."

"Very impressive!"

While Roger worked with his laptop, the detective looked over his notes again. He got up and prepared to leave.

"Mr. Essay," said Detective Beche, in a somber tone. "The more I review this theft the more you fit my criteria defining the likely thief. You certainly had the opportunity as the holder of the original and the creator of the fake. You were at the gallery at crucial times. Your motive is money since you don't collect Mauritius stamps. Why don't you finish up what you started here and give me a call tonight. Your matrix might just lead somewhere."

Roger was crestfallen; he had failed to convince Beche.

* * *

Stanley and Olivia left the hotel to visit the original Dockside store in Georgetown. A taxi dropped them off at Wisconsin and M Street, Northwest, where they started walking amid the throng of people sightseeing and shopping.

This section of Washington housed a diverse and affluent population surrounding prestigious Georgetown University. Old streetcar tracks were still imbedded in some streets while cobblestones covered other streets. In the business area, the merchandise was pricey; the restaurants unusual. As they walked past Au Pied de Cochon, a well known French restaurant, Olivia told Stanley she had to bring Marie there for lunch.

Olivia wondered if this street was like Rodeo Drive. No, although there were exclusive stores, the clothes were not as trendy. It was more like Soho in London. The variety of shops, eateries and night club was as varied and there were several jazz clubs. On Halloween, Wisconsin Avenue looked like a mini Mardi Gras with thousands parading in costumes.

Stanley and Olivia commented that the area unique as they turned and walked toward the river where the Dockside store was located. Inside, Stanley looked at the products sold by his company. A large blackboard listed incoming ships, their cargos and when they would dock in Baltimore and other East Coast ports. Stanley steered Olivia to the jewelry section and bought her a uniquely designed pin from India.

Olivia wandered around while Stanley studied the blackboard. When she came back to the front, she was startled to see Stanley talking to a very attractive, younger woman.

"Oh, there you are," said Stanley when he saw Olivia, "I want you to meet Virginia Couvert. She is a manager with this company and will be visiting us on business next month. She is also a collector."

They exchanged pleasantries.

"I was telling Mr. Roulette that I came here today to check on a problem with the wicker furniture."

Virginia explained the problem. Olivia appeared to be listening but her eyebrows knit into a frown as she ogled Virginia. This is what worries me, thought Olivia. Stanley's face was illuminated as he hung on to Virginia's every word.

Stanley and Olivia said their goodbyes and headed back to the hotel. During the ride back Stanley chatted cheerily about Dockside but Olivia sensed he was enthusiastic about Virginia as well. She looked forlornly at the pin that Stanley had bought her.

*　　*　　*

When Virginia returned to her condominium, she found a message on her answering machine from Detective Beche. She stiffened with apprehension as she heard his request to call his pager as soon as she returned. She thought she had seen the last of him after the interview in her office. What, she wondered, could she tell him about that stamp theft? A bit of anger flared as she recalled that Roger had told the detective she had been in his office. She was still angry at Roger for last night.

She called Beche's pager and, while she was in the kitchen to get a bottle of coke, he called her back, saying he would be at her place within a half-hour.

"Ms. Couvert, I'm sorry to bother you on your day off," Beche said as he sat on the sofa, "but I must get some information from you."

Looking at his notes he recounted her involvement with Roger Essay and her trips to the gallery. While he was talking, Virginia thought, it was a good thing he didn't know she'd gone dancing last night with Roger or he'd even find that suspicious!

"You collect Mauritius stamps, saw the forgery in Essay's office and were a the gallery at crucial times. You could've taken the forgery and somehow replaced the original with it."

Virginia blushed deeply at the mention of the forgery, but she sat quietly, maintaining her composure.

"Much as I would like to own that stamp, I did not take it. I wouldn't know how to remove it from the exhibit. I know how valuable the one penny orange is so why would I take such a chance? Anyway, I'm not the avid collector that Roulette is."

"How do you know about Roulette?"

"Roger Essay told me about his threats when I was in his office."

Virginia stood, crossed her arms and tossed back her hair. She wanted an end to the interview. Detective Beche had no more questions and left. Virginia sat and drank some coke, contemplating the strange relationship she was having with Roger.

* * *

After Detective Beche left, Roger got right into the mess as if it were a new problem on Project 006. Even if he couldn't help Beche solve this theft he must at least sway suspicion away from himself. Roger poured himself some coffee and sat back on his sofa to think. Then, he got the phone book, looked up a number and dialed.

"Hello, Mr. Watermark? This is Roger Essay. Sorry to bother you at home but I need some information. Detective Beche was just here and went over the whole scenario again."

There was a long pause.

"I need your help so that I can reconstruct the way the theft was executed. If you will think back on each time the stamp was out of your vault, I can construct a timetable."

Winston began talking and went over each occurrence since he and Postmark had retrieved the original from Roger's office. Roger entered the data in his laptop. The screen showed two occasions when the stamp was on display. To help him recollect events, he set up a minute-by-minute timetable. Once the stamp was on the glass, the chart showed there were four hours during which the stamp could have been taken but it also showed there were two guards there at all times and hundreds of people looking at the stand. Then, around 8 p.m., there was a diversion. The guards were helping Winston remove the glass sheets holding the stamp.

Staring at the screen he suddenly snapped his fingers! *The spotlights were turned off at that moment. I remember it was suddenly dark in that area.* Roger made his own estimates of the time it took for Winston and the guards to close the curtains, shut off the spotlights and go behind the exhibit to remove the glass sheets. His numbers showed that at least ten seconds were available. In that time, he concluded, someone already behind the exhibit could have separated the glass and replaced the stamp.

Roger then set up the same display for the day of the auction. He didn't see any opportunity at that time. By coincidence, he had been watching the stamp and had, in fact, discovered the forgery on the exhibit before it was removed. He concluded the stamp was stolen when the exhibit was closed the day before the auction.

Adding to the notes under the chart, he typed in there were scratches on the glass and that something was used as a lever to pry apart the two panels of glass. Any flat, stiff and thin object could have been used. What would be handy to a person, an everyday object? Of course! A serious collector would have a pair of stamp tongs!

Roger got up and stretched. He poured some fresh coffee and went back to his desk.

Next, he opened his catalog to study the other clue, the stamp Beche had found on the floor presumably left by the culprit. The stamp was from Mauritius, catalog number 88b, and not an expensive stamp. Who would collect that? One who collects British Colonials, of course, and that, according to the matrix, would be Roulette and Virginia! Was it even remotely possible that Virginia would steal a stamp? Roger had to admit to himself that he hardly knew her. She certainly was an avid collector, recalling her desire to see the one penny orange.

The afternoon was waning; Roger still did not have a solution. He decided to take a break, eat something and then come back to it later. While he was eating, something almost subconscious told him to look at the catalog again. Then the light bulb flashed on the page! The stamp was an error. Now he had three possibilities!

He checked the catalog again and then looked at one of his albums. *Now, I can connect the two clues and I have a high probability as to who did it! But I have no proof. Lt. Beche will have to take it from here; he has the resources. This will get me off the hook!*

Roger grabbed the phone and dialed Beche's pager.

Detective Beche was at home watching the football games. Between commercials, he reviewed his notes on the case. Then the pager beeped.

"I know who and how!" cried Roger as soon as Beche called him back.

Roger rushed to elaborate on his analysis. The detective interrupted again and again to challenge his reasoning. After Roger finished, Beche conceded he had a good theory.

"What you say makes sense but I have no way to prove it. I could have gotten a warrant to search the premises of all of the suspects but I am sure the stamp is well hidden. It is so small it could be hidden anywhere. I need another way. I need a lure; some way to trap the thief."

Roger's mind was doing acrobatics; he had to convince Beche!

"Wait, maybe I have an idea. Assuming the thief is still in the area, suppose you plant something in the morning newspapers which hints that the original will be displayed tomorrow at the gallery, but, of course, the forgery will be shown instead. The thief is probably following the articles on the theft and will be curious; did he steal the original or another copy? It's a long shot."

Beche did not respond immediately.

"Assuming the thief is on my list of suspects, reads the paper, gets curious and shows up at the exhibit, then we can easily spot the culprit. I don't know; that's a stretch."

Roger looked again at his laptop screen.

"As a collector I would certainly be curious. There's no convenient way for the thief to compare the stamp with another original or with a forgery to make sure the stolen stamp is an original."

Beche began to pace, thinking it over.

"I also checked my Internet E-mail, "continued Roger, "and no one has indicated that the stamp was sold. So there's a good chance it's still in the area."

Beche stopped pacing.

"Okay," replied the detective. "They say 'curiosity killed the cat' so maybe it'll work here. I'll call the director to set it up and call the newspapers."

Beche rang off, but Roger felt deflated; he sensed that he was still a suspect.

*   *   *

At the Watergate, Peggy noted Winston's appearance was rather haggard. He had just gotten off the phone after Roger called about the sequence of events which surrounded the robbery. Peggy was making him a light dinner. Knowing Winston was in a depressed mood, they would not enjoy a fancy meal out today. After she had the food ready, she waited on the couch in the living room for Winston. She admired that room because it was furnished similar to his office, decorated with Oriental objects. The furniture throughout was in the style called Chinese Modern.

"Come on, Winston, I have a nice hot meal for you."

"Thanks, Peggy, but I can't eat much," said Winston, coming out of the bedroom. "That was Roger Essay on the telephone. He is trying to come up with some answers for the detective. I worry about the insurance company. Will they pay off or will they haggle the price down? Will they accuse me of insufficient protection?"

"I don't think they will argue. You'll get the full amount."

"I had hoped the police could find the culprit by now. The robber could easily have skipped the country. The chances of selling the stamp overseas were certainly greater than selling it in the states."

"Come eat something. You're working yourself into a tizzy!"

"I cannot figure how the thief could have gotten to the stamp. Am I overlooking someone obvious? I thought about the sequence of events all night and who could have had the opportunity. But I keep coming back to the fact that I alone handled the stamp."

Peggy was sympathetic but she could see that coddling him was not helping one iota. Once he got back to work tomorrow he would be diverted.

An hour later, the telephone rang, startling Peggy, who was reading the Sunday newspapers. Winston, who was pacing in front of the picture window, picked up the instrument. It was Detective Beche. He explained what he needed to do, and Winston agreed to call the press right away to get the article in the morning papers. Monday morning he would set up the exhibit again and be ready for the display on Monday noon. Winston expressed his doubts about the plan's success. In his opinion, the stamp was likely on its way overseas where it could easily be disposed of. This was a long shot but he had no other choice.

Winston hung up and began calling his press contacts even though it was Sunday. He discussed the pros and cons with Peggy and gradually became more enthusiastic about the possibility of the trap working. Peggy loved to hear his British accent when he was excited.

"This could work, Peggy. It would be a snare and a delusion."

Chapter 17

> *"Unlike doctors and lawyers held in awe,*
> *We take our engineers for granted;*
> *Think on that driving high on a bridge,*
> *Held only by beams that are canted."*
>
> *- Engineer's Lore - Anonymous*

Roger looked for the article in the morning paper. Sure enough a small blurb appeared on the front page which read:

RARE STAMP ON EXHIBIT

The London Gallery announced it would exhibit the rare Mauritius one penny orange. Last week the police were called in to investigate what appeared to be a theft of the rare stamp which reached a record sale of $1.5 million. The exhibit will be shown at the London Gallery today between 12 noon and 4 P.M.

Roger's electronics went through their ritual and got Roger off to work at the usual time. At his office, it was showdown time for his contribution to Project 006. He set up an early meeting with his three engineers so that it would end before the 10 a.m. staff meeting. Following the staff meeting, he would then take off for the gallery at noon to witness the display. He had to be there to make that trap work.

Roger's meeting started on time. His engineers reported that they had worked on the suggestions made by the technical director and one of them showed promise. They needed another week to complete the changes and run the tests. Roger expressed dissatisfaction with that schedule.

Normally, Roger was gentle with his staff. But suddenly he was snapping at his startled engineers. The pressure of being a suspect lay on his mind and made him impatient to solve the Project 006 problem so that he could concentrate on the trap. He put forth the idea which he had put in his laptop while on the sofa with Virginia. He frowned with a pang as thought briefly crossed his mind.

It had occurred to Roger that one of the software routines may have switched off a driver which made the instrument appear to be malfunctioning. The software was correct at normal, full power but when operating at reduced power, the instrument stopped working. This was a critical indicator which measured the temperature at the generator bearings. In the incident that Pamela had called him about last Saturday, the meter did not indicate the abnormally high temperature and the bearings nearly burned up.

It also had occurred to Roger that somewhere in the software code an unrelated instruction was switching off the driver. The instrument had been tested off-line and worked perfectly under all conditions. The software had been rechecked by his engineers to no avail. The suggestions of the technical director related to potential problems in the instrument itself, in the sensor or the converter. That was what struck Roger on Saturday night; something in the software switched off the driver signal that told the converter to pass a certain voltage to the instrument.

Roger went to the blackboard and hurriedly explained all this to the staff. He told his engineers to review unrelated areas to see if some code introduced a term into the equations when the power went below 100%. He ordered one of the engineers to call the power plant site and have Pamela set up a test which would confirm that the instrument driver emitted no signal when power output was less than 100%. That would strengthen Roger's theory that something was disabling the driver, but it would not explain what was causing it. The engineers took notes on the problem and left to look at the code. It was almost 10 a.m. so Roger headed for the staff meeting.

At the staff meeting, Project 006 was first on the agenda. Roger outlined his proposed solution and expected to confirm it by tomorrow. He said his team also was looking at a second possibility suggested by the technical director that would take the rest of the week. The vice president made some notes.

"Let me know as soon as you have the solution, Roger."

The vice president moved on to other problems while Roger read his mail and fidgeted impatiently for the noon hour to arrive. He kept looking at his watch. With all his multiplexing, Roger began to realize that he was at some upper limit of stress. He had seldom felt this irritable before.

The meeting finally broke up and the vice president asked Roger to linger a moment.

"Roger, I understand that a detective interviewed some of our people regarding an activity of yours. I trust it's not connected with work."

"No, sir. It is a personal thing. It'll positively not interfere with my work and I don't expect the detective will be back."

"I hope you're right; you have gained some notoriety lately!"

As he left the conference room, Roger looked chagrined; he could see the stares of the engineers as he walked to his office. He did not ant to speculate on what might happen if the trap failed. Imagine the commotion if Beche arrested him in his office!

* * *

Edward had a quick breakfast in the hotel coffee shop and

then left to see the sights. He failed to see the announcement in the newspaper about the exhibit of the Mauritius stamp. He had earlier placed a call to Winston to hear if there was any news about the theft but the gallery was not yet open. He then tried to reach Detective Beche but he was not available.

* * *

In the hotel suite, Stanley saw the notice in the paper and showed it to Olivia over breakfast in their suite.
"Look at this, Olivia. What do you make of it? Why are they showing it? This does not add up."
Stanley was disturbed; he could not finish his breakfast.
"What will you do, Stanley? Are you going to see it?"
"P'r'aps. I am thinking about it."
Olivia finished her breakfast. Stanley began pacing and then went to make a telephone call.

* * *

It was late morning when Marie saw the notice of the exhibit in the newspaper and showed it to Andre who suddenly paled.
"I shall call the detective. This cannot be; something is wrong!"
He tried to reach Detective Beche but to no avail.
"Andre, why do you not call the gallery?"
"I do not know what to do yet. I must understand what is behind this exhibit."
"Well, Andre, I have to do an errand. I shall meet you here this afternoon.
Andre made no comment; his mind was elsewhere. Marie put on her coat, blew him a kiss and left the suite. She took a taxi to her friend's apartment to rendezvous with Pierre Inverte. As soon as she opened the door, the forlorn look on Pierre's face

told her this tryst was not to be.

"Pierre, what is wrong? You look terrible!"

"I am concerned with a notice in the morning paper about the one penny orange stamp."

"Why should that concern you? You did not bid for it."

"Yes, but I must return to the Embassy and then visit the exhibit. My regrets, cherie; I shall explain later."

"Au revoir, Pierre."

They embraced and left the apartment to go their separate ways. Marie thought how strange it was that both Pierre and Andre reacted the same way to that notice in the paper.

* * *

When Virginia got to work, her computer flashed a message that she was to meet with the vice president, her supervisor, as soon as she returned. She took off her coat, checked her hair and went upstairs to see him as requested.

The vice president was free and she went right in.

"Have a seat. I've some news for you. I have to tell you that I've been directed to cut out a level of management as a result of the reengineering effort that is taking place. Regrettably, your position will be combined and absorbed by another manager."

Virginia really did have to sit down. After all these years with the company she was going to be let go!

"I can't accept this. My work here has always been exceptional and now this!"

"It has nothing to do with your performance," he replied. "It relates only to the need to flatten the organization and reduce the complexity of how we do business. Please go to the Personnel Department and they will fill you in on the details of the separation package. I am sorry."

The Personnel Administrator advised her that she had to leave that day and take her possessions with her. Her salary would continue for six months. Her health insurance would continue if she paid the premiums. Details of her pension and other matters would be spelled out in her separation package.

Devastated, Virginia left the Personnel Office, picked up her briefcase and the few items she had on her desk. She was never one to clutter her office with mementos and pictures. She headed for the elevator. What a day! How could this happen to her, she wondered? The reengineering effort included several interviews regarding her duties. Being in the marketing department she could not conceive of a reduction in staff.

What a blow to her career, she thought as she walked toward the subway station. She had always thought she would achieve a vice president's position and participate in the corporate perks, especially the stock option plan. It had always bothered her that the new projects put forth by the chief executive officer were done for the benefit of Wall Street analysts to help publicize the company. That was one approach which often worked to get the stock price up. Telling the analysts about new projects or new products was a sure-fire way of getting positive recommendations to buy their stock. She had figured out that one of the objectives, often the main objective, of top management was to raise the price of the stock to enhance the value of their stock options.

She recalled the latest project put forth by the management to the analysts was a proposal to merge with an import/export house in Malaysia. The management made a number of trips there and talked to a half-dozen companies. This effort was spread over many months during which the president of Dockside International presented the Wall Street analysts with glowing charts showing how profits would grow after the merger. The stock started to climb up slowly to a new bias line. Virginia knew some of the marketing managers at several of the far eastern companies and found out from them that the discussions were superficial. After the stock went up, the trips stopped and the project faded away.

Virginia understood the game. She had wanted to be a player but it would have to happen at another company. She had some ideas and would sit down and develop a plan of action. She would take a positive approach to her career problem. Virginia got on the Metro car and decided not to brood. She refused to indulge in the time-honored traditional moping over a drink at the local tavern.

As the subway tore through the tunnels, she reminisced about her now-defunct career at Dockside International. It always bothered her that her salary seldom put her income ahead of the cost of living. The so-called "merit raises" that she had received every year were not really raises based on performance. They amounted to increases to keep up with the cost of living. One evening when she was working on taxes she reviewed her years of work and plotted out her salary growth against the inflation curve. When she subtracted the promotion increases, which were not merit raises, her salary was close to but behind the inflation curve.

In other words, the only way she could stay ahead of inflation was to get promotions. This was not easy to do for a female in a company that was mostly male. In fact, it would become harder to do even for men because there would be fewer echelons that one could be promoted to. The career ladder was getting shorter as a result of the downsizing activities in many corporations. The neatly packaged table of organization charts would soon be obsolete. A "flat organization" eliminates the "career ladder" that used to be discussed with employees as part of their annual performance reviews.

This thought reminded her of a date she had last year with a computer expert who was job hunting. He mentioned one company that had called him in for interview. During the session, he asked to see their organization chart to see where he would be placed. The lady from personnel interviewing him said there was no organization chart. In fact, to keep herself informed on what was going on she made up her own organization chart on a large sheet of brown paper! It changed almost every week, she said. The lady probably did not know it, thought Virginia, but that chart was a sign of the future corporate structure.

As she rose to get off the train, she said to herself, this move may be a blessing in disguise because she now has an opportunity to parlay her experience into a higher paying position. Had she stayed at Dockside International, her next stop up the organization ladder was the vice president's job. The present vice president was only ten years her senior and not likely to retire soon or leave the company. It was unlikely she would get that job over an older male.

She had to devise a way to set up a position where she was the prime mover. Her experience and her ability were her security. She must find a way to start in a company at the officer level so that her position would be protected by stock options and golden parachutes. Any other position would leave her vulnerable and insecure. She would find a way, she concluded as the Metro car arrived at her stop.

Back in her condo, she made a pot of coffee and sat down at her desk. She started to make an action list but when she wrote "Roger," she got up and stepped out on her balcony. Roger was on her mind, wondering if he was the right man. He was physically attractive and polite but one date was not enough to tell. His simultaneous romance with his laptop was upsetting but he did seem attracted to her. Did she find a friend at the same time she lost her job, she wondered?

Suddenly, Virginia remembered she had wanted to go back to the gallery to see the one penny orange display. She went inside to get a coat and yet, she thought, she had a lot of calls to make.

* * *

At the gallery, a crowd was building and excitement was

mounting. Some returned to see the rare stamp again; others came for the first time because of the article in the paper. Not long after Roger arrived, the guards got the visitors to form a line, which soon extended from the second floor to the first. Roger met Detective Beche, Sergeant Parcel and the director near the exhibit where they had a clear view of the line of people.

"I don't know who will show up," said Beche, "but I hope it will be one of the suspects or someone who might be suspicious. Mr. Watermark, you know many of the viewers. Please study them and see if any suspicions come to mind."

The parade continued as the crowd got larger. By 2 p.m. there were no clues coming forth from Winston. He knew many of the visitors but so far none raised a suspicious note in his mind. Occasionally, an expert showed up and confronted Winston about the authenticity of the stamp on display.

"Winston," said Dr. Seebeck quietly, "I am concerned that your stamp out there is a forgery! What is going on?"

"Hello, Dr. Seebeck," replied Winston, sotto voce. "I will explain as soon as the show is over."

The afternoon wore on. It did not look like the bait was going to be taken. It was now 3:30 p.m. Beche and Watermark began to pace restlessly. Winston looked forlornly at the detective and the detective looked at his notes. He huddled with Sergeant Parcel.

Beche was beginning to think about what to do if this ploy failed. He would have to re-interview his suspects again. He knew he could not keep Roulette, Setenant and Postmark in the States much longer. He would talk again to the women to see if one of them had something to hide. Not a pleasant prospect. He shunned the thought that the thief was successful.

In another thirty minutes, he would retain Essay, call the other suspects to come to the gallery and begin a long round of questioning. The detective called Sergeant Parcel over and then noticed Marie Setenant had entered the line and a well dressed man talking to her.

"Who is the man with Ms. Setenant?" asked Beche, turning to Winston.

"That's Pierre Inverte. He often comes here from the French Embassy."

"What is his connection with Ms. Setenant?"

"That I do not know, detective."

When he turned back to watch Marie, the detective noticed the man had disappeared. His mind was alert again. Was that man connected with Marie or did he meet her here by chance?

At 4 p.m. the line was shut down by the guards. Those still in it continued to move along. Marie stood in front of the one penny orange, studying it through the magnifier on the glass. The detective faced her when she turned and started to leave.

"Ms. Setenant, you may remember me, Detective Beche."

"Ah, yes, I do remember; you questioned me."

Beche's concentration was wobbling again. *The perfume and the accent! I must keep my mind on my work!*

"Ms. Setenant, where is your husband?"

"Why do you ask me this question?" Marie replied evasively.

Beche's mind was back on track. Did her husband send her to examine the stamp? Or the man from the Embassy? She had already seen the exhibit, he thought quickly, and recalling Essay's matrix, she did not collect Mauritius stamps so why would she return unless someone sent her? In which case he may be waiting for her.

"One moment, please." He turned to talk to Winston.

"Detain her for just ten minutes!"

As soon as Winston began talking to her, he and the sergeant quickly left the floor and went outside. They scanned the area looking for Setenant or Inverte. Beche spotted a taxi waiting across the street. He alerted Parcel and they walked slowly behind the taxi to surprise the passenger.

When the passenger saw Beche cross the street and turn toward the cab, he jumped out and ran to the subway station, dodging and shoving people in the way. Beche and Parcel ran after him but he was swift and was well into the subway station before his pursuers could catch up with him.

The suspect ran down the stairs, jumped on the five-story high "UP" escalator and pushed his way down through the passengers who were coming up. He turned around just as Beche and Parcel entered the stairwell.

"Wait outside!" yelled Beche. "Just in case he doubles back!"

He then ran down the stairs and walked on the "DOWN" escalator scanning everywhere for the sight of his quarry, who, with his sunglasses on and looking away, was now on the "UP" escalator and passing Beche going down. He got off the escalator and went up the stairs to the street. He started to rush away from the station but ran right into Sergeant Parcel who grabbed him, put one cuff on his wrist and the other on a metal sign post.

Detective Beche came back from the station and confronted Andre Setenant.

"Please empty your pockets, sir," said Lt. Beche. "I know you have the stamp there."

"No, I do not have it. You can search me!"

The search did not produce the stamp.

"Why did you run?" asked Beche, his face showing the disappointment at not finding the stamp. "You had a reason for running!"

"I was a suspect! I did not want to be arrested!"

The three of them were all sweaty despite the coolness in the air. Together, they headed back to the gallery where the others were waiting. Marie Setenant came forward quickly to meet her husband and addressed him sharply in French. Detective Beche held Andre by the cuffs.

"Sergeant, I want to book Mr. Setenant but the stamp is not on him," said Beche.

It was back to the drawing board for Detective Beche. He

and the sergeant huddled together talking quickly and staring at Roger, who was looking at his matrix on the laptop screen. The crowd was winding down and Winston was talking to customers as they were leaving. Roger looked up from his laptop and stared at the director and the visitor he was addressing. His eyes suddenly lit up and he typed rapidly on the laptop keyboard. He stared at the screen, looking again at the listed assumptions.

Roger went to Lt. Beche and Sgt. Parcel. He showed them his laptop screen and discussed his rationale.

"What if our assumption was wrong and someone did make a second copy?" said Roger. "On that basis, look again at the list of suspects."

Beche and Parcel stared at the screen, then went to talk to Winston's visitor.

"Sir, I'm Detective Beche and this is Sergeant Parcel. We're investigating the theft of the Mauritius stamp. We have reason to believe you might have knowledge of it and we need to search you."

"I object to this and will call a lawyer!"

"Alright, you can do that but I'll have to hold you until I get a warrant."

While he spoke, Roger noticed the visitor holding something behind his back, trying to place it in his briefcase on a table. Roger moved behind him, picked it up and showed it to the detective. It was a magnifier. Roger handled the magnifier and studied it. It was an unusual European make that looked like a small telescope because it carried three different lenses. He put it to his eye and peered at a light. Then he removed the other two lens and there was the one penny orange in a plastic envelope, small enough to nest on the lens!

Perplexed, Beche just stared at the stamp and at Roger. Winston studied the stamp and confirmed it had the right initials on it and thus must be the original.

"This is it!" exclaimed Winston.

"I'm placing you under arrest," said Detective Beche, "for the grand theft of the Mauritius stamp!"

He then turned to Parcel and told him to read him his rights. As the Sergeant was taking the thief to the police car, Lt. Beche commiserated with Andre and Marie Setenant.

"My apologies to you, but you were unfortunately a suspect."

He turned to Roger.

"Thanks for your help, Mr. Essay. If I need a counterfeit stamp I'll know who to call! "

He then addressed Winston who was still staring at the stamp in his hand.

"Mr. Watermark, I'll have to take both stamps with me. Why don't you come with me and after we document this I'll get them back to you as soon as possible."

The others stood around as though waiting for someone to tell them it was all right to leave. They looked stunned at what had just transpired, unwilling to acknowledge who the thief was.

Chapter 18

> *"Ye tradeful merchants that, with weary toil,*
> *Do seek most precious things to make your gain,*
> *And both the Indias of their treasure spoil,*
> *What needeth you to seek so far in vain?"*
>
> - *"Amoretti" by Edmund Spenser*

On his long flight home, Edward Postmark relaxed in the rear of the first class section. He had deposited his check from the sale of the Mauritius one penny orange into a Washington bank account. In London, he would transfer the funds to his own bank. With a scotch and water in front of him, Edward recalled the telephone call from Winston Watermark who had excitedly reported to him that the one penny orange was recovered. Edward had been stunned to learn who had stolen the stamp. He had suspected Roulette, given the strong arm tactics used by his hired hand, Joe Coil.

The flight attendant interrupted his thoughts briefly as she placed his meal on the tray, smiled and asked if he needed anything. She was quite attractive, Edward thought, shaking his head and returning the smile.

On the way to the airport, Edward had stopped at Roger Essay's office to say goodbye. To offer his appreciation for Roger's honesty and initiative, Edward produced his checkbook and wrote out a check. Roger objected and declined to take it.

"That check could certainly buy a lot of stamps," Roger said, "but it won't buy the one penny orange!"

They laughed and shook hands as Edward departed, leaving the check on Roger's desk.

At the airport, waiting for his flight, Edward had called Penny Cancel in London but had been unable to reach her. As he slowly ate his meal, Edward wondered if she had resolved her dilemma with two suitors. He remembered their intimate evening together before he left London. After he finished dining, he leaned back into his seat, closed his eyes and imagined Penny providing him with a warm homecoming.

* * *

Virginia sat on her sofa staring at the living room drapes which she had not opened. The semi-dark room reflected her somber mood. The memory of the firing still haunted her, as if a spider was crawling on her blouse. She had never been fired and, despite her bravado attitude upon learning the news, she was devastated. Being a suspect in the theft of the one penny orange had not helped her disposition either. At least that problem had gone away. Sergeant Parcel had called to tell her the case was solved and she was free to leave the city. She rose from the sofa, went into the kitchen to get some coffee.

To make matters worse, Roger had not called. Perhaps that was just as well. She liked him but did not know what to make of his propensity to multiplex things. And yet, he certainly had charm. Anyway, she needed to focus her attention on becoming gainfully employed. Roger would only be a distraction right now.

Slowly, in the silent room, she made some decisions. She would arrange to visit Stanley Roulette in London and convince him to set up a Washington distribution center for his U.S. customers. She knew a good deal about Roulette Traders, Ltd., enough to know that Roulette was ready for expansion. She believed she could put forth the arguments and numbers to show him the advantages of this move. She would develop a business plan that he could present to his board of directors. Stanley Roulette was impressed with her knowledge of the import/export market and she thought she could work well with him. She had confidence in her business acumen. Before the layoff, her boss had admitted that she had been right about the best way to salvage the wicker furniture. She had known she was right but she had to find a way to convince people she knew what she was doing.

Next, she made up her mind about Roger. Perhaps she would even consider becoming more involved with him. She liked him and he obviously was attracted to her. She began to perk up. Maybe all this would work out for the best after all. She rose from the sofa and opened her drapes. The sunlight filled the room, adding warmth to her thoughts. That was her plan, she thought, and it was that simple.

* * *

Roger was back at work. He met with the three engineers and learned that there was progress. Pamela's test at the site confirmed that the instrument driver signal was definitely dropped when the plant power went below 95% power. The engineers told him they had found some spurious code that was interrupting the signal. One more run through of all the input-output signals should confirm the solution. Roger was elated and told them to report back at 2 p.m. for a final review.

Detective Beche called to thank him for his help in solving the one penny orange mystery. He apologized for treating Roger as a suspect but Roger, he said, matched his own matrix, as he put it. After Beche rang off, Roger's thoughts returned to the trap and the realization of how close he had come to being arrested. He was still shocked at the identity of the thief. The memory of the theft began to fade from his mind but not so the memory of Virginia.

Roger picked up the telephone and dialed Virginia's office number but there was no answer or recording. Roger thought perhaps she was home so he looked up her number in the telephone directory and dialed. She answered the phone.

"Hello, Virginia, it's Roger Essay. I was calling to ask you out again," said Roger, tentatively.

"Well, maybe another time. The reason I'm home today is because I lost my job."

"I'm sorry to hear that. Why don't we get together Saturday night and talk about it. I'd like to help."

"Thanks, Roger. I don't think I would be good company. Perhaps another time."

After hanging up the phone, Virginia went to her balcony and gazed at the leaves still flitting down from the many trees which surrounded her building. Roger went back to typing a report to the technical director then stopped suddenly. He took out a small radio and tuned it to a big band station. He rang Virginia's phone again.

"Virginia" said Roger over the sound of the music, "I want you to reconsider. Let's go dancing again at the Nightingale Casino. It'll help clear your mind from your problem."

The big band music drifted over the telephone. Virginia hesitated.

"Well, okay, Roger, maybe you're right. Where's that music coming from?"

Roger quickly shut off the radio.

"I'll pick you up at 8 o'clock."

"Yes, that's fine. I want to show you the rest of my collection that you did not see."

Virginia hung up; her face lit up as she went back to her balcony. Part of her plan was already working.

*   *   *

Winston was back at the gallery assembling the next auction. He was busier than ever. The stamp theft incident had only brought more attention to his business and the telephone hadn't stopped ringing since early morning. The ordeal would linger with Winston for a long time considering it could have cost him his reputation and business. The memory of the identity of the culprit brought on a momentary pang and disbelief.

He interrupted his thoughts and work, picked up the telephone and dialed Peggy. He spoke to her for only a moment then hung up the telephone. Smiling, he thought about how he would make up for his behavior of the past few weeks.

* * *

In their hotel suite, Andre and Marie were arguing over the article in the morning paper.

"You see, Andre, it could have been your name in the paper and I would have been mortified! Whatever possessed you to try to take the stamp away from the owner? Forget about that stamp and get on with your life.

"Oui, Marie, you are right, of course. I am glad now that no one knows I tried to take the stamp. I know that I was quite obsessed with the idea of owning that stamp. I fantasized about it constantly but when you told me at the auction that the bidding was likely to be high, I realized then that I had lost the chase and so had Stanley."

"Why did you return on Monday and insist that I check the initials on the stamp?"

"Because the forgery fooled so many people, I began to wonder if the stamp was another fake. I was paranoid I suppose. I did not want to go myself because I was a suspect. If the stamp on display was another forgery I thought I might still find out who took the original and possibly negotiate a price!"

Marie allowed Andre to rant.

"I could not stand it," cried Andre. "Stanley was going to outbid me and I could not allow that to happen. I even tried to out maneuver him in London where I engaged an agency to get the stamp away from the owner. The twins failed miserably."

"Were you the one who dropped that Mauritius stamp at the exhibit?" asked Marie.

"Yes, I had purchased it - a seldom seen error - at the gallery and then accidentally dropped it in front of the stand. I went back to get it but fled when I saw the detective. Had he caught me I would have been arrested!"

Marie moved about the room, restlessly.

"And yet, Marie, had the twins been successful in London, I could have bought the stamp from the owner. I would have beat out Stanley Roulette!"

Andre was beginning to wind down and excused himself to another room. Marie glanced furtively at the telephone and then called Pierre. She arranged in code to meet him at her friend's apartment, as Andre returned to the living room.

"Andre, I must visit the Embassy before we leave Washington. I shall return in a few hours."

Andre paused to watch her depart, then called after her.

"Marie, what do you need at the Embassy?"

Marie did not reply as she closed the door.

Pierre was waiting for her with a bottle of champagne to wish her a bon voyage. They went straight into each other's arms, shedding their clothes as they inched their way to the bedroom. Their few moments of passion passed and, not wanting to linger, Marie began dressing.

"When we last met, Pierre, why were you so distant?" asked Marie.

"I did not want to upset you, Marie, but I had heard that Andre was a suspect in that stamp theft case so I wanted to get to the gallery and see what was going on. I arrived in time to see the detective chasing Andre! I reported back to the Embassy that we might have a problem, but of course we were relieved to find out that Andre was not involved in the theft of the stamp after all."

Marie could not stay any longer; she gave Pierre a long kiss goodbye. As he departed, he promised to call her on his next trip to Paris. Marie left the key to her friend's apartment on a table along with a thank you note. She would, she thought, send her a gift from Paris. She took one last look at the apartment, warming at the thought of Pierre in her arms and left.

* * *

On the flight to London, Stanley Roulette and Olivia Block sat in the front of the first class section trying desperately to relax. Two days ago, Stanley had received a telephone call from Sergeant Parcel's informing him it was all right to leave the city. The stamp had been recovered and the robber was in jail. Stanley was shocked at the identity of the culprit.

As they tried to relax, Stanley talked incessantly about the auction. Perhaps, he told Olivia, he should have bid higher; but Olivia reminded him that no matter how high he would have bid the Japanese collector would have outbid him.

"Olivia, Joe Coil called before we left. He had spoken to the detective about what happened at that exhibit yesterday. It was a good thing I did not go because it was a trap."

"A trap?

"Yes. The detective hoped the thief would return to make sure he had the original."

Stanley repeated the story to Olivia.

"I cannot believe it!

"Yes, it's true. The robber was a total shock to me. The mystery was solved by the detective with the help of that engineer who duped me with his forgery. In any event, I told Joe his assignment was complete."

"I spoke to Marie before we left. She was quite upset. She said Andre had become obsessed with the Mauritius stamp and had done some stupid things but she did not elaborate."

"Well, I can sympathize, Olivia. It would have been a feather in my collector's cap."

"I, for one, am glad it's over. When we get to London there is a new subject I would like to talk to you about."

Olivia looked to Stanley for a response, but he was lost in his own thoughts.

"I suppose, Olivia, I will have to wait until another one penny orange turns up. After all, the fun is truly in the chase! I shall make inquiries of the dealers for stamps from other countries that are missing from my collection."

Olivia rose from her seat to visit the lavatory. As she turned away from Stanley, she suddenly caught the eye of the stranger she had met in the Chinese restaurant. She blushed as he smiled and approached her.

"Stanley, this is Mr. Edward Postmark."

"Ah, yes, we have met several times. Olivia, he was the owner of the Mauritius stamp. I did not know you two had met."

When Olivia realized who Edward was, she felt her knees give way as though the aircraft had suddenly dropped a thousand feet.

"Yes," Edward was saying, as he winked at Olivia, "we met at the gallery. Small world!"

Olivia had said nothing to Stanley about the afternoon she and Edward spent at the Corcoran Art Gallery. Olivia excused herself as Edward turned to walk back to his seat.

"Wait up, Edward, here is my card," said Stanley. "Let me know where you will be staying in London. I would like to show you my collection."

"Sorry, old chap," said Edward. "I think I would rather not."

Edward returned to his seat. Olivia soon returned to her seat, avoiding eye contact with Edward.

"A pleasant chap, Olivia," said Stanley, not at all rebuffed by Edward's rejection. "I offered him my card and invited him over to look at my collection, but he refused. He was quite put out."

"Stanley, I had no idea he was the owner of the one penny orange."

Olivia turned her face away to hide the light of an idea in her eyes and the sudden blush on her face. Perhaps her plan to marry Stanley would work out after all, with Edward Postmark's help, of course. *Before we land, I will get Edward's address. In London, I will encourage him to accept Stanley's invitation to see his collection. While he is there I am sure I can get him to make a fuss over me. Stanley is possessive in all things as he is with stamps. This is the subtle approach I was looking for. When Stanley sees that Edward is interested in me, Stanley will marry me!*

She smiled at Stanley and rang for a drink.

* * *

The day was sunny, crisp and cool, the kind of autumn weather that makes the city look brighter. It matched the buoyant mood of Detective Ted Beche as he arrived at the police station. With a piping hot cup of coffee, he sat at his desk to wrap up loose ends on the case of the one penny orange mystery with Sergeant Parcel. Beche was enjoying the notoriety from his successful investigation. Some of his colleagues kidded him about his extensive knowledge of philately. For someone who knew so little of philately, he was now the precinct's expert and had gained the respect of his superiors. He told Parcel that perhaps he should start a collection. If nothing else he could learn about other countries, something he had never thought about, being confined to one city. Up until now he had never heard of Mauritius. Sergeant Parcel listened without comment. "Well, Sergeant, this was a unique case," said Beche. Without Essay's matrix, as he called it, we would not have set the trap."

"I have to agree, sir," said Parcel. "It looked like the trap failed until Essay pointed out the thief."

"Dr. Seebeck couldn't resist returning to the scene of his crime. Luckily, he had the original stamp with him."

"How come he wasn't on the list of suspects?" asked Parcel.

"After we arrested Dr. Seebeck, I remembered Setenant telling me about him when I interviewed Marie Setenant in their suite. Somehow my notes are vague about that interview."

Beche dared not confess to Parcel that he had been spellbound in Marie's presence.

"Why did Essay get so involved in trying to help you?" Sergeant Parcel asked.

"He told me he knew he was a suspect, which weighed on his mind, so he felt he had to do something to get off my list. We were lucky Essay was the type of person who liked to solve problems. He was driven to find solutions; he hated loose ends."

"That worked out; you had the suspect working on the case!"

"Essay had made up the matrix that identified my suspects, what stamps they collected and if they saw the original and/or the forgery. I told him of two clues: a Mauritius stamp was found behind the exhibit and there were scratches on the top of the glass panels. The stamp clue pointed to Roulette or Virginia Couvert, both of whom collect Mauritius. Essay suspected Setenant because the stamp was an error."

"How could one have gotten the forgery?" asked Edward.

"When Roulette, Coil and Setenant left Essay's office, any one of the three could have taken it. Virginia Couvert was also in his office and could have taken the fake, except we now know a second forgery was prepared by Dr. Seebeck. Essay still doesn't know what happened to the copy that he'd made."

Beche paused, sat back and stretched. Then he went on.

"Of those four, Essay thought he had it narrowed down to

Roulette and Ms. Couvert because of the dropped stamp. He looked in the catalog once more and then realized the stamp had an unusual error which he'd missed earlier; the surcharge was inverted. Now he had three candidates because Andre Setenant collected errors on stamps."

"How did he pin it down to one?"

"Since Roulette had a nearly complete collection of the British area, he assumed he did not collect stamp errors. Essay said most errors or variations are not illustrated in albums. He knew that Virginia Couvert didn't collect errors, so he eliminated both of them. That left Andre Setenant. I had noted that Setenant was in the experts' meeting before the stamp went on display so he'd gotten a close look at how the display was assembled. Essay also figured he'd used his stamp tongs to separate the glass panels. That was the theory Essay presented. He was right about the tongs but wrong about who used them."

"Did you buy it?"

"I wasn't impressed. I agreed that Setenant, like Roulette, had plenty of motive but we had no proof. Essay then suggested the trap and, fortunately for both of us, it worked."

"And, of course, Setenant sent his wife to the trap."

"Yes. He sent Marie to check out the initials on the stamp. I suspected he was outside and we caught him at the Metro Station. It appeared that Essay's theory was correct but Setenant did not have the stamp. Luckily, Dr. Seebeck showed and, when Essay saw him talking to the director, he recalled Dr. Seebeck's curiosity about the forgery and how it had been created it. At that point, Essay assumed there was a second copy with Essay's initials on because Dr. Seebeck did not have access to Essay's forgery. That made him fit the matrix and luckily he had the stamp with him."

"That was a close call! He could've gone back to London."

Sergeant Parcel looked at his watch and got up to leave.

"Why did Dr. Seebeck steal the stamp?"

"He told me he began his scheme after appraising it in London.

After all those years of expertising so many of the world's most valuable stamps, he finally decided he would own one himself. By the time he decided to go after the stamp, Postmark had already left London for the U.S. Seebeck came to the auction seeking a window of opportunity to somehow steal that stamp. He even hired someone to grab Postmark's briefcase when he arrived at the gallery. He said he saw the blow-up of the one penny orange in the director's office when he attended the preview. After Essay told him how he had made the fake, he slipped into the director's office, borrowed the print, made a reduced copy and then returned the print to the office."

"So Seebeck left Essay's initials on the second copy to confuse us," said Parcel. "Why did Dr. Seebeck enter the trap?"

"Seebeck had no reason to believe he was a suspect so he thought it was safe for him to see what was on exhibit."

Beche turned his mind back to his work; he had to complete his report on the now-famous one penny orange robbery. It was a crime with a strange motivation. When he had interviewed Dr. Seebeck, he realized the motive in the case was even stronger than he had anticipated. Dr. Seebeck was absolutely driven by an increasing envy of collectors who owned rare stamps.

"Well," said Parcel, "I admit I learned something about stamp collecting."

Sergeant Parcel stood for a moment staring at Beche, who obviously was distracted, and then left. Beche leaned back in his chair and grinned as he thought about Marie Setenant. He sniffed as though her perfume was still there. Lieutenant Beche finished his report and opened the file of his next case.

*   *   *

During the drive to the nightclub, Roger chatted about the new band playing there while Virginia was unusually quiet. Roger didn't mind; he knew she was blue because of her job loss and he wanted to divert her.

"Roger," she said, changing the subject, "did you go the London Gallery Monday to see the exhibit?"

"Why, yes. I did go."

"I'd planned to go there for a last look at the one penny orange but I stayed home instead to work on finding a new position. I had to make a lot of telephone calls."

The hairs on Roger's neck stood up. He said nothing but thought, what if she'd been there? The detective would've arrested her! He changed the subject back to music, not wanting to rehash the unpleasantness of the theft.

The night air was chilly, almost frosty, as Roger and Virginia left his car, trampled the brown leaves, and entered the Nightingale Casino. The warmth on the dance floor and the music contrasted with the cold silence outside. During dinner and between sets, Virginia told Roger of her plan to set up a company with Roulette Traders. Remembering his confrontation with Stanley Roulette, Roger was not enthused about her involvement but felt it was not for him to discourage her.

As the evening progressed, Roger kept looking at Virginia, convinced that he wanted to spend more time with her. This time, Virginia appeared less awkward dancing to the music which was new to her. She smiled, swaying in his arms as they danced nearly every set. Finally, they left the casino and soon arrived at her apartment building.

"Well, here we are," said Roger as he pulled into her parking area. "I don't know if you want me to come up after last Saturday."

"Please come up, Roger. I want to show you the stamps you missed last week."

In her apartment, Virginia went to her kitchen to brew some coffee. While she was there, Roger wandered around the living room apartment. On his first visit, he was so keyed up about the stamp theft and his first date, he paid little attention to her apartment. He felt comfortable, he thought, amid the modern furnishings. The room was furnished with blond, contemporary furniture throughout. She had a Japanese doll, several brass objects that looked to be from India and a wooden Chinese warrior carving. A large porcelain camel sat on the floor supporting a green plant.

The aroma of brewing coffee soon filled the room as Virginia brought in a tray holding a bottle of brandy, coffee and pastries.

"I like your decor, Virginia. I didn't take a good look the last time I was here. You are adventurous with this modern furniture."

"Thank you. I've had the advantage of buying from my former firm. You were right, Roger, going out tonight did take my mind off my problems."

They sat on her couch to look at her albums as they sipped coffee laced with a little brandy.

"We were looking at India when you swept me into the bedroom!"

She finished turning the pages of India stamps and then pulled out her Mauritius album. When she opened the album Roger sat up and stared. There on page one was a one penny orange!

"Where did you get that?!" he shouted, spilling coffee on the tray.

"It's your copy. I meant to tell you last Saturday but we didn't get to it! This is the copy that was in your office. I wanted to use it as a space filler. I wanted to surprise you by highlighting it in my album."

"I'm shocked! If you'd told me you had the forgery, I could have gotten off the detective's suspect list! He could have arrested me! We thought all along that the original was replaced with my copy!"

"I'm truly sorry. When I read about the theft I assumed another copy was made by the thief."

"Didn't Detective Beche ask you about the forgery when you were in my office?"

"Yes, he did, but I told him I didn't see it because I thought another copy replaced the original so I saw no reason to get involved."

Roger got up and paced. Virginia went to her bedroom, changed into something more enticing and returned to the living room. Roger stopped pacing and stared at her standing near the couch.

"I can't believe this! You thought it was another forgery and that's the way it turned out! If only I'd seen this copy last Saturday."

"Well, we never got to see my Mauritius collection. You got to me with the dancing and the music."

"Well, it's over. It's your's to keep, Virginia."

They sat down on the couch again. Her long bare legs hardly hidden by her negligee. Sudden desire overwhelmed him. They kissed and fumbled their way to her bedroom. She had an electric warmth that made Roger tingle. Snuggled together on the bed, Roger plunged into the ecstasy of penetration. Roger had finally found the right woman at the right time. Someone who would help him multiplex less and even share his hobby. Somehow the events of the past week seemed trivial next to this single most important discovery. Roger was a happy man, wrapped in her arms. He looked into her eyes. Perhaps, he fantasized, they would spend their honeymoon on the far away island of Mauritius.

*   *   *

Back in his home the next morning, Roger awoke late. He stared at the telephone then picked it up and dialed.

"Good morning, Virginia. I hope you have no plans for today."

"Hello, Roger. No plans. What do you have in mind?"

Multiplex man and his new girlfriend were still talking on the phone an hour later. Outside, the wind was gusting, pushing more brown leaves in front of Roger's house. The cool, windy days of fall continued, not yet Indian Summer. The first frost of fall was nipping off the remaining leaves from the half-bare trees. Only the maple tree leaves lingered on the branches with their brilliant yellow and vermillion colors as if to reflect the warmth inside Roger's house.